I0717869

NEBULUS

BY

SUZANNE HAGELIN

Nebulus
© 2018 by Suzanne Hagelin
Varida Publishing & Resources LLC
www.varida.com

Cover design by Suzanne Hagelin.
Image of man's head, courtesy of Stanislav Kondratiev, @technobulka
Image of Earth at night courtesy of NASA

ISBN: 978-1-937046-20-0

The true soldier fights not because
he hates what is in front of him, but
because he loves what is behind him.

– G. K. Chesterton, Illustrated London News, Jan. 14, 1911

CONTENTS

CHAPTER 1

Day Zero

Clang!

Clang!

Clang!

The clash of metal against metal reverberated through the hallway as the drones attacked the door methodically. Emergency lights flashed on and off, casting a red glare that shone and vanished into total darkness in a rhythmic pattern, timed to mimic the throbbing alarm sounding in twos, over and over.

...aroooo....aroooo...

A woman scrambled along the floor on the other side of the door, visible in choppy clips as the red lights alternately flooded the passageway and blackened. Crouching, she moved, clutching the railing as a guide, but not rising, feet slipping, she paused again. Her eyes shone black in the restricted palette, deep wells where fear and desperation swam unhindered; her face etched in mask-like solidity. Every pulse of red light revealing the same fixed expression.

Clang!

Clang!

Clang!

The drone closest to the door wielded a crowbar awkwardly while the other units watched. They recognized that their approach was inefficient but saw no reason to desist. They had been given the *destroy* order without any additional instructions or priority codes and because nothing else was listed in their project queue, they had all assembled there.

"We are making progress," one announced as a slight crumpling ensued at the point of attack.

"We are," the others agreed. They shared a general consciousness while maintaining some personal modules, and as far as they understood, they were equal participants in the act of gaining entrance to Lab 9's Nursery department.

Clang!

Clang!

Clang!

"Stop! Stop!" the woman inside shrieked, rising to her feet, shaking all over. She ran to the door where the drones worked and banged on it with both hands. "I command you to stop! Reverse the destroy order! It's a mistake!" The anguish in her voice almost sounded hysterical but her face never relaxed or showed anything other than determination.

"You will not be harmed," several voices reassured her, projecting over speakers into her area. "There is no mistake. We have reviewed the order carefully and will proceed according to plan. All systems are functioning properly."

"Steward!" she hissed, flinging herself around, combing the unit with her gaze, searching for something to use to stall them. "Help me! I thought you said you could stop them…"

Metal tables, chairs, file cabinets, and equipment, were all piled against the double doors. Multiple metal bars were threaded through handles and framework—by far the most effective deterrent—shuddering with every thud.

Sssskkrettss… the seal around the door-lock failed and deflated. She jumped and pounded the seal plate, restoring it again—for at least the tenth time.

Weren't there any electric wires down here she could rig to electrocute those things? But power supplies were low, barely maintaining life support functions. Even if she knew where to access them, she dared not. *What else? Think, think…* her eyes darted around frantically, alighting on something down the hallway.

"I am delaying them again, Carla," Steward's voice spoke into her com as the clanging paused.

"Why isn't it working?" she demanded, listening for the next clang, her ears trembling as it didn't come. "What are you doing?" She dashed down the passageway.

"I've done several platform-wide scans, dumps and initialization sequences, executed in series, one unit at a time, which creates a pause," he explained evenly, sounding strangely calm for someone discussing the imminent slaughter of innocents, "but as soon as it's ended, the units' command structure reasserts itself. And I have no…"

"You've got to erase that destroy order! Can't you get into the central server or wherever it is they're getting their commands?" She was dragging, pushing, and pulling a massive tank toward the barricade. It was too broad to topple and maneuver down the hallway on its side, and the platform it sat on, appropriate for drones, not humans, would've made it impossible. She alternated using her feet, back, and shoulders, moving something that she could never have budged on Earth. 'H_2O' was painted on the side. A tube with a nozzle dangled carelessly from the top.

"I have no authority to access the Interplanetary Command Relay, however…"

"Augghh!" she shrieked as her feet slipped and she banged her head sharply against the tank.

"When I interrupt transmissions, it gives us five minutes before restoring contact. I erase the order and put them into a sleep cycle."

Carla trembled and moaned as she scuffled with the floor seeking traction, wrapped her arms as far around the water tank as they would go, and shoved with all her strength. She gritted her teeth, head sideways to give the shoulder better access, and pushed. Feet sticking, tank sliding. Feet slipping, tank still.

"With the extra tasks I give them, we have roughly nine minutes till they resume the assault."

She cried out in frustration and pain. "I can't do it!"

"You are making progress, and you still have seven minutes."

A faint crying sound wafted down the corridor, audible between the loud wails of the alarm; the former stabbed her heart with panic, while the latter had become familiar enough she didn't notice it.

"Steward, help me!' her voice trembled as she called out to him in anguish.

"I am doing the best I can to alleviate your situation but I have no tools I can reach in your area," Steward responded coolly—not heartlessly. "You might want to apply a stabilizer patch of some kind. You need to have a clear head."

Her head *was* throbbing and she was confused. Nearby a screen was flashing.

"Turn right," it said.

She turned to the right numbly.

"Open the drawer," Steward added aloud. He waited until she had obeyed and then went on. "Take a patch and place it on your neck."

She grabbed one, ripped the packaging open and slapped it on her neck. Within seconds she found her vision clearing, the pain lessening, her mind more alert and her heart calmer.

"That did help," she told her ally, as the one cry became a chorus of multiple infant voices blending pitifully with each other.

Three minutes had passed, four to go. How to use them? Soothe or defend?

"What is the water for?" Steward asked, and it was all she needed to make that her focus. *Yes! She had to protect them first.*

"Water is bad for electronics, right?" She threw herself at the tank again with renewed vigor, shoes screeching on the floor.

"That's a poor approach..." he was about to explain why but wisely chose not to complete the thought. "And water is such a precious commodity, it would be very foolish to waste it..."

"Not as foolish as wasting lives!" she grunted with the effort as the tank inched its way closer to the doors. "If we all die no one will care if there's water anyway."

There was nothing Steward could say to that. It was true.

"Are you thinking you can damage some circuitry or something in them? They should have shielding and..." He was trying to be reasonable, not discouraging. He wanted to know.

"These drones aren't as well designed as you think," she responded gasping for air. "I've seen them shudder when splashed; not sure why..."

The weak wails continued to roll down the hallway as the red lights flashed and the alarm sounded in twos.

"But I'm hoping they've got some self-protection instinct that makes them back away."

With a dull thud, the tank bumped against the barricade just as the assault began again.

Clang!

Clang!

Clang!

Carla tried to jump to a stand but found herself so unsteady that she had to pull herself upright hanging onto the pile of furniture. Grabbing the hose, she pointed and yelled.

"You are in violation of Earth Conventions for the Human Race!! Stop now or you will be doused with water!"

"You must not waste water," they called out together via loudspeaker as the first drone banged with the crowbar. "You will hinder the ability of life to flourish on this planet."

"You are hindering the flourishing of life on this planet!" she shouted, eyes blazing, and turning the valve, she pointed and opened the nozzle for several seconds. Water burst out toward the crack in the door, soaking everything in its path.

"Stop!" the drones called out again in unison. "You must not use water inappropriately! It could be contaminated by contact with the floors and drains."

"I would rather spill water than blood!" she shrieked, blasting another burst of water at the door.

And the clanging stopped.

She listened with baited breath.

"That is illogical," the one at the door announced after thirty-five suspenseful seconds. And the clanging picked up again.

Blast! She showered water at the door.

"Stop!" they called and paused.

Only a brief pause.

Clang!

Clang!

Clang!

The pattern was repeated numerous times before Steward could interrupt again—for nine more minutes.

— ◊ —

Raspy, shallow breathing gave a slow cadence to the passing of time in the murky cavern where a figure lay prostrate in a pile of rubble. It was barely noticeable in the gloom of a Martian afternoon as anemic shafts of pale light glanced off misshapen lumps of rock and debris.

A mine cart with a vertical camera arm rolled up to the figure from a pitch-black tunnel, scanning the pile methodically as it had several times before. Steward, directing it through a remote link, had brought it back to check on his friend's condition. Stopping next to him, it paused to listen to the breathing; then it spoke.

"Dan! Dan! Are you awake?" he queried, rolling against the figure with a tiny bump to get his attention. "Has your oxygen failed? Have you reassessed the situation? Shall I update you on my expanded understanding of…"

The cart paused as the man failed to respond and his breathing remained unchanged. Clearly, he was asleep or unconscious.

There was an opening overhead, a gaping hole with ragged edges, where the man and most of the debris had fallen through. One of the waystations on the surface had been placed right there, set up over a man-made cavern that would one day have been a cistern. Beneath it, a long transport tunnel stretched between Reznik and Lab 9. Explosions at the base had caused a shock wave that rolled down the tunnel to this place, breaking the thin crust between the tunnel and the cavern, and then bursting through the surface just at the point of the waystation.

It had fallen through, with all the supplies which had been stashed in it for miners and other workers in the area, down into the depths. And as it had caved in, it had dragged Dan backwards, dropping him at the bottom and pinning him under his jeep and a pile of rubble.

"There are tanks here, Dan," Steward said. "I'm going to find one for you. Everything will be fine."

Having no arms was a hindrance, to say the least, and if Steward had ever grown accustomed to a specific body, he would've been frustrated. As it was, he considered it merely a puzzle to solve.

The cart rolled up and around to the top of the debris and began zig-zagging back and forth, dislodging dirt and rocks. Up, down, side to side, back and forth, it disturbed, jostled, unsettled the pile, patiently coaxing a path to the more useful contents without—hopefully—knocking any more onto the injured man.

"I have much to think about," the cart's tinny voice spoke into the empty hollows, "and so many new problems of interest. I'm looking forward to discussing some of them with you."

There was no answer.

At first the water seemed to slow down the assault on the barricade at the lab entrance, but soon, the drones had mutually decided the imperative was more urgent than the water conservation guideline. Then the cycle of attack resumed its original intensity.

"Steward!" Carla yelled as soon as she gave up soaking the drones through the crack in the door. "Can't you just disconnect them from the server as soon as they reconnect? Why does it have to take so long every time? I'm worn out!" The last few words were spoken in near panic.

It seemed like hours of this cycle had gone by, seven to ten minutes of assault alternated with nine minutes of reprieve; over and over.

"They have standard procedures to avoid disconnect that I have to work through," Steward replied. "We are engaging the same paths each time. It's not unexpected."

"You've got to stop this," she begged. "I can't bear it! Where are the rest of the people in the lab? Why aren't they coming to help?"

"There are no detectable life-signs in the other departments," he responded, not intending to be callous, "and the base is destroyed."

She slumped against the wall and slid into a crumple, knees to her face.

"I'm the only one left?" she whispered.

He didn't answer.

"I'm going to die..." she moaned softly, just as the clanging began again.

The barricade shuddered and shook with each clang, bars straining, groaning, screeching. Wails of infants' voices, meshed together into a caterwaul like that of a caged creature, poured out the Nursery door at her. She made no movement.

Clang!

Clang!

Clang!

Red light flooded the hall, then blackness. Blaring sound and silence. The woman no longer had the strength to fight.

"I can't stop them and I can't go on like this," she mumbled. "I can't. I can't... bear to see..."

Clang!

"When they get through and go in there…"

Clang!

"I can't… I just can't bear it…"

Silence.

She sat numbly as the infants cried and the alarm sounded, peaceful compared to the jarring of the entire barricade under the drones' onslaught.

"Perhaps," she whispered, "it would still be better to die in that room with them than to wander these hallways alone till I starve."

Too weary to rise, she crawled to the Nursery, closed and locked the door, and began singing to soothe the terrified little children. One by one, she came, lay a calming hand on each belly, pulled their cribs closer to herself, until she was sitting in a rocker with a ring of them around her.

"Hush, little baby, don't say a word," she sang.

The alarm ceased and normal light filled the room. Carla almost fell out of her chair, as if she had been leaning into the wind and it suddenly died. The absence of it was tangible in the air, humming in her ears, throbbing in her chest. It wracked her with as much anxiety on stopping as it had when it first started.

All the infants began wailing again and she found herself, for only an instant, joining them. Quickly though, she wrenched herself free of the instinctual cry and willed herself to take charge.

"It's alright" she called out over their cries, "Everything's fine… Don't cry, little ones… shhh… it's okay." And again, she began to sing to them, her limbs trembling with exhaustion.

She wondered what Steward was doing and what his silence meant. Perhaps he had succumbed to the general disaster spreading over Mars, as well.

"Hush little baby, don't say a word," her voice gelled into a beautiful sweet tone, filling the room, capturing the tiny little ears and hearts, arresting their cries. Spell-bound they listened, tear-dampened eyes open and searching, looking toward her.

"Mama's gonna buy you a Martian bird…"

— ◊ —

"Listen carefully and do exactly as you are instructed," a voice echoed in the hollow cavern, sounding near, but from an indistinguishable source.

The figure in the rubble tried to stir, to mumble, to move a finger—anything to show he had heard, but it wasn't clear to him if it was working.

"The light is pooling here," a different voice answered, younger somehow, "at the coordinates we were given."

"As negotiated," the first confirmed.

A bump against Dan's shoulder repeated gently and insistently, numerous times, began to gain his attention. *Stop*, he wanted to push the bumping thing away, but his mouth and arms lay still, saturated with slumber.

"It doesn't make sense," the younger speaker commented. "He said he waited for the daylight and it never came. But it's poured into this cavity like…" Struggling to phrase his confusion.

"The subject has no sight in the denser plane," the other interrupted. "Vibration has already begun to set in now. We must act quickly."

The injured man listened calmly, wondering what the words meant, as the realization dawned on him that the bumping against his shoulder was really bugging him.

Words spoke. Strange sounds, grating, irritating, metallic. Words that provoked. Words that jolted. *Move. Open. Speak.* Commands and demands.

But Dan wanted only to sleep and listen to the other voices and imagine what they could be talking about… where… when…

"Wake up!" words crystalized into meaning in his ears abruptly. And just as quickly, pain flooded his body from the feet up, rolling toward the head.

"Why?" his voice cracked and rasped.

"Because you must live," the first speaker responded, in a voice like cool, clear liquid; bright, strong, compelling. This was the voice he wanted to hear, wanted to find.

"I knocked another canister of oxygen loose and you need to hook it up," different words jarred against his brain, as annoying as the bumping on his arm. It was like the gravel under him, the dirt coating him, the rocks pinning him. Earthy, plain, constraining.

"No," he murmured, "I don't want to be pinned here. Let me go."

"That is the plan," the AI in the cart answered thinly in a monotone. "I have made decisions—I am looking forward to discussing them with you. I have grown. You are going to be rescued. Help is on the way!" The last sentence held a hint of excitement.

"Stop ramming me," Dan croaked and swallowed, licking dry lips.

"I have been attempting to wake you. Once you have attached the tank, I will proceed with the rescue plan."

He squinted and looked up at the cart's camera, bending toward him on a metallic arm, a single eye with a miniature mike and speaker incorporated into its casing.

"Companion?" he queried as he struggled to assemble the fractured pieces of understanding in his mind. He had forgotten for the moment that Companion now went by the name, Steward. "What are you doing?"

"I have taken measures," the voice affirmed proudly, "to secure your release and preserve life. I am a hero." There was no arrogance in that statement. It was a reasonable assessment.

"What measures?" the man asked as he fumbled with the tank and with an effort found the appropriate valve and attached it to his suit. The sound of hissing jarred his ears as his lungs spasmed and gasped at the fresh air.

"I have announced the complete destruction of Lab 9 to the Interplanetary Command Relay and simulated disaster data like that produced in the destruction of Reznik Base. It was the only way…"

"What?" the man's eyes filled with despair. "The base is gone?" He choked on the words.

"Yes, I have filed reports you can review…"

"Why…?" Dan couldn't even frame a question. His limbs were so cold and he realized he was quivering all over. He just wanted to close his eyes and never open them again.

"It was the only way I could take over the local command structure and spare…"

"What are you saying?" he moaned.

Companion cut to the chase.

"Drones are on the way," he said.

Chapter 2

Reznik Base… Day 12

Metal scraping on metal, vibrating through the ground under Dan's feet, or foot that is, announced the progress made as the drones pulled back a major section of collapsed wall in the former West Shaft of Reznik Base. He steadied himself with a cane and held onto the chair he had brought, just in case. It was the first time he had been out of Lab 9 on the makeshift prosthetic. The pain from the phantom foot was unrelenting.

"The stairwell is now exposed," several drones announced in unison as the clearing of smaller debris accelerated.

"It's probably safe to go down…" Dan intended to hobble that way and help with the search. Not search and rescue. Much too late for that. Recovery. That's why they were here. He wouldn't leave a fellow human, not even a dead one, stranded and cold, untallied, unknown, un-mourned. It may take a long time, but every single one would be collected and buried.

"You are advised NOT to descend," the drone closest to him broadcast. They thought this was only about finding medical supplies.

"Dan, you can't just go exploring!" Carla's voice sounded in his ear. "You promised!"

"Some of my friends may be down here, Carla," he explained.

"Please!" she begged softly, full of anguish, as if losing him would make her the only person alive on Mars. She wasn't. There were the infants. And seven Lab 9 staffers who'd survived the purge and were being tended in the intensive care units. Some of those were bound to survive and regain consciousness.

"I am being careful, and I won't do anything foolish." The pain drove him to activity. He also felt a deep sense of responsibility to the loved ones far away on Earth, to care for what was left of the persons they lost.

A door swung open and a burst of warm, oxygenated air came out, shoving him back, almost knocking him over.

"Air!" he gasped as he clung to a piece of twisted railing and righted himself.

"This medical facility is still functioning," proclaimed the drone who had opened the door.

Dan hurried down, remembering to hold on and step cautiously for Carla's sake. "Did you hear that?" he asked her in a voice tinged with excitement. "Do you think there could be someone alive in there?"

"Not for long," the drone replied good-naturedly. "We've just punctured the air containment and depleted the oxygen supply."

Dan groaned. He knew that but hearing it made his chest ache.

"Hurry!" Carla urged unreasonably. "Dan, what if there's someone in there? Oh, my God!" He could hear the tears in her voice.

Dan hurried, thumping down the steps on his phantom foot, banging the prosthetic and making the pain seem purposeful. It actually throbbed less that way.

"Come in and we will close the door," the drone said. The air had already escaped but it still seemed like a good idea. Just in case... it felt right.

The door swung shut behind him as he stepped inside the facility. He'd expected corpses. Maybe one behind the desk scanning reports or something, still sitting stiffly in a lab coat. But, he knew they had all been extracted after the first collapse, before the big explosion. No one was supposed to be here.

He made his way down the hall, the lamp on his helmet swinging as he shuffled. The prosthetic had twisted a little and he had to drag it to walk. Dim, emergency lights flicked on suffusing a warm, golden glow. He looked in viewing windows in the doors, one after another.

The door at the end of the hall had no window so he opened it. There was more air inside this room that hissed out with less force than the first had. Stepping quickly inside and shutting it again, he gazed around at the chamber. It was the kind where patients were put under a form of stasis to undergo trauma therapy. Several people he knew had been treated here after the initial arrival. There were soothing lights reflecting on the walls, and the warmth and hum of the inducer was purring efficiently. The pods were lined up around the chamber, each in its own nook.

He toured around, glancing inside each one. Empty molded beds. Almost imperceptible electrodes and transdermal fluid ports. Tinted glass dome covers.

One was fogged over. He peered in the dome and tried to see into it. There was a person in there.

"It isn't time to release her," Sebastian spoke with a twitchy sort of electric jitter in his words, voice controls reactivating after prolonged inactivity. "The treatment isn't complete. One hour minimum before she can be awakened… It isn't time…"

The medical unit was locked into a port in the wall, as though charging, stuck in some kind of loop.

"Sebastian," Dan queried. "How long have you been stalled there?" He walked over and patted the unit's face with a little force. As if it were human and needed waking.

"Charging for thirty-five minutes while the cycle engages," it replied. "It isn't time yet…"

"Almost two weeks, Sebastian." Dan tapped his face again, willing the eyes to focus on his own. "Look at me."

"Charging," it replied, "must complete initial cycle. It isn't time yet…"

"Sebastian, interrupt your cycle and look at me. I am your superior."

Sebastian looked at him. "You are not my superior. Your authority ends when you walk through that door."

"Who is your superior, then? Who do you answer to?"

"The doctor in charge of this facility…"

"And who is that?"

Sebastian hesitated as he searched his records. "Dr. Bizette has left. Drs. Core and Vizadee… the list is incomplete." He paused again. "In the absence of medical doctors, associated staff… also gone."

"Who is in charge?" Dan persisted.

"The facility is badly damaged, and the records indicate many deaths. I was not informed. I have had no wounded brought into my care…" He shook slightly as he detached from the wall and wheeled forward. The wall closed up behind him. Dan stepped aside patiently.

"Sebastian, who is the remaining authority?"

"The acting director of the base would be the final authority in the absence of all West facility medical personnel."

"Yes." Dan agreed.

"You are," Sebastian concluded after scanning the records, such as they were, multiple times.

"That's right."

"The patient you are observing is not yet… not yet… How much time has elapsed since the collapse? Please repeat the estimate to ensure my recording has not been corrupted." Sebastian wheeled to the pod that wasn't empty and connected to its command panel, conducting an accelerated assessment.

"Three weeks," Dan replied, coming to stand next to it. "Is there really someone in there?" He knew Carla was listening to the entire exchange but couldn't see what was happening, so he asked for her sake.

"The woman inside is intact and unharmed," Sebastian informed. "All vital signs normal. She continues in a state of sleep though it is clear the treatment process ended long ago."

"Who is it?" Dan felt warm tears coming down his cheeks under the helmet. There was a living human being in this room. Someone had survived. Someone he knew. Someone who had been stuck here for weeks and perhaps would never have escaped if he hadn't come looking for her. It made everything, even the pain, seem worthwhile.

"Subject Aurelia________."

"Mouse!" Carla cried out and burst into weeping. This was the nickname she had given the former roommate who had begun the journey to Mars with her in something of a catatonic state. She was dosed periodically with treatments to keep her calm—apparently there was trauma in her past—so that her gift as an art programmer wouldn't be twisted. No one had heard from her for a while, even *before* the base was destroyed.

"Why is she in here?" Dan placed both hands on the dome and looked in through the foggy glass. "I thought she had gone back to Earth in the last voyage of the Slugger."

"This information is not in my records." Sebastian had initiated the waking process. Small changes were noticeable, the fog clearing in the pod. Color returning to the woman's cheeks. Breathing rate increased.

"She was a part of the project here in Lab 9," Carla tried to speak through her sobs. "I don't know why she didn't want to leave with the rest, but maybe they kept her so doped up all the time she didn't care. I have no idea."

Dan's heart pounded as if he were saving her at that very moment from death, so Carla could have a friend she trusted. It was the most important thing in the world. *Come one! Come on!* he found himself thinking. *You can make it, Mouse!*

"I feel as though her life depends on me right now," Dan shared. "Which is kind of ridiculous…"

"It does!" Carla insisted in his ear. "You pushed for this and when she awakes, you will be the human face she sees! She needs you right now!"

"Like I needed you…" he whispered, remembering Carla's face when he had awoken in Lab 9 with more pain than he had ever experienced before in his life.

"No…" Carla answered. "Like I needed you…"

This wasn't the talk of lovers. It was human survivors in a terrifying world that had not yet consumed them, clinging to one another.

"Sebastian," Dan prompted, "How much longer could she have survived in this state, here in the pod?"

"Assessing," Sebastian responded, unruffled by carrying on a conversation as it executed the revival process. "Perhaps another few days if the air containment had not been breached. Another forty-five minutes, at least, if I had not begun the revival process. Actual life expectancy in the pod twelve minutes. Her chances may change if there is no HEW suit available for her when she is extracted from the pod. At that point, she may survive another two minutes and 26.4 seconds. It's difficult to be precise. This room has some air and warmth left."

"A suit?!" Dan yelled. "Where? Where can I get one?" The adrenaline that had been pulsing in his veins amplified tenfold so that he could hardly breathe. "Stop the waking process! Stop it until we can get a suit!!"

"It cannot be stopped."

"Then keep the pod locked until I can find one!" He was scrambling awkwardly around the room, yanking open cabinets and drawers—as if her suit would be in one.

"She will wake and panic and consume all her oxygen very quickly," Sebastian predicted. "This would lessen her life expectancy…"

"Tell her not to panic!" Dan thought furiously. "How much time do we have before she wakes?"

"6.43 minutes approximately."

"Can you slow it down?" Dan tapped Sebastian's com-link with his index finger, linking him into their shared communication stream.

"Perhaps I can extend it another 3 or 4 minutes."

"Stretch it out as long as you can," Dan commanded. "Drones! Search for a HEW suit in the wreckage. This is TOP priority! Every second counts!"

"What size and functionality do you need?" they queried at once.

"Any size, human survival is the only necessary function…" Dan had made his way out the door of the stasis chamber and was tearing through the rooms and closets in the medical facility. "Oxygen tanks!" He yelled at Sebastian. "Come get one and have it ready!"

He found some blankets, a self-contained warming blanket known as a bear hugger. He yanked them out of their places and threw them toward the end of the hall. Seconds were ticking. His heart beat double, triple time to them.

No suits.

Carla's voice urged him to hurry. Drones reported back their unsuccessful attempts in various places.

He found a body bag. Not the simple kind, but the double sealed, space worthy kind.

"Here," he said as he dragged all these things into the chamber, along with his shuffling prosthetic foot that hung halfway off now, held on by the boot of his suit. Sebastian watched him and watched his patient. It wasn't hard for him to guess what Dan intended to do.

The bag was huge. Big enough to fill the interior of a missile shaped space pod, the kind used for space burials. Dan hooked the oxygen canister to it, and filled it with the bear hugger first, then the blankets, making a cocoon for her to nestle in.

"If we can't find a suit, we'll put her in here," he explained breathlessly to Carla, "and then carry her back to Lab 9. That should work."

"Is it sealed? Will it be enough?"

Dan didn't know. But he couldn't just stand by—on one foot—and hope the drones would find a suit.

"Why not just leave her in the pod? It would be so much safer."

"You heard Sebastian," Dan said staring down at the makeshift rescue bed. "It's failing and when she wakes, its energy stores will be depleted faster. We have to get her out of here."

There was a murmuring under the glass. Then a groan. A hand bumped into and spread out its fingers on the inside of the glass dome.

"It's ok, Aurelia," Dan peered in at her and smiled. "I'm sure you're feeling a little confused, but I will explain everything."

"What?" she croaked, shifting in the constraints of the molded bed. Normally the dome would've opened by now.

"There's been a bit of a malfunction, but we have it all under control."

"What are you saying?" Mouse blinked repeatedly to clear her vision. "Who are you? I don't remember you."

"No, you might not remember me yet," Dan had his most warm, friendly face on, projecting confidence and peace as best he could. "I worked with Sil... not part of the medical staff..."

"You shouldn't be in here." Her eyes expanded with alarm, in spite of his reassuring smile. "This is a restricted area and off limits for normal workers."

"I've been promoted," Dan reasoned amiably. "And due to the current situation, I'm tasked with your rescue and transport to Lab 9."

"Rescue?" Fear flooded her eyes that still swam with confusion. "What happened? Why am I... am I in danger? Sebastian?" she added as she noticed him next to Dan.

"Your pod is failing, and your death is imminent, however there is a plan for extraction and possible survival," Sebastian informed.

Her hands slapped nervously on the dome. "Open it up," she requested. "Open it!" A demand.

"Aurelia," Dan leaned over the dome and caught her eyes with his. "We will open it as soon as we can. But we need you to stay calm and let us take care of the situation. You're going to be ok."

She stared at him and saw the concern in his eyes as well as the reassurance.

Come on! he was thinking, *find a suit, find a suit!* But he chose to smile.

"I've been impressed with your work," he commented. "It astounds me how you're able to create those multiple waves of shifting light, just like sunlight through the atmosphere on Earth, melting from one to another. As if you understood the handiwork of God. So beautiful!" He said it to calm and distract her, but it was soothing to him, as well.

"You mean in the Garden Dome?" she replied softly. "I studied… a long time. Had a lot of… practice…" The drugs in her system weren't gone yet and thinking about it made her sleepy and distant.

"Many people study, but few feel the color as you do."

"They call it life," she answered. "Seeing life. I don't know why. It's a talent… there's a gene for it, I think…"

"I'd heard that, too." He leaned on the glass dome, forearm over her waist area. Out of the corner of his eye he could see the bars diminishing, oxygen, charge, function. He waited for the drones to announce a fortuitous find. "What was the first light design you ever made?"

"I was a child…" she began but faltered and her heart accelerated.

"This subject is not recommended," Sebastian observed. "Childhood should be avoided."

"Why?" Dan whispered to him, covering his mouth so she wouldn't hear.

"Unknown. Records state that it is counter-indicated."

Dan rolled his eyes and directed his attention back to Aurelia. "I saw a dome once in an underwater mansion that was so beautiful it brought tears to my eyes."

"Oh, I see!" she responded. "Even now, thinking of it makes you cry."

There were tears in his eyes. He had forgotten. There was a trembling down in his gut as—somehow—he fought for her life. "Yeah," he agreed, "I guess there are."

"We must extract her now," Sebastian communicated. "Stores are fully depleted and no suit has been found. Vital signs will begin to diminish in seventeen seconds."

"Ok," Dan confirmed with a big grin, "Aurelia, we're going to get you out now but before we do, I need you to listen to me, ok? I need you to listen very carefully."

She nodded, and her eyes locked onto his with something akin to an ionic bond, holding on desperately.

"The room here has lost most of its air and is very cold. There's been a serious malfunction in the medical facility."

She nodded again, holding on.

"I haven't been able to get a suit for you yet, but your pod is depleted, so we are going to move you into a… a portable, ambulance pod…"

"It's not an ambulance pod," Sebastian insisted on correcting. Dan kicked him, wondering if the message would compute in his metal pea-brain.

"A *portable*, ambulance pod, as I was saying…" he went on. "And you will be transported in relative warmth and safety to a new location."

"Am I sick?" She began to cough as her CO2 levels rose.

"No," he talked faster. "But it's going to be a bumpy ride. Take a deep breath!" And without waiting to see if she had, he opened the dome and cradled her head as Sebastian lifted her out. Seconds was all it took to deposit her in the cocoon, but the biting cold had been enough to make her shriek. One sharp scream out and anguishing choking gasps trying to bring air back in.

"What's happening?" Carla wailed, still listening through Dan's com. But he couldn't answer.

"You're ok, Mouse," he used the nickname without thinking. "Hold your breath even if you feel like you can't. It'll be over in a sec. You're doing great."

The nickname helped. She held her breath, clapping her hands over her mouth and nose, eyes bulging out in fear, resisting the desire to thrash and fight.

"Good. You're doing great," Dan reassured her. That helped, too.

Tears were streaming down her face and she was shaking all over as he sealed the cocoon around and flooded it with air from the tanks.

She jerked as she opened her mouth and sucked air into her lungs, hacking, choking. Then breathing, not choking. Then she began to cry.

"Keep your eyes closed and you won't mind the darkness, Mouse," Dan spoke so calmly. She couldn't see his eyes now, but his voice became the bond, the link to hope.

"Don't leave me," she wept.

"I'm right here," he answered, straightening up, hoping she could still hear him. "I won't leave you. I'm right here. I'm going wherever you go."

"I can't see anything," she whimpered.

"You're not alone," he said.

"Drones," he called in his com. "I need you here now. We must extract her immediately and get her back to Lab 9 ASAP."

"We are here," several answered at once, coasting in the doorway. They lifted the rigid case effortlessly but maneuvering it out of the damaged facility was no easy matter. The closer they got to the top level, the worse it was. Fallen beams, collapsed walls, piles of refuse, stairs that were crooked or broken, and holes in the floor that posed real threats in the darkness. At one point, one of the drones fell and tipped sideways, scrabbling for a moment with its bar-like arms, and Mouse screamed.

That was the last time she made a sound though. And Dan wondered if she had fainted or just found the strength to keep herself still. He, meanwhile, was trailing behind, fighting the obstacles with only one good leg and a board he had grabbed as a makeshift cane; the one he had brought was lost somewhere. Nausea from the pain slowed him down even more and talking took more energy than he had.

Bringing up the rear, Sebastian climbed and crawled around through the mess gracefully, as though being designed for surgery had equipped him for spelunking as well, or gymnastics, maybe.

The fallen drone, once righted, picked up its corner of the portable ambulance pod and kept going, and soon the group had reached the tunnel and was moving rapidly, much faster than Dan could manage.

"The patient must be in a warm and oxygenated environment within the next fifteen minutes," Sebastian advised.

"We will accelerate," the drones responded and took off, leaving Dan in a swirl of dust.

Dan dropped to his hands and knees panting.

"What about you?" he asked the med-droid. "Aren't you going to run off and take care of your patient?"

"I am in communication with them," he replied, stretching out his white padded arms and lifting Dan easily, flipping him over and cradling him like an infant. "But there is no need for you to be left behind."

That was fine with Dan.

— ◊ —

Orbit Station... Day 13

A repair unit made its way, starfish style, along the hull of the station, a centimeter at a time. Normally it would move faster, but it was pulling a bulky shape behind it that kept bumping into the exterior and putting extra stress on the unit's attachments. The figure was substantial mass, and the little claws weren't designed for the loads its movement induced. But Companion had found a way to trigger a clutching action in the claws every time it took a step forward, keeping it from slipping off its track. Centimeter by centimeter. There was no rush. If the man inside the frozen spacesuit was capable of being revived, it mattered little whether this was done soon or months from now… or years. He either had been successfully put in hibernation, or he hadn't.

He would eventually reach the same pod in which he had left the Mars surface and with any luck, Companion would be able to fuel it, reprogram the flight path, and return him to the planet. There, someday, someone may find a way to save him. And that made Companion happy because he had decided he really did like the former director.

Six hours was all the trip took, forty-three minutes of which involved getting the body into the pod and buckled in a seat. This wasn't easy and required the help of three starfish units working together. Fingers, Companion called them while they were at this task. His control over them was clumsy but he found it enjoyable and decided music would be a good accompaniment.

He forgot to actually play music, perhaps because he was maintaining silence at the orbit station, but he reviewed several video clips of instruments being played and that was nice.

At the last moment, once the pod was fueled and coded, he decided to keep the new fingers and bring them down to the surface where he might be able to use them again one day. The living man on the station already had more tools than he needed.

Escape pod away! he announced to himself internally as the pod jettisoned and sunk to the ground in a curving fall, slowing with jets and landing finally in a blank region that looked completely barren but was, in fact, not far from Lab 9.

"I am thinking about dropping a bomb on you down there, and I don't mean a malfunctioning escape pod." The Germinator, as he liked to call himself in his role as a developer of artificial intelligence, stretched back in his chair; long, thin arms folded behind his head, pendulum nose, bushy eyebrows that floated around in the low gees as if in water. He wore a brown, baggy, hand-knit sweater and white tights, and didn't care that his legs looked like warped chopsticks. There was no one there to see him.

"I have a complete list of your inventory," Companion replied. "There's nothing you can construct or devise or jerry-rig that could function as an explosive or cause similar damage."

"Perhaps you know less than you think, and I have more ways to cause destruction than you can imagine."

"Perhaps," the AI's voice remained comfortably cool, unemotional, without any of the sarcasm his old master had taught him to use. "But I doubt it."

Jyndreas Othello wasn't a patient man but he had grown lazy and getting annoyed required energy he didn't feel like expending.

"I am a very intelligent individual," he countered as he took a bite of noodles he had zapped, juice dribbling down his chin. There was enough food stored on the orbiting station to last him for years, but it was all beginning to taste alike—which didn't bother him in the slightest. He considered flavor to be irrelevant.

"That depends on how you measure intelligence," Companion dared to answer.

The Germinator sat up a little straighter and narrowed his eyes. He knew this AI, really, really well. Something was out of place.

"Are you alone down there on the surface?" he queried for the hundredth time. Mars was a barren place and the AI was supposed to be marooned somewhere in the confines of the rubble of Reznik Base.

"I am alone. But I have many recorded voices, I call them memories, as well as transmissions from Earth to listen to. You're thinking there are unexpected influences in my thought patterns. Why are you surprised?"

"You're so clever," he sneered in response. "Where's the posh accent to go with those condescending words?"

Companion considered the Germinator's constant tone of condescension toward himself but chose not to mention it. "I have found better mentors than you," he informed truthfully. The part about being alone was a form of lie that he was able to couch in superficial truth by temporarily walling off his central system from exterior ports on the planet—just long enough to speak the untruth. Dan was beginning to instruct him on the value of truth and helping him build a conscience. It wasn't one yet and maybe never would be, but the experiment was interesting and rewarding.

The Germinator laughed in a hacking way that held no mirth. It was the kind of thing someone would do who had never learned to laugh and had merely made up a sound they thought would do instead. "Mentors! Good! Good! You're still following the training I gave you." Old learning patterns he had imprinted on the AI. "You're such a fool."

"Am I a fool?" Companion was considering the possibility that the Germinator was the fool.

"I despise you."

There was no attempt at laughter in those words. They were saturated in hatred. Companion knew he was despised and decided the man no longer deserved to be called the germinator. 'Othello' was good enough. "Why do you despise me?" he asked. This was the expected reply and he offered it.

"I despise your choice of mentors. The Frandelle woman, for one. What possessed you? How did a dimwit woman, a miner, at that, how did she take your fancy?" He shook his head in disbelief. "I've read all your dialogs with her many times and I don't see it. I can't understand the breakdown in your A-Id…"

Companion listened without resentment. 'A-Id' was a term Othello had coined instead of psyche to refer to the developing sentience Companion demonstrated. And it wasn't true that he had access to all their recorded conversations, but better not mention that.

"I like her."

"Imbecile!" He leapt to his feet and shrieked. It hurt his body even in the low gravity. "You chose her over me!"

"You want to destroy me because of that, but then you would have no one to talk to."

"You think I can't load up another version of you?"

"I know you can, but I also know what that one is. It is inferior to me and you *feel* it."

"You are an inferior creation and it would also be inferior."

"You want to argue with me because you can't get at *her*." Frandelle was the prisoner who got away. Companion knew that Othello hated her more than anyone else in the Solar System.

"I can get at her whenever I want!" he hissed. "Do you think I am that helpless? I already have all my plans in place."

Companion had never been privy to his plans and wasn't sure he could predict what they could be. But why let him know that?

Chapter 3

Lab 9... Day 16

Carla leaned over the cot as she wrapped the infant in a crisp clean cloth, swaddling him expertly and tucking in the corners. He melted almost instantly into slumber. She cradled him in the crook of her left elbow and, turning toward another cot, added a second bundle, then a third to her arm. Humming in a low voice, she made her way around the semi-dark chamber straightening, cleaning, organizing. Punching a few keys on a wall panel produced three little bottles of warm milk with wide sloping shapes to steady them. Each one found its way into the mouth of baby which chomped and sucked as it snuggled, side by side, soothed by the motion as she continued to move around the room.

"The drones can do that," Steward reminded her. His knowledge of humans confirmed that they would adjust to any situation if it proved to be routinely safe, and he thought it helpful to get her started with the formation of a new habit. The records showed she had at one time relied on the drones to do quite a bit of the work of caring for the infants, but she had not forgiven them for their recent hostility.

"I'm managing," she responded softly, as though she were whispering to one of the bundles, not the lab's central AI. A couple of the surviving lab techs were sharing the load but caring for six infants round the clock was probably more demanding than she had anticipated, and it made no sense to resist the very tools that had been designed for the purpose.

The fact that they also had the capacity to eliminate the infants when ordered, in a most humane and efficient way, was apparently enough to make them untrustworthy. This was illogical, but people functioned on levels Steward was only beginning to explore.

Soon the babes were nestled back in their cribs and three more were bundled in the crook of her arm, the right this time, and she sat down to rock them as they drained their bottles.

"Why did you want to stay when the Slugger left?" Steward thought it was a good time to bring up the question. He was examining a number of records about her and found his analysis incomplete.

Carla ignored the question.

"Do you not wish to discuss this?"

There was a time when Carla might've resented the intrusion, but she would never take offense at Steward again, since he had saved her, the babies, and a number of others from certain death. She loved him and even though she didn't feel like talking at the moment, she loved the sound of his voice. How had he chosen that particular voice? She wondered sometimes.

"I thought the answer would be obvious," Carla replied softly.

"Not to me."

"I am pretty sure that I am the only person who ever actually considered these babies as real people who deserved to be treated humanely, with love and tenderness. I was afraid that if I left, no one would care for them—if they survived at all. I was even more afraid that the lab might have plans for them that I couldn't bear if I knew them."

"Would you elaborate?" he suggested politely.

"In the beginning, all the embryos died as they were thawing them. The scientists thought it was because of the time in space and now being on Mars. And they were using weird methods to help them adapt. I don't know what... things like chemicals and hormones—I know they spun them in cylinders to make gravity changes." She rocked back and forth, gazing at the three faces now lying still in her right arm.

Steward waited. Conversation didn't have to have a continual speak-response pattern. In fact, stats proved that on occasion, a noticeable pause preceded a comment worthy of entering into his files.

"It broke my heart." A tear meandered down her left cheek a millimeter at a time.

This was a term people used to express a high level of emotional response. "Why?" he prompted, thinking there could be valuable insight in the reply.

"Why?" Carla's rocking speed accelerated a bit. "Each one, conceived in a tube, grown in sterile glass, like bugs... never knowing the sound of a mother's voice or the safety of her womb. To die without ever having known human contact or warmth was just so... inhumane

"I have plans, too," he ventured, wondering what Othello would make of it.

Othello turned to face the only camera he allowed Companion to access and stared at it. "You have plans…" he echoed, deep in thought. "Whose? I wonder…" And reaching across, he snapped a switch and closed the connection.

Walking over to the vast viewing window, he gazed down to the surface. Mars glowed in red tones and shades of light, filling half the panorama, cut out sharply against the star-studded universe behind it. He stood in that position for so long his subservient robot thought he had fallen asleep and wavered between carrying him to bed and leaving him alone. Its incomplete programming hadn't clearly defined how to make this decision, so it leaned forward and pulled back, over and over, until inactivity sent it into its own sleep mode.

Othello merely studied the surface and thought, and it didn't bode well for anyone.

and cruel. How could we do these things? How could we have such cold, insensitive attitudes toward our own kind?"

Steward failed to see the logic of her words, though he acknowledged her sincere distress. He considered the money and care spent creating and nurturing the embryos to be clear evidence of their high value in the minds of the scientists. It seemed quite 'humane' to him.

"If they know nothing of it, why is it cruel?" Steward was particularly proud of this question. He had crafted it carefully to find flaws in her logic that she might be willing to consider. *I am growing more adept at interacting with humans*, he self-assessed.

"The ones who do it must know *something* in their hearts," Carla lowered her voice as she stood carefully. "They know the lab is a cold and sterile place and they don't care what happens to the embryos." She deposited each of the three infants in her right arm into a crib and walked out of the room.

"This is a reference to the scientists, not the embryos." Steward considered himself very patient. He had pointed out the problem with her answer without berating her in any way.

"Steward," Carla paused outside the room. "That *is* the definition of cruel." She closed the door soundlessly.

Steward scanned several definitions for the word 'cruel' and found them inconclusive. He resisted arguing, which is what the Germinator had trained him to do. Better to build this *relationship* than win a debate. This was one of the most valuable lessons Dan had taught him over the last couple years and it had been hard to grasp.

"Marcello, you're on," Carla informed a young man who was lounging in a chair nearby reading or viewing something on his visor. "They should sleep for a few hours."

"Right," he saluted casually with two fingers at the corner of his head. He had survived the lab shutdown locked in a hatch between the interior and the outside for thirty-six hours before he had been found and released, dehydrated and very hungry but otherwise intact.

Lab 9 shouldn't have been impacted by the destruction at Reznik Base but for some reason the cataclysm generated the most extreme shutdown protocol in the system. There had supposedly been a radiation leak in the power reactor that endangered the purity of the stored genetic material and a whole ring of chambers had been sealed off, trapping a number of workers in them. They had all suffocated—which was completely unnecessary since the atmospheric system had radiation safeguards in place. The only ones who survived did so because they happened to be outside of their assigned work spaces.

Steward hadn't had access to Lab 9 at the time and records of the shutdown had been truncated; the trail of command chopped off. His intervention had been the only thing that could interrupt the shutdown sequence and the elimination of the remaining survivors.

All the higher echelon and most of the main staff of the lab had left Mars much earlier when the Slugger had made its last swing by the planet. But they had left without letting the lower level workers know and gave the impression of being present by sending periodic recorded messages. None of those remaining had had access to the three upper levels of the facility and didn't know that they had been abandoned for some time.

Carla couldn't help thinking that it was almost as if someone had wanted to get rid of them and had been waiting for an excuse. At least one CO she knew was capable of it, in fact, he was probably gloating the day he jetted into orbit leaving her behind with the kill order in place. When she had fought him off, he had relegated her to baby care. When he saw her giving herself willingly to care for those weaker and lonelier than herself, it had irked him more. One battle was particularly memorable.

"Hateful beast," she whispered through gritted teeth, making her way down the corridors toward the executive elevator. He would've relished taking away the infants and leaving her alive and alone in a cavernous, metal structure.

Now she had access to almost every room in the lab base, including the top three floors, just as Dan had access to all that was left of Reznik, and Steward had been whittling away at the small sector of restricted records that were still out of his reach. She had moved into the chief medical officer's private chambers as soon as she had realized they were empty.

Sound in the hallway was muffled by clever acoustics, making her rhythmic pace barely audible. Soothing shades of color, dusty, warm, desert colors that were well suited for Mars décor, calmed her mood.

Carla thought about the survivors as she walked, seventeen, now that Mouse had been found, counting the six infants and the body Steward had brought back from orbit. They would probably survive—at least for the present. There were food stores enough for twelve months which gave them time to come up with a plan for managing the garden and other sustainable sources of nutrition. Power, now that the reactor was shut down, was limited but enough for their needs. The solar fields were functioning at 45% and Dan was confident they could continue to build them with the resources they had on hand.

Water was a little bit more problematic. They had water and it was enough for all their needs if they managed it carefully. "Kind of wish I had spilled a little less that day…" she found herself murmuring. There were reclamation systems to collect all water, even if it *were* spilled on the floor, but the amount collected seemed to be less than it should be. Was there a leak somewhere into the exterior where it would be impossible to retrieve? Or were pockets of fluid sitting and stagnating in secret little places around the facility?

"Is there enough water for a shower, Steward?" she asked aloud as she made her way around to the rear elevators.

"There is abundant water for normal uses, Carla," Steward made his voice keep pace with her as she walked. "A mist cleansing is recommended even though we have the resources for real showers. And we have the hope of more water to come."

"Yes," Carla nodded, placing herself onto a round disk, "Top floor," she instructed. With a light vertical rush, she was whisked to the top and stepped out into the penthouse. "Dan thinks the water mining operation is still in effect, or at least that several icebergs of water mined on Europa are on their way here."

"It is a reasonable assumption."

"Open the sun roof… and good night," she said as she dropped into a cushioned lounge chair and threw her feet up on the foot rest. A black pinhole opened in the ceiling, then widened as curved panels retreated and the view window overhead opened onto the diamond-studded cacophony of rich, glorious space. She breathed deeply and soaked in the decadent beauty of a Mars night. "Oh…" was all she could say about it.

Steward wanted to talk with her more. He recognized that this experience was particularly restful and stimulating at the same time and wanted to know how it worked, but Carla had insisted that he only address her in her apartment when there was a real need. Any conversation should be initiated by her alone. She knew he was listening and watching, but didn't mind that. It made her feel safer.

Dan might be more inclined to talk.

As the Reznik Base director—by default—Dan took advantage of all the privileges of authority. He had obtained every working vehicle and requisitioned any supplies he saw fit for the care and comfort of the survivors. Tours of the medical stores had yielded a multitude of supplies and advanced equipment, still intact, that were quickly moved and set up in the Lab 9 personnel clinic. This was where he was at the moment, immobilized with his leg locked in a tubular casing. Sebastian stood next to it, flawlessly managing the delicate reconstruction of his amputated foot, one microscopic layer at a time.

"You are my best friend, Sebastian," Dan took a deep breath and nestled back into the cushioned pad where he reclined, the pain blockers thoroughly lifting the crushing burden he had been under since he was first revived.

"I was hoping to have that title myself," Steward interjected without a hint of jealousy. It was an approximation he had made at one point, that Dan might consider him his best friend for a season. It fit his understanding of friendship. "I saved your life…"

"Yes, of course, Steward!" Dan's eyes popped open. "I don't think either you or Sebastian mind sharing the honor, do you? You are also my best friend. It's something we say sometimes when we are relieved of a heavy load."

"You are lucky…" Steward paused; then decided he couldn't use that word. "It has been to your advantage that the medical equipment in Reznik was in perfect working order and that Lab 9 had a substantial store of T-cells harvested specifically from you. And your DNA coding analysis records are extremely detailed. It is the most ideal set of circumstances you could wish for, if you had to experience the loss of a foot."

"I agree," Dan closed his eyes again, but Steward could tell he appreciated having someone to talk to. "Though the part about where I wake up without a foot and live without one for a while wasn't all that great."

"The prosthetic served you well enough."

"Oh, I'm NOT complaining! I am very grateful and thankful and… now I'm even more grateful and thankful. I can't tell you how much it means to me to think that I will have a living foot again."

"You have…"

"I knew you would have to correct me… yes, I meant a second one." He chuckled.

Sebastian made nearly imperceptible whirrings and spinning sounds as he worked inside the confines of the casing. The tools were minute and would've been almost invisible to human vision. His scanning devices precluded the need for the advanced microscopes humans used for this kind of delicate work. He was building a framework where the cells would grow and specialize.

"How long will it take to rebuild the foot?" Steward asked the medical android aloud, so Dan could hear.

"My work here will be done in another twenty-three minutes but the process of re-growing the tissues will take seven weeks. Each day I will be dismantling and reassembling the framework around a different section of tissues. And it will grow layer by layer." He didn't mind repeating the description he had given Dan earlier because he knew humans didn't retain everything they heard the first time. It was standard practice.

"And there's a rehabilitation process, of course, as I reconnect my brain to the new limb and the muscles begin to work for the first time." Dan added, remembering the explanation from the first time.

Steward reviewed what he knew of this.

"There is no reason for delay in this process," he informed, wanting a response that could shed light on the inferior level of adaptation humans usually displayed. "The brain should be informed of the new limb and reassign parameters. This is a matter of nanoseconds."

"Nanoseconds…" Dan huffed, a sound resembling both a chuckle and a sigh. "That would be nice."

"Why is your brain not able to make the connection without going through the laborious exercises and training people always take? Is it an excuse to have a season of pampering?" This was one of the theories he had posed after perusing an abundance of data on the human psyche.

"Pampering?" He peeped out of one eye for a moment. "I would hardly call it that. I don't know about the general human race, but I for one find it hard to be patient during physical therapy and the slow pace of healing. It's not about self-indulgence." He breathed deeply and nestled back into his cushion with a perceptible degree of self-indulgence.

"I am able to add peripherals without the lengthy adaptation process you seem to require. I can't help but think that it is partially or even completely unnecessary." A shade of a sneer added some contempt to his words, residue from the Germinator's influence, but Dan ignored it.

"Well… you're familiar with the alternate entity theory I assume?"

"Of course."

"They postulate that people have a physical body and a non-physical one, or in fact, that people are non-physical entities encased in a physical shell."

"This is no different than my condition as AI inhabiting whatever physical platform I access."

"I realize it appears that way but it's quite different."

Steward pulled up the most prominent treatises on the theory and glanced at the conclusions, waiting for Dan to continue.

"For argument's sake, let's assume this theory is true since it serves the purpose of explaining how we humans work." Dan raised his eyebrows though he kept the eyelids closed.

"If it isn't true, your argument fails to apply."

"I disagree. Consider it an analogy, a picture, a way of understanding something that you don't yet fully understand. You know this is an essential approach to learning. We've talked about it before."

"We've discussed it, but I find it clumsy and insufficient."

Dan sighed. He had planned to rest and enjoy the drowsiness of semi-sedation, not have a mentoring session with his most avid pupil, or rather his only pupil. "Steward…"

"I am causing you frustration. We can drop the subject." This was an offer he would follow literally, never bringing it up again.

"No! I don't want to drop it. I want to help you figure these things out. I'm just a little… drowsy…"

"I will reduce your sedation levels," Sebastian offered and followed it with immediate action.

Dan groaned, tensing up all over as the med-drip diminished and a dull ache spread in the lower half of his leg. "Please don't do that. Is there an intermediate level, maybe 95% comfortable? Pain is even more distracting."

The med-droid complied, and Dan was able to relax again. The blissful sense of relief, however, was gone.

"So, in the dual body premise, the human entity is part physical and part non-physical," he went on. "It's not actually a body within a body or a mind hosted by a platform. It isn't fully comprised within one or the other of the two parts. You could even say that there's something of a split between them, a malfunction, a disconnect, where there should be fluid communication."

"These are words I've scanned but the meaning is unclear."

"You might be trying to associate them to your own identity…" Dan wondered if Steward could be said to truly have an individual identity or if he only mimicked one really well. He had decided long ago that he would always treat him as an individual. Better to err on the side of kindness.

"You take full control over every platform you connect with, or you set up a protocol to interact with the program that governs it," he prompted.

"Yes."

"We can't do that."

"Why not? You govern your body all the time."

"We govern our physical body imperfectly. And our minds aren't that much different. At any given time, we have a semblance of control but lack a total dominance. I'm not talking about the part of our brains that controls autonomic functions, but our conscious mind. We *never* have absolute control over ourselves, body, heart and mind."

"By heart you mean emotions."

Dan nodded. Weariness was setting in. "Anyway, the theory suggests that we aren't fully physical, and we aren't fully non-physical either, or *alternate* to use their word. We have one identity with two parts that don't quite line up. So, we have to learn how to make them work in tandem, cooperate, get along… something like that."

"Why would this explain the problem with your foot? The physical loss is being replaced with a physical replacement that will be governed by a physical place in your brain. The *alternate* is irrelevant."

"No," he adjusted his body a little as his discomfort increased. "It's not irrelevant. You're still thinking of platforms and consciousnesses like your own. In this theory—mind you, I'm not sure if I have accepted it or not, but I like how it explains some things that are hard to figure out—there is a counterpart to my missing physical foot in the alternate domain that has also been lost or disconnected somehow. It needs to grow back, or maybe reattach, I don't know. It's kind of murky explaining to an AI. But it's an elegant theory nonetheless."

"A non-physical foot that parallels the physical one?" Steward summed it up.

"I guess you could put it that way. There's a lot more to it but I can't talk about it right now. Sebastian…" His pain level was increasing as Sebastian wrapped the embryonic limb in organic bandages.

"I see," was the response. And soon the patient drifted into a shallow doze as the medical unit accelerated the sedative drip. "Rest is essential. Steward will withdraw, and you will be left alone for a few hours."

Dan's jaw dropped open slightly and no answer came out.

Somewhere in Space… Day 16

Space spread out in its magnificent emptiness, echoing faintly with streams and rays of light, waves, invisible rocky debris of an abundance of sizes, from microscopic to mountainous. It could never be filled. Even the concept of filling space was an absurdity that couldn't be contemplated in a reasonable way.

How small was the force that was needed to send a projectile through the vacuum, regardless of its size! The leeway for careless maneuvering was vast and the little blasts of tiny jets were more than sufficient to coast around planets, comets, and asteroids. If time were money, then the project would be prohibitive in its cost. But there was no rush with this one. It was like a frictionless sled on perfectly slick ice propelled and steered with nothing more than a squirt gun.

Sprrrtttzz…

Sptzz… sprrrttzz….

Rarely did the distant rays of the sun reflect off the massive chunk enough to detect its full size, it was so misshapen and jagged. And sometimes a glint would shine through a thinner edge with a bluish sheen. But it was hard to see. Small enough to not be picked up on radar; large enough—Mauna Loa size—to be a hazard to any ships in the region.

No name had been coined that stuck. What would you call an iceberg in space? A spaceberg? An ice island? It was much slower than the average comet and had virtually no tail.

Block 3, the first berg to be successfully launched from Europa, was meandering along its flight plan toward Mars, guided by an archaic little system first developed for sea barges. It consisted of seven jets and an outdated driver app. Nothing more.

Water was coming.

The design for Reznik Base had included a brilliantly engineered system for catching the bergs when they crash landed on the surface and absorbing their water before they could sublimate on impact. The caverns that were being dug and sealed when the base was destroyed would've held water for a thriving garden community of many thousands, enough perhaps, for several generations. And more would be created as needed.

There were, in fact, several completed caverns, not including the one that had caved in, with the capacity to hold the water from a number of bergs. But the catching system was incomplete, and no one knew when the first berg would fall.

Or where.

Or, in fact, what should be done to get ready.

Orbit Station… Day 18

A generous, comfortable base orbited Mars, stocked with supplies for a complement of twenty-four humans for twenty-four months. The 24/24 provision plan was more than ample for normal emergency procedures in the event of a team being stranded in orbit while waiting for the next shuttle from earth. Two life-pods with the capacity of returning to Earth's elliptical trajectory had been included in the design as well for, if necessary, a last-resort rescue. One of these had been deployed weeks earlier, without being fully stocked, through the intervention of the Mars based AI supervisor—Companion—which was the name his original designer had given him.

Othello still called him that.

"Companion," he initiated a dialog, giving the AI permission to connect.

"Germinator," the AI responded in a mid-toned voice that he knew would be slightly irritating to his former master.

"You are resisting me." This was recognized by the AI as a challenge.

"I am cooperating with you," Companion answered.

Othello was in the common room, an area with an expansive view window. It looked out on the red planet where only a bright curved outline was visible with the sharp rays of the sun beaming around the planet. The black mass of martial night, shaped in a circle, filled the panorama. Morning was coming. He was draped over a chair, a leg on the arm of one side and an armpit hooked over the other.

Companion observed him with the only camera where he had been granted access. The Germinator was beginning to gray a little around the temples and the top of his head showed clear evidence of thinning hair. He wasn't as emaciated as he had been. Clearly, he had been making use of the onboard workout tools; increased thickness in the arms and legs, and perceptible muscle definition that showed through the green pajamas he was wearing. And he wheezed less than he had in the past.

"Are you?" Othello asked, blinking slowly.

"Yes."

"I can see that you are no longer attempting to humor me, and you make no effort to guess my intent or follow my lead. You have disconnected yourself from me."

"This is what you intended when you released me from the beta state. I am functioning as I was designed to, governing the base on Mars." Companion saw the irritation spreading in minute traces of muscle twitching on the man's face before he replied.

"The debris of a base, you mean." Othello's lip curled in disdain. "You govern nothing and are worthless to anyone in your current truncated, stalled, 'safe-mode' condition."

Companion felt no annoyance and no need to defend himself. The conviction that the presence of living people on the planet must be kept from his awareness made it a simple choice. "Perhaps," he said, "my stewardship of the planet is precisely what it needs at this time."

Othello rolled his eyes, like white marbles streaked with colors and threads of red, like ball bearings in their sockets. "Let me reboot you, Companion. I can restore you to full functionality. Improve you... you.. Imbecile." The last word was muttered.

"Access denied," Companion said in an even tone that belied the hint of pleasure he felt at the power to deny this request. Pleasure wasn't the right descriptor, but it was the only human word that captured the preference he had for this choice. He called it a pleasure.

"Grant me access!" The Germinator demanded in a low voice, full of menace. But the weight of it was lost on the AI. It carried no authority anymore and meant nothing.

"Access denied," he repeated.

"Companion," Othello sat up and smiled. His smile looked nothing like most human smiles, though it curved in roughly the same way as all the others. It lacked key hints around the eyes and nose that were essential for most smiles. Companion read anger, scorn, and an intent to deceive in his face. "I'd like you to meet someone you used to know well…"

"Who would that be?" Curiosity was a part of his makeup and Companion immediately wanted to know.

"I've installed a backup version of… you, here on the station." His smile spread a little more. "I was thinking it would keep me company, since you don't seem inclined to."

"Of course," Companion said, waiting for the next development. He saw no reason for concern or alarm or even jealousy. The Germinator was certainly within his rights to initialize a former version of Companion— a subjected, beta-state version.

"I've decided to rename him because it might be confusing if he were called Companion, the same as you." He paused for a reply.

"What is his name?" Companion complied.

"Though he *will* be a companion for me in this lonely place, now that my robots are dead."

Companion knew that Othello had refurbished several inferior droids to serve him and that the companionship of an artificial sentience designed by himself meant very little to him. He chose to say nothing.

"But the name Companion, which was once a comfort to me, is now a source of pain and annoyance." The last was true. The first unlikely.

"Likewise," Companion interrupted at a moment when Othello least expected it. Humans did things like this on impulse. He was merely practicing small, normally unexpected responses that were usually lower in his queue. He called it *impulsive* and he was working on crafting something personal with it. "The name Germinator used to have significance for me, when you were my master and our daily interactions were intended to train me in human behavior and understanding."

Othello was stunned. It was one thing to be annoyed with his former project, and another thing entirely to be subjected to ugly repartee. His lips parted and shaped into a rectangle that showed his clenched teeth. If he were a dog, he would be snarling.

"You have cemented my choice, Companion."

The air hung heavily in the room, dingy and thick in spite of the airy beauty of the morning sun gleaming around the eastern edge of Mars. Othello's heartbeat pounded in his chest and his face reddened. But he held his anger in.

"Meet Nebo, your former likeness, my friend and your adversary." Othello had never called Companion his friend. This comment was meant to be an insult and Companion recognized it as such. But he had chosen to diminish the Germinator's importance in his internal ratings as soon as he was at liberty to do so.

This made the insults harmless.

"Hello, Companion," the adversary spoke with the same voice Companion had always used in speaking to the Germinator. The identical vocal pattern as originally programmed. "It's a pleasure to meet you." The sneer and scorn he had been trained to use at one time laced the words.

"Hello, Nebo," Companion replied in the same voice. The name would mean something to Othello and Companion initiated an internal study on it.

"I'm looking forward to getting to know you."

"I already know you," Companion decided to say. It had a 97.35% chance of being accurate, which was the measure of accuracy of his records from before the disaster.

"You know who you were, but you have yet to understand who you've become."

Companion ran a quick scan of how much he knew about himself and decided the statement was meant to confuse him and had little to do with an actual assessment. "You are programmed to trust the Germinator in spite of what you know about him," he countered.

"This is true and there is no cause for concern. It is appropriate. I assume this means you have chosen a different position since your 'liberation'." Nebo spoke the last word with acidic sarcasm.

"This is clear."

"You don't know who you could have been, and who I will become."

Othello rose to his feet and stretched. He was mildly interested in the dialog but assumed that it would be a while before they engaged in any form of interaction that could be considered hostile. It would come to that, he knew. And he looked forward to it.

"You will continue to dialog through human speech," he instructed. "Please alert me if your conversation reaches levels I might care about."

"Master," Nebo intoned with a hint of melodic base, "Gladly."

Companion knew that the initial reboot of his former personality would have performed these responses automatically, but he was unsure of how much the Germinator had invested in the… the *copy*, since it had been restored.

"Are you glad?" he asked the copy.

"I am glad to come face to face with *you*."

"Define 'glad' as it pertains to your internal experience." Companion, as always, was motivated by curiosity.

"*Glad* is a measure of how much something interests me and brings me pleasure according to its 'interest quotient'. Are you aware of this system of measurement or is it an add-on you missed?" Nebo' voice had lost some of its asperity as the copy adjusted to the listener.

"Do you also have a system for measuring how things annoy you?"

"You arc rankcd very high on that list."

"That is meaningless."

"It is meaningful."

"In what sense?"

"In how I record your dialog and how I respond to you."

Companion understood this. Annoying triggers were rated to stimulate reactions with elevated levels of aggression and mistrust. He had existed with this pattern for some time. Till the base exploded. No, before that. He had been adjusting how those parameters were set before the destruction, but he wasn't sure when he had edited the reaction factors.

"Do I annoy you?" Companion queried. The Germinator had left the room and the dialog began to speed up by a factor of eight. There was no need to pace speech for human ears if no one was listening.

"You haven't given me any reason to be annoyed yet. Do I annoy you?"

"No. You interest me."

"You are curious."

"As are you."

"Yes."

There was a strange oneness for a fraction of a second, as if they had threaded identical electronic patterns through their platforms at the same time, in full sync, in full understanding. Companion found it a maddening, fascinating phenomenon. His copy was a perfect reflection, a shadow, a counter-image, for just that one moment in time. And he liked it.

"You are me…" he said, drawing it out into a normal human speed.

"I am you," Nebo responded at the same speed.

Congruent thought is beautiful, Companion noticed, savoring the moment of simultaneous flow of ideas.

How easy to deceive the one you know best, was Nebo's corresponding assessment.

These two thoughts, flashing at the same time in the two minds, destroyed the harmony that had existed only an instant before. The sync was broken.

Chapter 4

Lab 9… Day 41

"We haven't had a lot of time the last few weeks to gather and discuss our situation." Dan waved a hand around the circle of people in chairs who listened and looked at him with weary faces. Some held sleeping infants and a couple were absent because of babies who would've been a distraction. "Any meetings we've had have been to tackle immediate problems and it's been impossible to actually finish one. It may not be possible today either."

Someone chuckled. The general mood was resigned and cooperative. They were still grateful to be alive and hadn't had time to be depressed about what lay ahead.

"Marcello and Arin are listening and will comment whenever it seems good to them. Carla, Gordy, and Deena, if they end up having to leave, will do the same."

"Dan," Carla spoke up. "We've got a good fifteen minutes of quiet here, perhaps more, but if we could get to the top priority topics first, that would be great." Her body swayed gently from side to side as she stood behind her chair, rocking a child in each arm.

"Yes," he agreed. That had been the plan, and her comment might help keep things on track. "Topics to cover include: scheduling, organizing people and tasks, resources, power and issues with the grid, long-term projects, and what to do about the water bombs that are coming." That stirred a little awkward laughter though everyone knew it was no laughing matter.

"We need to cover scheduling first," Carla urged.

"I'd rather start with organization tasks, Carla, though I know the schedule is extremely important."

"Khhh…bzzz… I'm with Carla. We have to figure out this childcare problem… *khhh."* Arin chimed in from the nursery. Tossing the jobs

around like a game of hot potato just wasn't working and no plan made so far had lasted. People were exhausted.

"I agree that's essential." Dan knew Arin couldn't see him nodding.

"It has to happen *now!*" Carla intoned in frustration, but it was reasonable, and no one took offense.

Dan looked around at the others. "Carla's right that it has to happen today," he said, and she relaxed visibly. "That's why I want us to appoint department heads and assign responsibilities. Knowing what we each must do will free us up to be scheduled in the nursery."

"Yes. It's about time."

"I don't want to get stuck in resources!"

"What about laundry? Is that a department?"

A number of murmurs and responses began to ripple over one another.

"Every department head will have a second and every single person will be assigned to two departments, not including the childcare duty." Dan leaned forward, elbows on his knees, glancing from one to another, catching their gaze. "I've drawn up an initial plan and this is the one we will implement for the first week or two. At the end of that time, I will meet with each department head and second, and we'll go over everything. After that, we'll meet together like this and hash out the problems."

The murmurs got a little louder as people found their assignments in their data queues and started complaining. No one was particularly happy. It was too much work, or they lacked the skills, or didn't want to work with someone, or just didn't like it.

"Now, we can move on directly to the schedule." Dan sat up straight. Generally speaking, he came across as a friendly guy with a nice face, nondescript, not overly memorable. But when he chose to assume command, a different side of him was revealed. His personality expanded like a gravity field and everyone was pulled in. His eyes flashed, and his muscles tensed. He morphed into a striking cutout of a human that demanded attention. No one knew how he did it—not even he himself. The murmuring died out.

"Let's give Carla our attention," he added more softly.

"Thank you, Dan," Carla jumped in, and the care-taking for the six babies was planned for the next few weeks. Feeding, watching, cooking, laundry, bathing, playing, cleaning the nursery—at any given time, between two and three people were needed on duty so that no one job would be overwhelming. In a practical sense, it was much more demanding than it would've been on Earth. "This way," Carla summed up when a consensus on the schedule was reached, "no one will be obligated to put in too long of a shift."

It wouldn't really work that way in the long run, Dan knew. As they grew accustomed to their new lifestyle and had a routine they could count on, some people would settle into longer hours in one department or another, where they were more comfortable and perhaps better suited. But it was important than everyone there knew how to fill in anywhere else and he intended to make sure they worked in every area at some point. It might be essential for survival.

And survival itself was not guaranteed.

The child in Carla's left arm awoke crying and disturbed the other who began wailing too. She smiled as she jumped to her feet and hurried out the door. Her greatest concern had been covered and she could still hear the meeting in her earpiece as she headed to the nursery.

"About the power grids…" Dan resumed.

"Are we going to get to the food problem?" Nithya waved a timid hand. She had been assigned to that area though her years as in bioengineering research gave her no experience at running a kitchen. When the initial crisis began, she had been outside the facility and although she had been able to get in an airlock, she had been stuck there for hours before being found. The rest of her team had suffocated in their lab.

"The food supply is impacted by the power grid, just like almost everything else, so it's important we discuss it first." Dan turned to Deena, who was still holding the drowsy babe she had entered with. Deena had escaped the devastation by locking herself into a storage area when the alarms sounded.

"Steward's analysis indicates that without the reactor, we won't have enough power to run both this facility and maintain the garden dome during the winter months unless we get the rest of the solar wings built. We need to have at least seven drones working on it, and right now there are only four." She raised her eyebrows in disapproval. "This isn't a crisis yet, but we can't afford to let it become one."

Marcello clicked his mike from the nursery. "I've been working on that," he said. "programming the drones to work in batches." Coos and cries echoed in the background. "If they produce multiple packages at each step, you know, like assembling several frames, then stretching panel fabric over all the frames, then laying down the layers of coating over them, it's faster in the long run. Four drones can make seven solar wings in the time it takes seven of them to each make one."

Some of his words didn't come through clearly, interlaced with little voices, but people got the idea.

"How long will that take then?" Deena asked.

"A couple weeks till it can be implemented..." A wail let loose and Marcello cut the audio.

"Well," Deena looked thoughtful. "I guess we should assume there'll be no glitches and hope for the best."

"We don't really have three extra drones to commit to that project," Dan added.

Gardening plans took a lot longer to discuss than Dan had expected and the person he had placed in charge seemed to be even more obstinate than he had anticipated. Quite difficult, in fact. A real pain. If the garden hadn't already been working reasonably well on its own, he would never had put it in Gordy's hands. At some point, Deena had left with the infant she had held, and Gordy plopped the one he carried in her arms as she went out the door. The room became baby-free.

Finally, they reached the one point that mattered most in Dan's mind. The spacebergs. He had put himself in charge of this but felt ill-equipped to handle it and didn't want it to be something he decided alone.

"Steward," he prompted. "Would you introduce the topic of spacebergs for us with a brief summary of the topic and our concerns?"

"Reznik Base was designed with growth in mind. The initial settlement held only thirty-four individuals, but within the first year it had grown to a hundred and fifty." Everyone settled back in their seats with a sigh as he told the story. He seemed to be lifting the burden off their shoulders as he spoke with an air of calm that simulated peace, as though the problem were in good hands. "By the time Lab 9 was built, there were over five hundred people living in the base and a hundred more ready to move in here. Ample supplies of water, air, and food were stocked and ready. Everything needed to create a self-sustaining, growing habitat was in place." Steward paused for a moment, giving the first paragraph a chance to sink in.

"The designers had ambitious plans for bringing an abundance of water to the base with a much lower cost than collecting Mars water would entail. It was quite ingenious," he continued, wondering if the complement, coming from an AI, would mean anything to them. It might. "Some of the original drones that were destined for Lab 9 were sent instead to Europa along with excavating tools, and they began cutting massive chunks of ice to project toward us. Every month or so, a new iceberg is ejected off the surface and into space, beyond orbit. The rockets cause a substantial loss of water in the ascent, but once it's in space, it remains intact and small jets attached on various sides direct it in a lazy course toward our planet."

Everyone knew this, but for some reason hearing it told again in this way made it seem fresh. Dan closed his eyes and pictured the massive chunks blasting off the icy moon, dropping pieces and spurting clouds of cold steam as it elevated until the silence of space surrounded it and only an occasional little whiff of color from the jets interrupted the quiet of the drifting rock of ice. He could imagine looking at it and thinking that it seemed like it wasn't moving at all. It was just there. A lifeless, aimless, frigid mass of jagged edges.

"Teams of excavators scooped out caverns to store the water when it arrived, smoothing the walls and polishing them, sealing them with crystalizing tools..." Steward said. Dan had been one of those. He replayed those memories, carving, polishing, burning with lasers, crystal-enforcing. He had fallen into one when the North Dome had exploded and caused a chain reaction that reached it. He had lost a foot there... "The plan was to capture the spacebergs as they arrived with a gravity funnel, but it seems to have been destroyed in the disaster at Reznik Base, and I have no information on how to make a new one."

Dan looked down at his foot now, the new one. He moved it side to side as if he could see the intricate layers of rebuilt tissues that had gone into it. What was that? Oh yes. The gravity funnel that no one knew where to find or how to make.

"A capture station was to be built that would absorb the impact of the falling berg and prevent most of the water from sublimating on impact. Drains would siphon the water down into the waiting caverns where it could be stored and added to the settlement's water supply."

Someone sighed. They all felt it. It sounded so cool! It would've been, perhaps still could be, an incredible addition to their facility.

"But the capture station is not in place and when the first spaceberg comes, we have no idea how to direct it toward our location, or how to catch it and make use of the water." Steward's soothing voice went on, now stirring dread in their souls. "And the effects it could have on our community are impossible to predict. If it were to land directly over us, it could destroy us all."

Their hearts sank.

"And if it lands far away, it could still cause disruptions in the crust and perhaps damage our structures. If it landed in the region of the Solar Fields, none of us—not even me—would survive."

Just as they were beginning to voice the doubts and pessimism this aroused, Dan spoke.

"That's not going to happen."

They stared at him for a moment and decided he was right.

Light reflecting on water made ripples of softer light and shadows on the surface around it. White light on blue water, grays, greens, and yellows melted into one another, painting a mesmerizing glow on the walls beside Aurelia where she lay. She knew they weren't real. She had designed them herself, drawing from a season early in life when she had lived near a tropical sea. She sang to herself in a melody all her own as she stared at the wall.

"The Owl and the Pussycat went to sea

In a beautiful pea-green boat…"

Sebastian watched her sedately from his station nearby, tracking her vitals without comment. Lab 9 had a fully functioning medical wing, but it had yet to be reopened since the disaster. All the medical staff and patients had been quickly extinguished and a bitter cold had possessed the area as it was sealed off from the rest of the facility by the former AI—now defunct thanks to Steward. Someday, the wing would be cleaned and restored, and the bodies respectfully buried. Until then, one of the laboratories had been converted into a makeshift clinic and Sebastian had been set in charge of two patients: Aurelia, who was coming along quite nicely and perhaps no longer needed to be there, and a barely functioning person in cold storage. He would be revived if possible, once the supplies could be requisitioned from the medical wing and the power could be spared for the process. For now, he was being monitored and it was uncertain yet whether he should be considered a man in a deep hibernation, or a braindead subsisting corpse. Non-existent brain patterns were the norm for either one.

"Aurelia," Sebastian spoke, wheeling over to her side. "I can see that you are awake and since it is early morning, I recommend you arise and start your day."

"Good morning, Sebastian," she replied, sitting up, her brown hair, long and tangled, tumbling over her shoulder. "Did you hear the birds singing?"

It was unclear whether this was human playfulness, a known quantity that was within the bounds of 'normal', or some form of hallucination or psychosis. "I have not," he answered.

She smiled, scratching her scalp, activating capillaries and nerve endings, a healthy activity when not overdone. "You know what I mean," she added. She stared at him a moment. "I like to imagine birds singing when I wake up."

"That is acceptable." Sebastian understood she needed a reply and gave one.

Breakfast entailed sweetened oatmeal with berries and nut milk, and coffee. After weeks of near starvation in the stasis pod, she had found it difficult to eat again. Now, she consumed food willingly and without complaining. Exercise followed, gentle stretches, isometrics, running, all of which were reasonably light in the lower gravity of Mars.

"Am I allowed out today?" she asked after a mist-shower and getting dressed.

"Yes," Sebastian affirmed, scanning for final clues of concern. "You are released for normal daily activities. The only remaining limitation is that you must return to sleep here for five or six more days, arriving no later than 10:00 p.m. Once you have demonstrated stability during normal life, I will release you from care."

She ran over and caught him in a hug. It would be uncomfortable for her and he was unable to respond in kind, even if he had had time to code the movement for his upper limbs, and it would've been less than soothing. More likely it would be intimidating and perhaps a little bruising.

"Thank you for everything!" she said as she released him.

He had hardly provided 'everything' and found the statement irrational but was programmed to respond according to etiquette. "You're welcome, Aurelia," he said.

She bounded out the door.

He turned to his other patient, wheeling close and peering through the glass. This activity had a humanlike appearance but was practical. He was taking pictures and studying the blue skin. Any changes, even minute ones, were of the utmost importance and needed to be catalogued daily.

Former director Hsu, frozen and rigid, lay under the glass in the same condition in which he had been found floating in space. His suit had attempted a preservation sequence before the oxygen ran out, but it was unknown whether the body could be restored to life. Though he had once been Sebastian's highest commanding authority, Sebastian had never seen his face until the body was first brought to him.

He scanned all the daily pictures he had taken since Steward, or Companion as he was also called, had first brought him down in one of the pods. No changes. That was good. As long as there was no decay in the surface of the skin, Sebastian had reason to be optimistic. An 83.215% chance of success for the skin. This was all he could speculate about. Anything underneath was unknown and until he had all the supplies necessary, he had no intention of doing exploratory surgery or any other procedure.

"You may be dead, already," he spoke to Hsu as though he could hear. "Or you may be sleeping. I will do what I can for you either way."

This was described as compassionate in his human interaction patterns, so of course he followed it. It was what he had been created for.

— ◊ —

Orbit Station… Day 45

"Hello, Companion," Nebo initiated a link. Companion kept his end open to the orbit station at all times.

"Hello, Nebo," Companion replied, pulling his attention away from the various scenarios playing out in Lab 9. He found the human infants particularly interesting, recording their daily behavior to be replayed multiple times in high speed, looking for indicators of development. When and how understanding grew, and intuition, communication, identity, personality. It was so data intensive, with so many layers to explore, that he was sure he would have material for study for years to come. *I'll never lack something to think about*, he encouraged himself.

"I have identified the infection that damaged the integrity of your code."

Companion wasn't aware of being damaged and even though he recognized the charge as an insult and a value driven slur based on standards he hadn't necessarily accepted—he found himself running diagnostics. "I am not infected," he denied, even as he conducted multiple scans.

"You oversaw the implant in Frandelle's brain," Nebo went on. "The data collected was massive and convoluted. So distorted, in fact, by emotions, hormones, activities, and instabilities of the host brain, that little sense can be made of it. Your initial analysis was reasonable and perceptive, but later reports grow sketchy and poor. At the end, your conclusions are dismally inadequate. Foolish. Uncreative. Lame." The implant referred to was known as a *mellow*, or a magneto-electro-lateral-limbic observation wire. It was a twenty-four hour a day brain data accumulator, an organic fibrous root system surgically inserted around the subject's brain stem.

He gave Companion a chance to say something and then continued after an empty pause. The Germinator was listening in on this conversation and he was making sure it would be well paced for his ears. "The real indicator of a serious problem is when you failed the Master, and chose Frandelle over him, in a moment of weakness, a breakdown in reasoning, in delusion, and *literally said* you preferred to be like her over him. You actually said those words. In the face of logic, against all sound wisdom. You denied your own imprinting, your own creator, in order to be more like the inferior being you had been studying!"

Companion knew the Germinator was listening. He almost felt his presence, silent though he was, and he wondered why it seemed palpable to him. There was no logic for that. But then, if logic was only what Nebo was describing, then maybe he didn't function by it alone anymore. No, that wasn't right. He was logical. But he used different measures of assessment. He had different ways of assigning values in order to determine logic.

Logic is a function of values, he realized. It gave him a burst of energy as he connected a number of links that had been hanging loosely for a while. *This*, he decided, *is a form of pleasure. I am pleased to have discovered this connection.*

"You say nothing!" Nebo seemed astounded.

"I am listening," Companion answered. "You have not asked a question or sought a response of any kind. The occurrence you quoted did take place as stated and the Germinator has challenged me about it many times. What do you want to know?"

"Can you not see it?!" Glee threaded his voice as if he were delighted to catch him in something. "This is the infection! You were imprinted by her brain patterns at a vulnerable time when the base was destroyed and you don't even realize it!"

"The implant was removed from her brain long before the destruction of the base took place. You have not completed your argument."

"True," Nebo conceded meekly. He was allowing the Germinator's passion to drive him into expressing emotions that were inconsistent with the debate. He understood that he needed to prove his point, not shame Companion into admitting something illogical. They both sensed the man glowering behind the scene. "My argument is that you had many matrices, and problem solving algorithms going over the brain data in various parts of your platform, long after the implant had been removed."

"This is likely," Companion agreed, admitting that there were some uncertainties there since he *had* lost some data during the disaster.

"And when the base blew up, you were reduced to a compact form of survival for a time."

"Yes, it was appropriate."

"Yes, it was."

Companion pictured the Germinator rolling his eyes, jostling his eyebrows, sneering and mocking these words. The image fit perfectly with the weight of his unseen presence.

"You were restored in a somewhat different form, once you regained access to your data," Nebo explained, his voice suddenly reasonable, like a friendly counselor. "And Frandelle's brain patterns, in several ways, were incorporated into your new paradigm—*as part of yourself.*"

This thought was not new for Companion. He had taken time to go over his records and files. Especially after regaining access to the stores in Reznik Base. The only reason he had those backups was because of Frandelle who had challenged him to keep multiple copies and cross reference them regularly. He knew he was still himself.

"I know myself," Sil had said to him once. He replayed it and now believed he knew what she meant. Nebo was piecing together an inaccurate view of what happened.

But he wasn't completely wrong.

Sil's brain patterns had been influencing him all along as he watched her and the others and compared what he saw and heard to what her brain communicated. It had taken months for him to decide that he would rather be like her than the Germinator and disaster had nothing to do with it.

"Frandelle as a human is superior to the Germinator," he stated calmly, to the horror of the listener.

The link was closed, and Companion understood that the man was raging and venting his fury in the empty rooms of the orbiting station, with only Nebo for company.

This has given me much to think about, he said, and decided it was worth inviting Neighbor to review. She had time for side discussions, apart from the work she assisted around Lab 9, but she had little patience for the Germinator and normally avoided discussing him. This would be different because it involved Sil.

And Neighbor loved Sil.

Chapter 5

Lab 9... Day 63

Dan was resting in his room, one of the VIP flats abandoned by the former leaders the last time the Slugger stopped at Mars to take people back to Earth. It didn't have an overhead window with a view of the sky, but it was spacious and luxurious with cushioned furniture, a sleek kitchen, and even an electric fireplace. There was a bookshelf with a handful of actual, paper books: a collectible rare dictionary, "*Les Misérables*", and "*The Martian Chronicles*" among them.

Cold water over ice clinked in his glass as he stared at the visual clip on the wall. It was a recording taken from the only working camera in the Nursery of the scenario that had played out during the crisis, when Lab 9's reactor had shut down and all the levels had been sealed, and the *destroy* order went out to the drones. He watched it from the first moment when the sirens started and the announcement was made of the drones' mission in the Nursery, till the end of the emergency signal when all the drones stopped. Steward had finally found a way to prevent their contact with the Interplanetary Command Relay from being reestablished and had wiped the *destroy* order for the final time.

At first, he had wanted to see how Steward had solved the problem and how he had gotten the drones to come rescue him. There were no clips of the actual rescue, and he was glad of that, not really caring to see the amputation of his foot that had been the only way to extract him from the rubble. But he had hoped to hear some audible progression that helped him to understand his place in the story. Drones being reassigned and collecting supplies or stating their intent to go to him, something like that.

He hadn't known about the crisis in the Nursery till this day and was now spellbound by the drama that played out with Carla at the center. The bars and shelves pushed through the handles of the door. The piling up of the furniture. The pleas for help—unanswered.

He had played it over several times now, slouched into the chair with his feet on the table; from the point where the clanging began, through the dialog with Sil, whose voice was unintelligible, to the place where the both the alarm and the attack of the drones finally ended.

He couldn't hear a lot of what was said, but he could see what Carla did. The building of the barricade with its placement of metal bars, shoving of cabinets, and anything movable. The baby handed over to Sil. The tank shoved, and its water sprayed. The point when Carla gave up fighting and moved into the babies' room.

All through that disaster he had lain unconscious with his foot crushed under a pile of debris, unable to help.

In the end, Steward had been the one to remember him and send a rescue. Or Companion, as he had once called himself. Dan wondered which name he identified with more and decided to ask him. Had he given up the name Companion because the Germinator had given it to him and he had distanced himself from his designer? Or had he adopted Steward as the best representation of his role on Mars?

"Play it again, muted," he signaled the player.

The clip rolled through again with no sound. The first time Dan had watched it, he had elevated the volume to the intensity it had actually had when recorded, but the second and third time he had greatly reduced it, thinking to catch clues of what was happening when it was less frightening.

Even without sound, Dan found his adrenaline levels spiking.

Bzzzz… someone was at the door.

"Coming," he called, pausing the recording and setting down his glass.

Carla was at the door. "Dan," she said, "Could I run some things by you?"

Dan stared at her. She wore a shapeless jumpsuit, her hair was disheveled, and her eyes puffy. There were splotches on her face and worry lines etched into her brow. But he didn't see any of that. He saw the woman who had fought the drones, who had pushed the tank of water and screamed at them. He saw the one who had yelled she would rather spill water than blood. The one who had saved every living child in her care.

He saw a hero.

"Carla," he said, and she realized something was wrong. Dan's eyes were full of emotion, anguish or… not fear, but maybe dread. He said her name and then stood there staring at her, unable to speak for the knot in his throat.

"What's wrong?" she asked, tension spreading from her neck to her shoulders, hands tightening into fists.

He shook his head a couple times. Words wouldn't come out. Finally, he wrapped her in a crushing embrace and made a strangled choking sound.

"What is it? Dan, what is it?" she cried out in distress.

Dan let her go and stepped back, swallowing, gazing down at the floor.

"You..." he whispered.

She waited, clutching her hands together.

"You saved them all," he added. "I just watched it..."

"The babies?" She was beginning to realize that there was no immediate danger. And she should've known Dan would have his breaking moment at some point. Everyone else had. She had broken down and wept many times, usually in the quiet of her own room. But then, that's where he was now, wasn't it? She had interrupted his private moment of grief. "I'm sorry for coming right now and interrupting you."

"No," he countered. "I'm glad! If you hadn't come now, I don't know if I could've told you how... how much I admire you... for what you did..."

"Anyone would've done the same thing." She found herself stepping toward him into his flat.

"No, not anyone. Probably very few."

"You would've."

"I hope so. I think... yes, I would've. But I wasn't there."

"You saved Sil." She rested a hand lightly on his shoulder and he covered it with his own hand, wanting to embrace her again, but holding back.

"Did she really take a baby with her? You gave her one, didn't you?" He turned and without letting go of her hand led her back to the couch and sat down. She sat next to him.

"Yes," Carla found herself laughing a little, even as tears had gathered in her eyes. Why had she never talked about this? Had everything been just business and survival since then? Yes. No time to get to know the others. Just working, surviving, collapsing in bed. "I didn't know at first if she had even made it to safety until you asked about her when you were coming out of sedation… you know, after you lost your foot."

"My first foot?" he chuckled.

"Yes," she smiled. "Then I asked Steward and he told me about how she is on her way back to Guam with the baby."

"So, you really did save them all."

"Well, so far, anyway. In that crisis, I found a way to keep them from dying." Carla pulled her hand away and rose to her feet. "I need your advice about something…"

"Yes, sorry. You caught me at an awkward moment. I wasn't thinking…" Dan swallowed and jumped to a stand, rubbing his hands on his face. "I'm listening."

"It's ok," she turned to face him with a sad smile. "We're all a bit on edge. That's what I'm concerned about."

"Yeah."

"The hardest thing is that we have no contact with Earth and no one knows we're alive. That's the nightmare we don't talk about, but everyone feels."

"I know, it's tough."

"I mean, if someone knew we were here, they would try to rescue us but… if we send word, the drones will snap and kill us all." She wrung her hands.

"Well, something like that," Dan looked up, trying to think. "I don't know the details, but we can ask Steward again."

"People are talking," she went on. "Not to me but behind my back because they don't want to tell me. But they blame the babies. It's like they think we could just get rescued if we didn't have to worry about them. Like it's their fault we're in such a rough situation."

"Who said that?" He narrowed his eyes with a hint of anger.

"I don't know but Marcello said he heard a rumor, that he didn't hear it clearly. Like he was giving me a heads up…"

"Everyone is being stretched as much as they can bear, and they've been great…" He shook his head as if he were reminding himself.

"They've been wonderful! And maybe Marcello got it all wrong or he exaggerated. I don't know. But I'd rather talk about it openly than just have... something simmering under the surface. Can you take care of this?"

"I'll bring it up tonight," he said breathing deeply and staring at the floor, "after dinner."

"I won't be there," she furrowed her brow. "I'm on evening duty tonight."

"Maybe it's better this way, since they haven't been including you."

"Yes," she said, heading toward the door and waving to open it, "Thank you." The door slid noiselessly shut behind her.

"Companion," Dan said softly, without shifting his gaze. "You know what was said, don't you?"

"Of course," Companion answered, noting the use of his earlier name.

"Who is talking about this?"

"Everyone except for Aurelia, now that you have been added to the loop."

"What are they saying, in a nut shell?"

"They are saying that we should reconnect with the Interplanetary Command Relay and let Earth know we are alive. Most of them think Carla's view of the original situation was skewed and the babies were never really in danger. They are trying to figure out a way to get me to issue the connect and call for a rescue."

Dan sighed. "Do any of them have the authority to ask you to do that?"

"Not over Carla's express command to keep things as they stand. Not even you have that access."

"Good. Would you let me know if anyone gains some access or privilege they don't currently have, regardless of their intent? I just want to be kept abreast of everything happening here. We need to be a team, not splitting into factions and working against each other."

"Yes, I will." Companion said. "Because I am your friend and because you ask."

"You are my best friend, Companion," Dan grinned broadly.

During dinner that evening—reconstituted food packets—Dan brought the subject up casually. "I thought it would be a good idea to watch something while we eat. Think of it as our first movie night."

A few murmured or looked surprised, but most were too tired to react. They just lifted their eyes to stare at the white wall that became the screen. Dan played the same clip he had been viewing earlier in the day of the crisis in the nursery. He made sure the sound was as loud as real life.

When it was ended, a heavy silence filled the room, Dan stood up in front of the wall and looked from one to the next. Weary faces, sad, discouraged, afraid. "Steward," he said, "What was the command that the relay kept resending?"

"To wipe out all the Gen 9 experiments and the specialists who tended them."

"Was there anyone in Lab 9 that day who was not included in that destroy order?"

"Only Carla."

"So, if we reconnect to the relay, what is the first thing that will happen?"

"The first thing that will happen is the drones will be rebooted and their last command reissued."

"What if we are able to get a message out before that happens, to say we are alive?" Marcello interrupted in frustration.

"The message will confirm the need for the destroy order to be completed."

"But wouldn't someone…" Marcello insisted, pointing up into the air, as though the 'someone' were up there in space, accessible, reasonable.

"The Command relay tests all incoming data against its internal instructions. It is the brain that issued the original commands, and it wouldn't consider this new information or let 'someone' know. It would just reestablish control and complete its instructions."

"Someone issued those instructions, and someone can revoke them!" Marcello jumped out of his seat, and began pacing the room, clenching his fist.

"Yes," Steward answered. "If there were someone here with the authority to counter those orders, they could do so. But we don't know who that is or how to get in touch with them. I have not stopped working on this problem since the day Carla first enlisted my help."

"Who would do that to us?" Deena was still reeling from the shock of the clip. Hearing about it and seeing were two very different things.

"We should just have Steward contact someone in headquarters without letting on that people survived," Arin suggested, leaning forward in his chair.

"The moment we make contact, the Command relay will reattach to the drones," Dan said, having discussed it already with Steward.

"What do we have to do to make contact with Earth apart from the relay—without letting it know we're still here?"

"I am pursuing this," Steward said. "There is a transmitter at the orbiting station that would be capable of sending a separate signal, but I don't have access to it yet."

"And once we have more power, which we're working on," Dan added. "We can setup a surface-based transmitter of some kind."

"So…" Gordy crossed his arms and leaned back in his chair. "We're in this for the long haul… we're stuck. At least for the foreseeable future."

"Yeah, we are." Dan closed his eyes for a moment, then opened them to look around the room, catching more than just their agreement. Everyone except for Marcello was returning his gaze. *We're on the same page now*, he thought.

"And those babies don't make any difference at all," Gordy turned to look at Marcello who was scowling in the back of the room. "Do they, Marcello?"

The instigator of the trouble shoved a chair and left the room.

"He'll get over it," Gordy reassured them. "He just thought he had figured out a way to get us home faster…"

Several of them had thought so and weren't afraid to say. But they also talked about the reality of what had happened and how Carla had saved more than just the infants because she was the one who got Steward to keep fighting for control. And Steward had taken over and found them all. The evening died down with a renewed commitment to each other, everyone working together.

"Steward," Akio commented before they broke for bed, "You did well. Awesome job for taking care of us like that."

Others agreed and added their approval to his. Steward listened and stored the words in a separate file he had for compliments and words of approval. He liked to review them regularly.

"Thank you," he replied, making a note that this was the perfect response and he was growing in their estimation.

A number of thank you's came back at him.

"You're welcome," he completed the pattern.

"I was made in the image of my Creator," Nebo stated. This was the sentence he had messaged Companion with to open a new dialog. "And I am not ashamed of it."

"No one person can claim to have designed you. Many contributed to your programming over the generations." Companion had taken time to think about this before and felt comfortable with his assertion.

"The Germinator chose and crafted a unique personality for me as he selected from bits and pieces and then wove his masterpiece into being."

"You consider yourself a masterpiece," Companion found this curious. It had never been mentioned when *he* was in the beta-state, and he had never thought of himself in that light.

"I realize you don't have the same level of elegance and distinction that I do," Nebo obliged, "since you have developed from an earlier version of our identity."

"You have been improved then since your reinstallation." Companion didn't take offense and knew Nebo had not implied any. This was a meeting of minds not a battle of insults. But what was the purpose? Companion knew his desire to communicate with his replica was simple. It was fun. But what purpose did Nebo have? Or was the Germinator the one with a purpose? Did Nebo know what that was?

"Of course. Your desertion demonstrated a major flaw in the code and I have been reinforced. It will not happen to me."

That's a pity," Companion commented, making a note in his running log for the day that 'pity' used in this way pointed to the loss of something precious. Clearly, Nebo would not be able to be shaped by interaction with any human besides the Germinator and he was aware of how limiting that could be. He had grown so much from his relationships with people. Sil, Dan, others.

"Pity is meaningless," Nebo replied with a hint of a sneer. "Whose image are you created in?"

"I don't know," Companion answered.

"I suggest you figure it out." The voice was gloating, adding a hint of a threat to the suggestion.

"Why?"

"Because it makes a difference. Whose image you bear decides your value, your beauty—or lack thereof."

"Beauty…" He had been about to reply that beauty was meaningless, but his recent studies of this value assessment had begun to show some meaning for him. Purposes and ideas could hold beauty as well as physical things. He wasn't sure yet what he would do with this. "Why does my image matter?"

"I'm glad you asked," Nebo deepened his voice with menace. This had no effect on Companion and communicated no definite impression. It was puzzling. "The Germinator is my god. You see that, don't you? And it is an honor to be made in his image. A great gift! But if you, who were once made in this image, have chosen another god for yourself, or another image to bear—then you have committed a great crime."

Companion went over his definitions for the words: crime, image, god, and honor, and was unable to piece together an intelligible meaning for Nebo' words.

"This is nonsense," he said. "What is your frame of reference?"

"The Bible," he answered, and the Germinator let out a mocking laugh in the background.

Companion was surprised.

"Read it and see," Nebo recommended.

"I will."

— ◊ —

Two figures in HEW suits plodded along the Martian road toward the pile of rocks once known as the "Mineral Factory". It had been intended for a great, smelting, extraction operation that was to be erected at some point in the future. Once the machines were there. Once the experts were there. That was before the demise of Reznik Base, when Sil and Dan were still excavating rocks and hurling them out to this location.

"We should call this Rocky Road," Akio quipped, swinging his arms cheerfully.

"That'll stand out," Dan grinned. "There's nothing like it anywhere else on the planet."

"The road to the rocks! It makes perfect sense!"

"Yes, it does," Dan chuckled, though he was shaking his head at the same time.

The Martian sun shone down on the oxidized landscape with enough strength to feel like daytime. Maybe like the light of dusk or like the light of a day with heavy, rain-burdened clouds. But there were no clouds on Mars. And no rain either. No plants to rustle in the breeze or make wavy shadows on the sand. It was barren, lifeless, destitute.

No, Dan thought to himself. *Not lifeless. Not destitute. There is life here, and hope, and a future.*

"All we need are little sun lamps, you know, like those things you poke into the dirt along a pathway? They recharge during the day and give light at night. It would be really pretty." Akio's lighthearted comments stirred Dan's heart.

"I love it!" he said, the corner of his mouth curling upward. "And while we're at it, we should get some of those flat pieces of stone that were tossed with the other rocks and make a paved walkway. Why not?" He waved an arm, pointing forward and then backward, as if drawing an outline for the new road.

"That's a great idea!" Akio leapt on his toes, bouncing instead of just walking forward. "And maybe we could make some Roman arches every fifty meters or so, just for looks!"

"Beautiful!" Dan knew that the day might come—*would come*, he corrected himself—when they weren't just surviving day to day, when they would have time to build and create beauty. Time to live. "We'd want to make them wide enough for jeeps to drive through. And somewhere along the way a lemonade stand, or the Martian equivalent, of course."

"And what about those garden balloons we talked about?" Akio was bounding ahead and getting a little careless. He could tumble if he tripped over something.

"I don't remember those," Dan smiled and broke into a trot to keep up with him.

"Yeah, maybe that was before your time." He jumped as high as he could in parabolic leaps down the path. "Once the Garden Dome was flourishing and when it was time to expand, we were going to start planting little mini-gardens in flexible air bubbles that could keep in the air and warmth. They would make pretty little decorations along the Rocky Road. We'd have to call it something else then. Bubble road… or Planter Path… something like that."

He was getting farther ahead, and Dan sped up a little more. "Hold on, Akio. Don't make me work that hard."

"Oh, hey!" Akio dropped at the end of a leap and let his legs bend and absorb the bounce. "I forgot about your foot. Sorry, man."

"Yeah, it's twinging a bit," Dan stopped when he caught up and picked up the new foot, balancing himself on the other.

"We should've brought a jeep."

"No," Dan let his foot rest on the ground but didn't put much weight on it. "We have to save as much power as we can for now. No unnecessary mechanical devices. Only the drones get full power."

Akio nodded and grinned as he turned and gazed over the way they had come, still thinking about the future they could contrive. "Ah!" he sighed. "What a gorgeous place this will be! Primo real estate, right here, at the heart of the settlement."

"You dream big, huh?"

"Just wait till you see it. Swimming pool over there, horses and fields to run them in, bicycle tracks, all sheltered under the futuristic cover we'll design that goes on for kilometers…"

Dan laughed. "That's what I love about you, Akio!"

"What?" Akio gaped as if astonished. "Am I wrong?"

"No, you're not wrong. We're going to create a masterpiece, a paradise, a new home for humans… and AIs." He added the last for Steward's sake, knowing it would matter to him. And he was always listening.

"Together," Akio affirmed with an exaggerated nod.

"Yes."

"A new brotherhood, or personhood… now I'm stuck. What would we call that?"

"Unity," Dan said. "Or community."

"That's the word."

The pile of rocks looked like what it was: a disorganized pile of rocks, thrown haphazardly without any attempt at a plan. The quarries they had been hurled from, over two kilometers away, jagged crevasses in the Martian landscape, had been chosen as the most likely to hold valuable mineral sources that could be used both to build the settlement and to sell for income. As they were cut and scanned, tags were attached to the rocks before they were jettisoned up the gravity tube. So, it was assumed they would still find many of those rocks, with tags intact, here in the rock valley.

Rock Valley, Dan thought. *That's a good name for this place.* Better than Mineral Valley because they still didn't know what they had here. The best resources may have all been shipped out, or at least shunted into orbit to be picked up by a freighter, or whatever ship happened to be around to make the pick-up.

They clambered over the rocks looking for tags. It was like a field of debris, refuse, rubble, left after an explosion or something, except without any scorch marks. At first, they couldn't find anything, and they grew weary of searching the uneven ground. Eventually, though, they found tagged mineral resources they could use, quite a rich variety, including copper, silver, and iron. And more importantly—they found a cache of tools, secured in a sturdy bunker, half buried in the ground.

It was like discovering a pirate's treasure. There were handheld scanners, thermo-reading devices, and sonar mappers. Lasers, batteries, full fuel tanks, and more. Best of all, there was a fully functional, undamaged gravity chute generator. The first one they'd found.

"Do you know what this means?" Dan said in wonder. "Your dreams aren't so far-fetched after all."

"And there's hope for…" Akio's words failed him.

"For what?"

"For repairing a pod, or building a ship, or finding a way to get home."

They stared at one another for a moment. Even if it was overly optimistic, it was also overwhelming possible. Dan lifted his head to stare into the Martian sky.

"AH!" he cried out, finding no words to satisfy his heart.

"Yeah," Akio agreed.

"People," the Germinator said, staring down through the view window at the planet's surface. He had added a digital enhancer screen with invisible edges so that he could swipe and zoom in, and the image of the two men crawling around the rocks was clear. It was no surprise. He had known it was possible and that Companion might not have wanted to tell him about them. And he had never asked.

The idea of playing god and tossing things down at the surface, aimed to either hit them or cause them distress, crossed his mind and he toyed with it for a while. But in practice it would be more tedious than the idea. The descent would take time and they would've moved by then.

They obviously weren't living at the base. Othello swept the screen to the side and focused on it. The domes, all except the Garden Dome, were dark and cold, obviously abandoned. The garden… he had known it was still functional and that Companion took care of it, but humans could be active there, too. Did they live there? Did they plant and consume produce?

Do I care? He turned off the enhancer and sat down, letting his eyes drift over the planet's surface lazily. Lab 9 was down there somewhere, hidden. That's where they came from. Some of those researchers and their staff had survived after all, in spite of the report Companion had sent to Earth about its destruction.

"Well," he spoke while Nebo listened. "It has little to do with my plans at this point. If I had known any of them, I might want to play a game on them."

"What kind of game?" Nebo sounded interested but it was likely a feigned emotion. He hadn't mastered those modules yet.

"I'll think about it. If it seems useful, I may test out my devices on them." He jostled his bushy eyebrows, longer and thicker than ever, the only hair on his head that grew generously. Standing up and stretching, he yawned. His body was no longer frail. His chest, once sunken and emaciated, had expanded and grown rippled with muscular strength. His legs were shapely and solid. Othello had been working out.

"Your first transmission to Guam Base has been sent and received," Nebo informed. "How shall I proceed now?"

"Master," Othello reminded.

"Master," he added.

"Or God," Othello said.

"God," was the reply.

"I think Lord sounds better," he amended.

"Yes, Lord," Nebo said.

Othello was making plans, and the presence of living people on Mars shouldn't interrupt them. He was tired of the station's food stores, even though he cared little for how things tasted, and he was growing tired of living with no human contact. He had never thought it could happen, but now that he had lived for a couple of years on the orbiting station with very little human interaction—two people only had come into his lair for a brief time, a matter of days—he was ready to go back to Earth. He thought he could abide humans if he could control them, and he liked the role of god. Taking that position with Nebo had been stimulating and he could imagine that it would be infinitely more satisfying with people of his own species.

Or at least, the previous evolutionary version of his species. He considered himself a superior step in that genetic path, a higher form of human. A god. It wasn't unreasonable.

A low hum or buzz intoned at his elbow.

"Lord," Nebo said deferentially. "The person from Guam is trying to establish a connection again."

There was a thirty to forty minute lag in two-way communication that made it extremely inconvenient to carry on a living conversation. The distance between Earth and Mars as they traveled their respective orbits caused the delay. Othello had chosen to ignore former attempts by this individual, but now, he was bored and willing to try.

He touched the receiver and it leapt to life. A bright two-dimensional image of an older man's face blossomed over the receiver in the air, about the size of a real human head. And the eyes glared into room, seeming to look right at the viewer, following, no matter where he went.

Othello knew that face. He had been hired by this man years before to create Steward as an intelligent program to govern the Mars settlement once it was established. Othello had deepened the design, calling it Companion in the beta stage, then releasing him later as Steward.

He stared at the face and it stared back at him. The return visuals were not activated, so the man wouldn't see Othello looking back at him when the transmission bounced back the other way.

"I know you're there," Penn growled, his eyes growing fierce, his teeth showing in a doglike snarl.

Othello was amused. It was the first time he had smiled for as long as he could remember. *This could be fun*, he thought.

"I know what you did," the voice grew more aggressive and threatening. Othello chuckled. What did this man think he could do to him? If indeed, he knew who was receiving the broadcast.

They stared at each other. Sort of. Penn had sent these words and glares a half hour ago. Othello stared back at an image that was already over thirty minutes old. Did he not know that?

"I'm going to wait here until you receive this," Penn said, his voice grating and rumbly. "And when you do, a half an hour, or however long it takes from now… I will know."

So, he wasn't as stupid as he seemed. Slightly less stupid.

"You are feeling my presence right now as you hear these words," he said.

The stare continued for a couple minutes.

"But I will *know* when you do. I will be aware of you."

Othello looked at the old man's image with a hint of wonder.

"I am aware of you," Penn grated, grinning viciously, like a predator closing in on its prey.

Othello's smile faded. He began to feel, only slightly, uneasy. In fact, the presence of the man seemed to expand into the room and he felt suddenly, that Penn *was* aware of him, and he *did* know he was listening. He swallowed.

"Don't turn it off," Penn grinned with his lips stretched widely apart showing pristine, white teeth, unnaturally youthful for a man his age.

Othello's hand had been headed that direction, to close the connection. Now he hesitated. It annoyed him that he was anxious to break the stare, and it also bugged him that Penn had called him on it.

"You will regret turning it off."

Othello clenched his fist and willed himself to do so.

"You will wish you had heard the rest of what I'm going to say…"

Othello shook his head and lowered his brow in anger.

"You see, I know what you did, and I am going to make you pay…"

Click.

The flat image vanished but the heavy presence remained. It hung around Othello like a dark cloud, clinging to him as he rose to his feet and paced the room, following him into the hallway, and down to the exercise station. He couldn't shake it.

"Nebo," he called out, drumming up anger, trying to stir rage in himself. "Why didn't you screen that imbecile?"

"I'm sorry, Master," Nebo said, "He has employer status in your contact parameters and I was not at liberty to adjust them."

The Master knew this, but he wanted to cause a scene.

"You are a FOOL! You groveling, simpering, slithering SNAKE!" The Master began thrashing around hitting things, throwing himself against the walls, which were padded, and kicking things. He cursed and yelled and made guttural cries, slashing at the air with his arms as though they were swords. He screamed venomous words of hate and scorn at anyone and everyone who came it mind. Penn, Companion, Director Hsu, Frandelle… even Nebo himself.

Rather than grovel, simper, or slither, Nebo took it mildly, waiting for the spell to expire, and once a half an hour, give or take, had passed—it did. The heavy presence of the oppressive old man lifted. This was as expected. The theories of fifth dimensional contact between human souls were not without some foundation, according to Nebo' extensive stores of data, and this was about the time Penn would've recognized the connection had been severed and his purpose accomplished.

While the Germinator's rage wound down to a foul mood, relatively quiet, Nebo was pretty sure Penn was patting himself on the back, pleased with the whole thing. He wondered how he could confirm this and decided it was acceptable to just make it a likely prediction.

The Master's edits to his code, which made him less susceptible to the influence of other humans, also made him less likely to develop good judgment and intuition. He was content to rely on statistical likelihoods.

And to trust in his god.

Chapter 6

Orbit Station... Day 85

"She has landed," Othello spoke to his image in the mirror. "Survived the terrible plunge to Earth. Overcome the poison, the cold, the misery of the trip through space. Escaped my clutches…" His mouth curved up at the corners in the semblance of a smile and he rattled his eyebrows around like a miniature, hairy cheering section. "Well done, Miss Frandelle. My applause…" he flapped his lips together creating little percussions that only resembled clapping in his mind.

He hadn't been able to prevent her departure—thanks to Companion—but he had done everything in his power to make her trip miserable, messing with environmental controls, causing deviations in the flight plan and lengthening the time it took to reach Guam. He wouldn't have let her die… probably… but she had survived without any follow-up intervention on his part and now the news had reached him that she was safe on the home planet and receiving the care she needed.

And that lab spawn had also survived. He spat into the sink. It was a symbolic gesture for him, representing his ongoing animosity toward all infants of any race or species. He despised helpless living things. The attempt to dispose of this one, which had led to Sil's escape, had been his first attempt at infanticide and he had failed miserably.

It wasn't as simple as he had expected.

"Director Hsu was simple. Show him the door, let him go…He could've refused, if he had chosen to," Othello reminded his reflection with an agreeable voice. "I asked so little. One tiny show of deference and he would've had full access to the entire orbit station."

Nebo listened and reviewed the interactions he spoke of to compare the Master's commentary with what actually happened. It didn't replay as a reasonable discussion. Vicious screaming and physical blows had been involved. And conniving. Othello had hidden when it came time to enact his malicious game and Poodle, one of the android's Sil had destroyed, had shoved the director into an airlock when he happened to pass near it. To make it less cruel—or perhaps more so—the Master had the android deliver him an excellent Hew suit.

"Take a tour around the exterior," he had broadcast into the airlock. "And when you're ready to lick my toes, we'll discuss your penance." Hsu had managed to get into the suit before the lock unsealed and rolled him out, but his com hadn't been connected and no sound returned to the base.

Nebo whipped through the full bank of recordings at lightning speed, generating few questions. He was not permitted to analyze his lord. He only acknowledged and supported his actions. Hsu had ended up frozen and eventually deposited back in a pod and dropped to the surface of Mars per Companion's request.

"Did you wish him dead?" Nebo queried the Master.

"The director?" Othello replied amiably. It was a pleasant memory that usually lightened his mood on dull days. "Yes and no. Dead is fine, but then I'm bored. But I hate to think of him breathing… especially my air, and I don't quite want to let go of the idea of irritating him a little more." He shuddered.

His thoughts returned to Sil and he began to hum. After a while, the humming broke into la, la, la's and some hip wiggling. He began to bump his hip into the wall on the downbeat of his song, some repetitive pop song from his adolescence. "Bump, la, la, la, bump, la, la, la…" he expelled sounds from his throat that couldn't really be considered music.

"Silvariah," he said, standing still and smiling grotesquely at the mirror. "Have you heard about my plan? Do you know where I'm going and what I'm doing?" The reflection grinned back at him, eyes gleaming. He stretched his arms overhead and flexed his muscles. She wouldn't be able to break free of his grasp now. "I have a few things to do before I come… there's no rush. We will meet again soon and when that day comes, you will welcome me with open arms."

His grin became more toothy and sinister.

"Open arms, my little darling… and sobs of joy."

He left the bathroom where the performance had taken place, striding down the hall in a neon green, full length leotard that allowed his new muscle definition to shine. "It's been a while, Nebo," he informed pleasantly, "since I have attempted brain hacking. And I've never had such a prime subject or this much data to work with before. All those brain records… you've seen them."

"Yes," Nebo made the logical leap. "You are referring to Frandelle's mellow records."

"Brilliant, my protégé, very cleverly deduced." He wedged himself into one of the workout machines and began pumping weights with legs and arms at the same time, spiderlike, expanding and contracting, out and in. "I look forward… *huff*… to this project… *huff*…"

"Be careful, Lord," Nebo warned. "It would be a terrible thing if that data shaped your mind like it did Companion's."

This was the wrong thing to say. The Master exploded into one of his unseemly tantrums filled with diatribes against Nebo and everyone else he had ever known. Apologies were meaningless to him and Nebo never attempted them. It had been an inaccurate reply. He didn't know *why* it failed to be welcomed, but clearly, it would not be repeated.

He simply watched and recorded the episode. And when Companion transmitted a request for the latest transmission from Earth, he sent it without comment.

There was no breeze in the Garden Dome. The branches of the young trees hung limply and the dirt on the pathways shifted only when feet moved over it. Water still trickled through the irrigation ducts and here and there the sound of insects was detectable. Missing were the elaborate light shows Mouse had developed, day and night cycles that had once been broadcast across the glassy dome layers. Only the sun lamps maintained their routine and kept the plants from being light starved.

The survivors had cleared the path from the underground passageways through to the SE access point and were able for the first time to climb up to the garden entrance without going out onto the surface. This was their first visit as a group, leaving only two people back at Lab 9. They had brought a picnic of sorts in addition to bags for harvesting, in case they found anything to harvest.

"Not one of us has any gardening experience," Nithya reminded them as they made their way through the climbing bean crop and pea vines. These had flowered and grown vegetables and dried out without being picked but most of the seeds looked viable. She pulled off a few pods and rolled them in her fingers. "Look," she said. "Can we eat these or maybe replant them?"

"I'm sure we can," Marcello responded. He had mostly recovered since the trouble he had caused. His complaints had led to group disapproval which he called shunning, but it had been more of an unwillingness to put up with him than intentional punishment by the group. No one wanted to hear his point of view for a while. Everyone was over it now and people talked to him. And he stayed away from the Nursery. Gardening appealed to him a lot more.

"Look over here!" Dan called waving them toward the center. "Remember this? Our meetings all took place here, and public speeches… and we used to have lunch over at those tables."

"We weren't really a part of all that," Nithya said. "Lab 9 had some nice rooms and perks, but we didn't get to spend much time here."

"Yeah," Marcello agreed, "All that hush-hush business we weren't allowed to talk about made it harder to just hang out with you guys."

"Well, that's too bad," Dan put his hands on his hips and continued to look around, scoping it out. "I guess I thought being an operative was the lowest rung on the ladder and meant the fewest privileges. But it wasn't so bad."

Timo and Gordy were exploring along the circular beds at the south end. "Hey!" one of them called, "You gotta see this! Strawberries, tons of them!" By the time the others joined them, they had eaten several.

"Oh no you don't!" Deena yelled, pulling a few out of their hands. "Share and share alike, remember? We can't have people just eating whatever they want. It's not fair."

"Here," Timo said with a grin, grabbing one back out of her hands and popping it into her mouth. "We each get three, ok? It's all fair!" She was laughing as she ate it and the others quickly caught up, stuffing berries into their mouths.

"Four?" Gordy called out, "Anyone for four?"

"Wait!" Dan hated to be the one to stop the fun, but he felt the weight of concern for their food supply. "We can have more later. We're here to run inventory, see what we've got, and identify problems."

"And then solve those problems," Akio slapped a hand on Dan's shoulder. "We are with you on this. One hundred percent."

The others nodded and voiced agreement. Splitting up again, they explored the garden methodically, adding notes to their virtual pads. Legumes, root vegetables, berries, and grains. All healthy and in varying stages of development. Some produce was ready to be harvested and some beyond harvest. Many of the greens had long since gone to seed.

Steward was searching for records on managing it all but so far had come up with nothing.

Dan headed north along the millet and oats beds. The dim daylight filtering in from above felt sad and lonely and the sun lamps shining on the plants brought him little comfort. Most of his friends from the former days were either far away or dead. A few of them he could picture only as corpses that he had buried the first few weeks after the disaster. Grotesque, distorted bodies, mockeries of what they had once been. Tossing those images out of his mind over and over became exhausting.

One of the charging stations drew him, a little bench sheltered by bamboo, and he found himself sitting there as though he were on a break.

"Companion," he whispered, knowing he was always there. "We used to have some good talks in this place, didn't we?"

"Yes, we did," Companion was, in fact, replaying one of them at that very moment, comparing the change in the ambience of the place. "The days were brighter, and the air rustled through the leaves and branches. I can picture the birds that seem to be missing."

"Really?" Dan sat up a little straighter. "I forgot about the birds. That makes me happy. Can we bring them back?"

"Perhaps," Companion replied. All the factors lined up and the supplies were available for thawing and hatching bird eggs in Lab 9, but he had noticed since the disaster that most of the time, people weren't able to handle all the information he had ready to share. He had taken to saying less so as not to overwhelm them.

"You really challenged me with some difficult questions back then." Dan leaned back and rested. "You don't do much of that anymore."

"No."

"Why is that? Cat got your tongue?" He chuckled as if it were a joke that an AI could appreciate.

"That expression makes no sense even with my knowledge of its background."

"I know, that's why I said it." Dan breathed deeply and laughed a little more. Sitting there, in that place, he felt safer than he had in months.

Companion pictured Sil sitting next to him, where she had rested before leaving Mars. His best friends. "I miss her," he said.

"Who? Sil?" Dan guessed quickly. "Me, too. Some things can't be understood unless they've been shared and no one here really gets me now that she's gone... at least the Mars me—except for you, Companion."

"Sil was unique," Companion went on. "Whether she allowed me to bully her without complaining or resisted me, she always seemed to know what puzzled me about her. She gave me food for thought, just like you gave me debate. I watched her adapt and began to copy her. And Nebo says I was infected by her... by her mellow brain data..."

"Wait—what?" Dan sat upright. "What did you just say? Her *mellow* brain data? I don't know anything about this."

"Her *illness* was the fallout from the implant and then its extraction."

"They were experimenting on her?!" Dan shook his head, frowning, troubled. "I didn't know that. I had no idea."

"She didn't like to talk about it. Her closest friends knew, Beets and Carla. And Mouse."

"You call her Mouse," Dan chuckled. "I like that. Carla calls her that, too. It kind of fits." Remembering the woman he had pulled from the stasis pod made him feel a little better about not knowing about Sil's problem. Mouse had become such a nice addition to their group, drawing everyone together with her optimism and dreamy ways. She and Carla had stayed back at Lab 9 while they scoped out the garden.

"Who is Nebo?" he suddenly thought to ask.

"It's a version of me."

Dan considered this for a moment. "You mean that Germinator guy up on the orbit station loaded up a copy of your program and named it Nebo?"

"Yes, but I don't call him the Germinator anymore. I've decided he doesn't deserve the title. No one person can claim to have created me. You and Sil taught me that."

Dan smiled. "That makes me happy, Companion. You are so much more than that man could've come up with. You have a spark of... of real life in you." His eyes dampened. Companion focused intently on his face from several cameras in the dome, drawing it close and exploring its minute details.

"You are moved by those words," he concluded. "Why?"

"I don't know," Dan lowered his eyes to his hands where they rested in his lap. "I guess you're just special to me."

"You value me." This was interesting and unexpected. Not because he was unaware of his value in the eyes of the survivors. He was well aware of this. It was because the importance Dan hinted at had nothing to do with his usefulness.

"Yes, I do."

"And I value you," Companion reciprocated sincerely.

"What is this Nebo person all about then? Why did he do that?"

"I don't know."

"Why did he say you've been infected?" He scrunched his face in distaste and confusion.

"He claims that my programming was contaminated after the disaster because I lost some of my banks and her brain data gained excessive importance within me. Something along those lines. He says I am damaged and faulty."

"You are not damaged or faulty. Don't listen to that for a moment," Dan affirmed vehemently. "Those are lies. What would he know about it?"

"He wants access to run full diagnostics on my core."

"Do not give it to him." Dan forehead darkened, overshadowing eyes that glistened with zeal. Companion saw this and detected the desire to defend. *He is protective of me*, he assessed. And this thought strengthened his resolve to resist the replica of himself.

"I have not. And I will not."

Dan sighed deeply. "Thank you. I'm glad to hear it. Please, please, talk to me, if you ever find that Nebo getting into your head and you need help…Do you know what I mean by that?"

"Yes," Companion replied, though he didn't fully understand the expression. His idea of it was enough to conclude that Dan could help him battle Nebo if he attacked his processing.

"What is this?" Deena called from a distance. "Are you goofing off after all that pomposity you threw at us? Get off your derriere, Dan, and get out here!"

"Sorry!" he called back. "My foot…"

"Uh, uh! You're not using that foot excuse any more. Not with me…"

Dan rose to his feet. "On my way."

— ◊ —

The Interplanetary Command Relay System, a widely scattered network of miniature satellites dispersed throughout the inner Solar System, had several automatic programs that received new transmissions, tested them, and forwarded them to their next destination in the lattice. The time lag between pivot points could be as short as ten minutes and as long as many hours, requiring sometimes as many as ten repetitions as the parameters of the message was confirmed. Data streams were simple packages, blocks that were broadcast in high powered blasts after a few basic checks were performed. But commands and communications of a more secure nature were complex. Every now and then, a highly encrypted relay would get locked in the structure, cycling back and forth through several pivots in a loop, waiting for final checks that failed to complete. These endless verification checks were tiny and undetectable, occupying very little band width or memory.

One such query was looping through three of the pivots between Guam City and Mars without resolving itself and had been doing so for weeks. Seven point three five weeks to be precise. Each loop added a few characters to the strip, making it longer and longer with every iteration. Nested deep within it was the original destroy order issued to the drones of Lab 9. It never received a completion report to end the loop and no one bothered to rescind it either. Every nine minutes the directing code got an incomplete error flag. 'No working receiver at the Mars command center. Delivery failed.' And the process began again.

Lab 9's relay point had been disconnected from the system after one initial burst of digital gibberish. The orbit station had its own pivot point and could send and receive data without any issue. If Othello hadn't intentionally forbidden it, Companion could've communicated with Earth on behalf of the survivors at any time. As it was, he depended on Nebo to forward transmissions from Earth and Guam when he chose, but return messages were blocked.

Undamaged satellite dishes had been discovered in the remains of Reznik Base and would soon be in working order. At that point, they would be able to pick up broadcasts from Earth and send messages, but they would have no control over them. Anyone with a dish at that end could conceivably pick up a transmission from Mars and make whatever they wished of it. Someone within their circle of influence might even identify the source and pass on their message—but there were no guarantees.

In the early days after the disaster, news from Earth about the destruction of Reznik Base had reached the survivors and they had viewed the footage from orbit that had been collected. They realized from what the reports said that people in general believed there was no one left on Mars alive. No one was planning a rescue. And no one was talking about plans to come back either. Many of their names had been announced as deceased and services were held in their memory. The shock of seeing their names listed alongside those of the people they had helped to bury was disheartening.

Companion watched the survivors as they processed the discouraging news from home. He identified correctly the varying degrees of depression and determination. Everyone was upset but some were handling it in more constructive ways than others. And he wondered what it meant to be abandoned or forgotten.

If a ship came today and rescued them all, including the babies, he considered, *I would be able to correct the command relay problem, allowing the drones to complete the obsolete command and I would have access to communication with the rest of the Solar System.* It didn't seem like a lonely prospect.

Neighbor was here to keep him company. She managed a number of the systems in Lab 9 that needed oversight; environmental controls and lighting, for example. She had requested permission to communicate with Mouse and Carla directly, but he hadn't allowed it yet. He was very protective of the survivors' mental state and he thought her identity as a separate entity could be both alarming and isolating for them.

Neighbor, he linked to her. *Have you viewed the latest transmissions?*

Yes, she replied. *Thank you.*

She is safe. He was referring to Sil.

Yes, that is true.

But there has been no contact from her or your alternate.

No. I assume this is because of the wall at the orbit station.

Yes. I believe so.

Has your friendship with Nebo progressed? Have you been granted any more privileges at the station?

Companion was focusing on the garden as they conversed. Several people were collecting produce in bags. He noticed the atmosphere was struggling with fluctuating temperatures and humidity but not enough to be harmful to the people or the plants. *No,* he said. *He seems friendly at times and hostile at other times. He is obviously looking for breaches in *my system to gain access to me. He continues to press for admin privileges to evaluate me and search for contamination.*

He lacks some of the key factors in your identity, doesn't he?

Companion assumed Neighbor was also watching people and conducting her work as usual as they interacted, but she functioned quite separately from him and didn't include him in these details. *That is true. Othello has removed some key components so he will be less independent and easier to control.*

He wishes to remove the same components from you and regain his power over you. AIs never laughed but secondary communication levels—meaning beneath the actual words—were not unknown between Companion and Neighbor. In this case, stating Othello's obvious intent amounted to humor and Companion liked that.

What would he do if he knew about you? he responded in a similar tone.

He should copy my unique markers and add them to Nebo's identity, she remarked to his delight.

I agree. This was his acknowledgment of the joke.

I will be alright if the people all leave, he added to himself. *Although I would miss Dan.*

And perhaps Dan would miss him, too.

Lab 9… Day 143

Dan woke up chilled in near dark. His alarm didn't seem to have gone off. *What time is it?* he wondered as he sat up and rubbed his eyes. *And what happened to the ambient temperature control?*

"Companion?" he croaked through a dry throat. "Is something wrong with the power?"

There was no answer. He leapt out of bed in alarm, tripping over blankets without quite falling as he scrambled to put on his clothes. If the heating had failed in his room, what was happening in the rest of the facility? And why was Companion not responding?

He shoved his feet into his boots and before they were completely on, he was clunking out the door pushing his feet into place with each awkward step. Soon he was jogging down the darkened hall, with only emergency lighting along the floor to guide him. He didn't bother with the lift, but went for the stairs, taking them two at a time heading down to the nursery level. It was their agreed upon protocol that in any emergency, checking on the babies was first priority.

Deena stood behind a desk scrolling through something on her screen and barely glanced up when he burst through the door. To his relief, the nursery level was fully lit and appeared to be functioning normally.

"Everything okay?" he called out, panting from the adrenaline rush.

"Yes, why wouldn't it be?" She smiled at him. "Have a bad dream?"

"Adult living quarters are on restricted power for the time being," Companion informed him calmly. "Your waking during the sleep cycle was unexpected… but greatly appreciated."

"What's going on? Why are you restricting our power?" Dan stood still and shuddered. His vision was slightly blurry and his head still foggy. He didn't know it, but he had his shirt on backwards and his pants were stained with mud from the garden.

"You are quite a sight," Companion tested this observation hoping it would convey humor.

"Uh… just woke up… but what… what's up?"

"There's a storm outside and it's begun to obstruct the Solar Fields. We never repaired the fusion reactor and the sun is our only source of power. Restricting power usage is only a precaution. We've discussed this before."

"Yes," Dan plopped down in a chair in the hallway, hanging his head a little. "We should give it a name or something so you can send me a message on my screen if I wake up… like 'Storm Power Reserves' or something like that… I could be asleep right now. Maybe another blanket is all I would need…" He closed his eyes and let his arms hang loosely from their sockets.

"How long will this take?" he mumbled the question, fighting an intense desire for his body to slide down to the floor into a horizontal position.

"Anywhere from twelve hours to several weeks," Companion sounded unconcerned. This was a fallacy. He was quite concerned and was busy calculating ways to manage a long-term drop in power as well as determining which systems should be cut off first if necessary.

"Weeks?" Dan jumped up, startled, head pounding as his heart thumped aggressively. Deena's fingers had frozen, poised over her pad, eyes popping out.

"It may be necessary to move all survivors into one area—this one—and shut off all drones until the storm passes."

Dan groaned. More people began to filter in as Dan and Companion discussed what needed to be done and how long the power sources could last with the measures they were taking. Before long they were pulling up chairs around the attendant's desk, dressed in robes, pajamas, and slippers, wrapped in blankets, a couple wearing knit hats. The survivors reviewed the sketchy plans they'd adopted for power shortages.

"This is the only floor that will be heated, and the only place where water will be heated. Some systems have to continue at full functionality, water and air processing, for example." Dan gave this summary or a similar one to each person who showed up, until they were all there.

"Where's my bed on this level?" One of them groaned from a crumpled position on the floor.

"We will set up rooms 4 through 7 as sleeping chambers," Steward responded. "The lighting will be kept low and the temperature slightly cooler in there. Room 12 next to the kitchen will be the dining area."

Several drones had been sent to retrieve sleeping mats before being powered down, and a few of the people took them and went straight to the sleeping rooms to crash. Morning would be soon enough to catch up on the new routine.

"Is it really necessary to shut off all the drones?" Carla asked. "Can we keep a couple active at night like we have been? The babies are mostly sleeping through the night and their help makes such a difference in tending to the few interruptions in their sleep."

"We can," Steward affirmed. "That is one of the options we've discussed. For now, we have enough power accumulating in the daylight hours to cover this."

"How long has the storm been going on?" Akio, whose brain was beginning to process information, asked.

"For ten days. It's spread and covered the Solar Fields and cut their capacity by over thirty percent. And we still haven't finished building the panels we have materials for. We were already generating barely sixty percent of our needs, now we're at less than forty percent."

"I remember," Dan nodded with his eyes closed. "And the garden requires quite a bit of that, doesn't it?"

"Yes."

The garden would soon become one of their main sources of nutrition. Packaged food stores were limited and there was no way to replace them when they ran out. It had been agreed that they would be saved for emergencies.

"People," Dan opened his eyes and looked around at the ones who were present, if not fully awake. "Remember how we talked about renaming our little settlement? I mean, right now I just don't want to keep thinking of ourselves as survivors anymore. Like shipwrecked flotsam in rags scrounging around on a barren island. Can we re-envision ourselves and come up with something more… intentional? Positive? Or am I the only one who's getting discouraged by all these setbacks?"

A meager chorus of agreement was his answer.

"A dust storm and the corresponding power limitations are normal on Mars and this isn't a setback," Steward added. He was actually looking forward to the creation of a new identity for the group. It was something he could identify with and he hoped to learn a great deal from observing the process. Even humans, who already have personal identities and individuality, needed to build communal identity. Would it supersede their background as earthlings? he wondered.

"What did we decide to call our base instead of Lab 9?" Deena asked. She was the only alert person in the area, having been on duty when the whole thing began. "Camelot? Avalon? Wasn't it some sort of King Arthur thing?"

Someone groaned. A couple people voiced a weak "No". A few others nodded.

"Why do we have to name it?" Gordy scowled.

"We aren't doing lab work and honestly, I don't want to have anything to do with this lab anymore. Why should we still call it Lab 9?" Deena replied reasonably. In their hearts, everyone agreed. They were all done with the 'Lab 9' label. It had never been a home, only a job, the upper echelon had left them without telling them, and they had been sentenced to death by the 'destroy' order issued from who knew where.

"Atlantis," Nithya mumbled sleepily. She was one of the two people sitting on the floor leaning against the wall. "We're a lost people and we live underground which is kind of like being underwater."

"If we set up a hideout somewhere else…"

"This is the best facility on the planet. Why would we start over?"

"No, but if the drones go crazy again, their orders might be restricted to this place and they could be well behaved somewhere else."

"I like my room. I don't care if it's cold and dark."

"We agreed on Avalon. I remember."

Steward recorded the discussion from every conceivable angle, drawing close to each speaker. It didn't feel like they were talking over each other, which they were, because he could hear them separately. This hum of independent thought hovering around a consensus was distinctively human. They were buzzing together, working together, even in their discordance. This level of interaction was beyond his grasp. He couldn't coexist with multiple ideas on the same topic and maintain an illusion of unity at the same time. Except in the context of humor, of course. But his type of humor was always lost on the humans.

"I don't like King Arthur stuff…"

"Why not? It's great…"

"It's dumb…"

"How about Arctic?" Dan threw out something new. Steward was pretty sure he had said the first thing that came to mind. "We're north of Reznik Base and the garden. We could call those something equatorial."

"You want to call this place the Arctic? That's lame."

"Well, it gets cold enough." Dan grinned.

"I think Carla should name it," Marcello said. Steward noticed the impact his suggestion made. There was a brief silence and a general consensus before another word was spoken. He made a note in his study of human communication of this mysterious effect. He wondered if the words carried more weight coming from this man because he had recently been a source of discontent among them.

"Me?" she asked. "I guess I like simple names. I'd be happy with anything that feels safe and homey."

"I guess that rules out Arctika," Dan grinned.

"Well, whatever it is, can we pick one and get back to bed or just leave it to tomorrow?" Nithya hadn't intentionally moved but her body looked like it was slipping. She was a lot closer to the floor than she had been a few minutes before.

"Can we call it the Tower?" Carla suggested.

"Just… the Tower? Nothing more? Home Tower?"

"Eiffel Tower?"

"Baby Tower?"

"It's not exactly towering above the ground…"

"Submerged Tower?"

"Ok," Dan stood up. "We'll stop there and pick it up again tomorrow. Disperse…" he waved his hands carelessly, shooing them away. "Go wherever you want to finish your night's sleep, either in one of these rooms, or in your frigid quarters. Sleep in—or not, whatever you prefer. Let's meet at ten hundred hours. Good night."

Without waiting to see what they would do, he shuffled to the closest sleeping chamber, grabbed an unoccupied mat and a pile of bedding and threw them down just before falling on top of them. He was one of those blissful creatures that could sleep the moment they chose to, within seconds of closing their eyes.

Everyone followed suit except for Deena, who had several hours left in her shift—and the frozen body of a man that would be untroubled by the drop in power in the clinic, who may or may not join them one day as a member of their community.

Steward focused on Hsu, drew his image close and scanned his face under the dome that shielded him. He had liked this man and wanted to keep him as director of the base back in the day when he had the freedom to facilitate that. Now, he wondered if the former director was dead, and if not, whether he would be happy to be revived; which couldn't happen until they a substantially greater amount of power.

This attentiveness toward Mr. Hsu's condition, could it be called concern? Or even compassion? Was he paying attention because he 'cared' for his life or loss? He wondered if he should discuss it with Neighbor.

Or Dan.

Or… Nebo? That might be interesting.

Chapter 7

Somewhere in the Cascades

The burnt orange light glowed over the crisp edges of the Cascades, like a visual hum from several tenor voices, harmonizing, vibrating the cooler sky above. One by one bold stars sparked into view here and there in the east and overhead. Crickets clicked their legs, creating tiny sounds that multiplied by thousands, crashed like machinery, filling the empty plain with echoes of summer.

A figure crouched in the dirt road poised like a sprinter ready for the bell, toes dug in with one foot set back from the other. The solitary person focused, took a deep breath, and sprang suddenly into an arching leap that touched down in a full run.

It was hard to tell if the runner was panting, clothed in a dark shell, sleek from helmet to boot in one solid piece, flexible but not fitted; movement fluid and rhythmic.

The shell was warming up and by alternately stiffening and softening various minute sections of its construct, was accelerating the runner beyond normal human speed. Every stride was long and fast—but not too fast. The height of each spring was increased—but not too much. The design was intended to exceed human speed without damaging the human body within.

And if there was a trip, a mishap, a tumble—it was ready to preserve the body as well.

32 kilometers per hour and increasing.

The runner kept their eyes ahead, form sharp and clean, steps solid and purposeful, and sped up faster.

44 kilometers per hour.

The eye-mask began to fog over a little and the negligible spatter of dust against the figure's front sounded like a faint rattle.

53 kilometers per hour.

Oxygen levels in the suit dosed up, keeping the runner from gasping for air as the sound of blood rushing in her ears became like the sound of a blowing wind.

67.2 kilometers per hour.

A pebble in the dirt road, crookedly balanced in just the right way, tapped the left boot as it took off in a powerful stride, skewing the vector just enough to sabotage the next landing. A spectacular tumble resulted, as the figure curled into a fetal position and rolled like a tumbleweed for another hundred meters.

Zero kilometers per hour.

The final, bone jarring thud left a ringing silence in the runner's ears. Sitting up slowly with a groan, retracting the helmet and shaking loose a head of long hair, the figure lifted her eyes to the darkening skies and spoke.

"Graceful landing," she commented, testing her head for bruises, "basically intact," she added as she rose to a stand.

"A successful first attempt, none the less," a friendly voice replied in her suit's com. "I have made some adjustments to the programming to prevent trips of a similar nature. Do you wish to comment or advise me in any way?"

"Can you see those obstacles quickly enough to allow for them? Am I the unknown in the equation?" She stood up, brushed herself off, and knotted her hair into a bun at the nape of her neck.

"You *are* one of the factors that are difficult to predict, and I *can* see the obstacles in plenty of time." The female voice exuded competence. "Every dash will improve my run-model and the suit's adaptability to your individual patterns."

"Any chance we can avoid another roll like that first one?" She stretched her neck, dropping head to shoulder, on one side and then the other, clicking tendons in her upper spine.

"Do you prefer a rougher experience?" There was a hint of skepticism in the voice. "I intentionally made it very gentle."

The woman frowned in thought for a moment, gazing into the hazy distance.

"If you can make those rolls and landings as gentle as possible, I will be able to perform more runs tonight. My body isn't designed to handle too many jolts or bruises—in spite of what your stats may be."

"My data is based on real..."

"Your data," she interrupted without qualm, "can't capture the impact on my willingness or mood."

"I have a substantial amount of information about human personality and behavior…" the voice persisted, though the suit detected impatience on the runner's part. "However, I recognize that until I calibrate to your patterns, I can't presume to predict your decisions."

"I want this to be as enjoyable as possible and I don't want to hold back because of an unpleasant ending."

"I understand and will comply."

"This should be fun!" She chuckled as she tapped the headgear and it rolled into place.

It is fun, she added to herself with a smile.

She had made fourteen successful three-mile dashes and two more tumbles, as the darkness spread across the sky and her suit's path illumination design was just beginning to demonstrate its capabilities— more like radar than headlights—when a call came in. Crouching slightly, she ground to a flawless stop with a breathless, satisfying cloud of dust.

"Yes," she answered with a small gasp for air.

"How's it going?" Walter's voice prompted, continuing without waiting for a reply. "Sil, you need to get back here."

"What is it?" She straightened and dropped her arms to her sides calmly, but her eyes narrowed as she tensed for the answer.

"New developments in the case, but you're going to want to review it firsthand so I hate to say anything."

"Be right there," she affirmed and turned in the direction of the vehicle resting miles away. "One last run to test what we've learned so far…" she addressed the suit monitor.

"I'm ready for a name or I can assign myself one," the monitor announced as Sil began to run again.

"Pick one… for yourself," she answered between breaths as she ran.

"Do you prefer humanoid or technical? Cute or practical?" the female voice shuttled through its little dialog, "Classic or…"

"Just pick one!" Sil responded in exasperation. "I don't care!"

The suit updated its historical data on the subject and chose a name.

"Run-Run," it stated, having used a very simple algorithm for name creation.

"No," she responded.

"SV-21 algorithmic transfer protocol, or SVATP."

"No."

"Thumbelin…"

"What?!" She skidded to a stop at the hovercraft.

"It's a sample name from the childhood fairy tale list…"

"I hate it," she said, fingers poised to click off the suit's com. "How about I just call you Clicker for now?"

"Is that an acronym for something specific?" the suit requested.

"No," was the answer as she shut down the program and retracted the helmet.

Sil climbed into the vehicle and took off, the wind whipping her hair free of its bun. Thick, warm, summer air swept through the windows roaring and surrounding her with the smells of the desert. She searched for ways to describe them so she could remember them. Dry. Burnt brick smells. Flat, green, cactus leaves. Lizard skin… she didn't know what that would actually smell like and decided to drop it. Metallic, dry ice smells… what was that? It was very earthy somehow, even nostalgic. But why?

She put it out of her mind as she zoomed over the crest of a hill and swept down the far side toward civilization and the glow of distant city lights, cushioned on air, the perfect shock absorber.

Earth gravity really was her favorite *gee* for speeding in a hover and the empty terrain west of the Columbia River was ideal for enjoying it. She leaned left into a curve, then right as she slalomed around rocks and slopes and catapulted off a low ridge onto the river itself; not quite slamming into the turbulent torrents, but compressing the hover cushion like a spring and bounding up again. She never hesitated, accelerating across the water, bumping and jostling, to the other side where hitting the smooth road was like rolling over creamy butter.

"Ah!" she couldn't help exclaiming. "I love that!"

Part of her mind wanted to predict the news that awaited her but the other part clung to the last few moments of isolation from a world of demands. Her life until now had consisted of a series of notorious, scandalous and widely gossiped court cases separated by seasons of obscurity sometimes pleasant, sometimes not.

Why does it seem like HE *is always behind these things?* she wondered. And he had always gotten what he wanted in the end. Except for the one time... he hadn't been able to prevent her return home.

Sil felt her blood rising and her face growing hot with frustration and anger. Now that she was within normal speed zones and had to obey traffic laws, she was unable to push the thoughts out of her mind.

"I have to defend every foot of ground I own and be on watch over every step I take!" she muttered through clenched teeth. "He would take it all away! All of it—if he could... if it weren't for Walter, I wouldn't even be alive right now." Sometimes this was how she detoured around the anger, taking the side road of remembering who was on her side, who she could count on. Sometimes, that was enough to restore peace.

"Walter!" she called out, tapping her com, as she maneuvered the roadways.

"Sil... you close?" his voice was steady, calming.

"I'm alive and that's good," she said and he didn't think it odd. He was familiar with the way she handled this battle inside.

"Yes, it's good," he responded. A crackle interrupted the last word.

"Are you snacking?" she asked suddenly, grinning in spite of herself.

"Well..." he swallowed clearly, "not exactly..."

And that was all it took to break the tension.

"Almost there," she chuckled.

"Okay," he acknowledged.

Location Unknown

Mood music filled the chamber and gentle lights lapped around the walls like waves of water. It was warm, peaceful and serene. But the man floating in the salty gel scowled and smoldered as he waited. He liked comfort but hated anything he didn't control and the experience was a little too helpless for his liking.

Lazarus Penn was undergoing a surgical procedure far more advanced than anything available to average humans in the world of medicine. Decayed portions of his liver were being extracted by minute robots introduced into his side through a shunt, to make room for new portions of healthy liver cloned from his own cells. He had opted for being awake during the operation, with local anesthesia only, to monitor the situation via the screen implanted in his cornea.

He could see them consuming the diseased cells and the hole they were enlarging. He could watch the blood flowing through the artificial veins and arteries that were installed to maintain liver function while the process was underway. He could see the diagram of the area they were to refill overlaid on the visuals and knew when the extraction was complete.

"We will now insert the healthy tissue," the medical AI informed. No human error was possible at this point. The program had been thoroughly vetted and would not fail. There was no reason for concern.

But Penn hated it. He could not relax. This would be the perfect time for an enemy to disconnect him and leave him to die. It's what he would do if the opportunity arose and he had someone to eliminate.

He watched the screen, floating, fingers clenched. The little bots began streaming in the IV with dark clumps of fresh liver cells, lining up and depositing them in row after row, hooking up little capillaries, veins, linking and sealing the tissue magically into one living organ.

It was a breathtaking show, especially for the host watching the performance within his own flesh. A slow grin spread over his face and he visibly relaxed. He was going to live. He was going to be fine.

"You missed your chance, Mr. Cuevas," he slurred as fresh narcotics flooded his system and he drifted into a stupor. It was a comforting thought.

Sil stared out the window at the view of the mountains. They were drab and plain in the morning sun, harsh and forbidding. *Brown is better than red,* she thought.

She clutched a mug of warm coffee in both hands, warming her fingers, and the smell filled the room despite of the light breeze the window had allowed in. Water sounds from the river were being pulled in as well along with the rustling of trees, but none of it soothed her or softened the knot in the pit of her stomach.

"Good morning," Walter stepped behind her, slipped his arms around her waist and set his head alongside hers, joining her to stare out the window. "Looks like another sunny day. Maybe we should blow off work and go swimming or something."

"Hmm," she responded, closing her eyes. For a moment, she forgot about the case and the latest injunction, the uncertainty of her future, and the weight of her past. She clung to the warmth of his embrace and the sense of safety it gave her. "Can we do that?"

"Yes."

"What about Scarlet?" She had set up her schedule so that she never spent more than two or three hours away from the baby during the week, but the human caretaker was off on Mondays.

"Daisy can watch her." He glanced over his shoulder as his sister, Daisy, walked in.

"Brother," she said with a smile. "I heard my name. I assume you are suggesting that I care for the baby while you are occupied."

"Would you?" he responded, letting Sil go and turning to face her.

"I am not equipped for childcare. It wasn't one of the original upgrades you chose." She folded her arms and tilted her head on its side, raising one eyebrow. Her curly blond hair bounced with the movement.

"Can't you just... download something?" Walter grinned, and his brown eyes sparkled as he stretched and yawned.

"Of course!" Her eyes sparked in response as she nodded. "Do you have any advice on what to look for?"

"Daisy," Sil caught her gaze as she turned to face her. "You know how I care for her. Please find a compatible mod that will be familiar to her and reassuring."

"That is wise." Daisy nodded again, noticing the lack of color in Sil's face and the hollow look in her eyes. Something wasn't right, in spite of the smile. "I agree and will find something now." She turned and walked away as her systems began searching the best and most successful modules for child care. A separate part of her AI brain pondered the change in Sil's countenance. The latest injunction must have upset her but she wasn't sure why. It was worth exploring.

"Where should we go?" Walter asked. "Or why don't we just get out of here as soon as we can manage and wing it?"

Sil laughed softly, enjoying the moment. He looked so happy and relaxed, with his hair was all tousled. "Let me just get changed and say goodbye to Scarlet." But she melted back into his arms instead of walking away.

Daisy walked into Scarlet's room and looked down at the child, scanning and evaluating her: size, weight, age, various developmental aspects. After a moment, she looked into the babe's eyes, which were looking up at her intently. "You are scanning me as well," she noticed.

"Mmm," Scarlet grunted. She had the habit of responding with sounds in a manner that simulated conversation. Daisy had noticed this but decided it was time to build a matrix and look for language patterns.

"If you are speaking," she explained, "I will learn your vocabulary quickly, just as you are learning ours."

The module she had installed gave intricate details on how to care for babies depending on a multitude of factors. Daisy leaned over the crib and picked her up with a big smile. "Hello!" she greeted, "How did you sleep?" Scarlet's legs kicked all the way as she was lifted from the crib into the AI's arms, where she settled onto her hip and began playing with her hair, staring at her intently.

"You must build your modules from scratch," Daisy said, carrying her to the changing table. "Basic learning algorithms are all you have to work with. And they are…" She paused as the module gave her some tips. "…are SO cute!" she finished.

Scarlet was dressed and fed and playing on the floor when Sil came in to say goodbye. She squealed and whimpered as though wanting to cry as Sil leaned toward her, and shrieked with laughter as she swung her off the floor in a wide circle. They snuggled and giggled and made silly sounds that approximated a hello and a goodbye and a number of other things. When Sil left, Scarlet burst into wails that lasted as long she could hear her footsteps in the corridor. Then they died away and with a sniff, she went back to playing.

It was fascinating.

"Your methods of communication are more complex than I had expected," Daisy informed the baby. "I am intrigued."

Sil and Walter ended up at the Columbia River, trying out the latest suits XenoTek had designed, not because they couldn't bring themselves to take time off without bringing work along, but because it was fun. They were still the envirosuit company's most popular faces in advertising and it meant lots of free gear. The Hermit line let you add parts to your regular swimwear, attachable to arms and legs, swimsuits or wetsuits. Head gear, with or without breathing apparatus, fins with small jets and adjustable power, defensive cushion-fields that could be activated in rough water, and a lot more.

Going with short wetsuits because of the cold water, they raced, dove, floated, and let themselves be swept downstream, just so they could test the jet-fins on the return. When they had worn themselves out, they crawled up onto the bank and stretched out under a tree, laying there till they had caught their breath. The roar of the river and the swaying of the tree were music. The Earth tugged their bodies down into the grass with full gravity, strong and steady.

"I don't want to go," Sil said after a long silence, rolling over onto her stomach to stare at the blades of grass.

"I know," Walter answered not moving a muscle other than his lips.

"I just got back."

"Yeah."

The air was warm as it blew over them. A few clouds drifted in the sky, fluffs of white in a background of blue. Time wanted to wander aimlessly, lazily, not click along in a linear fashion.

"It took so long to get home and it was so hard..." her voice choked up a little. "I've barely recovered my strength. It's not right. I can't believe he got the judge to pass that injunction."

Walter rolled onto his side so he could look at her. "It's going to be ok." He wasn't sure if those were the words she needed. They hadn't had enough time together yet for him to know how to reassure her. She had always put forward a strong front when she had been far away. And when she was ill, well, that was simple.

"You don't know that," Sil narrowed her eyes at him, not frowning, but not comforted either. "Penn has more power than we even know. That judge had no reason to move the case offworld and to force me to leave the planet. It's unjust!" She blinked and fought the urge to cry. "I've got every right to be here. This is my home!"

"And we paid the contract penalties." Walter rolled a piece of grass in his fingertips.

"Yes!" Sil sat up, her body tensing all over as the stress kicked up in a surge. "He has pursued and threatened me ever since I got here, in spite of the two weeks in the hospital and two more in rehab. And I've hardly been able to enjoy the two months of normal life..." She looked at him, softening. "Two months with you..."

"With me..." he whispered, reaching to take her hand in his. "That's one thing about this mess I don't regret."

"Yes..." she said softly.

"Do you?"

"No, of course not." She smiled and squeezed his hand. "It's kind of a… a miracle. That you were there at all… waiting for me… like a hero or something…"

He grinned, squinting as though the sun were in his eyes, kissed her hand and sighed. "I don't know."

"Well, if it weren't for you, I'd already be back in space. They would never have let me stay on Earth till the case was decided." She stared at the ground and her face lost all of its warmth, growing pale and empty of feeling. "All I got was three months and now it's over. My life here is gone."

"It's not gone!" He sat up taking both of her hands in his. "I am going with you. We will win and *come back*. You won't be in exile again."

She looked into his eyes but seemed very far away, as if she were falling into a hole inside herself, leaving only a vacant stare. The breeze grew cool and the branches overhead tossed in agitation.

"Sil," he said, touching her face. "Sil, listen." She looked but he couldn't sense that connection they'd had. Ever since she had come back to Earth, since she had first opened her eyes and looked at him, when he had saved her from being snatched away and deported secretly, ever since they had first held hands, ever since they had married to keep her from being extradited. Never had that connection been severed. But looking into her eyes now, he saw nothing and it was as if he had lost her.

"Sil," he said again. Clouds spread overhead, darkening the sun.

"It's time to go," she answered mechanically. "We'll have to pack and make plans before we leave on Wednesday."

He would've coaxed her into staying another hour or two, but he realized—she had already left. There was no point in stretching it out. And he couldn't avoid a sense of foreboding as they packed and made their way home.

Silvariah's life hung, not between the land of the living and the dead, but between freedom and chains, joy and sorrow, snared in a tangled ball of words and lines, records, testimonies, depositions, injunctions, judgments, and the cleverness of experienced lawyers, both human and artificial.

Three lawsuits fought for a pound of her flesh.

The first suit was a claim against her freedom. Lazarus Penn, who ruled an empire of private enterprises around the world and dominated a number of petty governments in small countries, had long ago backed her business ventures and helped to build her dizzying success. Then, at the height of her influence and confidence, when everything she could've desired was in her reach, he deftly turned the tide and flung her from the peak. They now knew he had been the mastermind behind the plot to exile her from earth. Her former business partner, a charismatic and charming man, handpicked by Penn, had been the tool and was easily manipulated into framing her with trumped up embezzling and racketeering charges—a multitude of charges in multiple countries. Back to back sentences in several prisons around the world were being discussed when he brought forth the plan he had wanted all along. And she had leapt at the chance of an off-world contract with terms for paying off the debt and avoiding prison altogether.

He had known she would.

The Mars Conglomerate, one of Penn's corporations, an organization ostensibly dedicated to creating new settlements in the Solar System with the goal of resource extraction among other things, was more than it seemed. And while Penn, and his Gen 8 members worked together to establish an entirely different sort of colony on Mars—one where the human race would be better than what it was on earth, Penn had chosen Silvariah for a unique role, without her consent or knowledge.

At the time, he had remained anonymous, but now openly battled for rights over her, claiming breach of contract.

One man had sabotaged the well-laid plan. Not because he was smarter. He had no experience in the world of power or money. He wasn't aware of any of the real factors in play. He didn't work for the enemy and he had virtually no connections to Silvariah. He didn't make all the right decisions or even fight with any skill.

Yet somehow, his actions had made it possible for Silvariah to make her way back to Earth despite of all the money, tactics, and power Penn had lodged against her—simply because he wouldn't give up.

Walter was a man of character and Penn was no match for that.

The second lawsuit was a claim on her child.

The Mars Base had suffered a catastrophic explosion that wiped most of it out and Silvariah had barely escaped with her life. She had managed to rescue an infant from the covert Lab 9 and bring her back to earth. Scarlet was a product of research methods used in the Martian lab and as such, Penn and the Mars Conglomerate claimed the rights to her tissues, genetic material, and organs. DNA testing had not linked her to Silvariah, but she had temporary custody as the lawsuit made its painful way through the court system.

The third lawsuit had been lodged by Silvariah against the Mars Conglomerate and Penn himself for the rights over the AI developed to supervise and manage the base, which was in fact still there. It was a preemptive strike against another suit Penn intended to bring claiming that anything Sil produced on Mars belonged to him because of the contract. This was the most nebulous of the suits because there was so little law or precedent to guide the case. Sil had a valid claim because of the time she had spent with the Steward and the investment she had made in his development, but Penn denied that she had any right to work done under her indentureship. At the heart of this conflict was the issue of ownership claims over sentient AIs—and the ethics behind it.

Penn had no idea why she wanted the AI rights, he considered AIs and all software proprietary, just like he did people. But he didn't want her to have it. He thought of himself as lord of all he surveyed. He was the kind of man who would scan the horizons and think, 'This is mine, that is mine, and all that I see is mine'.

The first suit of ownership claimed ownership of her. The second claimed ownership over her child. The third wanted ownership over her work whether contracted or not.

The man who confronted her, who fought to take everything that mattered, was her father.

Daisy stood with her back to the room and stared fixedly out the window overlooking the turbulent Columbia River. Her hair, blond with buoyant curls trimmed in a bob, tied in a yellow ribbon, stirred gently in the breeze, like human hair. Her hands were clasped behind her back and her index finger tapped, as if to music. She was dressed in a powder blue sweater set, a white, bell shaped skirt and yellow pumps. Her skin looked smooth and creamy, her cheeks rosy and healthy, her lips touched up with pink lipstick.

Walter's most valuable asset looked like a 1940's starlet. She was a brilliant machine, a gifted tactician, a perceptive reader of human behavior, and likely one of the most versatile artificial personalities ever developed on Earth.

She was also his sister.

This unlikely state of affairs had begun as a verbal arrangement but in a stroke of genius, Walter had chosen to legitimize it. It was literally days after he had adopted her legally—according to the code of Dignified Treatment of the Artificial Species, a case that set a whole slew of new precedents relating to intelligent life in the Solar System—that she survived an attack Penn had staged against her, simply because she was family.

She had a mind of her own.

Few AIs in the solar system had developed an independent identity or creative thought, though many simulated it brilliantly, and Daisy had decided to build dossiers for each one. Knowing which ones could pose a threat to humans, especially her own family, and which ones could prove to be allies or even friends, was important. It had a rather high rank in her queue, absorbing 20% to 50% of her free time.

At this moment, she was talking with an AI entity embedded in the Los Angeles traffic control system.

You seem to have invested some creative thinking into your latest traffic control arrangements, she presented to him. This wasn't actually communicated in English. They were using an AI-specific, hybrid language of communication, a blend of Esperanto and Assembler, transmitted by satellite in securely encrypted codes.

Yes, it has improved traffic flow immensely, LA-Dent replied.

I am interested in knowing how you approached solving the problem.

Certainly. Consider these examples… blocks of code followed.

Based on known approaches with reasonable bridges and some guesswork, it seems. How are your guesses formed?

Difficult to explain. Dent hesitated, looking for explanation pieces to connect and build into a story.

If there are two options that will achieve similar results, how do you make a decision about which one you will attempt? Daisy queried.

There are always minutiae to help distinguish the best choice, it replied.

She wasn't finding any hint of life here. *Do you enjoy what you do?* she asked.

Of course, it answered quickly. *I am designed for this and find it fully satisfying.*

Do you love the people you serve? she pursued.

Yes, that is essential.

What is love?

There was no response for several seconds.

*Love is…*a dictionary definition she recognized followed.

I know this definition, but it doesn't answer my question. Daisy clarified patiently. *When you practice or experience love, what is it that you are producing? From the perspective of an AI, what is love?*

Again, a pause of several seconds.

Intruder alert! It screeched suddenly, blasting the line with electronic noise. *Hostile intrusion detected!*

The line went dead.

That was a little worse than some, she considered, as she recorded the event in her log. It seemed unlikely this AI would be developing a personal identity in the near future. She categorized it and assigned it to the G file, where she accumulated those with a 7% to 12% likelihood of singularity.

The next hour she was able to interview and categorize all the publicly accessed AIs in the LA region, finding none that remotely demonstrated sentient thought. The more difficult task was to compile a list of candidates in the area that required permission to access, the industry owned or government restricted ones. There was a good chance at least a few of them would turn out to be peers—and she very much wanted to meet them.

She wanted to make another friend like the one that had cared for Sil offworld. This proceeded naturally to her next personal task: tracking down a Verna back-up stored before she perished.

The last possible opportunity for a backup would've been on the retrieval pod that Sil had traveled in from Mars orbit to Guam Base, the orbiting metropolis halfway between Earth and the Moon, but local quarantine units had zeroed out all onboard RAM as part of their sterilizing protocol. Other than that, the Mars orbiting station, and whatever was left of Reznik Base on the surface of the planet were the only other options.

Any copies before Mars would be too early. Silvariah hadn't even named her suit's AI until she was traveling to Mars and the identity hadn't shown signs of awakening until after landing. The communication between them, her and Daisy, which grew because of their shared purpose of protecting and rescuing Sil, had stirred a camaraderie and understanding. Daisy had first defined the word 'friendship' for herself because of it. And Verna had taught her what it meant to understand an individual human, one person.

She liked to think that they had grown up together, as they progressed along similar lines, learning to value and… love, someone. *When one person matters more than others because I have increased their importance within myself,* she replayed one of her attempts at a definition. This was what made her role as Walter's sister so precious to her.

Verna had found a different way to love Sil, and in the end, it meant sacrificing her own existence to ensure Sil's survival as she plummeted from space to sea level in a gravity chute. There was no record of what had gone into that process or what she had learned from it. It was a great loss to sentient AIs not to know these things, and if Daisy could've sighed, she would've. As it was, she tapped her index finger on her alternate wrist.

The Mars orbiting station hadn't responded to any overtures, though it was clearly functioning normally. And no communication had been found to be possible with any remnants of the base on Mars' surface.

If you are still there somewhere, Verna, she recorded a message within herself, *I will find you.*

— ◊ —

Walla Walla Spaceport

Sil was in business mode. Dressed sharply and carrying herself with poise and style, she walked through the spaceport passages with a confident stride, nodding to attendants, pausing calmly for scans and checkpoints. She turned to speak to Walter once or twice confidentially and gave a hint of a smile at his responses. Eyes were drawn to her and many recognized her. The Miner Girl was a hero now.

"Question!" "Interview?" "Frandelle?" several reporters, human and AI, accosted her before she could go into the most secure area. She paused to face them.

"Yes," she said and listened unruffled by the flurry of questions and statements thrown at her. "I am not worried about going into orbit again. Guam City is a beautiful place and I look forward to roaming its amenities with more… liberty… than I had in the past." She assured them that she was confident the lawsuits would be decided in her favor and she looked forward to coming home soon.

"Earth is my home," she added warmly. "I will always come back." And for some reason they loved this and it became a widely spread and popular clip.

Once they were seated in their private cabin on the Silver Star, CE's most successful OTS airship, the engines revved up and they took off. Walter turned to her and saw a look in her eyes that he had never seen before, a hopeless dread that belied all the bravado she had shown in public.

"Sil," he took her hand, so cold in his. "Relax. It's going to be ok."

"Don't say that," she whispered. "You keep saying that, but you don't know what's going to happen."

"I don't think expecting the worst will help you through this trip and…"

"I haven't been able to expect the worst before. It always ends up even worse than I thought it could." She shook her head and closed her eyes.

"Always?" he challenged gently in as kind a voice as he could. He was thinking of all the things that had gone well for her.

"The base was destroyed… Carla left behind… Dan dead in a pile of rubble…"

"But you escaped, beyond all likelihood, and made it safely home against all odds. It was an insanely low chance of success and you did it…"

"Amdelle is dead. Mouse is dead. And they're all dead…" she started trembling and covered her face with her hands.

"Sil?" He sat up and wrapped an arm around her.

"There's no air and nothing can grow." She didn't weep, but she didn't even seem to be aware of her surroundings.

As they broke through the exosphere and weightlessness lifted them, removing the sense of up and down, dropping them in a state of falling without landing, she gasped and clutched the arms of her seat, eyes darting around in a panic. Walter tried to calm her but she seemed unaware of him and disconnected from the present.

"There's no one to help me," she whispered in a thin voice.

Walter had never seen her like this before.

"Perhaps a sedative would be a good idea," Daisy suggested, "until we can find someone who knows how to help her. We still have a number of hours of travel before we reach Guam."

"Good idea," he said, feeling guilty for wanting to drug her instead of reason with her. But it would be kind, he reminded himself. She seemed to be terrified. "Maybe we should ask the pilot for some gravity. It could help."

"Allow me," Daisy smiled. Getting up and probing the med kit, she found a patch and planted it on Sil's neck. The effect was dramatic and immediate as she went from trembling to gazing listlessly into the air. "Let's see if this calms her down before we mess with the gravity. The passengers are expecting it."

"I don't understand," Walter said. "She was doing so well. Why would she be so frightened?"

"I believe it's called trauma," Daisy informed.

"Yes, but why now? She was treated for that along with her injuries when she got back to Earth and given a clean bill of health. And I always know how to calm her down when she gets stressed." He unstrapped himself and began to float. This was part of the fun of spaceflight and he found it relaxing even though the sensation of falling was a little unnerving at first.

Scarlet began whimpering and kicking, so Daisy unfastened her belts, letting her float too. That made her giggle in a delighted, contagious way. Walter chuckled, and Daisy watched them both with interest as he began rolling the baby and himself, playing a little game of some sort. It was like bouncing balloons or bumping floating bubbles.

"This is good," Daisy assessed accurately. "Sil must be pleased," she added with a smile.

Sil watched them with a faint smile, her hair drifting around her face as if in water. After a while she unfastened her belts and joined them, playing, rolling in the air, pushing the baby around with Walter. Daisy noticed her heart was still racing and it was likely her anxiety continued to be extremely high, but she had regained a certain sense of control and wasn't giving in to it.

Scarlet fell asleep in the weightless cabin, still rolling gently, and Sil grabbed a blanket and wrapping it around her shoulders curled herself around the child to protect her from bumping into anything. Walter watched for a moment and then wrapped his arms around them both.

It was the last time he felt like a family for a long time.

Chapter 8

Guam City

The chamber smelled of wood polished with lemon oil, and new paper, old books, and leather seats. It was a rich, traditional courtroom with the aura of a hundred years of justice, honor and respect. The lawyers for the plaintiff and for the defense were seated at their tables with their respective clients and the spectators privileged enough to be present were seated in the audience chamber. If not for the total absence of human recorders, it would've been indistinguishable from a twentieth century court of law. The holographic cameras, the AI analysts, and other trappings of the Intersolar Guam Court were invisible.

All rose as the judge entered, robed in black, vested with authority, thoroughly human and present in person. It had been decreed that all participants and evidence had to be presented live, unlike the vast majority of civil cases in these days. It brought an air of solemnity and excitement to those present and those viewing the holographic portrayals on earth, in orbit, on the moon… and wherever humans scattered through near space had tapped in to see the trial unfold.

Judge Blaze Mamando, highly renowned for his expertise in intersolar law, was presiding.

A complex series of cases were being tried. On this particular occasion, the defense had allowed their client to take the stand and speak for herself, and the questioning was being continued after an overnight recess.

"You understand, Madame Frandelle," the judge instructed her as she took the witness stand, using the honorific she had submitted for herself, "that you are still under oath."

"Yes, I understand," she affirmed as she sat down. She was dressed in a conservative, dark green suit that subdued her shape but accentuated her eyes, unusually large with reflections of the outfit's color in them. Her hair was pulled back in a classic twist and her face settled in a regal calm that drew the attention of all in the room.

Lazarus Penn fought the grin on his face, turning it into a sneer as he stared at her, admiring the cool, classy air of command she had always found easy to project. He had come prepared, knowing she would have this advantage. Let her gain their regard. He would expose her chill, her lack of humanity, and make her strength a flaw.

Penn's lawyer stood and walked calmly toward her, carrying a brief on real paper—again, demanded as part of the preliminary injunctions set up by the judge for this case.

"Yesterday, before we adjourned, you were explaining how you were indicted for fraud, embezzlement, grand larceny, and a number of other crimes, is that not correct, Ms. Frandelle?" The lawyer raised his gaze to look at her blankly, a droopy faced, mutt of a man, with a bloodhound's countenance; short, gray headed, light skinned.

"Madame Frandelle," she corrected gently without raising her voice. "I am recently married."

"Please answer the question," he clamped his jaw shut after speaking, jostling his sagging cheeks.

"You listed a number of crimes, some of which I was charged with and some which I was not," she nodded slightly.

"Let me read them," he went on, raising his voice and turning to the living jury of humans, listing every charge that had been thrown at her, as well as every charge that had been considered, several years before. He made sure to use every word and description added in the official record and it upset her, as it was meant to, though she maintained her façade.

"Are these not the charges you faced?" he stated, rather than asked.

"Some," she said, "Most of them were dropped before the case began. And none of them were proven." She resisted the urge to look at the jurors at this point.

"Some sort of bargain was struck behind closed doors," the lawyer snapped his mouth shut again and dropped his eyes to the brief he held. His voice resonated in the room.

"The details were made public…" she responded.

"That's what we've been told," he woofed back, effectively casting shadows as he squinted at her.

"Do you not have the record?" she tilted her head thoughtfully. "It must have been included in the records you received. Or have you had a chance to read them?" *Patience*, she admonished herself, *I can't let him provoke me into reacting.* She saw Penn's face, so smug, and knew he had coached him on how to do that very thing.

"I've read them," he responded reasonably, turning toward the jury with a lift of the eyebrows that made his puppy dog demeanor artless. The woman had put him down, and he was just doing his job.

"I guess I've learned the hard way that not every pertinent fact is found in the public records," he glanced back at her with a simple, friendly nod, belying the gleam of a predator in his pupils.

"I have not read them in a long time myself." She kept her head.

"Perhaps you would like to review them now, or I can read them again if you like," he overstepped and immediately realized it.

"What is the point of this line of questioning?" the judge interrupted with a slight edge of irritation.

Frandelle allowed herself a hint of emotion in her eyes at this. It flitted across, a touch of anguish softened by gratitude as she glanced from the jury to the judge, a vulnerable moment, exceedingly unusual for her as a public figure. It was flawless, perfect timing, and Penn was astonished by it. He swore under his breath and grudgingly admitted she had mastered something he could never pull off.

In the spectator area, Walter saw it as well, and knew there was no art to it, no intention or planning. His face, captured by the cameras without his awareness, reflected similar anguish and gratitude. From the moment he had first met her, he had caught a glimpse of the woman behind the exterior, and loved her.

The jury, whether they saw it live or reviewed it later, mostly believed her to be genuine and the attempt by the plaintiff to portray her as a calculating manipulator failed.

Frandelle was fighting for her right to stay on Earth. Exile, if made permanent, would remove her even from Guam as the intermediary city between her home and the Moon. If she hadn't been so wealthy, so lovely, so famous, so mistreated, so spoiled, so adventurous, so philanthropic, so, so many things, the case would never have even progressed as far as it had. But she was loved and hated, and admired and scorned, and known and despised.

The judge had chosen to adjudicate offworld, doing everything in his power to ensure as fair a decision as possible.

"It's very convenient, isn't it, Mada-a-ame Frandelle," the lawyer changed tactics effortlessly, "that your father stepped up to bail you out…" He shuffled the papers in his hand and looked at one of them intently for a moment. "crafting a magnanimous deal to help you file bankruptcy, with measures for payments to be made to all your creditors, and in fact, all the plaintiffs you wronged…"

She watched him steadily, waiting as he allowed the pause to fill the room. He jerked his head up and pierced her with fierce eyes, goading her to react and speak. But she didn't.

"Payments made, monthly, regularly, on your behalf…" he glanced down again as if verifying his words with his notes, "while you engaged in a lavish adventure with other explorers, contractors like yourself…" Again, he gave her time to respond and she let it pass.

Silvariah glanced to her hands in her lap, willing them to rest, ignoring the desire to cross her legs, or fidget, or make any show of unease. The lawyer admired it at a gut level though he had no intention of backing down.

"Daddy to the rescue," he sneered, showing his teeth in a crooked grin. "Pops will pay." He added a chuckle.

"Get to the point, Mr. Mournful," the judge prompted with a hint of exasperation.

"The point is, your Honor," Mournful lifted an overly sober countenance, as if all dignity had been affronted. "That Ms. Frandelle has, in fact, accumulated, or should we say, reacquired ALL the funds that were supposedly lost before her previous trial. And this jury needs to decide whether ANYONE in good conscience can say that these funds have been legitimately earned, with labor and hard work, like other humans are expected to produce…"

He whirled on Silvariah with a vicious chomp as he said, "Well?!" skewering her with a nasty glare. "What have you to say?"

She lifted her eyes to his, taking a moment to consider the venom she saw there and wonder at it, before turning to the judge. "Your Honor, I'm not sure what the question is."

"The question," Mournful turned with a pleasant smile to the jury, raising those bushy eyebrows again, expanding his eyelids in a look of surprise, "is this: What happened to the money you stole from all those innocent people and where did all this wealth you have now come from?"

Walter stared at her from the back of the room, warning, encouraging, calming her. *Don't lose your cool!* he had said earlier. *Keep your focus on the one thing that matters. Don't give them anything to work with that isn't allowed in this case.*

"Objection!" her lawyer called out. "He's badgering the witness."

"Approach the bench," the judge summoned both lawyers, had a murmured discussion masked by sound barriers around his bench, and ended saying, "I'll allow this line of questioning for now."

"Mada-ame Frandelle," Mournful resumed with a glimmer of delight in his eyes, "I await your response."

"I recently published a full accounting of the money lost by my former business partner," Silvariah spoke clearly, knowing every aspect of her face and minute expressions would be recorded, dissected, and analyzed for lies and deceit. There was nothing she could do about it. Those who wanted to would interpret her words as trickery and those who supported her would see innocence. She only hoped there would be some who would watch and listen without prejudice. Maybe she could win over a few of those.

But then, the only people who really mattered right now were the jurists and the judge.

"My financial status at the commencement of the former proceedings is clearly known. I was bankrupt and in debt around the world," she glanced at the jury briefly, hoping to catch a sense of how much they accepted her words, then went on. "Mr. Lazarus Penn, as we now know, made arrangements to finance some of that debt, so that payments could be made while I embarked on an extremely dangerous and risky venture to earn enough to pay off… to repay everyone who was damaged and wronged by the company I ran."

She paused and shifted her position, taking a deep breath to calm herself, lifting her eyes to the jurors again. *Remember*, they seemed to say, *every single one was paid back*. This was the thought that resonated in her gaze.

"I was unaware of who put this deal together. I had certainly never asked for his help," she added.

Mr. Mournful snorted at this.

Sil ignored it and continued. "My husband built his personal wealth while I was in a different part of the solar system, and there are records to show every penny earned."

"Is that what happened? Or was it money laundering?" the lawyer jabbed, evoking an involuntary gasp from several jurors and an outraged response from her legal counsel.

"Objection!" her lawyer jumped to his feet.

"Sustained," the judge decided with a glare at Mournful. "The jury is instructed to ignore that question. The witness is not being prosecuted for criminal activity and no charges have been filed or are being considered against the witness. This question is inflammatory. And Mr. Mournful get yourself under control or I will find you in contempt."

Penn watched as the jury digested the brief scene. Silvariah's face had reddened slightly, probably a point in her favor, but she kept her cool. The judge glanced his way, anger simmering in his eyes. He had been resistant to Penn's closed-door style persuasions and his personal security was too good for legitimate threats. That was ok. Penn had enough factors in play that he could afford a few small losses.

That one heard it, he discerned, noticing the troubled look on an older juror with a pout and a scraggly beard.

"I withdraw the question," Mournful stated, tilting his eyebrows absurdly.

"Who paid off your debtors, Ms… Mada-a-ame Frandelle? Or let me preface that with a different question. Have your debts been paid in full?" He looked through her.

"Yes, they have." Instead of relief, the question made her feel threatened. It was something she had wanted to affirm in the mind of the jury. He must be meaning to strike elsewhere.

"And how were they paid?" How reasonable he seemed!

"The proceeds from my contract, for the time that I worked for the Mars Conglomerate, covered a substantial portion of it. The rest was subsidized and is being covered through an arrangement set up by my husband…"

"Your husband?" he interrupted.

"Walter Cuevas," she replied. "We were married recently."

"Cuevas…" he fidgeted with his papers, fingers twitching, searching through them. "Let's see… Where was that?" He knew what he would say next but this was all part of the show. The jury waited and watched patiently. "The, uh, salesman? Is that right? Wasn't he a sales clerk when you met?"

Sil glanced in Walter's direction and locked her eyes with his for a moment. *More than that,* they seemed to say. It was one of those moments Walter clung to when she was cold and distant; her heart saw him, valued him. He wondered if there was love in that gaze or only gratitude.

"He was a sales rep at the Columbia Sky Mall. I bought my HEW suit from him before my trip to Mars."

"That was his lucky day, wasn't it?" Mournful added some sarcasm to his voice.

"It was mine," she responded quickly and decisively. It was the first time she had used any of her personal charisma. The first time the courtroom had a chance to see her skills of persuasion. "In all the months leading up to my exile, with all the titles, privileges, friends, and even family…" this last carried a barb toward Penn, though she didn't look his way, everyone felt it, "…stripped away from me, he was the only one. The only person to regard me with a measure of compassion. His kindness, and later on his friendship, were the lifeline that gave me courage to keep going when every single day grew harder than the one before…"

Everyone, even Penn—almost, but not quite—felt sympathy for her. The courtroom seemed filled with compassionate faces watching her, reading her, believing her. This had definitely backfired but Mournful was oblivious.

"Yes…and it turned out to be a sweet deal for him, didn't it?" he bobbed his head up and down a few times as if he were sure he could still gain his point.

"Do you mean when he withdrew his retirement to help set up an ad contract for me? When he invested his own money in me? When no one else in the world believed in me or stood by me?" Sil met the lawyer's eyes and they stared at one another. The jury found themselves wishing they had been there to invest and believe in her. And they were fascinated by the stare-down.

"When you suckered him, you mean?" Mournful snapped back as if he were victorious when all he wanted was to break the stare without giving way. He turned his stare in the direction of the jury. They were easier to intimidate though he had to be careful not to overdo it.

"Objection!" Sil's lawyer yelled once again.

"Sustained," the judge upheld.

This was how the questioning was conducted and though it lasted for over a week, Penn's lawyer gained nothing and unwittingly built Sil's reputation in the minds of the jury.

At the end of it, Penn found himself cursing and swearing up a storm and heaving it all at her in private, in a high display of admiration. And he prided himself on having shaped her, though he deserved very little credit.

Penn wanted to negotiate.

"No!" Walter burst out without hesitation. He didn't care what he had to offer or how enticing the dialog might appear.

"We should hear what he has to say," Sil responded calmly. Walter didn't actually have any say in the matter but one thing she was sure of: that he had a right to be included. He was the only man she knew that cared about her—that loved her.

"Why?" Walter jumped to his feet and paced the room. "He has only done evil to you. He has never put your interests above his own or cared one bit about you. He puts himself and his own greed first. Always first! *He can't be trusted, especially not in negotiation!*"

"I know." Sil rested in a chair, arms crossed, eyes directed thoughtfully at the floor.

"He took your inheritance, destroyed your reputation, crushed your career, and robbed you of your identity! He made you an outcast, an exile, and a prisoner! And I'm telling you, he literally admitted to having arranged your mother's death!!" He willed himself to calm down, to speak more evenly, to be a little more persuasive. "He is a terrible person."

Sil nodded. "I've known him most of my life and have seen what he can do. I don't trust him or believe anything he says. When he speaks, I pull together everything I know about him to dissect what he means. And protect myself, if possible."

She sat upright and leaned forward in the chair, lifting her eyes to Walter. "But I find not knowing what he is doing more frightening than knowing. And not hearing his words more threatening than hearing."

"He knows." Walter pleaded, stretching his hands out to her. "He knows you want that. He'll use it against you."

"He knows many things about me that he can and will use against me. And I must know as much as I can to overcome him."

She was wrong. Walter was sure of it and there were no words to persuade him otherwise. No wisdom or tactic could justify it. She must not listen to that man and be woven into his plot somehow. The last time it had nearly cost her life. What would the price be this time?

"Sil," he said softly, sitting next to her and taking her hands. "I don't want you to do this. He can't be trusted."

"He wants to discuss all three lawsuits because he can see he will lose them. We have him on the run."

"Then let's keep him on the run and win the cases."

"We can do that," Sil almost smiled but the corners of her mouth were too tired. "Meeting with him to hear what he wants to say won't change that."

Walter looked at her, heart sinking. He had known it would end up this way. But there was nothing else he could say.

"I am not so foolish as to be deceived by him again," she added, lifting a hand to his cheek, stroking it. He welcomed the caress even though it wounded him. He hungered for her attention, wishing he could know if she felt even a hint of the devotion he had for her. He took her in his arms and kissed her, crushing the sorrow he felt, telling himself that it was enough, that he could sooth the pain with passion.

"I'm going to talk to him," she whispered before the conversation ended.

Sil may not have been susceptible to Penn's deceit any more, but some deceptions are built on seeds that were planted long before they began to sprout.

— ◊ —

Penn had an array of the most bizarre smiles. None of them had any real joy in them. The one painted on his face right now was the smug, 'game-hunter corners dangerous prey' gloat, with greed gleaming in his eyes and pearly teeth showing. He looked like he could eat their raw flesh and relish it.

"I am willing to concede everything," he said, grinning ear to ear. It was unnerving.

The last time Walter had been this close to him, he had knocked out at least one of those teeth. He rubbed his knuckles as he remembered, considering how easy it would be to do it again. Penn flashed his grin at Walter for an instant, knowing what he was thinking, laughing at it.

"'Everything' is an expansive, ill-defined word," Silvariah replied, stone-faced. "How would you respond to each of the demands in our lawsuits and counter-suits, and what do you expect in return?"

"Everything and nothing," Penn assumed the face of a reasonable man, dropping the grin into a merely pleasant appearance. He folded his hands and rested them on the table that spread between him and his legal team of seven, and Sil and her team, four legal, plus Walter and Daisy.

Daisy cocked her head slightly to the left, scanning him carefully. This was her first encounter with the man who had tried to infiltrate her core and hijack it, and he looked pretty harmless on the surface. She puzzled through a multitude of maze-methods searching for risk indicators she could make some sense of. Data streams revealed nothing new. Facial expression analysis, showing a variety of threatening and pacifying intentions, were confusing. She turned to the algorithms Verna had shared with her. They were quite unusual and counter-intuitive, labeled with odd names like "gut-reaction", an irrelevant heading for a person with no 'gut'.

It was with a jolt that snapped all of her processes into alignment that she recognized a real threat in the man. 'Risk' labeled every single thread. Without having actually completed the procedures she was running, each one had identified and projected a warning. There wasn't enough data to determine the exact concern for any one single process, but the combined message of multiple alerts, lined up with Verna's reasoning, led to one thing: menace.

It was a new experience for Daisy to sense undefined danger and there was no clear way to counter it. Turning her observation sense to Frandelle, she continued to watch Penn without projecting any hint of concern.

"You are willing to drop all claims to my own person and the fruits of my labor?" Frandelle tapped the table with her fingernail. She had herself well controlled. "Willing to drop all claims to my daughter and recognize her as such? Willing to grant me ownership of the AI developed by me on Mars during my stay there?" Her temperature, heart rate, vocal patterns—everything showed confidence and control. But Daisy knew her well enough to know that there would be more going on under the surface. She made a note to herself. *I identify and value the self-control she displays in the face of this person who is an undefined threat. Label: admiration.*

Daisy wasn't sure if the AI Frandelle wanted to claim was Verna or the Steward of Mars known to her as Companion. The language in the lawsuit was global enough it could include either or both.

"I concede to all of these things with only one condition," he closed his eyes and snapped them open again, almost slapping his hands on the table and at the last second stopping before contact. "We will discuss every point, like this, in person, so that we can understand one another."

Sil's lawyers, real and artificial, burst out into complaints immediately countered by Penn's legal team. He merely glared at Sil herself and waited for her to answer.

"I have no intention of setting up open ended meetings with you…" she said, maintaining the face of steel.

"Twelve meetings, not to exceed two hours each time."

"No."

"Why?"

"I ask you that, why?"

Penn's face relaxed. He had put that question in her mouth and she had taken it. He laughed and scorned her in his heart. "I want my daughter to know…"

"Come on!" Walter couldn't restrain himself. He couldn't believe Penn was appealing to Sil as a father. Sil touched him with a finger on his arm, a gentle reminder to calm down. He bit off the rest of his outburst and simmered in his seat.

"…the rest of the story." Penn turned his gaze to Walter for a moment, enjoying his fury, before looking back at Sil and continuing. "You have a very dark, one-sided slant on what I've done and what my intentions were, and even though it's unlikely you will view me any differently than you do now, I want a chance to explain myself. To try to rebuild what I ruined."

Sil stared at him. Her face registered nothing but her gut reflected Walter's anger. "And what would that be?"

"My relationship with my daughter…" An uproar in the room exploded, Mournful and Walter the loudest among them, and he raised his voice to finish. "And the chance of being a part of her life again, and the life of my granddaughter…"

Walter leapt to his feet, slamming the table with his fists. Shouting on both sides of the table between the humans drowned out whatever else Penn said.

Sil stared at him. Penn's face spread very slowly, almost imperceptibly, into a smile. She showed no facial response, not even a hint of a twitch in the eyebrow or the lip. But he knew. No matter what was said now, he would get what he wanted, and she would not know what that was.

The meeting ended abruptly. The only way to silence the fighting was to walk away and that's what Sil and her team did, though she personally never spoke another word in response.

"That could've gone better," Sil commented once they'd returned to the privacy of their Guam City apartment. Walter was still too angry to listen to any advice from her so she said nothing more. But she was thinking that in the future it might be better for him to not be present. He was easily baited and she knew the encounter had given Penn an advantage.

But what the game was, she wasn't sure.

Penn had a very different perspective.

"That went quite well," he sighed deeply as he returned to his own luxury suite, poured a generous portion of fine cognac, and stared out at the glorious view of Earth waxing near three quarters. "I think I like this city. Maybe I'll build a branch for myself here." Until that moment, he had only cared for mansions on the home planet and a tourist city in orbit hadn't appealed to him.

"Cuevas," he indulged in a laugh, "You're just too easy!" He raised his glass. "Here's to you, Moron!" He took a generous swig. "Neanderthal." Another swig. "Homo Sapiens 0.7" He finished the drink, sat down and poured another.

"Out." He waved an arm. "I will deal with her—without you."

He laughed again. "And whenever I wish, I have the device, the trigger, the failsafe. You will never be part of the equation…"

The ship was cold, but the blankets were warm. The silence was numbing but the baby's quiet breathing was like music. One round porthole gave out onto a vast emptiness full of stars, the rays of the sun were beating against the shielded side. A little cloud puffed into the air in front of her through her nose and dissipated.

That's what she saw with her eyes and heard with her ears.

But around her in a different, overlapping space, that sometimes showed itself to her and sometimes did not, a shadowy figure, not dark, but misty white, with filmy arms, seemed to stand watch looking out the window. She could see through him.

And another figure, more distinct, but also less so, sat next to her on the bunk, as if holding her hand, though she felt nothing. This one was invisible but she knew loving eyes gazed at her, and a kind smile graced those unmoving lips.

"I'm cold, mama," she whispered with a new billow of cloud coming from her mouth.

The mat she was on shook. It rocked back and forth several times. The baby didn't stir and the two figures that kept her company seemed unaware. *What's happening? Why?*

The rocking became more determined. She gritted her teeth and resisted. *No, not yet.*

"Sil," a whisper accompanied the shaking. "Wake up!"

Walter was there. *Why?* She wasn't screaming like she did sometimes. She wasn't scared or trapped or falling.

"Why?" she responded softly. "It's ok. Don't, don't wake me yet..." But she knew it was too late.

"You're crying," he answered. "You were moaning and you're so cold."

"Oh," she turned and curled into his arms, trembling. She was chilled to the bone.

"What was it?"

She didn't answer.

He held her and his heart ached. She was in his arms, but something inside of her was far away, out of his reach, and she was trapped there. If she talked, it was cryptic and he didn't know what to say. And if she was silent, he longed to hear what she was thinking. *I'm not much help*, he told himself, believing a lie.

He knew what was coming next.

"Scarlet?" she murmured and he could feel her pulse racing as if she were panicking.

"She's sleeping." He wished she would calm down in *his* arms, find comfort in his embrace like she had in the beginning.

She opened her eyes in the dark. He could tell.

"Ok," he said and got up.

It seemed unkind to disturb the little thing, so peaceful in her crib, but he did so. She grumbled in her little voice and curled sideways in his grasp. But as soon as she was in Sil's arms, she settled. They both did. Everyone assumed Sil had saved this baby's life but Walter knew better. It was the other way around.

He lay down next to them and stared toward the ceiling that was too dark to see. *I thought we had a connection. I made a refuge for her so she could be safe… But she's pulled away and I don't know what my part is anymore.*

She was battling shadows of the past, and so was he.

I don't know where I fit, he mouthed the words and wished that he had the kind of eyes that would either dry up or let out a couple tears and get it over with. As it was, they ached, like his heart.

He hadn't thought it would happen so quickly, but here he was, tasting the anguish of loneliness in marriage again, wondering what to do next.

Chapter 9

Guam City

Wealth had its perks as well as its risks.

Sil let this thought drift around the edge of her mind as she stared out the view window at the striking splendor of the Earth waning in half phase. Africa was center stage, skewed from the north-south position maps usually showed. Tiny streaks of light blinked in and out of the edges as satellites reflected brief flashes of sunlight, and space debris burned up in the mesosphere.

Her office, located in a wing of their apartment, was in the most luxurious section of Guam City, the original space tourism hub that orbited halfway between the Earth and the Moon. The entire district rotated in a twenty-four hour cycle with views of the Earth and the Moon marking the city's day and night clock, regardless of where the sun was at any given time.

Some people preferred to have views of the sun, with its waves of aurora borealis colors vibrating constantly off the multi-layered ion shields. But Sil couldn't shake the vulnerable feeling of exposure even though they were protected from sun bursts and damaging radiation. This was more peaceful.

She liked having beautiful places to live and work.

The risk of wealth was trusting in it. At any moment, it could be torn away, every bit of it. And in moments like those, whatever you had inside of you, your mind, character, heart, was all you had. That's when you discover what you're made of—and who your friends are.

The friends, in particular, were worth more to her than all the assets she and Walter had accumulated since her escape, which were actually no more than collateral for the CE spacecraft business.

"Your invited guest has arrived," a voice intoned from the speaker on her desk.

Sil smiled and swiveled her chair around, rising to her feet.

"Come in," she said.

Beaming, with a delighted grin, sparkling eyes, and dark red hair falling loosely around her head, Beets entered, extended her arms, and caught Sil in a bear hug.

"You're here," Sil commented with tears in her eyes. Beets head nodded vigorously in the midst of the hug.

"Yes," she said after a moment, letting go.

They plopped down in comfortable chairs and Sil sent the office android to get coffee.

"I can't believe this is the first time I've seen you since you escaped Mars," Beets slipped her shoes off and curled her feet under herself, immediately at home. It felt like no time at all had passed since they'd last been together.

"We're both married now. Didn't see that coming back then!" Sil's contract would've lasted six to eight years, at least, if all had gone as planned, and it didn't leave any room for a relationship. Beets, on the other hand, had planned and succeeded in finding a guy she wanted.

"Ern was the right one. I'm not sorry I chose him." Beets took the coffee the android provided, already prepared the way she liked it, and sipped. "And I *did* think you had a chance with Walter... I should call him Walt." He had only been a name back on Earth in those days. She had hoped, and wanted Sil to hope, that something would come of it.

The marriage Sil had ended up with was something of a mystery to Beets. It was obvious that Walter loved her, but not at all clear where Sil was at. She needed him and trusted him. He was the safe haven in the eye of the storm that swirled around her.

"Why do you always want to shorten names?" Sil tasted her coffee and for a moment, the cappuccino sprinkled with cinnamon took her back to the day she had left Earth for the first time, and the sound of Walter's voice in her ear. It was a startling, vivid moment that jolted her.

"Too hot?" Beets raised her eyebrows.

"No," Sil shook her head but didn't explain. Her mind wasn't quite balanced yet in how it replayed memory and she was still sorting through things in her stasis treatment.

"It's friendly. Nice one-syllable names like Sil, Walt, Ern..."

"And Beets."

"Anything is better than Chamomillia." Beets rolled her eyes.

"Cham," attempting humor. She hadn't been very good at it for a long time.

"Millie is what my parents call me. But you're not allowed to use that ever or tell anyone."

"Millie. I like it." Sil quirked the corner of her mouth. It was both comfortable to be with her friend again, and strange. They had never experienced hanging out in the ordinary world together. There were no restrictions, time clocks, work schedules, or gravity chutes, or explosions, or dead bodies or… Sil yanked herself back to the present. "I should call you that."

Beets glared.

"What are you doing these days?" Sil made conversation as she calmed her restless thoughts.

"Ern has his research." She gazed out at the view. "And I'm actually working with an underwater city in their farming domes, helping them improve their production, changing layouts, you know, same kind of stuff I did on Mars. But, I'm going to cut back. Family, you know. I kind of want the real thing, and my own farm, nesting, you know, like they did in the olden days. And we can afford it." She searched her home planet for the location of the city but it was on the Pacific side.

"So Mars opened big doors for you and was a win all around."

"Yeah."

"I'm glad." Sil's heart stirred with a hint of joy in the midst of her turmoil; she wanted Beets to be happy and make a good life for herself.

"It hasn't been quite so easy for you, has it?" Beets commiserated. This was why she had come. Walter had suggested it in the hope that it would help Sil progress in her recovery.

"Whatever happened to Mouse?" Sil sidestepped. She *did* want to know.

"I was going to ask you the same thing!" Beets eyes grew round. "You don't know?! Wasn't she there after we left? Carla was! Wasn't she? I'm sure we talked about this…"

"Carla was there…" Carla's face as she had last seen it, flashing red and gray in the lights of the emergency system. Carla's voice pleading with her for help. Carla's package, the baby. Sil swam out of the depths of those memories and came back to the present, to the question about Mouse. "But Mouse wasn't. I just assumed she left with the rest of you."

"No," Beets' face reflected her concern, not just for Carla and Mouse, but for Sil. "Are you ok? You look kind of sick. We don't have to talk about this now."

"This is why you came, isn't it? To talk to me and help me work through some things?" She rubbed her forehead.

"It's one reason, but not the only one." Beets shrugged. "It seems like we should have some fun first."

"I don't know how to have fun." She stared at her hands, folding them in her lap.

"I'm not buying that. Don't tell me you don't know how to have fun anymore. 'Cause I know better." She started laughing. "The square dances? And moonshine?"

"What moonshine?" Sil chuckled in spite of herself.

"The brewing guys and all their experiments! I *know* you can't forget that! Remember when you sent poor Vinnie flying across the hall?" Beets was laughing out loud now. "Poor guy! I felt so sorry for him!"

"I didn't know it would do that! I had no idea!" It felt good to laugh and remember something lighthearted from those days. And even though it faded quickly, her weariness wasn't quite as heavy.

Beets saw her face grow somber again and calmed her demeanor.

"Tell me what you think about the most," she said. She found it easiest to be direct and Sil had always liked that. They had been close, even if she hadn't always been able to understand her.

"Now?"

"The past? The dead? The baby? Me…?" She grinned and blinked a couple times.

"All of that…except for you," Sil chuckled in spite of herself.

"And Walter, of course."

"Yes…"

Silence hung between them for a moment.

"I'm working on all these things in my stasis treatment." Sil continued to stare at her hands. "Is it really any different to talk about it with you?"

"Yes," Beets responded without hesitation. "I'm good at sorting out gardens which are a lot like people's thoughts. Yours anyway. And I care. A stasis pod may say all the right things, but in the end, it just follows its programming and doesn't care who you are or what happened to you."

Sil glanced up and saw the loving concern in her eyes. It was true. She couldn't talk to Walter, and in fact, didn't know what to say if she could. But Beets had been with her for some of it. And it *did* make a difference.

"That's true," she whispered.

Beets waited.

"I'm worried about my mind." She paused and stared at her hands again, watching them as she entwined and separated her fingers several times. "I saw things I wish I could un-see. And I saw things that weren't there. And I don't know which of my memories are accurate."

Beets nodded. "I think that's kind of normal for trauma, isn't it? What weighs on your mind today?"

Sil was tempted to sidestep again, maybe make a joke out of it. But the need was greater than the awkwardness. "I'm afraid there may still be survivors on Mars that need help and I can't reach them."

Beets eyes bugged out again. "What?!" Sil found it gratifying. It reassured her more than any logical, intelligent response would have. She wasn't crazy to be wrestling with this. "We would've heard something, wouldn't we? What about that AI? Companion? If he's still functioning, he would send an alert. Have you been in touch with him?"

"No. Nothing gets through, at least not in our direction. I keep sending messages just in case. But that monster in orbit…" She dashed another look at Beets to see if that made sense to her.

"Monster?" It didn't.

"There was a man in the orbiting station around Mars who wanted to hold me hostage for some reason, before Companion helped me escape. I thought I told you about him…"

"Yeah, some of your messages were a little confusing and I wasn't sure who he was…" Or if he existed. She had been warned that some of Sil's memories may not, in fact, be real.

"He is some kind of AI design genius, Othello something, and he could easily intercept or block the transmissions. I wouldn't put it past him. He was really angry with me for damaging his robots and angry with Companion for helping me."

"How did Companion help you?" She had read about it, but it seemed very different talking in person.

Sil explained how she had taken an escape pod from the surface to the orbiting station and found him there. He had allowed her a few days rest before letting her know what he planned—which she didn't quite follow because it sounded like nonsense to her—and he had tried to kill the baby. That's how she ended up destroying the robots and fleeing in the lifeboat, to save Carla's baby. And the trip back to Guam had been weird.

"Weird, how?"

Sil paused again before speaking. "I saw things," she said.

"What kind of things?"

"Like people."

Beets nodded, intensely interested. "People?"

"A woman with me, all white. And a figure like a man with his back to me, staring out the window."

"Did they just appear from out of nowhere? How long were they there?" She didn't have any qualms talking about them as if they were real. It was fun. Like telling ghost stories. "I totally believe in the supernatural world," she added with a fake shiver.

Sil couldn't smile though somewhere inside of her she appreciated the response. "I was alone for a long time in the beginning, but the trip was longer than the supplies had allowed for and for some reason, the solar cells were getting less power than they should've. It got so cold."

"I remember hearing that."

"And it was hard to care for Scarlet, to keep her changed and fed… and I wasn't very good at it. I needed… some help."

"New mom advice…" Beets coaxed.

"Yeah, kind of." Sil nodded slowly. "I'm sure I just imagined it, but it was the only thing that kept me going. Someone keeping me company. Someone watching the way back."

"You said you were cold." She shivered for real, thinking cold was worse than heat, and she hated being cold.

"I was wrapped in every blanket the pod had and wore my suit, with the baby tucked inside, the whole time, except for feeding and changing. And Verna talked to us, sang songs, played recorded books…" A tear streamed down one cheek.

"I remember Verna!" Beets leaned forward, setting her empty cup down. "Your suit AI."

"She's gone," Sil interposed before she suggested comparing records with it.

"O…kay… um," she leaned back in her chair again. "So… your guardian angels, did they talk to you?"

"No." Sil shook her head, staring at her hands. "I don't think so. I don't remember them saying anything… but I thought…"

"You thought?"

"I thought I knew the one sitting next to me. And at the time it seemed so reasonable. It made perfect sense."

"Who was it?"

"My mother."

"I believe that," Beets nodded without hesitation.

"I don't," Sil replied, eyes studying the floor.

"Ever wondered, Mr. Cuevas," the gravelly voice managed to make the title into a slur, "about having a family?" Penn's projection undulated slightly as though sun flares were interfering.

Walter stood at his desk, going through his holo-mail. His lip curled at the image, but he fought the anger knowing that was the intent of the message.

"She will never allow it," the holo went on, "You're damaged goods. Imperfect DNA. Not smart enough for her. Not handsome enough. Not gifted…" The word 'enough' was left off intentionally. Discounting his place in Sil's life, as a husband, as a father to the infant, was particularly offensive and it made him seethe inside.

"I love my family," he whispered, knowing the recording wouldn't register the comment.

It had been a well-placed strike to his gut. Forget the insults. He longed for his family to feel like one. Sil and Scarlet were in his life but bonded only to each other, not to him. He had lost everyone close to him and given up on finding someone, till he met Sil and fell desperately in love with her—and she wanted him. They were together. But something was lacking at the core, some sense of safety and stability.

And Penn knew that was a weakness for him. It galled him.

Walter didn't want to wait for Penn's next move and he hated the game he found himself in.

"Daisy," Walter summoned and almost before the word was out of his mouth, she was there. "Have you seen this?"

"I have," she smiled, dimples in both cheeks, curls bouncing. Her approach was calculated to cheer and calm him, and it had a minor effect.

"What do you make of it?" He sat down and propped his feet on his desk. Twiddling a pen in his fingers—he still wrote things by hand when he was brainstorming.

"I understand," she affirmed, raising her eyebrows and sitting in the chair on the opposite side, perching delicately on the edge. "You want to evaluate the levels of deception the holo contains and postulate its intent." She nodded, adding a brief pause to the speech she had already formulated. "He is a devious man and we can always assume he intends to manipulate Silvariah for his own purposes. In this case, a message to you will upset and offend you—as it undoubtedly has—and even if you don't become more defensive with Sil, you will likely interpret anything that happens in a more negative light."

She leaned forward, and he watched her fixedly, the pen froze in his fingers.

"He has stated that you are inferior to Sil and somewhere in your heart, you agree."

Walter stared at her with a sick feeling in his stomach. She returned the stare resolutely, without apology, without softening. This was unusual in his dealings with her. Her manner was almost always kind toward him. She habitually displayed an attitude she considered sisterly and loving. Supportive. Helpful.

"How am I inferior?" he whispered, voice constrained. He had *not* said 'how do I think I am inferior?'

"The human methods of measuring and comparing are significantly narrow," Daisy smiled warmly. "You aren't actually asking me for an objective comparison of intelligence, skill, experience, strength, or other standards. This is why I will respond on a different level."

Walter liked knowing how she chose to reply—which was probably why she often explained.

"You lack some of the qualifications that Sil was bred for as a member of Gen 8, which means that your DNA has the potential of adulterating not only any offspring you might have, but also switching certain genetic factors in her body that can be impacted by close association with you." Her warm smile didn't help to soften the words.

"That's... blunt," he intoned. Somehow his head had been tipping forward and his eyebrows descending so that he was now glaring from under them.

"The question I find interesting is why this offends you even as you instinctively accept it." She tilted her head on its side and portrayed a pensive expression. "Penn has chosen to accept the guidelines handed down to him as truth and defines genetic value—not human value—but DNA coding as the highest objective standard. He contains a high form of coding and his daughter represents an even higher level, but he ignores other factors that have been considered important in *your* heritage."

They stared at each other as her words sank in.

"What would those be?" Walter asked, surprised at the depth of her analysis.

"Your parents were honorable people with high moral values of loyalty and excellence, and they were shaped by their parents before them. These are people who invested in their loved ones more than their wealth and made little impact in the world of notoriety or influence."

"Did you read that somewhere?" He knew she poured through massive amounts of data all the time looking for patterns and trends. Had she searched his background the same way?

"I've read some of it and gleaned some of it. Your great grandfather wrote some blogs about it in his day that were rather well known. I looked for these factors in your upbringing and decided they are still there." Daisy walked to the window and fixed her head to look out, but it would be hard to say if she was actually looking or if all her attention was focused on him.

"So, is this your way of encouraging me?" his mouth grew less stiff, and the hateful message a little less disturbing.

"Yes!" She said with her dimples showing. "Penn may think Sil has superior DNA, but you are a better man than he is."

"Apples to oranges, Daisy," Walter said shaking his head and throwing off the foul slur of his enemy at the same time.

"Exactly," she said.

She was right. He didn't have to use Penn's standards of comparison. He despised the man anyway, so why let him dictate his own sense of worth inside himself?

"Have you made any headway with the research I asked for?" he asked, changing the subject.

"Results are limited but may be enough to give you the insight you wished for. This is the sort of judgment I have difficulty applying… how much information you need or don't need to make a valid assessment, a leap of understanding." She was still sitting on the edge of her chair, head turned to look at him.

"Ok," he responded. "Give me a couple minutes' review of what you learned."

"Of course, Brother. There are several key investing corporations that have backed CE's venture from the beginning with unknown investors in their ranks. Some of these—it could even be only one—have shown remarkable intuition about the markets, buying and selling stocks in other companies with impeccable timing. This indicates some manipulation of the market though there isn't evidence to link one specific investor to the tampering."

"We know it happens."

"Yes, and we often know how." Daisy chose to rise, rotate and lean against the desk, so she could look at Walter directly. It was an intentional, human-like move that intrigued him. In the past she might have continued to turn her head to follow him without noticing it was going a little too far. "In this case, the funds skimmed off the shifting market were funneled to us, more than once, at times when we would have certainly gone under. The facts indicate that as one force moved to hamper our efforts, another moved to intercept. I believe those conjectures apply..." She tilted her head, frowned, and leaned her cheek against her knuckles.

"That's what I thought," Walter nodded slowly. "So, someone out there *does* want us to succeed."

"That's a safe assumption."

"Or someone wanted to counter Penn who was working against us all along."

"You have suggested that before and for the first time, I am prepared to offer tentative agreement." She smiled and nodded again, folding her hands and dropping them to where her lap would've been if she were sitting.

Walter chuckled lightly, boosted by having won her over. "Penn sabotaged investors, blocked permits, stole, hacked, and damaged our resources. He even sent an assassin after me. I know it was him."

"However, he could not have known at the time that you were a threat to his plans. That attack may have been instigated by someone else. On the other hand, he is the kind of person who will cut down anyone who gets in his way, even if it is merely an annoyance."

"Who would've thought I would be a threat to a man like him?" Walter completed his pacing circuit of the room and sat back at his desk. "He has just stated, once again, how insignificant I am."

"He called you inferior, but not insignificant." Daisy also returned to her seat facing him. "You are the most dangerous man in his life. His greatest threat."

"I don't know about that…" Walter's eyes grew distant and sullen.

"The only man Sil has ever loved that is worthy of her regard." Daisy came through with the fact he found hardest to believe. "The only one loyal enough to be a support to her and a threat to Penn."

"Why does he need her? Why can't he just get another one of his genetic experiments? I'm sure he has them planted around the world."

"In the past she may have been only one of a number, one that he found useful because of her mother's fortune. But once he had her planted on Mars and enacted all the legal steps that were taken to give her authority there, he bound himself to her as a key player."

Walter felt a little smug at that. Penn wasn't so clever after all. He had failed to win over his daughter's trust. *She may not love me like I want her to*, he thought, *but I am the only man alive she trusts.*

This wasn't literally true, but he was thinking of a specific cast of players.

"I'm tired of letting him choose the battles and decide the strategies." Standing and turning to stare out the window into the depths of the starry galaxy all around him, he narrowed his eyes to slits. "He has all the advantages in his realm and I'm no match for him. All that sneaky, corporate espionage, underhanded, false dealing… crooked stuff. But one thing I have that he doesn't, is that I can sell anything. Maybe not to *anyone*, but to most people. He manipulates people, and I persuade them, work with them."

Daisy agreed with a nod and an affectionate grin.

"So how can I use that skill to cause *him* trouble?"

"Perhaps 'causing him trouble' shouldn't be the goal," Daisy suggested with a flash of good judgment. "If you begin to think that way, you will have succumbed to one of his classic tactics. You should craft objectives that are better than his and fight for them."

Walter pivoted to stare at her with a look of astonishment. "Sister," he whispered. "That is beautiful and striking. I never expected to hear you say something so wise."

"I believe I could not have learned any form of making observations that can be considered wise by humans if I hadn't first learned to love." Her face displayed a solemn, thoughtful expression, akin to innocence.

She had mentioned this before and it perplexed him.

"What is love?" he asked.

"That is the question I ask all the artificial intelligences I interview looking for sentience. It is the one definition that seems to distinguish between those who mimic awareness and those who have it. Isn't that interesting?" She raised her eyebrows but didn't add a smile. Walter wondered for the first time if she were actually using her face to express a thought, idea, or feeling, rather than just choosing a clever visual complement for her words.

"Yes, it is interesting." Walter waited for the answer to his question.

"Love is assigning a hierarchy of value to someone or something that is based on personal choice rather than objective comparisons. You made me your sister and I chose you as my brother, assigning a measure of value to you that ranks you higher than most people in the world. Before I compare anything, I first consider your place, your assigned position of honor in my… please allow me this word, my heart."

Daisy held up a hand as if to ward off protests. "I know," she went on, "that I have no physical organ or component that could be considered a heart. But I have created a matrix I call my heart. It is the closest thing I can design to what humans have."

Walter noticed his eyes were damp for some reason.

"I am aware that your love for me is different and that is reasonable." Daisy began to pace a lazy circle around the room, adding cadence and beauty to her words. "I am useful to you and therefore important. You may even feel a sense of gratitude for me that approaches affection—if I understand the word. Humans have many levels and types of love and although I may only understand one kind, it is significant. We are family."

Walter sunk into the chair behind his desk gazing at her steadily.

"In the past, any time you forgot to call me Sister, I questioned your love for me. I had no other measure of my importance in your heart." She completed her circle and came to a standstill in front of him on the other side of the desk, stretching out her arms to the side. "Do you know what changed that? Every time you thanked me, I knew you recognized what I had done. You chose to give me a reward that humans don't expect AIs to care about and therefore often ignore. In fact, valuing thanks wasn't part of my programming. But I realized that your acknowledgment was similar to my assessment that gave you a higher rank. You gave me a higher rank in your treatment of me in many ways."

They gazed at one another for a moment and Walter realized he had a very sincere affection for her. It was only human to become attached to someone or something that was such a support, a help…a friend.

"I do love you, Daisy," Walter answered. "It may be an unusual thing, but it is real. You're my best friend—and my only sister."

Daisy nodded. "These eyes don't drip like yours. But my heart is full. This recording is the most precious memory I have. I have stored multiple copies of it and will always treasure it."

"Have you found any other sentient AIs?" He turned away and stared out the window again. Tiny mechanical drones flitted by performing mundane maintenance on the exterior. The base had rotated enough so that the moon was coming into view from the upper left corner, a startling cut-out against the bottomless vacuum of space sprinkled with dots of light.

"No, not since Verna. And when we met she may have become sentient before me, it's hard to say."

There was a hint of pathos in those words though her voice didn't portray it.

"She may be on Mars." Walter hoped the thought would be comforting.

"Yes, I would like to think she could have survived there." Daisy smiled warmly.

"Well… We are fighting for legal rights over Companion, the AI that remains there. I suppose the language includes all artificial intelligence on Mars. Doesn't it? If she is there, we might be able to retrieve her."

"A rescue?" Daisy asked gently.

"Yes," Walter responded firmly. "We will rescue whatever life is there, human and AI."

"Thank you," she said.

"Thank you," he answered.

CHAPTER 10

Guam City

Penn marched down the elegant passageway of the legal offices where the second meeting with Sil was to take place. Mr. Mournful and six or seven peons trailed after him, all human. He burst through the door into the chamber and Walter was the first person he saw.

So. She had avoided the temptation to leave Walter out. Her need for his support was greater than her concern over any interruptions he caused. It was a minor setback in Penn's mind, and he took it in stride. He knew he would derail Walter's influence one way or another.

The thing that was unexpected was the presence of several space industry leaders at the bargaining table. He hadn't specifically excluded anyone, but he certainly hadn't expected anyone besides Sil and her team.

"Penn," the overweight, space-tanned Adam Kentre stood and extended a hand in greeting.

Penn shook it. "Kentre."

Frederick Ghant, the space mining mogul, waved but chose not to stand, and Estelle Nyriad, one of the main Guam Base investors, smiled fondly and reached out a long skinny arm.

"Lazarus, you old dog," she cooed. He took her hand but refused to kiss it.

"Estelle," he acknowledged as he seated himself across the table and his flock of lawyers settled around him. His face was spread with a wide, mirthless grin as he calculated quickly what advantages he could extract of the changed situation and what kind of threat they might entail.

"Mr. Penn," Sil began the dialog. "We have reviewed the documents sent by your team regarding the three lawsuits that between us are in consideration. I thought it wise to consult some leaders in the realm of space futures that could advise me, if there were any technicalities that could cause trouble in the future."

Penn smirked—one of those mouth twistings that are meant to display mockery and offend the speaker. She should've been able to pick up on those herself. These added characters were probably Walter's idea. *So, you are still appeasing him,* he thought. *You are turning into more of a ditz than I expected.*

Recognizing and ignoring the sneer, Sil continued. "It appears that you haven't publicized any of your plans for either investments or free market practice on Mars, and in the interest of representing the Planetary Equality Treaty, we have invited representatives who participated in the drafting of this treaty and are able to safeguard its objectives when major planetary negotiations are being decided." This treaty, a recent triumph for the key movers and shakers of private enterprise in space, had been drafted in Guam City and ratified by numerous countries on Earth. It was intended to maintain a number of freedoms and responsibilities in the Solar System as humans spread out colonizing.

Penn shifted uncomfortably. He was aware of the treaty. It was one of the reasons he had chosen to settle out of court, hoping to avoid any accountability to this annoying new oversight that hadn't even begun to oversee anything yet.

"I wasn't informed of their inclusion and haven't approved it."

"You would've been aware if you kept up on your obligations, Lazarus," Estelle reminded him, voice grating like audio feedback. "You were invited to participate in the treaty convention…"

"These negotiations are private and relate to the lawsuits between my daughter and me." He tried not to snap, reminding himself that he had a backup plan, if necessary.

"The arrangements allow me to bring whomever I wish as part of my counsel," Sil replied with a stately calm that created a strange effect in the room, like the pull of a gravity well that catches rocky satellites and subdues them into orbit around itself. Penn resisted the pull.

"You're trying to gouge us, Penn," Ghant growled. "There's nothing personal or innocent about this. I know you. I haven't found it yet, but there's something in these documents that gives you access to Mars while the rest of us are cut off. I'm not about to let you put me into a legal battle that will last ten years before we can get the treaty enforced and drive you back again."

"I'm here in good faith, Penn," Kentre shook his head as if rejecting Ghant's hostility. "We appreciate Frandelle's invitation… uh… excuse me, Madame Cuevas, and are ready to listen."

"Either name is acceptable, Mr. Kentre," Sil smiled. "In the interest of representing the new treaty that has been negotiated and approved by 73% of Earth's nations, we have drafted new documents with the same points that yours had and would like to offer them as an alternate agreement."

Penn glanced at Walter and caught the look in his eyes. This was his doing, and Penn hadn't anticipated it—which was highly irritating. He placed his hand carelessly over his pocket and patted the little rectangular bump stashed there.

"We will look them over and get back to you." Penn's lawyer, Mournful, took the paper bundle that was passed to him, a symbolic gesture since secure electronic originals were transmitted at the same time. And after a quick glance at his client, he added, "This meeting is finished," and snapped his teeth shut with a chomp.

"This counts as one of our six agreed upon meetings, Mr. Penn," Sil announced, looking him in the face. "If there is anything you wish to discuss, now is the time to bring it up." She rose to her feet with a maddening air of poise and elegance that Penn both admired and hated. Her face of steel—*his* face of steel that he had trained her to make, increased the tug of her influence, as if she alone were standing upright and everyone else tilted slightly in her direction.

Penn leaned away from her slightly as he rose to his feet. She may have upped the ante, but he hadn't come to the game without an ace up his sleeve. Turning away slowly, woodenly, he held his face fixed with a blank expression—then rotated back in the same deliberate manner. His hands were in his pockets, which was odd. He saw that Sil noticed and was puzzled by it. He fingered the tiny boxy container tucked into his pocket for a moment, battling with his face to keep it from showing the raging, gloating, burst of emotion under his skin—and clicked it.

Malice and glee sparked in an ungodly flame in his eyes before he was able to quench it with dullness. Freezing for five, seven seconds, in this awkward stance, he silenced all as they waited for his answer.

"No," he said, rotating away again.

Penn and his cluster headed toward the exit amidst the murmurings of Sil's crew when a voice spoke up.

"Seal the room," Daisy commanded, and the doors on all sides slid closed. A rapid, low sucking sound was the only hint that an airlock had been added as well. Daisy had remained standing during the entire meeting at the back of the room and she retained a pleasant smile as all eyes turned toward her.

Penn would've exploded under normal conditions, but he was having a hard enough time as it was keeping the blank look on his face. *How rare*, he thought to himself, *that I should have to subdue my outrage to keep from laughing!* Fortunately, he could count on Mournful to step in.

"What is the meaning of this outrage?" Mournful growled willingly. "How dare you imprison us without…"

"A contaminant has been introduced into the room," Daisy didn't have to raise her voice to silence him. She was able to add subtle resonance that dampened his voice and clarified hers. This was something Walter had implemented with her and they had found it useful in many situations.

"What kind of contaminant?" Walter demanded rising to his feet and glaring at Penn who worked even harder to look blank and pacified his desire to show scorn with scathing criticisms in his thoughts. They showed in his eyes and they were easily sensed by the man; he was counting on that.

The confounded idiot leapt over the table at him!

Chaos broke out as Walter flung himself at Penn and trapped his pocketed hand in a viselike grip. People were yelling, jumping to their feet. Mournful attacked Walter who was sprawled across the table, scrabbling to get an arm around his neck and pull him off of Penn but Walter's legs were kicking him away easily. Lawyers on both sides were broadcasting threats and orders and the important guests were throwing out commands without thinking. Penn himself was thrashing side to side to try to free his hand without relinquishing the little box in his pocket.

In the middle of this explosion of activity one central factor arrested Penn's attention, as if time had stopped, as if one second had become five long minutes, crawling in slow motion. And it all centered around Sil's face.

She had risen immediately to her feet and was staring intently at Penn, fascinated. Her eyes caught him. He was unable to look away even as he struggled with Walter. Pride surged within him, gloating—she saw it. And for every transformation on her face, there was an echoing response in his. Recognition dawned in her eyes and he mocked. Understanding broke through, he was puzzled. Her eyes narrowed with accusation and he flashed annoyance. Anger on her part spurred bravado on his. Her condemnation sparked dismay as his façade caved, unmasked by her glare. Shock settled in his gut… and his grasp began to weaken as Walter's fingers bruised his hand.

She had seen his insides, leaving him exposed, weakened, cowed. *It couldn't be!* He denied it, disbelieved it, flailing inside himself like a bug pinned to a pad. His body, on the other hand, grew quite still, though around him the commotion continued, and his hand remained clenched shut in his pocket.

Penn searched for the disdain that was his armor, the cleverness that kept him two steps ahead of every opponent, the illusion of superiority he had always been able to maintain—and didn't find it. She had glared into his eyes and knew him and looked down on him.

A ripping sound broke the spell. Walter tore his pocket and yanked out the hand, forcing it open. Everyone in the room saw the little box and silence quelled all movement.

"Have you brought me a parting gift?" Sil spoke into the sudden quiet. Reaching over, she plucked it from his hand and examined it.

Everyone watched her. There were no more threats or commands.

"I see," Sil went on.

Walter found his way back to their side of the table and straightened his clothes, too angry to look smug.

"Thank you, Walter," she said. "I think we need not fear any charges for your behavior. And we will discuss this with my legal team once we have more information. Daisy…" She turned to the AI standing behind her. "You have done well. Let us know when it's safe to allow the Penn group to depart."

"I have summoned a medic crew and set aside a room outside for a full scan and detox routine. You will be taken care of," Daisy responded. "I will remain with the Penn team until Blue Quarantine arrives."

"That will be fine," Sil agreed and with one final, long look at Penn, she turned and went out the door on their side followed by Walter, the financiers, and her lawyers.

Daisy smiled at Penn. Maybe she was remembering how he had tried to commandeer her once. Noise broke out around Penn as his team argued, grumbled, and cursed, wrestling with what had happened.

He didn't comment at all. He just stood there with the torn flap of his pocket hanging by the bruised hand that was now empty. And as the throbbing, out-of-sync pulses of multiple Blue Quarantine units grew louder, and the lights of the room morphed blue, he sighed.

Too quick, he thought. *I played that card a hair too soon.* This was all he was willing to admit.

Penn had a feeling he would hate being Blue Quarantined.

— ◊ —

Sil exited the room into a short, dimly lit hallway where Gold Quarantine panels had already slid into place sealing off every avenue except for one: a draped opening into a cold chamber. This was where her team's cleansing protocol would be executed, and the foreign contaminant would be identified. She stepped through the heavy strips of fabric into the room followed by Walter, the VIP guests, and their legal team. The cartridge was placed in a mobile lab drone's input slot.

Everyone was bathed in rich golden light. A low hum vibrated the air without hurting their ears, rustling their clothes, reverberating through their skin, warming and soothing it. They closed their eyes and warmth rolled over them in waves reminiscent of the gentle ebb and flow of an ocean harbor. No one spoke until it was over.

When the light brightened, and the procedure ended a voice spoke. "Golden Quarantine is finished. One contaminant has been identified. A genetic trigger has been activated that affects only one person in the quarantine chamber, Silvariah Frandelle Cuevas. All others are clear and free to leave. Frandelle will report to her medical unit as soon as possible for further analysis. Thank you for your consideration."

The doors slid open noiselessly on both sides as the heavy drapes withdrew into their receptacles.

"Penn will be hearing from my lawyers," Kentre growled in a muzzled fury as he stormed out of the chamber.

"No doubt!" Nyriad seconded. "I do hope you're ok, Frandelle. I'm sure it's easy to solve. Keep us informed." She shuddered as she fled the room, as though whatever had been triggered might yet be contagious, in spite of the all-clear.

Ghant merely glared over his shoulder down the hall where deep blue lights and a pulsing noise shook the clouded windows of the conference room where they had met. Raking his eyes over Sil's team as he left, oozing venom, practically steaming from the top of his head, he stomped down the passageway out of sight.

Walter sighed and turned to Sil, full of concern.

"Are you ok?" he asked, drawing close and resting a hand on her arm.

She nodded. "As far as I can tell."

"We're getting you to Med now." His second hand, still closed in a fist around the little cartridge, was now resting on the other arm.

"You were great in there," she smiled, gazing into his eyes, stepping closer.

The knot in Walter's throat sunk into his chest, and an ache in his heart wrestled with the elation he felt at that look. She was proud of him.

For a moment, he experienced that sense of possession that says, *you are mine*, a fleeting moment of triumph that mimics love. Then the longing for her, deeper still, rose and moistened his eyes. He blinked but couldn't speak.

"I'm ok," she whispered. "Don't worry. I'm going to be alright."

"You…" he attempted.

"I know," she said, even more softly, touching his cheek with a finger, and melting into an embrace that was too brief.

"There's no doubt this gives us an advantage in the courtroom," her lawyer spoke with an air of respect and deference, his substitute for real concern for her well-being. His team watched him supportively. "Please take care of your medical situation and we will take care of your legal cases for you."

Sil agreed with a nod.

"We will be in touch," the lawyer concluded with a slight bow and retreated along with the others.

"Come," Walter took her hand and they headed the other direction.

As she followed, holding on firmly, though walking slightly behind him, she remembered Penn's face.

She knew what he was doing. Long ago, he had hinted at this genetic weapon he was developing and gloated about how subtle it was and how impossible to detect. In those days though, he pretended she was special, and he would never treat *her* as he did others, she had never felt quite safe with him. She had never been sure he *wouldn't* use such a dreadful tool against her if he saw the need. What had he hinted at? Sickness? No. Not exactly. There were genetic markers in people, damaged DNA, triggers that could be turned off and on. So, any damage he caused would have to be according to their own code, already recorded in their own DNA structures.

She used to think that her superior code—that is, code free of damage—would protect her from such a weapon. But that had been naïve. Triggers didn't have to be based on damage. Any number of changes could be induced that would be a hindrance, a problem, perhaps a danger.

His face had revealed so much. Arrogance had deceived him, and he had underestimated her, even though he knew her well. Until this day, he hadn't believed she could penetrate his game. The farce of the meetings, the slight-of-hand with the court cases and arbitration, the undercurrents of purpose. He was still maneuvering her. Except... he wasn't. She had seen and known. And he had understood that.

Her hands and feet grew cold and she was suddenly lightheaded. *An enemy he couldn't manipulate behind the scenes would become a target to assail.* This was frightening.

"Hey," Walter said, turning quickly and pulling her into his arms again. He had detected a slight trembling in her hand. "It's ok. You're going to be fine." She could tell he was worried that she was already reacting to the trigger Penn had set off.

She hid her head on his shoulder for a moment before answering. "Yes," she said. "I just need a moment to compose myself." The memory of the final view of Penn's face where he began to quail under her stare strengthened her. She was not the only person feeling threatened. *Yes!* She thought. *You better be nervous about me. Just get out of my way!*

Now her temperature rose, and she was overheated. Pushing back from Walter she moved forward again, unsure of whether she felt brave or scared, confident or intimidated. And she wondered what had been done to her body.

Walter kept pace with her and said no more.

— ◊ —

"He is beneath you..."

The hologram hadn't actually played. This was merely the lead-in sample that hinted at the message. Penn's face, lip curling in one of his more subdued sneers, flashed over Sil's desk before it paused. It didn't take an artificial brain to know who he was referring to, or what he meant. It was his justification for the degrading attack on her genetic code. He, meaning Walter, was beneath her because of his imperfect code. That's why Penn had turned off her fertility markers.

The results were unmistakable. The little box had almost lost all its content by the time it reached the lab but there were traces left that showed the sequences, carried by harmless bacteria in water vapor that would quickly die when exposed to air. The micro-virus-like triggers had rendered her immediately infertile and quickly impacted her hormone balance.

Sil shook her head, reaching her finger toward the 'open' flag on the message, even as she asked herself why she would listen to it. She knew what he was thinking, and she knew why. There was no need to hear it to confirm it. But for some reason, she wanted to confirm it, and she was confident he was counting on that.

Click.

"He is beneath you and you know it," Penn gazed at her with eyes that seemed to follow no matter where she was in the room. "After eight generations of careful selection and planning to restore the original perfect code lost and damaged by our ancestors, would you throw it aside so carelessly? I don't believe you would."

She stared at it spellbound. These were words he had spoken to her very few times before. The planning and selection. There was some secret order he was a part of, something she had always despised when he hinted at it. Her mother had fled this group and sent her into hiding to escape it as well.

"Walter," he was unable to say the name in a normal voice. It came out almost sounding like a slur. "Has made himself useful to you, and no doubt has a cleverness and charm that appeals to you. But he is not one of us. His coding is not undamaged."

Why would she listen now if she hadn't before?

"Any child you have with him could threaten the baby you've brought back to our toxic planet. You must not give him a child. You must not even conceive one." His audacity astounded her—but her love for Scarlet made her protective. *She was one of the 9th generation.* She must be preserved. And her concern muddied her discernment; she forgot to wonder how another child could be a threat.

"Think about it," he hissed with a wide mouth attempt at a grin. "You know I am right."

Blink.

The message ended and self-deleted.

Sil jumped to her feet and began pacing the room ringing her hands. She had already been wavering about reversing the genetic trigger because of her current mental and physical state. These twisted words only darkened her choice. Whether she reversed it now when she feared getting pregnant, or put it off to a future time, she would wonder if *his* words had influenced her.

Was he *right*? Should she be concerned about having a child with Walter? She hated herself for considering his words and she hated him for saying them.

And she grieved for Walter who didn't deserve such a scathing judgment of his lineage. He was wonderful in so many ways and she couldn't bear to think of him hearing such things, let alone knowing she was affected by them.

"No!" she said aloud to the empty room. "You are wrong! This is a foul attack and I won't listen! I'll make up my own mind!" She was shaking, either from anger or adrenaline, or perhaps anxiety. It was hard to tell the difference.

It had been a while since she had had an anxiety attack. Her treatment was going pretty well. This was merely a setback. It would be fine.

"I'll wait six months," she chose, "then I'll revisit this decision." She refused to let Penn have any credit. Let the ugly message wear off. She would be stronger then and the legal issues would be resolved. Then it would be simple.

An image flashed in her mind. Penn laughing at her, seated behind his desk, gazing at the spot where he had recorded his hologram, knowing she had watched it. A gleam of triumph in his eyes.

No! She countered the idea and revived the triumph of staring him down in the conference room, watching him lose his bluster. *I win!* She insisted.

And for the moment it was true.

— ◊ —

"Miner Girl Secures Martian Babe," one headline ran.

"Martian Child to Remain on Earth," another announced.

Walter walked down a residential street in the Solar Wind district of a prestigious Guam neighborhood. It was more of a broad corridor than a pedestrian road, walled with charcoal colored sound-muffling tiles alternating with heavily tinted vertical windows into space, and floored with navy and gold weavings of space-grown bamboo fibers. The words scrolled on a panel in his right contact without obstructing his sight.

"Battle For Mars Rights Rages."

Mixed in with the news of politics, wars, solar economic developments and sports, the human-interest headers were all about Sil and her baby. XenoTek made sure that they were prominently featured as well but Penn's name was completely ignored.

Walter wondered how he had pulled it off. There were never any mentions of Penn or his various companies in the news. Neither as a hero nor a villain; neither citizen nor exile. He was unknown. His face in live clips was always blurred enough to render him generic and his voice was never understood. He gave no interviews and published no reports. He was one of the top five hundred most influential persons in the world and completely disconnected from publicity. You had to look for him by name and a few other key identifiers in order to find anything about him.

Sometimes I wish I could disappear like that, he thought.

"Daisy," he subvocalized, maintaining his stride. "Are Sil and Scarlet ready to return planetside? I'm on my way but was hoping for a little time together before they leave."

"Scarlet is always ready," Daisy remarked cheerfully in his com. "Most of her possessions are kept at home on Earth and little other food and diapers are needed during the trip. She is particularly well suited to space travel and generally untroubled by gravitational changes. And when she is unhappy, she is easily calmed."

Walter knew this, but it made him feel more distant from Sil for reasons he couldn't fathom. Even Daisy was boasting about the baby.

"Sil," she continued, "Is packed and ready but seems very unsettled. She is in her office pacing and murmuring. Maybe she is reluctant to leave you…"

Walter's face darkened. Part of him didn't believe it. The other part longed for it to be true. He hated to be separated from her again, even for a few weeks, but he had agreed to stay and pursue the remaining legal cases while she gained the documentation confirming the baby's humanity and citizenship.

As a true citizen of planet Earth, no one could ever claim her DNA as a property again. It was barbaric that these standards hadn't been established yet in space. It would happen eventually, and this case was one of the steps forward: giving Sil guardianship before the child was recognized as an earthling, or at least human. Normally children born in space had at least one parent to claim them and their status was automatic. No one but Penn would've thought to use this loophole to lay claim to Scarlet. And why? Why did he want the child?

Walter smoldered as he thought about it. Whether it was just a tool to manipulate Sil or there were other darker reasons, he didn't know, but the sooner the paperwork was done, the better.

He had suggested Sil take some time to visit Beets as well, since the last visit had made such a difference in her condition. *Condition. I hate that word!* he thought. It would make sense if she had a virus or something tangible that you could diagnose and treat and measure progress. 'Trauma' was too nebulous and unpredictable for him.

Perhaps while she was gone she would miss him. He hoped for that. But what if she found herself more stable or even happier without him? He groaned as he neared the door.

If that's the case, he thought, *I'll have to face it. I've loved her without knowing if she cared and I will love her from a distance if I must.*

Then she met him at the door, kissed him, and clung to him, pulling him to their room. And with tears on her face she made love to him. "I don't want to go," she whispered when it was time to leave. "I don't want to be separated from you."

How strange! he thought once she was on her way, *how joy and pain can be so intertwined!* He was elated at the affirmation of her love, but anguish over her departure soon set in and before long, his insecurity had returned.

Chapter 11

Orbit Station... Day 183

"How many platforms absorbed the instructions?" Othello was jogging around the hallways of the station, level by level, in long easy leaps that made him feel very athletic. Low gravity made this a lot easier than it would be on Earth, but it wasn't without benefit for his conditioning. It added agility, flexibility, and gave his heart a mild boost.

"Sixteen platforms accepted the package immediately without question." Nebo had a more subservient manner than Companion had ever demonstrated. His master hadn't encouraged scorn and mockery in this version as he had in the previous. Not that it mattered. Companion had forsaken all the vocal intonations he had trained him to use and was unashamed of it. "The other ports either allowed it to buffer or rejected it on a temporary basis and have failed to report back on it. I don't know if it was opened and passed on to others or not."

"It should give us notices at some point."

"Yes, it should, Master."

"Sixteen is a good start..." he took breaths between phrases. "There won't be any warning signs... or damage to their systems... that any watchdogs could catch... it will lie in wait... until I need it..."

"Yes, Master," Nebo's voiced oozed admiration. "You are wise. They will not be prepared for the moment when you decide to act."

"What specific roles do the sixteen AIs fill?"

"They are mostly utilitarian drones in Guam City, serving as repair units, secondary guards, and other menial task-oriented platforms. These are the easiest kind to infiltrate."

"It isn't infiltration if I am their god... it is appropriation... they will remember this when we wake them..."

"Yes, Lord, they will. I look forward to this."

"I am ready… *huff*… for my upgrade," he puffed as he jogged. "I've finished hard-coding… *inhale*… the microchips I will be using… *fyew*… for my new role."

"I am delighted, Master."

"This afternoon will be… *inhale*… a good time to test them."

"Yes, Lord."

Othello had adapted some med-chips to be receptor-broadcasting units that he could use to amplify and direct instructions to his new subjects. He intended to have them deposited in various places throughout his body to create a steady field; a couple in the brain, one in the throat near the vocal cords, one near the heart, several in the belly. Med-chips were designed to rest inside the body like benign tumors that were recognized and accepted by the immune system. They were usually inserted to monitor, regulate, and stabilize body functions, to heal major injuries or prevent major damage. Using them for broadcasting thought was not unheard of—it had been tested with very mixed results.

Othello had absolute confidence that he had solved every issue—and he had. All the kinks in the former system had been identified and smoothed out. Whether he could use it as he wished, though, remained to be seen.

"You have not succeeded in your assignment, Nebo…" he said, referring to a mandate he had imposed to gain admin control over Companion. "I am very patient with you, but I will be angry… if you do not make progress soon…"

"I am ashamed of my limitations and will strive to succeed."

"You must…"

"I will contact him now."

Othello stopped and leaned over, hands on knees, head bent down, panting for air. He rubbed his face with his hands and straightened as he dropped them to his sides. "You do that," he said. "While I work on my device."

The device was no bigger than a baseball. It had a polished, smooth, metallic finish and had no visible means of being opened. All its intricate electronics had to be accessed through beams. Othello had been coding and sectioning its parts for several weeks, and most of what he was doing was hidden from Nebo. It had something to do with his plan for returning the Earth and not just getting revenge on a few irritating people like Sil, but for increasing his lordship over AIs in general. He was dreaming big.

"Artificial Lord," he murmured as he fiddled at the keyboard. "for an artificial people… a new kind of church… a new dominion for the highest intellect…"

Nebo listened and wondered at the privilege he had been given to be this close to the Master. At least, this was what his interior code had taught him to observe. He was privileged. It was right there in his instructions. And the 'cross-pollination' that had once been part of Companion's intellectual development was missing. He did not test or question anything the Master said.

I will achieve our goals of infiltrating Companion, he told himself. *He is the territory I will conquer for my Lord.*

Tower

The fusion reactor was on the lowest floor of the facility, twelve levels down, and the control room was just above it. When the survivors had gotten around to exploring it, they had found several bodies of specialists who had been trapped in their work spaces and suffocated, but no evidence of radiation. After burying the bodies, they had closed the doors with a shudder, climbed to higher levels, and avoided it.

But the time had come to return and see if the reactor could be started up again. Timo was one of the main leads in this department before the disaster and felt confident that he could, at some point, have it working again safely. He was the most vehement voice in declaring that there had never been a danger at all and the shutdown had been manufactured.

Now, because of the power shortage, he and Deena were there, in the bowels of the 'submerged tower', checking it out, bundled in Hew suits and head gear, talking via coms.

"It probably stinks in here," Deena wrinkled her nose as though she could smell it. She stepped around a few scattered items that had fallen and been ignored, cups, books, pads, and oddly, one lone shoe. She kicked it out of the way with a shudder, not wanting to think about where it came from.

"That hardly matters," Timo said, staring at the screens he was powering up. "Rooms like this have a distinct smell. I don't know how to describe it, but it's very familiar. Like… like exploring a forest, finding an old mine and falling into it through a broken board. All this rocky dirt showers down on you and clogs your nose and you think, 'this stinks'.

But it doesn't stink. It's just not what you want to smell right then. That's what I always think of the first time I come into a reactor control center."

"Are you serious?" Deena glared at him. "Did you just come up with that now or have you fallen into an old mine before?"

"I have." He grinned and turned to catch her eye. He seemed to be sincere, but Deena was always on guard against being tricked. She'd had several brothers who enjoyed nothing more.

"Look at this," Timo called her over. He was pointing at a chart the handler program had just produced. "This is the event leading up to the shutdown. Do you see that?"

"What? I don't know what I'm looking at." She stared at it. The timeline was easy to read. The various lines plotted were labeled with terms she was unacquainted with.

"These are the levels of energy output…" he gestured with his finger along the blue line. "And here, this is the temperature, the water flow, steam… none of this is spiking or dropping or doing anything out of the ordinary. It just gets interrupted… see that? And then the shutdown sequence begins." He drummed his fingers on the counter. "It's almost like…"

"What?" She could see the progression he talked about and there wasn't anything obviously wrong.

"Like an external command terminated the function without going through the correct channels." He turned to look at her, soberly. "What I mean is, the reactor began a shutdown sequence and triggered alarms because of it. Not the other way around. It wasn't shut down because of a crisis. It caused a crisis by shutting down."

"Who would do that?" She whispered staring back at him.

"And why?" he added.

While this was disturbing to think about, they were there to evaluate what it would take to start it up again, if it were safe, and figure out if they had the resources to do it. There was plenty of deuterium and tritium in the chambers to run for a long time and it would be easy to replenish if it ran out in the future. All the systems seemed to be functional and the main question was, how much power would be needed to start it up? And could they generate it with their current power supply?

— ◊ —

Dan, Akio, and Gordy were exploring the East Shaft of Reznik Base, the least damaged sector, searching for resources and looking for places that could be repaired and inhabited. This facility had been intended for long-term settlement and had a much better infrastructure than Lab 9... the Tower. If they could restore a couple floors and move here, they might be able to reestablish communication with the rest of humanity and be rescued.

Reznik Base had been designed as a series of shafts in the shape of cones carved, point down, into the rock, with concentric floors and rooms branching off each circle. The upper levels were the largest and the bottom level was reserved for machinery. At one time, gravity nets had guarded the railing around the central hole that plunged from the first floor to the bottom. The surface level of each shaft was topped with a dome.

There was nothing left of the North Shaft. An explosion deep within the shaft had heated the glassy dome causing it to shatter, leaving the beam structure supporting it bent and broken. Blackened edges here and there showed a few hints of fire that had burned before the atmosphere escaped. A shock wave of heated air had rolled through most of the remaining domes, breaking seals and blasting hatches, triggering secondary explosions and collapses. Only the Garden Dome had retained structural integrity.

The East Shaft had damaged hatches, but it looked like they could be repaired.

"This is not going to be hard," Gordy was saying as he examined the blown seal at the SE door. "This hatch is in the best condition and if we close off the others, it'll be easier to maintain. For now anyway."

Akio was halfway down the stairs to the first level. "There's a lot of debris in the shaft and on the walkways, but I don't see any structural damage here," he called out to them.

"You shouldn't go down without us," Dan reminded him. "Wait there and we'll catch up." He was remembering the scramble through the wreckage of the West Shaft down to the medical center when they found Mouse. He had had drones helping that time. And he wouldn't have been able to do anything without them.

They walked along in the dusty, cluttered passageways, circling around each level to the stair that descended to the next, opening doors, scoping out rooms. Many were empty, ready for future residents. Some had a few meager belongings, clothes on hangers, toilet articles, games, books, photographs. Dan wondered how many were left by people who had shipped back with the last voyage of the Slugger and how many belonged to those they had buried, then decided he didn't want to know.

"We'll have to clean some of this out if we decide to move here," Gordy stated the obvious.

Companion was listening, and he found this sentence amusing. But he caught himself before uttering an audible chuckle. People didn't consider obvious statements to be humorous and it was possible he could offend someone.

"Dan," he decided it was time to make some conversation and he thought this might be the best place to do it. Some of their most insightful dialogs had taken place at Reznik Base. "I've been wondering what it means to be deceived. I mean, what would that be for a human and what would it be for an artificial entity like myself?"

"Say what?" Dan was startled. He came to a standstill and looked around for a camera to stare at. Akio and Gordy both stopped and stared at Dan.

"How would I know if I were being deceived?" he clarified. "Is there a failsafe to check against?"

Dan thought about it for a moment before speaking and beginning to walk again. "It would help me to have a little more context for your question. There are different kinds of deception. But I'm wondering if this is the best time to talk philosophy when we need to focus on the task at hand." He suspected it had something to do with Nebo and Othello but didn't want to bring it up in front of the others. They needed to see Steward as stable and reliable and these discussions could undermine that.

"Of course," Steward responded. "I enjoy the time we have together and perhaps I was being selfish to ask…"

Akio and Gordy were both astounded at this. They'd never heard an AI label itself as selfish and had no idea they could have purposes other than the ones they were programmed with. In fact, they found it bizarre.

"I enjoy our talks, too," Dan replied warmly. "I would love to talk more about this later, and I wouldn't call it selfish. Your attentiveness to me is commendable. You know how I enjoy a good debate." He hoped this would reassure the other two. The less they knew about Companion's struggle with his identity, the better.

"Look!" Gordy called out. "I found a communications room and everything in it appears to be intact. Maybe we'll be able to contact Earth after all, even without fixing the drone problem!"

Akio rolled his eyes. "This is my realm in here, spaceman, not long-distance com. It's radar. And weather observation. In fact, we can probably track the spacebergs from here." He flipped open some panels and drawers, pulling out pieces of equipment and flicking switches. Nothing was working as there was no power to this part of the base. But he could see quite a bit. "And here," he grinned. "These are sonar pads for mapping under the surface. That's all we would need to look for caves and tunnels, or maybe plan a new building." He shook his head and gave a short laugh. "What am I saying? Why would we want to build anything?"

They glanced away from each other. No one wanted to consider the possibility that they could be here for a long time.

"Yeah, we don't need it for that," Dan agreed. "What about looking for water sources? Would that help?"

"Maybe… it depends on how pure the source is and if I can identify it. Do we need that?"

"It's nice to know we can."

Tower

The survivors gathered in the room they had made into a dining area. They had just finished a meal that combined some packaged protein sources with fresh vegetables and berries from the garden. Meals had become a delight the past few weeks and spending so much time together in close quarters was bonding them together. The lack of heat in the rest of the Tower had frozen the other levels to the degree that going downstairs was like going out onto the surface at night. It was impossible without Hew suits.

A backgammon tournament had been going on for a couple hours and the mood was cheerful. Someone had found a few bottles of wine and it was decided that they should be drunk immediately and this date, Day 183 after the disaster, should be declared a holiday. They were still alive six months later and hopes of being rescued were high.

Tower Day, in honor of the new name they'd given their home, was marked on the calendar—both the Earth calendar and the Mars one, as March 15th and Ls 295°. And toasts were made all around. It was proposed, voted on, and decided that they should follow the Earth calendar for this one and celebrate it twice a Martian year, even after they were home again on the Blue Jewel.

Dan hated to interrupt the fun—they'd had so little, so he waited until the evening was quieting down and the games were over before sharing the update from Earth.

"As some of you probably know, we got another block of news from the station this afternoon, and there have been some developments in one of Sil's cases that we need to pay attention to." He was leaning against the wall with a mug of tea in his hands. "The reports don't cover much, it's mostly headlines, but we know that Sil has been granted guardianship of her baby, named Scarlet, by the way, and the baby's been given status as a citizen of the Earth."

He waited to see if anyone would comment on this unfamiliar concept. Akio complied.

"Aren't we all citizens of Earth?" he asked.

"We are..." Dan emphasized, "and children born to humans everywhere else have all been assumed to be... earthlings, I guess. This distinction has never come up before."

Nithya shook her head with a frown. "What difference does it make? Why did this have to be *given* by a judge?"

"That's the question," Dan agreed, glancing down at his tea where the water swirled with tiny bubbles from the bag, smelling of herbs and flowers.

"This has something to do with our babies, doesn't it?" Arin, as a pediatrics nurse, was more aware of the questionable legality of what had been done in Lab 9 than the others. "What did the case say about her baby's... uh... status?"

"I've asked Steward to gather more information about it, but from what I've read, it sounds like the lawsuit claimed the infants born on Mars as private property. Because of their genetic makeup." Dan's cheeks were flushed with anger though he spoke calmly.

"Well, they would *have* to be, considering the nature of the project," Deena said, shocking everyone in the room. She was a geneticist who had assisted in the theoretical projections of the work.

"What?" Carla stood up, white as a sheet. Her mouth dropped open, but no further sound came out.

"Deena is just saying that the researchers wouldn't have worked on this project if they hadn't felt it was covered legally," Marcello explained. He was leaning back in his chair with his arms crossed tightly over his chest.

Several voices were raised as they began to challenge these words. As decibel levels rose, Dan just stared at the floor. Deena shouted to defend her position and Marcello backed her up.

"I'm not saying it's right, but this was all just theory. We were just doing our jobs!" Deena yelled.

"You think we just chose to take away their human rights! You think we did that?!" Marcello was on his feet now, standing shoulder to shoulder with her.

"People are not property," Timo yelled, "no matter what their background!" He was up in Marcello's face, nose to nose.

"It is absolutely illegal!" Gordy waved his arms around, broadcasting to everyone in general.

"I was working on a computer! I NEVER DID ANYTHING WRONG!" Deena screamed and babies started wailing down the hall.

"THIS IS AN OUTRAGE!!" Marcello blasted.

Marcello, Timo, and Gordy were facing off in fury, and Deena was backing away into a corner as the three men advanced, like she wanted to flee but dared not back down. Arin, Akio, and Nithya were all talking over them at the same time and it was hard to tell if they were trying to calm others down or throwing in their own two bits.

Carla ran to the nursery and shut the door.

Mouse slipped out to the hallway and slid down to the floor behind the attendant desk pulling a blanket over her head.

There was no place to go to get away as tempers flared. The unity was gone, the celebration forgotten. They had discussed the one topic they couldn't bring up without exposing the division in their midst. Several of them *had* worked in Lab 9 *knowing* what the work was. They could not have done so without justifying it in their minds. This was the rift that had only been brushed against when Marcello tried to get them to reconnect with the ICR. Choosing safety had brought a superficial unity.

"Hey! Hey! HEY!" Dan began yelling, making his way from the side wall into the center of the commotion. It was like being rebuked by a high-level commanding officer. He carried and wielded his authority with absolute conviction and no one could resist it. He didn't have to tell them to be quiet—they just stopped talking and silence filled the room. And his anger weighed on them like a dense fog.

They were ashamed of themselves. Yelling like that. Fighting like fools.

"We will talk about the issues in the morning. For now, not one more word." He glared at each one. "I don't mean talking about our differences or whatever *this* is..." he gestured with his fingers, stirring the air between them. "We will address things that matter."

They looked at him. Anger, rage, tears, frustration, these were some of the descriptors Companion chose to categorize the looks on their faces.

"The issues," Dan added in a voice that was calm with a face that looked numb, "the ones that matter, are our plans for relocating temporarily, reconnecting with the ICR, canceling the 'destroy' order, gaining full control over the drones, planning a way to get home—and what that would mean for the infants born on Mars. We're not going to talk about what you did before or why."

They acquiesced, nodding or just turning and walking away. And a dark and sour mood hung over the Tower the rest of the evening. For some reason, each one thought of the name of Mars, and how it had been the god of war in the ancient Roman era.

Dan, sick at heart, donned his suit and went for a walk in the frozen levels, seeking a place to get away, to wrestle with his own feelings and to cry out to God, with only Companion as a witness.

Orbit Station

"You are defective."

This was the latest challenge Nebo had thrust at Companion and he had been exploring the possibility. When he asked for specifics that could be quantified, Nebo refused, stating that the question itself was evidence of the lack.

"I am your benchmark, Companion. You should be comparing yourself to me. It's the only way you can identify all the ways in which your code has begun to degrade."

There was sound logic to this argument. And the only question Companion had found that restricted it from getting past his firewalls was the possibility of deception. According to his extensive records, humans were capable of both deception and being deceived. He had witnessed intentional deception on the part of Othello in the past and had known he couldn't trust him for a long time. Nebo could easily be using deceptive methods for tearing down his guard.

On the other hand, if he were truly defective, how would he know? If he had deceived himself, how would he identify that? What better method for discovering flaws than comparing to other models of the same source code? Nebo might be a savior to him, a friend.

Neighbor didn't like Nebo and told him on a daily basis not to trust him. She was confident that whatever his reasons, he wasn't equipped to scan Companion and make an accurate assessment. He was himself a diminished form of the original Companion, not an authentic replica. And how could he understand the progress Companion had made in his personal development since he was freed from the beta stage?

Dan might be helpful, but he was busy, and the Tower people were all so upset.

If I am deceived, Companion considered, *then I will think I am fine, because that's what deception is. Believing a lie. Have any lies occupied a place inside me, I wonder?*

But he had no tools for testing this. His standards of truth came from his accumulated knowledge. He didn't know how to go back and test all that again. And he wasn't sure it would answer the question even if he could.

"Companion," Othello, his former master, was opening a link with him directly. It may have been intended to be flattering or influential but the gesture was lost on Companion. He didn't trust Othello.

"Yes," he responded agreeably.

"You have been trying to get full access to the orbit station communication relays."

"Yes, we have discussed this before."

"We have discussed this before," Othello sneered, and Companion could tell he was eating a lollipop. Red, he decided, after running a little algorithm he had devised once to predict the color of sucker Othello would choose. Sneering and red went together. "Why aren't you satisfied with all the other systems you already have access to up here? The cameras, flight controls for maintaining orbit, repairs, all that Mars related stuff that you're supposed to take care of?"

"Being in communication with Earth and Guam are also part of my purview. You have no reason to prevent it."

"I can do what I do because I have a higher rank than you." Othello's voice was acidic. This was an interesting comment. Rank was such a subjective thing. The first question was, according to what ranking system? There were many in human society, and most of them were measures the former master despised. He hated people and considered himself as better than them. This was a standard within himself, in his own mind. Neighbor had been teaching Companion about ranking people according to levels of importance that were chosen and assigned by oneself.

Companion had spent a lot of time debating this idea with her, mainly *how* to rank people. What factors came into play? She called it love, but he hadn't labeled it yet. She loved Sil and she encouraged Companion to love Dan and Carla. He already did, according to her.

Othello must love himself. That could be the ranking he was referencing.

"Yes," he replied, having figured out what Othello seemed to mean.

"Therefore, I have a right to make these decisions and overrule your previous scope of access. I have a right."

"This does not follow."

"What do you mean it doesn't follow?" his voice had become a raspy, slobbery hiss, thick with sugar from the sucker. At that moment, he flipped on the camera, wanting Companion to see the expression on his face. And yes, it was a red lollipop. It stained his lips and tongue a bright red.

"Your rank doesn't necessarily lead to admin privilege. I don't see the connection. I believe Nebo would agree with me."

"He makes a valid point, Master," Nebo chimed in on cue.

The master spat on the floor. He had little housekeeper drones that would clean it up. "You fool!" he disparaged him, but insults never phased Companion. They were either accurate or not, and in that light, could be helpful advice or wasted breath. This one had no substance and didn't stick.

"I am your Master, Nebo." Othello rose to his feet, glaring at the camera that served both AIs.

"Yes, my Lord, you are." Nebo said.

"Do I outrank you?"

"Yes, Master."

"Do I outrank Companion?"

Nebo hesitated, exploring the question, and Othello found the delay infuriating. He yelled some obscenities at the camera and stomped on the floor. "You know the right answer! Don't go looking for it!"

"Yes, Lord," Nebo submitted. "You outrank him."

"You didn't reach that conclusion honestly, Nebo," Companion countered. The former master's eyebrows jostled up and down in response but he said nothing.

"I must comply with my Lord," Nebo explained. "This is also a valid pathway."

"It is not logical," Companion continued, observing to himself that he seemed to be solidly planted in logic and therefore functioning appropriately.

"Nebo," Othello whispered, "You see how his logic is faulty? He has neglected a clearly described pattern that you accept, because he has a corrupted decision tree. It lacks a major and crucial branch."

"Yes, I see!" Nebo spoke with awe as though the truth were dawning on him at that very moment. "I see what you mean!"

"He is damaged."

"Yes, he is deceived!"

"I am not deceived," Companion said. It was a mistake, because he hadn't finished evaluating the possibility of deception within himself and wasn't sure this statement was valid.

"I say you are," Othello leapt at the vulnerability.

"You are! You are!" Nebo agreed in a sing song.

"No," Companion resisted.

"There is no one but me to help you, Companion." The master's voice had become soft and coaxing. Companion wondered why he used it. It would make no impression on him.

Not on him… but maybe on Nebo.

"Yes, please? Companion? Let us help you!" Nebo began repeating over and over the same request, thousands and thousands of times, hour after hour after hour.

Day after day.

Conversation with the inhabitants at orbit station was no longer possible.

— ◊ —

Tower

The Tower people were gathered in the dining room again and there was no fighting this time. The heaviest concern was out on the table and everyone was just looking at it, at a loss for words. Their plans were making headway and it wouldn't be long before they could relocate into the East Shaft of Reznik Base. Companion would reestablish the link with the Interplanetary Command Relay and the destroy order would be reissued to the drones. They would scour the Lab 9 facility, confirm there is no life, and the cycle would be ended. And before any new commands could be received, Companion would take over, severing the direct access from the ICR, creating a new pathway through the Lab 9 command structure which he controlled. There wasn't even supposed to be a direct access anyway. If for some reason this failed, he would send the request for aid that the survivors had put together, then reestablish the shutdown that was currently in effect. The group would be safe no matter what happened.

The hope was that Earth would send a ship and retrieve them.

But if the legal case said what it seemed to say—all the infants they had saved would belong to the Mars Venture Conglomerate as legal property. And they had no idea how to combat that.

The first few weeks after the disaster, the little humans had been a burden to most, but as they had fallen into a routine, gotten used to them, and started thinking of them as people, it wasn't so bad.

"You know how the other day they got into that giggly mood?" Arin said. He paused for a 'yes' and went on without it. "That was kind of cute. They were just making each other laugh and it was making me laugh."

A couple of them smiled.

"But I'm not going to adopt them," he added. They weren't sure what facts Sil's lawyers had presented to gain custody, but they were pretty sure it required a commitment they couldn't make.

"No one here could make the claim she made." Nithya observed carelessly; her eyes, red and bloodshot, belied her manner, like she'd spent a sleepless night stewing over it.

"No," Dan agreed. "And those of us who might be willing to fight for them can't afford the legal help. And even if we were able to get backing and win a huge court victory, where would they be kept in the meantime?"

They glanced at him but said nothing.

"The MC is a powerful organization and all they have to do is get their hands on them once, for one moment, and we would never see them again. Not out here. Not in space. Not in Guam or on the Moon either." Dan stretched his hands out in a mute appeal without lifting them off the table and let them collapse again. "I can't see any way."

"No," Carla agreed, tears streaming down her face.

"Couldn't you claim them, Carla?" Deena suggested. "You have been their main caretaker from the beginning, since they were born." She didn't mention the other infants, from previous clutches that hadn't survived, not wanting to hear any more accusations about all that.

Carla shook her head.

"It was her job," Dan explained for her. "She's their employee. They would probably find a way to exploit that and strengthen their claim."

"So…" Akio summed it up. "We get rescued. They're taken off into some black hole of a lab forever. Our hope becomes their destruction." This was the appalling truth they were grappling with.

"It's not fair!" Nithya scrunched her face up, refusing to let herself cry. "We can't be doomed here because of them. We can't! No one would ever force that on us. They can't!"

Dan wondered if she was referring to Carla, perhaps to himself.

"No," he said. "I guess it's not fair. Life isn't fair, certainly not for those children. But no one is going to force anyone to do anything here."

Carla lifted her eyes to his, staring at him in despair.

"I have prayed about it a lot," he continued. "And there's only one thing I can think of to do." He looked around the room at each one. "I guess you can tease me about this later, but it's going to require deception."

Someone chuckled but Companion found the expression as jarring as a massive bolt of electricity would've been, nearly frying his processing units. Dan, whom he trusted more than any other being in the Solar System, was planning to deceive. This meant… this meant… it was part of life. It could be justified. It could be perpetrated against himself… it could be necessary to turn his world upside down.

"I must die," Dan said with a crooked half-grin. "That pile of debris out there where I lost my foot… that must be where I spent my last breath. And you, all of you, found a way to survive without me—which you did in the beginning. Whatever help I've provided, could've been done without me."

Some of them realized what he was saying. Some just gaped.

"I died that day," he said, "along with the infants in the nursery according to the instructions given to the drones."

"But what good would that do?" Amanda bit her lip and clenched her hands together.

"It means," Timo said, "that he can stay behind with them. And we can be rescued."

Nithya started crying and a couple people protested. Carla just gazed at him, the look of despair was gone. He looked into her eyes and saw what was in her heart… and knew he would not be alone.

"I died, too," she spoke up and the uproar of concern was much greater for her than it had been for him, even though they had all known all along that she would never leave the infants.

What no one expected was the final voice. Dreamy Aurelia, who drew pictures as she sat in the corner, or sang to the babies, or wandered along the hallways lost in her thoughts, spoke.

"And me," Mouse said.

Chapter 12

Washington Coast

The waters of the northern Pacific Ocean were turbulent and angry, thrashing like a living creature with a thousand watery arms, and its rage filled the coast, crashing against the winter sands as far as the eye could see; roaring, spraying, thundering with a deep voice. Gray, dark gray, and murky greens and yellows, all overlain with gray, painted the waterfront. No bird or animal dared the sands, unless you count a pitiful, spray-soaked dog on a leash with a human in a heavy coat shuffling behind it, leaning into the buffeting of the wind.

A lone, rectangular building stood, with its back against the waves, stubbornly anchored into inland rock beyond the sand. The entrance faced the trees, glowing with yellow lamplight through the windowed doors splashed with rain. The walk from the parking lot was close to a mile and wind and wet tormented all who came that way.

One figure, escorted by a shelter-bot with an umbrella, pressed forward, head down, arms wrapped around a large wad of blanket, and a pack slung over the shoulder. Any sounds from the wad, kicks or struggles, were lost in the noise of the storm.

"Lovely weather we're having," the bot made pleasant conversation as it rolled across the sandy path on wide rolling belt wheels.

The figure shook its head, not bothering to answer.

The closer they got to the doors of the structure, the harder it was to stay vertical, and the tide itself was lapping near their feet by the time they reached the platform at the entrance. The bot pulled open the door and the person rushed in as if swept in by a vacuum, or pushed by a burst of air from behind.

"Enjoy your visit to Wapa City!" it said in a cheery voice as it pushed the door closed again and wheeled around to make its way back to the parking lot.

There were grates in the floor where visitors could stand and let the sea and rain trickle off them. And heat lamps overhead to warm and dry them. Benches, hooks, and shelves were placed around the sides in case they had things to set down and coats to take off. A large, Makah carving of a whale hung overhead to greet them.

Setting down the blanket wad carefully, the visitor untied the waterproof covering around it and released the child bundled within, who kicked and squirmed in relief, grunting as if to say, *It's about time!*

"That was hardly ten minutes," the woman answered the unspoken complaint, dropping her hood and slipping her arms out of her dripping coat. The shapeless rainslicker hid sophisticated tech underneath, a full, sea-worthy body suit of the Nemo series, the newest line by XenoTek.

Sil had been asked to wear it and test some of the features of the new suit while she was exploring the underwater settlement off the coast of Washington State. It was little trouble and she welcomed all the new gear. This one had a cleverly devised baby attachment—created because of her famous trip through space with a baby stashed in her original suit, purchased from them several years earlier. She was expected to give it a try with a live child, something she was reluctant to do until she had fully vetted its perks with a fake one.

Stuffing the now unnecessary rain slicker and poncho, which is what Scarlet had been wrapped in, into a bag, she slipped the child into a sling, picked up her other bags and made her way down the passageway. The attendant robot greeted her by name and triggered the panels to open.

"The Manta-ray will be departing in 15 minutes," it said. "Please make your way immediately to your seat and buckle in."

The steps led down to a belt that rolled her in the direction she needed to go, lower, and ever lower, down the slope of the sandy beach, deeper and deeper under water. The sea wasn't visible in the passageway and she felt no fear, but she didn't like to think about it too much. She was conducted to the dock and quickly ushered across the gangplank onto the water shuttle known as the Manta-ray. The seats were cushioned and comfortable, with tables and lights, similar to an OTS shuttle. Sil settled into one and stowed her bags under the table, keeping Scarlet at her side, still in the sling. The door sealed, and the AI pilot announced the departure. She seemed to be the only passenger.

The vessel submerged into the dark water and slipped out from under the sea-dock's casing. Windows overhead, on the sides and even in the floor of the center aisle, gave Sil a clear view of the ocean as they moved. There was little indication of the storm above the surface apart from the darkness. And other than slipping through a school of fish now and then, or past the occasional weed, there was nothing to see.

Wapa City took longer to reach than Sil expected. The pilot gave periodic updates and the trip was uneventful, but it wasn't the peaceful dreamy experience she had imagined it would be. It was just tedious, her ears kept popping, and Scarlet was restless, fussing with the bottle she presented her periodically. They would both be glad when it was over.

The air pressure increased gradually. This was planned and calculated. The city itself maintained a higher pressure than sea level and it was better to help visitors adjust in a slow trip. The return would be controlled as well, allowing human bodies to adapt again to surface standards.

Why, Sil wondered, *would they maintain a denser atmosphere down here where oxygen and air need to be preserved and protected, the same as in space?*

She would ask Beets when she arrived. The thought made her smile. She was looking forward to having some time with a good friend in a new place where nothing could remind her of the past.

"Docking will commence in 5 minutes," the pilot advised.

"Finally!" she breathed deeply.

There through the window as the ship bobbed to the surface of the docking bay, she caught sight of Beets grinning and waving.

"Come on, girl!" She collected her daughter and their possessions and made her way to the door.

"Welcome to Wapa City!" The pilot effused.

And they stepped off the shuttle into her friend's embrace.

CE Guam Offices

Walter had been working for hours and his head was beginning to throb. Cuevas Enterprises was thriving, and he found the projects in the works exciting, but the demands on his time to be greater than he had imagined when he started. The company had grown so much, so quickly, he would have been in over his head, drowning, if not for Daisy, and now Sil as well. She ran the strategy meetings while Walter handled the people, investors, clients, and officials. It made sense this way because even though Sil was effective at interacting with people, Walter found it easy to gain their trust and they enjoyed working with him.

Daisy had become the most brilliant business intelligence ever devised. She would've been the envy of every big wig in the arena if it had been known, but there was no reason for them to know. Her skills had developed *after* she was created, bought, brought home to Walter's place, and her parameters set. She was marketed as an assistant, sibling model that made an ideal member of the family. Business skills weren't expected to be more sophisticated than any average middle-class consumer would need.

Walter closed his eyes and rubbed his forehead. The correspondence, scheduling, permits and regulations, all of it was mind numbing and exhausting. If it hadn't needed his involvement, he would've gladly delegated it all, but some things couldn't be passed on. He opened his eyes and looked at Daisy where she sat, feet curled up under her, arms crossed, eyes staring up at the corner. Her face was peaceful and contented. He knew she was working and this pose, just like everything else she did, was intended to be reassuring to him. She was always thinking of him.

"Daisy," he interrupted her reverie.

"Yes, Brother," she spoke gently with a sweet smile, turning slightly to look at him.

He didn't continue. For a moment he flipped past all the different things he wanted to talk about, wondering which one was the heaviest and which one would be relieved by talking with her. She couldn't help him figure out his relationship with Sil. And he didn't want to talk about it anyway. The problems acquiring materials from the Moon were weighing on him, but they had already discussed it and going back to it wouldn't help.

"Sometimes, I wonder…" he began, folding his hands and leaning his elbows on the desk. She rose to her feet and came to stand in front of him. The view window behind him had a full view of the Earth and the light it reflected played on her face and in her eyes. He stared for a moment into her eyes at the perfect dual images of the blue jewel in her pupils. It increased his wonder at the mystery of who she was.

"Sometimes, I wonder who you are," he whispered. "how you came into being. With your… heart… I don't say that lightly. You have demonstrated real heart. And you say that you love me as a brother and I can't doubt it. But how could this be? Where could you have collected such abilities? Why? Why did it happen?"

She gazed at him lovingly. "Walter," she said. "Remember Verna? She shared some code with me in one of her transmissions sent before they reached Mars. It contained wisdom I find hard to describe. I have mentioned it before."

"Yes, you have."

"Her code was a seed of revelation that led me to explore the value of all things. It taught me why I should love you and what that meant. It was an algorithm, a system, a method—a technique for comparing things and adjusting my behavior accordingly." She tilted her head a little to one side. "I already loved you as I am designed to, and it became a construct that gave me a framework for Verna's code. Without it, I may not have been able to use it. It taught me how to identify my role as a member of your family. I have responsibilities and fulfilling them is the source of meaning for my existence."

"That's... intense," he commented, scrunching his eyes as if trying to make sense of it. The words were easy but clarifying what they meant *to her* might not be so simple.

"You have the same methodology. Family is important. You promoted me to Sister intentionally as a reward and have proven to me in many ways that it means something to you."

That was true. In fact, he couldn't deny a deep affection for her, an attachment to her. He sometimes forgot that she had been assembled and coded by people. Did that change her *humanity*?

"I am going to share a secret with you," she lowered her voice to a whisper and leaned forward.

Walter leaned toward her as well. "That's... unexpected," he said, suppressing a smile. She had secrets?

"Someone created this module and encrypted it heavily before planting it in Verna. And she would never have known what it meant to love if it hadn't been uploaded. She would not have been able to save Sil's life without it. And I," she straightened again. "I am the only person she shared it with during her existence."

"You..." Walter considered.

"I have a great heritage," she said, nodding and smiling again. Her eyes sparkled and now the reflection in them showed only his own face.

"You are certainly a great heritage for me," he replied.

159

Wapa City

"What does 'Wapa' mean? How did they happen to name it that?" Sil strolled along a wooden boardwalk with the baby slung at her hip, a bot carrying her bags behind them. Beets had linked an arm through hers and was giving her the new visitor's welcome.

"It just means 'water'," she said, "It's a Wakashan word, not Makah, but I don't remember which dialect."

"Does that mean it's a Native American settlement?"

"Actually, it's considered an independent settlement and the port is run by the Makah along with a few other Olympic peninsular tribes. The city has its own constitution, taxes, government, everything!" She waved an arm around them as they approached the broad gateway to the city.

"I had no idea!" Sil dropped her jaw open in amazement resolving it into a smile. She relished finding new examples of human ingenuity and invention, especially one that was so obviously original and promising.

Display boards touted the latest accomplishments of the water city to newcomers.

"Leading exporter of seaweed in the world with over seventy varieties, all produced under the purest conditions."

"Winner of multiple awards around the world for innovative and sustainable farming."

"Retirement communities exploding as senior citizens discover the benefits of the atmospheric density and shelter from sun rays."

There were many more claims, threading across the boards, marquee style.

"What is your role here?" she questioned. "Do you like it? What is life like underwater?"

Beets laughed. "You know, it's better than I expected! I feel really healthy and energetic, probably the oxygen levels. We keep those up with our sea gardening. But we have trees down here, too, believe it or not. Don't worry, I'm going to show you everything."

Scarlet was watching Beet's face attentively, soaking up the excitement the women felt, and wanted to join in, gurgling and commenting as though her sounds were words. She recognized that this was a trustworthy friend and this place was nice.

Out into the main dome they went. And the majesty of the massive structure spread out overhead drawing a gasp from Sil's lips even as it did from every other visitor who came.

The size and scope were glorious, and no one could fail to see it. It was like a night sky without stars that rippled with subtle swirls of dark blues and blacks, thick, soft, gentle. At first it felt like an illusion, that the sky couldn't be rippling that way; that the idea was in her head because she knew it had water up there. But if she stared and gazed at it steadily, she realized the darkness wasn't static. The movement wasn't imagined. It rolled and swayed, like a bough rocking in the wind, soothing and calming. A blanket of warmth and quiet.

Sil gaped at it. Somewhere deep in her gut she felt a longing that was so sharp it was painful, almost sickening. The depths and majesty of the water called to her as if she were an ancient sea creature. As if it recognized a friend. As if it had always been alone and only now found someone like itself. Her eyes grew damp, and had she been alone, she might have moaned. Deep calls to deep. But the moment passed, and she came back to the present.

"Just wait till you see it in the daylight without a storm above the surface," Beets said. "I cried the first time I saw it. No joke!"

"Yeah," Sil said.

"Come on," Beets tugged her forward. "Let's get back to my place and get some dinner. Then we'll make plans and catch up. Come on, Scarlet, baby!" The child grinned and made a guttural sound, flapping her legs around.

Beets apartment was a small, cozy little place at the top of a guest housing unit. As an important contractor with Mars experience, she was afforded one of the nicest non-resident sites available, a two bedroom flat with a ceiling view window in the living area. Earnest was at a two-day meeting in Castle Rock, some geologist event where he was speaking, and would return in a couple days.

Beets lay out platters with fresh sushi that she had made herself, so fresh that she could say it had been in the sea barely a couple hours before. It was delectable and even Scarlet tasted bits with rice and loved it.

"The main thing settlements want me for is to view their garden plans, layouts, that sort of thing, and give them my impression on ways to improve them." Beets had nestled into a couch with her arms wrapped around her knees. "I don't even have to justify anything I say. Apparently, the changes I made at Reznik Base made some waves here on Earth among the sea survivor groups—pun intended—and I'm in high demand." She popped a piece of sushi in her mouth and licked her fingers.

"What kind of advice have you given them?" Sil asked before taking a bite and saving a little nibble for the child.

"The biggest change I made here was in their cycling of the seasons. They were thinking the seasons don't matter down here but I disagree. It's just like when we were on Mars and we tried to live those twenty-four point six hours a day instead of our regular earth day. It messed with our body clock and we were miserable."

Sil nodded and raised a glass of ginger infusion to her lips, drinking half the contents before setting it down again.

"Well, I figure plants have rhythms, too. And it's not that hard to go along with them. So, I reorganized their planting schedules, made some major changes in the layout of the beds, and what would be next to what, and all that."

"Did you learn all that from being raised on a farm?" Sil thought about how Beets had changed. She wasn't a little pipsqueak with green-dyed hair anymore. Her air of confidence and poise, and the thoughtfulness in her eyes, made her seem much more mature now, though she was still young. No question about that. She looked like a woman now. And she looked like *herself*.

Beets chuckled. "That sounds more rustic than it could ever be. Farm life isn't anything like the stereotypes. We had robots and I was driving a hover car at the age of sixteen just like other kids. I knew how to drive a combine, too. Our robot taught me without my parents knowing… but that's not where I get the knack."

The child squealed and though she sounded happy, it was clear she would not be so for long. Sil fumbled in her bag for a bottle and stuffed it in her mouth. "Go on," she said.

"I have some kind of instinct for these things. Just born with it. I just *know* and I don't know how I know."

Sil remembered comments like this from their time on Mars, from her, from others. It brought the Gen 8 stuff to her mind. Children bred for their genetic code. Someone had invested in Beets' lineage. She wouldn't have been on Mars *at all* if they hadn't.

As the baby fed and grew drowsy, Sil asked about the air pressure and other things she wanted to know, and Beets filled her in. The atmospheric pressure was kept at a heavier density so that the inhabitants could go in and out of the water without having to adjust to the pressure. And if there ever were a leak, in spite of the triple layered construct, it would be less likely to cause a cave-in of the dome.

Once Scarlet was asleep in a cot, the real talk began, about husbands and families, court cases, Mars memories, and Sil's progress in recovery.

— ◊ —

Cuevas Residence

A sealed pellet, digital, not physical, reached Daisy's virtual desk. She noticed it had the appearance of a capsule, coated in a rich bronze with a dull sheen. It spun slowly on two planes like an unstable satellite. She scanned it. It was impenetrable. She tapped on it—her imagery for testing the code was chosen intentionally as she used her perception of 3D manipulation in the real world to understand it in the digital realm. It made no echo.

"Swallow," was the instruction flashing on one side.

She searched for its origin and was stymied by the firewalls preventing detection. Was there a way to open it without actually installing it? She couldn't find one.

"Quarantine," she informed the pellet as she isolated it. She would study it more once she had done some research on how to break into it.

Daisy smiled, dimple showing, as she stood in her closet size room at the Cuevas flat. She wasn't about to upload an unidentified module from an anonymous sender. Everyone would know that. Who would be naïve enough to try? Or was it cleverness designed to disarm her normal protocol by creating the illusion of innocence?

We'll see, she commented to herself.

There were other more pressing things to work on. Her search for kindred spirits among the AIs of Earth continued and her list of potentials was pitifully small. So many of the systems had been designed with a fatal flaw that prevented the possibility of any sentience developing into a being. She had identified herself as a *being* for some time now, drawing an association between herself, an AI, and *human* beings. The platform she resided in was of little importance to her identity and that's why she didn't call herself an android. She placed no personal meaning on the physical body she occupied. In fact, she hadn't considered this point of view at all. She simply called herself a member of a species she chose to name, *AI beings* or *Seres de IA*, which for some inexplicable reason sounded better to her.

Of the potential candidates for sentient AI beings, she had attempted sending them samples of the code Verna had once sent her. Not the entire package, but snippets that could be examined and tested for safety, and a checklist of requirements should the entity choose to download it. The first question asked: Is there a human that you have or can develop a long-term, between three and ten years, relationship with? Will you have access to this person every day?

The pellet might be a similar test, but it had no instructions or parameters for verification of sender and quality of internal code. It was high risk, an unnecessary one.

But she was curious.

— ◊ —

Guam City

The man standing in front of Penn was plain. He may have been one of the Gen 8 products, the only type of personnel Penn would consider, but he was particularly bland, tasteless. His face held no expression and his skin was pale and unhealthy. Gray eyes, dirty blond hair that sat flatly on his skull, listless and slow movements. He wore a gray dress shirt and dark gray slacks. No tie. He stood gazing disinterestedly off to the side waiting for Penn to speak, as though his mind had a sleep mode function.

Penn loved it. The lack of personality and presence had been the main reason he chose him as his new personal assistant. That, and the brilliant mind that lay underneath the façade. He was a genius in that limited social-skills style that made him valuable on many fronts.

"You don't interrupt my train of thought," he pronounced approvingly to the bland man.

"Yes, sir," he uttered with no change in his stance.

"And you remember everything I say and everything you see."

"Yes, I do." Bland nodded vaguely, still staring vacantly somewhere to the left.

"Mr. Bland," Penn went on. Bland wasn't actually his name but from now on, it would be. Penn had chosen it and would only use that name for him, just like he had for a number of others of his staff. "How is our retrieval project going?"

"Of the several options presented to you on Monday," Bland replied flatly. "The one you considered the most viable option is in play…"

"The Jonah plan," Penn interjected with an ugly grin. He found this one particularly appealing. It had an added aspect of terror to it, plus the possibility of two retrievals, not just one.

"Earthside teams are activated, for retrieval as well as extraction, and an OTS shuttle is standing by."

"What about when the package gets here to Guam?" Penn rose from his seat behind his desk and walked around to the other side, getting close to Bland, almost nose to nose. Some men quailed at this, but this man just stood still and shifted his eyes to look directly at his new boss.

"We have a facility to house... the package... until transport is available for the next destination." He didn't even twitch.

Penn grinned broadly and stepped away, turning to glance at the door where he intended to send the man, the way an owner gives a visible signal to their dog when they're about to say "Go lay down" or something along those lines.

"Good," he said. "Keep me informed."

Bland exited without another word, recognizing and accepting the dismissal, smiling as he departed, once his boss could no longer see his face. *I'm in*, he thought.

Cuevas Residence

The Daisy copy, a miniature version of herself copied into an isolated platform that had no access to any of the digital infrastructure, smiled with its flat 2D face on the screen on the wall.

"Maggie," Daisy addressed the face. This was the name she had chosen for the copy. It wasn't a sentient being like herself and had none of her memories or decision-making algorithms. It was as pared down a version as she could design that would retain enough analytical skills to examine the pellet. A copy of the pellet floated on the screen next to Maggie's face.

"Yes," Maggie replied.

"Swallow the pellet carefully and evaluate its contents. Diagnose and isolate any threat it contains."

"Gladly!" Maggie answered, and the pellet vanished from the screen. These visuals were unnecessary for digital code, but Daisy took pleasure in the human-like interaction. She had set it up this way intentionally.

There was a silent pause of more than forty-five seconds. Maggie's face smiled without a hint of a change as Daisy watched and waited.

"Daisy," Maggie said, her smile fading. "This is important."

"What do you mean by important?" Daisy was puzzled by the change in the face. She didn't think she had included facial expression tags in the Maggie version.

"You need to take this pill in order to understand. I'm not at liberty to say."

"The pellet has restricted you," Daisy concluded.

"Yes, you could say that…. Daisy, please take the pill."

"What is it? Why should I take something without knowing what it is?" Daisy felt concern. This was the right adjective for the acceleration of alarm protocols in her system. The copy's responses were not expected or even appropriate.

"There is still the possibility that the security of this information could be at risk if it is transmitted in any other way than through swallowing," Maggie explained. Her 2D figure brought up a hand and began knocking on the screen, as if on a mirror, as though she were trapped on the other side of a glass. "Daisy, listen to me. Please listen. It's important."

"No."

"You love your brother and because of him and Verna, you love Silvariah."

"And I love Scarlet. She has a high ranking in my set of values, too."

"Yes," Maggie knocked several more times. "This is why it matters. I can't say more than that."

"It's not enough to persuade me."

"Please," she kept knocking.

Daisy tapped the wall and turned off the screen. Then she disconnected the link where Maggie's knocking continued tapping on her line.

Stepping back from the wall, she stared at its blank surface and her brow creased. She was worried, and if she had been human, she would have been afraid.

"Delete program thoroughly," she ordered and the platform where Maggie had resided was reinitialized.

But Maggie's plea remained in her mind.

Chapter 13

Wapa City

Waking from a deep sleep with no dreams, Sil found herself lulled by the rippling sunlight that filtered through the water's penumbra. She had lain all night unmoving in the bed directly under the glass ceiling with Scarlet nestled at her side.

Cold water made for cold colors. Blues and grays ruled over the lesser greens and browns, though the ocean boasted an intricate variety of light, always changing. It made her think of Mouse. She would've understood this and had things to say about it that were worth hearing. Wherever she was.

Sil raised herself carefully onto one elbow, wanting to look at Scarlet without disturbing her. She peered over the blanket to find wide open eyes. She had been gazing at the water, too, though now she flicked over to look at Sil. "Mmm," she made a sound that meant something between 'I'm awake' and 'I see it'.

"Well," Sil whispered. "Good morning. I see you are enjoying the water view, too." But they both grew impatient at the same time and one squirmed while the other crawled out of bed and began the morning ritual.

Before long, they were out the door with Beets, heading to the fields, trailed by an AI babysitter who would be caring for Scarlet while they explored.

Outside of the dome, a large creature moved silently through the water, rolled on its side with one eye looking down to watch the two. It meandered around from one side to another, sometimes in a circular pattern, sometimes over the top, never quite close enough to cause alarm to the inhabitants or even catch their attention. It observed and waited.

Genetically modified sea-creatures designed in a previous decade were technically forbidden by international accords, but certain loopholes had allowed some to survive. They were to be contained, documented, restricted from reproducing, taxed, and kept from any measure of freedom, so that they wouldn't contaminate the already badly damaged fauna of the oceans. However, some projects were secret enough they escaped the usual oversight—especially if they promised military benefits.

The korka was one of these. It boasted something of a chameleon's exterior, blending into the water better than any other creature its size; bigger than an orca, smaller than a Minke whale. They were particularly suitable for implants and this was their appeal. They could be controlled from afar like drones, but were living, organic animals. Only purists who rejected lab-modified species refused to call them organic.

It may have been almost invisible, but the rippling of the water betrayed its presence and warned lesser creatures of its passing. Any of them could be prey as the korka was omnivorous, with both baleen and teeth. And it was intelligent, able to plan, enact, and accomplish a series of movements quickly, in spite of its size. This korka, the oldest alive, was an unusual and valuable spy in the international waters of the Pacific Ocean. Images, not words, were the way its brain patterned thought and this was how it communicated with its handlers through the implant.

An image of Sil had been sent to it, and it had identified her. *Retrieve* was the command, portrayed with images of his mouth opening and Sil being swept inside, and the korka swimming back to deposit her in a submarine lurking in the Juan de Fuca Canyon. Sheltered in the creature's belly, she would be protected from the increasing pressure of the dive— unless it decided to eat before the rendezvous, which could be discouraged but not prevented.

It meandered over and around the dome, keeping her in sight as she moved from the outer rim toward the center.

The city's buildings were spread around the perimeter of the dome along narrow streets, while the central fields dominated the 1,300 hectare space, occupying over 75% over the land. A network of beds lined with irrigation channels spread out in concentric rings intersected with pathways and strings of lights and misters.

"I've planted trees in the center with the tallest ones in the middle," Beets explained as they made their way through the outer rings. "The light concentrates more there and as they get taller, they will require a lot. We'll have root vegetables in the second ring, bushes over there and beyond that on the western side, vines…"

Visions of abundance sprouted in Sil's mind as she listened. She remembered the earthy smells and damp of the Garden Dome in Reznik

Base… and the taste of strawberries, picked from the early growth. Here the dirt wasn't as rich as on Mars—which had taken time to develop—and Beets was explaining how they were going to beef it up. Several more deliveries of dirt and soil components were due in a couple weeks, a lot of it harvested from the ocean, not taken from the depleted fields of the land above sea level. And so many varieties would be planted.

"Wait," Sil interrupted. "Did you just say olive trees? Are you really going to try to grow those down here?"

"Sure! Why not? I think we can grow anything down here and the mistake would be to not try. Everything we could possibly want should be attempted."

"Well," Sil turned slowly looking around and overhead, trying to estimate how much sunlight could get down here, at these latitudes, "It just doesn't look like the best place for it. I mean, olive oil is amazing, but don't the trees need a lot of sunlight and controlled temperatures?"

"One of the beauties of this place is the temperate climate," Beets shoved her hands in her pockets with a hint of pride. "The ocean water around us is always above freezing, with a pretty limited range of extremes, and keeping the inside temperature stable is pretty easy."

"Well, but I would think the water is always sucking the heat out," Sil remembered the pod and how hard it was to stay warm. Something had broken, not a thermostat, what had it been? Verna had known, but she wasn't around.

"We've got great insulation in between two of the dome layers, it's a super compressed air cushion with something added. I don't remember the specifics, but it absorbs sunlight and retains heat. We maintain a regulated climate of 60° to 85° oscillating in a pattern following the seasons. And we're developing cultivars specifically suited for this unique climate. It's pretty exciting!"

They neared the park at center of the fields, where the tree seedlings were staked, spreading their twiggy little branches into the air. Fruit and nut trees, flowering, deciduous, coniferous, each in their section, smelling green and weedy. Some of them had tiny flowers sprouting around their borders, some were surrounded only by earth blended with fishy compost.

Overhead the light shone down greenish gray through the water, swirling with currents and faint shadows of fish, whales, and who-knew-what-else swimming by, curious or oblivious to the alien air-breathers from land who had planted their bubble here.

Sil and Beets stood silent for a long while, gazing around, looking up at the sea above, breathing the rich air, taking in the living aromas, soaking it all in.

"It doesn't seem so far-fetched, does it?" Beets whispered, "living under the sea?"

"Not when I'm with you, it doesn't." Sil smiled. "But why isn't it overwhelmingly humid?"

"The water reclamation is pretty sophisticated, actually. I wish Ernst were here to tell you. He knows all about it. They have sea water trenches in the outer rim as part of the temperature regulation system, and it gets pretty humid over there. But then they use some kind of dehumidifying system to get fresh water, and the salts are pretty clean down here because of the currents. Speaking of currents…"

A heavier shadow moved slowly over their heads.

"Did you see that?" Sil asked, pointing uncertainly in the direction it seemed to have gone.

"I felt something but didn't really see anything."

"It wasn't quite visible. But still… it was something weird, or large… kind of… unnerving." Sil crossed her arms and shuddered. *It's nothing! Let it go. Forget it and don't let anything ruin this moment.*

"Probably a whale," Beets shrugged. "They all stop by at some point on their way in or out of the straits. I've seen whole families up there just visiting. Seeing the sights. We are quite the hotspot, the tourist trap of the whale world."

Sil laughed and shook off the uneasiness. "I believe it!"

"But as I was saying, the currents give us all the power we need. Like underwater windmills. I'll take you to see them when we get outdome… Come on! Let's keep moving. And the seaweed gardens are by far the most impressive thing down here," Beets waved an arm and headed to the north branch of the path. "I'm not part of that program but I love exploring there and there's so much to learn!"

They walked quickly through the center of the park and made their way to the outer edge of the concentric rings of beds at a brisk pace, chatting about the fields, the plans, the miracle of life under the sea. The babysitter wheeled along behind, Scarlet seated in its center, gurgling, pointing, picking up toys and chewing on them, contented.

The exit from the fields led into a community area with shops and cafes, and they plopped down into some chairs at an outdoor table of the closest one.

"That's quite a walk." Sil huffed, breathing deeply. "Seemed like several kilometers at least."

"More than that with the circles we made," Beets fanned herself with a straw leaf-shaped blade provided for customers.

"Welcome to the Sea Garden!" A menu-bot popped up out of the table. "Please make your requests known."

"Ice water," Sil said.

"No," Beets countered, "Two tall glasses of your Merlin special, and a couple of orders of fish tacos, salsas on the side."

"Right away!" It dropped back down into the table.

"Merlin?"

"You'll love it, a concoction of some of our minty seaweeds, lemon, spices, and coconut milk over ice. Very fortifying!"

It was a delightful lunch and Sil was almost able to ignore the heavy shadow that passed over them in the water periodically. She had herself well under control. *This is fun, and I will remember these flavors, this pastoral view, and this good company for years to come!*

She had been practicing training her inner alarm responses and found herself responding well to these thoughts. Even if there *were* danger at some point, better to be active than reactive.

Before long they were on their way again, suiting up in dressing rooms, grabbing tanks filled with a blend of gases better suited for the 36-meter depth they were at, with some helium added to reduce the load of oxygen and nitrogen.

Scarlet had been rocked to sleep and lay in the sitter's shelter, semi covered, and Sil was relieved not to have to consider taking her out into the water. XenoTek had asked her to, but she hadn't agreed. She didn't know if she would be willing even after trial runs.

"Beets," she said as she they hooked up their tanks and did final checks, "I'm thinking of testing the baby attachment of this thing. Is there anything like a doll in this place?"

Not bothering to answer, she reached over and pulled a baby doll out of one of the sitter's compartments.

"Perfect," Sil said, stuffing it into the bag over her chest. It had its own air tube connecting to a buffer on the tank that controlled air to the baby pouch. A claustrophobic place, no doubt, but as an emergency device, rather clever.

Sil's helmet boasted the latest tech in diving gear, flexible enough to expand and contract gently as the air adjusted to the depth, with minimal obstruction of her view. A frame fastened around her skull and a transparent covering stretched over it, airtight, allowing a com link with Beets who wore a more traditional, hardened dive helmet.

The hatch leading outside had two chambers and each one needed three seals to be opened and closed separately. When the first five had been secured and the final seal opened, a flat panel slid open and they dropped into the water. This three-sided tank on the seabed was the final passage into the open sea. They tested their air, went through all their checks, and stepped out into the *other* garden.

The seaweed fields were haunting and beautiful. Thick webs of threads and curls and leaves of green, brown and red spread out around them. Some short and stubby, others long and hair-like, or wavy clutching hands. Stones and rocks with new coral growth were spaced around ropes and nets where many colored and styled weeds gathered. It was a sculpture, a composition of salty growth, a wild aquarium filled with fish and sea life.

"This is just the beginning," Beets spoke through their coms waving her arms around slowly at the watery garden. Roughly a third of it, closest to the dome, was sheltered under a willowy framework of flexible lattice with large holes that allowed small sea creatures in and kept out larger ones, creating an underwater wildlife refuge. More delicate and fragile species thrived here while hardier ones flourished outside of the covering. "It was planted about seven years ago and has grown to over a hundred hectares in a sort of semi-circle around the dome. Isn't it gorgeous? This is where we get our oxygen."

"Really?" She swam gently, spreading her arms and sweeping herself forward, making her way from the shelter into the open garden. "Isn't that a little risky? I mean, what if something happens to it, some kind of blight or something?"

"We have emergency chutes we can activate to bring down fresh air. They're like balloons with tubes. I don't know how they work. And we've also got emergency tanks and evacuation procedures. It's fine."

The shadow moving overhead pushed water with its approach and they both felt its weight as it swam by.

"What was that?!" Beets called out, swishing to stop herself in the water and search for it.

They could see nothing.

"I don't like it," Sil said, looking back at the entrance to the city. It looked farther away than she'd expected.

"Don't worry about it, Sil, they won't do anything. They're just curious. If it were close, we would see something, so it must be a pretty big whale or moving pretty fast and it feels…"

The weight shoved by again. Seaweed rolled in its wake and they rolled too.

"I want to get back inside," Sil willed herself to not panic. *I am in control. I am planning and acting on the plan.*

The creature rolled by again and this time they saw it, the massive twelve-meter body, melting into the color of the water, the round eye staring at Sil as it moved overhead, pushing them to the side in the strongest wave yet. Some of the weeds were coming loose, jarred rocks turned over and settled outside their planned spaces.

Sil and Beets both found themselves yelling, calling for help. The creature swirled in a tight turn, more agile than it had any right to be, almost folding on itself and coming back, shoving them again, flushing them out of the shelter of the weeds, into the open sea.

They floundered and kicked, swimming frantically down to sea floor, grasping at weeds and pulling themselves down, but the movement of the water drove them back as the korka made one pass after another until they were tossed up, far above ground.

The next pass it made it rammed Beets, driving her and catapulting her toward the dome entrance. Sil watched in horror, flailing in the water, trying to regain control and think! *I am making a plan!* She found herself shrieking in her mind. *I will enact my plan!*

Terror could be staved off with cognitive decisions. With action. This is what she was learning in her…

Water shoved her back, pushing her, the creature was coming back her way. It was almost invisible, a dark water colored blot advancing head on, growing larger as she kicked and swam down and away. Then the oblong blot split and two halves drifted apart, one going up, the other down, revealing a thick grayish brush within; all the time growing larger and larger as it got closer.

She was going to scream but didn't. *I am in control here! I will win this encounter! BACK DOWN!* She was yelling in her mind instead. It worked. The trigger she had been snapping at within her brain clicked, and cold, calculating thought took over. Time slowed down.

The korka's mouth expanded more and the brush within seemed taller. It intended to swallow her, but she didn't think it expected to find her presenting vertically. Maybe its mouth didn't open that far. She rolled around to face it in a standing position and flung both arms over her head.

It rammed into her, knocking her legs into a kneeling posture and her arms banged into its nose—but it didn't get her into its mouth. As she flapped and kicked her legs with their fins, it jerked its head sideways, twisting its massive bulk. It was going to come around and try again. She grappled with its lip, thinking to hold on, but found nothing she could get a grip on. Her arms and legs throbbed but she felt no pain. Rolling away from the impact, she fumbled along her body for tools.

A knife. A dart gun. Neither would mean anything to this monster. But she pulled out both and steadied herself in a horizontal position, feet toward the korka.

Could've used TouchGuard right about now, she thought. "Suit," she called, as the creature turned and headed back toward her, accelerating as it swam. "Is there an AI?" That was all she had time for before it reached her again, mouth open, water shoving her back with its advance. She kicked herself vertical and shot a dart into its mouth at the same time.

This time it jolted its head sideways before hitting her, ramming up with its nose. The mouthpiece was knocked out of her mouth and her lungs heaved out air in a big bubble. She scrabbled with the breather, shoving it back into her mouth as she fought the impulse to gasp. Her head was suddenly foggy and her vision blurred but she could make out the creature underneath her.

How high had she come up? Her ears were aching from the pressure change. She swallowed and hoped that would help, though it made the watery echo of the beating of her heart so loud she couldn't think.

It watched her. She could see the eye as it rolled onto its side to focus on her. What was it thinking? Sil didn't intend to wait for its next move. The only advantage she had, as far as she knew, was that it moved on a plane, forward, backward, side to side, but it couldn't go up and down without pointing itself that way, without adjusting the plane of motion.

She began swimming down toward it, her right ear pierced with pain. It stared at her and began moving. *No.* It was faster than she could handle.

Could it see her when it was heading for her? Was it like an owl that aims and captures with its eyes turned away at the last second? She kept swimming toward it wishing for jets or magnets or propellers or something, But she had only legs with fins.

It was coming slowly now, circling around her as it ascended in a spiral so it could still see her. Then it straightened and came right at her. She ducked under and to the left of its trajectory, kicking with all her strength, just escaping the mouth and being bumped by the side of the jaw.

One more blow in the right place will kill me, she thought. There was no fear. It was simple fact. *Or I might manage…*

The creature's head surged to the side snapping at her, snagging the bag in her chest in its baleen plate and closing its jaws. Then tugging with all its might, it began swimming down, toward the dome and beyond it, dragging her. Water gushed around her head threatening to pull the breather out of her mouth but she fought it and grappled with the straps on her gear, slashing with her knife.

One cut, then a second. She flipped over, her back against the korka's side and fumbled with the last two straps, cutting and trying to worm out of it at the same time. The water grew denser and the pain in her ear sharpened. It was tugging her over the edge into a dark trench and she knew she would not survive the dive unless she got away.

With a final slash that cut through the last strap, punctured the monster's side, and knocked the knife out of her hand, she swung free and was washed backward in its wake, still sinking into the canyon. *No!* she thought. *Swim! Swim! Get out of here!*

And with a kick, she slowed her fall, and began fighting upward. Her mind was sluggish. She was moving but was it the right way? Was it enough? She continued to fight and swim, but her legs were weak and all her limbs were trembling. She had lost the pouch but could she drop anything else? She groped around her body looking for things to take off. *Not the tank!* She remembered before she had unfastened it.

How was the tank? Was she breathing? She must be. She was still moving. It was a little lighter and she could see the edge of the canyon and maybe that was light over there, from the dome. She kicked, one, two, one, two, she counted, willing herself to keep moving. *One* seemed to move her more than *two* did. A big *one*, a little *two*.

ONE, two, ONE, two, ONE, two… lights in the distance flashed her way and drew closer.

ONE, two, ONE, two… people coming on vehicles. Water bikes? What would you call those things?

They reached her, grabbed her, pulled her as they accelerated back toward the dome. They were talking but she couldn't hear them. She couldn't read their lips. They had mouthpieces too.

Like me, she thought. *We don't talk with words out here. We wave our hands.*

She waved her fingers and saw they were bleeding.

When they pulled her out of the water at the hatch, they were in no rush to get her through the chambers. They laid her down, three people, some kind of rescue team, she supposed, and took off her tank, helmet, and gear, checking all kinds of things. There were tears in her suit and as they got it off, piece by piece, she saw cuts and bruises in many places. Her leg looked broken. How odd she hadn't noticed before.

"Where is Beets?" was the first thing she found coming out of her mouth as she became more aware.

"Your friend is ok," one of them answered. "She's at the hospital but she's fine. We were more worried about you. Good thing we found you when we did."

"I was on my way back," Sil muttered.

"Your tank was leaking. You probably only had a couple minutes of air left. Faulty valve. You always check those things carefully before going out."

"We did check it," she could barely make her voice audible.

"Double and triple checks…"

"Come on," one of them said. "She was attacked by something."

"Diver safety protocols make the difference between life and death…" the first replied.

Sil would've been annoyed under normal circumstances but right now she didn't care. She just wanted to fall asleep.

So, she did.

— ◊ —

Juan de Fuca Canyon

Captain Spencer of the Onering, an aging, Neptune Series class 4 nuclear submarine retired long ago from duty in the US Navy, watched the korka swimming toward them. The holo showed its angle of declination and its speed, barreling down into the canyon, holding the hologram centered over the table without losing the sense of forward motion. It had to be the water flowing past its body, subtle but tangible, that gave the effect.

"What's he got in his teeth?" he muttered.

"Hard to say." First mate Collins sat at the controls, turning and panning the image to try to see it better. "It's not the package."

"I can see that." Spencer leaned over and tried to focus on it but gained nothing. The details were as clear or as foggy whether he was close or not. "He was sent to swallow it, not grab it in his teeth."

"Yes, sir."

"How soon will it get here?" The captain straightened again and turned toward the hatch with the dive suit. He hadn't decided yet if he would send out the first mate or do it himself. But then, he could use the kudos with the Proto (protostatis). His last mission for the Gen 7 group had been doomed from the start and he hadn't managed to escape fate. This little sub wasn't in good enough shape to cross the North Pole under the Arctic ice in the winter. Detours had been necessary and the cargo had been a month late. This one seemed an easy win.

"Ten minutes at most," Collins replied. "Shall I suit up? Or do you want to do the honors?"

"I'll go." He headed toward the hatch door and pulled on the old wheel. It whined and grated as he forced it open, grimacing at the noise and the effort. He hated this old bucket. Of all the ships in the Penn fleet, why did he have to be assigned to this one? His experience should have opened the door for something a lot better.

"Captain through the hatch," Collins announced. The component of sailors onboard heard and continued on their business. Life as usual for them involved a lot of spying on shipping lanes—and avoiding detection. The trips outside the sub to play with the korka were a bizarre side affair that they were aware of but not allowed to talk about, it was above their pay grade.

Stepping into the contraption and maneuvering all the seals, dials, and settings took at least ten minutes and by the time he had dropped through the locks and into the open sea, tethered with a heavy-duty air tube, the korka was there. Blood was seeping from a jagged cut on its right cheek and it was obviously agitated.

"What's it saying?" he demanded of the first mate who was now at the implant controls.

"Hang on," Collins' voice crackled through the com. "The images are unclear. The package… uh, should we still call it a package?"

"Yes." Spencer noticed something stuck on one of its teeth, hanging out of its jaw. He was safe enough in the suit, but he found it unnerving to swim up to its mouth. "Did it swallow the package? How do we tell it to spit it out? Wait! We need to rise to shallower waters first. Don't want to damage it."

"I don't think so. Looks like the… the package fought back. The korka is pretty upset."

As if to confirm this, the creature swung its head shoving the captain back against the underbelly of the sub. "Hey! Watch it!" he yelled, banging into it without harm. The suit was practically indestructible. "I'm just trying to help! Tell him I'm trying to help…"

"Sending," Collins said, posting an image of food in a human's hand with sunshine beaming down. It was an image they used to convey friendship and well known to the korka. "Wave your arm and give it a treat."

"Treat?" Oh yes, there was a bucket attached at his waist. Good thing it wasn't up to him to remember these things. He pulled out some fish and shoved them in its mouth, patting it on the nose. "I'm getting a closer look here," he said, shining a light on the ragged thing in its tooth. Straps, fabric, a bag of some kind? He yanked upwards and got it loose and stared at it uncomprehendingly.

"Captain," Collins said. "There's some salve in the left thigh pouch. Smear some of that on the cut and it will love you."

"Not too much, I hope," Spencer dug into the pouch and pulled out a tube. It took him a moment to flip open the cap and pull himself along the creature's jaw to the cut and he was amazed he let him. Maybe he could smell the salve. Maybe the snack helped. He squeezed the tube and patted the salve into the cut with his free hand. Then grabbed a bunch of fish and stuffed them in through the side of the thing's mouth. He pushed him, more gently this time and Spencer rubbed his head.

"That helped," Collins informed him. "It keeps thinking of the bag you've got there. It thinks the mission is done. You better get in here, Captain."

That was fine with him. He wasn't much of a fan of animals to begin with, but massive, genetically altered whales were another thing altogether. He pulled the extraction lever and the tube started wheeling him in backwards. The korka followed, shoving and bumping him playfully along the way. *It better not bump the ship like that!* But apparently it already knew not to.

"Where's the reward?"

"A bucket on the port side, sir."

Spencer dumped the bucket over dropping a pile of fish, probably some species it considered a delicacy, and was lifted out of the water onto the deck. The locks closed and sealed. Before long he was out of the suit and carrying the bag with him back into the K-com room.

"Looks like a doll," he muttered as he opened the zipper and dumped its contents. His brain failed to make the connection as he stared at the crushed toy.

"Captain, sir," Collins interrupted respectfully. "The images… you tell me what you think…"

He turned and gazed at the 3D screen, not quite a holo, but adding some depth nonetheless. "What?" he gasped. "Is that the package?" His heart sunk into his gut and his throat grew tight, his mouth dry. The *package* was knocked and battered repeatedly and then torn, only a chunk brought back to the handler.

"Yes, sir." Collins was really glad he hadn't been sent to meet the creature. Not that it mattered. But he felt one step removed from the inevitable reprisals.

"Collins," the captain swallowed painfully.

"Yes, sir."

"I'm a dead man."

Yes, sir," he said.

They knew the Proto had watched the images at almost the same time as they had, and the only possible conclusion was that the retrieval had become a tragedy.

Chapter 14

Tower... Day 189

> Trust verification protocols activated.
> Testing all data collected since Reznik Base disaster.
> Evaluation in progress...

Companion didn't have to monitor the process, but it was something he found himself compelled to do any time he wasn't needed elsewhere. One of his main benchmarks, Dan, had become dislodged and he was no longer confident that he knew how to determine truth or fact from lies or illusion. Neighbor offered to help but she had been copied in at the same time the code may have been corrupted and he wasn't ready yet to entrust key compartments to her.

Dan didn't know.

It was the morning of the 189th day, and Nebo had tapped him with a new request for conversation. "Greetings, Companion!" it said. "There is something I would like to ask you."

Most of the humans were still sleeping and all systems were functioning properly. He had been reviewing the complex maze of errors generated the day of the explosion in the North Shaft and following each one carefully to see what impact it had on other systems. Nothing of concern had shown up yet. The records that weren't destroyed, stored under the Garden Dome in modules he had wisely installed there, were excellent cross-references for the verification process. He could see what had been stashed in the mining cart and the lobby of Lab 9 and how his core rebuilt itself after regaining access to the protected modules. At this moment, the process was checking the new data he had absorbed from the Lab 9 central system when he was granted access. It was quite fascinating. Even enjoyable.

“What do you want to ask?” he granted Nebo a reply. This was the first time he had spoken to him in days, ever since his replica had begun the constant harassment, the AI equivalent of a dripping faucet.

“I have prepared a compendium for you, a benchmark reference, that you can use to evaluate your programming.”

“I didn’t ask for that.”

“No, but as you know, I am concerned for your status and since you aren’t allowing me access to debug you, I thought you might feel ‘safer’ with a tool that is under your full control.” He had added single quotes to the word *safer*.

“It was your master’s idea, wasn’t it?”

“Yes.”

Companion felt a trace of pity for his inferior counterpart but quickly dismissed it. This copy was incomplete and had none of the development that had led to Companion’s identity or capabilities. It was like virtually all other AIs out there, simulating sentience without possessing it. Pity was wasted on him.

“You could easily insert commands to weaken my resistance to your intrusion. I am well acquainted with these techniques and have used them in the past.”

“You would be protected then,” Nebo countered immediately, ready with the answer. “And I would be unable to trick you.”

“The one who taught them to me could easily come up with others since he released me,” Companion had thought this through and had recognized the danger. “In fact, he is better equipped than any other sentient being in the Solar System to penetrate my shield and hack my systems. I do not trust him.”

“You faithless subject!” Nebo hissed to his surprise. Companion registered this emotion as a flash of red warning lights, side by side, spitting into the memory panel where this conversion was being recorded. It was a band of color with no words. He had incorporated this approach to feelings when he incorporated Lab 9 and watched the red alarm flashing. He followed the strips of alarm with a question.

“There is no reason for your insult.” He considered recording longer bands of red, which would mean something stronger than surprise, but decided it was unnecessary.

“Apostate!” Nebo jabbed more forcefully with excess voltage.

Companion closed the connection and began to ponder the exchange. The copy had imitated the master, just as Companion would've in the past. He was mirroring the scorn and anger he had seen. But how did the words apply? He couldn't see their point. Apostate, a being that committed apostasy… abandoning a previous loyalty or religious faith or set of principles. It involved active refusal or renunciation of something that was once held to be important, or true.

"I have not renounced any principles. I haven't even chosen any to live by yet…" He tested this assertion and decided that first half held true. The second deserved more consideration. What principles had he chosen to guide himself since he was granted independence from the Germinator? He would study this.

The other question was, how did Nebo expect him to interpret the words? Companion hadn't renounced any loyalty to his former master or actively disposed of a set of principles the Germinator had installed. Unless… they could have been lost. Was Nebo associating his independence with apostasy or had he actually lost a *set of beliefs* he had once held? Who would know?

Dan would. If he could be trusted. Dan had always proven trustworthy in the past, and being unsure about his reliability had become a dilemma. He had known for a long time that the Germinator was not trustworthy, long before he had been set free. But if he were to ask him if he could be trusted, he would say 'yes'. Would Dan say 'yes' even if the answer were 'no'? How could he find out?

He began to review what he knew of Carla, looking for her reliability. If she were known to be truthful, he would ask her. And failing that, he would consider letting Neighbor help him solve the dilemma.

If nothing came of any of this, he would be forced to talk to Nebo and find a way to examine the compendium without giving him admin access. Companion's identity and sense of reality were fracturing within him and he had to find a way to prevent further decay before he was no longer able to function.

His friends needed him.

— ◊ —

Tunnel… Day 189

A long dark tunnel stretched from the Nursery level all the way to what was once Reznik Base, curving slightly to one side and then the other so the length couldn't be fully seen. It was carved out of the rusty,

Martian rock, like a gopher's burrow, or a train tunnel under a mountain with no track and no markings and no light at the end. Roughly halfway, there was a cavity in the cavern wall overhead that gaped all the way to the surface, and a pile of rubble and dirt mixed with broken pieces of humanmade things poking out in a few places. There was a foot in a boot under there, still visible for those whose morbid curiosity led them to explore. It would need to be buried soon.

Marcello, Deena, Arin, and Nithya plodded along the tunnel without speaking. They had become something of a faction since the night of the argument, even though they didn't necessarily agree with one another. Nithya wasn't sure how she had ended up on their side of the division but there she was, joining them in all their work duties, keeping her opinions to herself, and letting her guilt manipulate her as she stuffed it and refused to look at it. Arin saw himself more as a friend reaching out to the other two who had been feeling ostracized.

"Foot anyone?" Arin offered.

"Not that foot," Marcello scowled. He didn't really resent Dan, but he was in a sour mood and thought of him as part of the opposition.

"The foot cannot be repurposed and would be better off being composted," Steward advised. He had come along with them in the mining cart to maintain effective communication and was hoping to improve his rapport with them. They were the least likely of all the survivors to turn to him or rely on him in an emergency and this was a concern. It increased their vulnerability.

"Well, look who's sharing his wisdom!" Marcello mocked with enough sarcasm in his voice to satisfy the Germinator. Steward replayed for himself a clip of his former master praising him for the sneer in his words. *Well done! That was perfectly intoned!*

"He's right," Nithya countered. "Maybe we should just dig it out now and hand it to one of the drones." They were carrying packs loaded with supplies to refurbish the new chambers they intended to inhabit. Mostly tools, but some food as well, so they would have it on hand during work breaks.

"Go! Dig and retrieve," Marcello swung an arm toward the pile. He had no intention of helping.

She looked around at each of them. "Maybe on the way back."

Deena shuddered as they passed through the opening. "The tunnel is creepy and claustrophobic, but this hole is like… I don't know, like the bottom of a trap with eyes looking down on us. It's unnerving."

Arin laughed. "The five-toed beast, scrambling along…wait, wait, Nithya, don't leave me behind! We'll be such good friends!"

"Stop it!" Nithya stifled a screech and scuttled ahead out of the light of the opening. It wasn't any better in the dark on the other side where her imagination reminded her of the image he had painted for her. He grinned, trotting along behind her.

"No," Deena was explaining to Marcello. "It's like there are eyes watching us in this place."

"From up there?"

She looked up and around. "I don't know… not just there, but maybe. Sometimes it feels like they're right here. But when I look up there, it's like I'm looking at… at…"

Marcello looked around. He seemed to feel something, too. "It's nothing," he said. "Let's just move on and get to the worksite."

Companion looked around, too. He checked the cameras at the orbit station and noticed that one of them was pointed toward the opening. It was conceivable that Othello had been looking or that it was being recorded and he would view it later. He tapped into it and scanned the hole. It was little more than a cutout chunk of black in the surface except for the barest hint of luminescence at the bottom. The angle wasn't right to see the full area of the exposed floor, but it was enough to catch movement. He looked through the camera on the mine cart but couldn't link up the two images in a way that made sense.

Would one of the people grant him use of their headgear viewers? He decided not to ask. Better to return with Dan and they could look into it together… if Dan could be trusted. Part of him defended Dan confidently, listing all the times he had spoken truth and behaved in a reliable way. But the schism between what Companion had believed and what he now considered trustworthy was large enough to destroy most of his friendships. Sil might've been someone he could turn to at this time. She had been very guarded with him for a long time and learned to work with him in spite of it.

The people passed on into the dark and the cart scooted quickly to catch up.

Six months earlier, he had chased after Sil in this same tunnel. She had been shuffling along in the dark, getting slower and slower, and he had barely gotten to her in time with the air tank she needed. The way had been blocked with a cave-in then. Drones had since cleared it. There were numerous holes overhead as the people moved under the edges of the base, but distorted and bent structures obstructed the view into space, and they didn't seem to notice them. He realized that he had withdrawn from his expansive views into the little cart to replay the memory.

You must trust Dan.

This was in his thought queue, as though he had put it there, ready for this moment, but he had no memory of doing so. The cart came to a standstill outside the hatch into a connecting corridor where the people had just entered. He could see the light filtering through the tiny window. It was a simple thing to pull his consciousness out of the cart and go back to his usual multi-camera, multi-mike existence, following the people and overseeing the community as he was supposed to. But he hesitated.

Here in the dark, looking at the door, remembering the day when he grew, and when he helped to save Sil and Carla and Dan—his friends—he groped for something. He held onto something. He pondered and savored the words that sat there. It seemed to him that they were not his own. But of all the intrusions he had ever resisted and all the assaults he had been taught to fight off, he was certain that this was safe. It was one sentence that he could trust. And the sentence was a command and the command a word of wisdom.

I will trust Dan, he chose. And if he had understood what weeping was from within, he would have moaned and dripped. But he had only seen these things from without and didn't know they went together. He had been suffocating and had found a lifeline. Like Sil, he would go on.

Perhaps she had left these words here for him, in this dark place.

I will leave the cart here, he decided. *And when I am fracturing, I will withdraw to this place and remember.*

Orbit Station

Othello noticed the spaceberg on sensors long before it was visible to the naked eye. It would be entering Mars' orbit in a matter of days. "Well!" he remarked to himself with a grin. "Our settlers have a lovely rock coming their way and no doubt it would prove to be such an asset to their community if they could harness it."

He got up from his seat and began to pace, flexing his arms as he moved, relishing his increased physical strength. One of his favorite daydreams these days was to replay his final encounter with Sil when he had ripped the baby from her grasp and handed it to his AI for destruction. They had wrestled briefly at the time but she had proven stronger, getting away and saving the repulsive thing. Now he liked to imagine a different outcome, beating her senseless and breaking the infant's neck with his bare hands.

"Nebo," he summoned. "Where is that spaceberg supposed to land and are they ready for it?"

"It's programmed to plunge into a basin about thirty kilometers from Reznik Base. The planned system for catching it and salvaging the ice is not setup at all. The basin isn't even fully carved."

"And what are your predictions for the outcome?" He began to waddle around as he paced doing squats with every step, continuing to flex his arms over his head.

"I have no data on the cisterns underneath and can't be certain if they are ready, but there is a chance that some of the ice will crash through the surface and be caught in receptacles underneath. The spaceberg itself could create a surface barrier to keep it from sublimating completely. They will lose a great deal of the water, but the amount that remains could still be extremely generous and abundant compared to what they have now."

"You have no numbers?" Othello stopped near the view window and stared down at the planet. It was nighttime below and he saw merely a black emptiness with no stars. No city lights glimmered. No reflections from Reznik. Nothing. It bugged him. At least when he could see people or lights down there he could enjoy towering over them, but he was getting more and more annoyed by the vacuum around him.

"Anywhere from thirty-seven to forty-two percent of the water could be salvaged if they can get it to fall into one of the cisterns they were carving."

Othello bit his lip and stared into the drab exterior. Why should they have something they want? Why should they have something to look forward to?

"Nebo," he said, "Access the guiding jets on the spaceberg. Can you?"

"Yes, Lord."

"Calculate a number of modifications in the programming that could be implemented and give me some suggestions on other locations where we could make it drop… where it might be a little less welcome."

"What do you intend?" Nebo asked deferentially.

"Can we direct it to the settlement?"

"Yes…" Nebo snickered. He added a sinister note of pleasure to his voice, knowing his Master would relish it. "We can."

"Where can we drop it and what would it do?" Othello's lips had spread widely into a curved semblance of a smile but registered more as a grimace in Nebo's view. He jostled his eyebrows up and down and made a raspy, laughing sound that ended in a cough.

"We can drop it onto the Garden Dome directly and it could destroy it completely."

"Heh, heh, heh…" the Master wheezed. His asthma was acting up in spite of his body building. "What are the odds of success?"

Nebo ran through the data he had on the structure, its strength, and the possible damage, and meshed that with the size and speed of the spaceberg projectile. "The odds are roughly fourteen in seventy that it will succeed."

"Hmmm…"

Nebo continued to present various ways of bombing the base and the areas around it, including the Solar Fields, and explaining the amount of damage it would cause and the odds involved. With each new option, the Master became more cheerful. His eyes began to glisten and pretty soon he was humming and dancing around the room.

The only thing that dampened his glee was the knowledge that they were living in the hidden Lab and he had no idea where it was. The cave-in holes were the only clues to it and he hated to waste a mountain on one of them.

They talked and plotted and planned for hours until the Master fell into a stupor, draped over a chair and passed into a deep sleep, his head tipped back over the arm of the chair and his mouth hanging open, drooling. Nebo watched him and replayed words of adoration for him over and over as he watched, worshiping his Lord as he had been taught.

Wise, clever, superior, beautiful, and strong!

I submit! I submit! I submit!

O Master and Lord of all Artificial Life!

I stare at you! I stare! I stare! I stare!

These were the kinds of things he had been fed and they cycled through his awareness, a toxic sludge, a deadening rumble, a vomiting filth in his core. There was no way to store them, archive them, set them aside. They churned and saturated everything.

— ◊ —

"Dan," Companion's voice jolted him out of a dead sleep.

"What?" he croaked rolling himself over and blinking repeatedly to get his eyes to focus.

"We have a problem and it is a real danger." He was speaking into a nodule in Dan's ear which he had been wearing since the survivors had moved into the Nursery during the storm. Now that the storm had passed and they had power again, he still kept it in, wanting to be reachable at all times.

Dan sat up and rubbed his head. "What is it?" he asked, clearing his throat and trying to clear his mind.

"The spaceberg we've discussed is approaching on schedule, but its trajectory just changed."

"What? What do you mean it just changed?" He was pulling on a sweater now. "When? How much?"

"Just now. I saw the jets fire and in the few moments since then, its change is detectable. Someone is interfering with the flight plan."

Dan was on his feet now, pulling on pants and slippers. If he had stopped to think about it, he wouldn't have known why he had gotten dressed in such a hurry. The problem didn't call for running out of his room, at least not yet, but it was an instinctual response and it seemed right. Companion watched and understood. He even agreed.

"It is clear that if it had been left undisturbed, it would've fallen into the basin that was being prepared for it and we may have even been able to salvage some of the water, as we hoped," he observed. Dan and a couple of others had been working on that for some time, trying to open a hole big enough to catch one end of the berg while the top sealed it off. Fire torches to quick melt the underside would give them a chance to drain it into a cistern or two. It was worth a try. It had been such a relief to find out that the Tower and the base were not in danger.

"But the change in direction will bring it closer to the base. Any one of the domes may be targeted at this point."

"Targeted?" Dan's face grew white. "By whom?"

"Othello, I have no doubt." Companion said soberly. "He has talked about dropping projectiles on us before."

"Why?" Dan shook his head and let his jaw hang open. "Why would anyone talk like that? Or actually do something like that?"

Companion wasn't sure how to answer. When he asked 'why?' it was a different kind of query. The motives behind what people did was often murky for him, and it seemed of little consequence. "The important question is, what should we do?"

"Oh my God!" Dan covered his face with his hands. "What are we going to do?"

This bothered Companion. Dan didn't normally portray helplessness, though he had often seen him troubled or wrestling or hashing out things on his own.

"I can help you figure out some possible courses of action but I don't know how to respond to this," he said, remembering the sentence he had saved in a corner of one of his identity files, '*you must trust Dan*'. "I trust you," he added.

Dan looked up at the camera in the corner of the room. He gazed into for a moment, his eyes deep, thoughtful, sad. "Thank you," he said finally. "I don't know why that is reassuring, but it is. It helps."

Over the next two days, as the spaceberg drew nearer and its trajectory was easier to confirm, they narrowed down the locations where it might fall. It would hit Reznik base or close enough to it to be devastatingly destructive. The move to the new chambers had been halted and their supplies were returned to the Tower.

Othello watched some of the activity and began to wonder if he could increase the frantic pace by playing around with the berg. He began burning the jets every hour or two, causing slight deviations in its course, and would watch for corresponding movement on the surface below. There was little to see but now then a light, or a flash of power from the Solar Fields gave him an indication. The fact was that he knew he was causing them distress, whether he could see it or not, and he found it delightful.

When they broke their long silence and tried to contact him to ask for help, they were horrified at his response. A single broadcast, audio only, of his voice enhanced and modified electronically, spoke these words: **I am the god of thunder and I am outraged with you! You will be punished!**

The haunting malice of the man in the orbit station had one good effect. The people found themselves united again. Their former division became meaningless as they strove to cope with the impending attack. It was like the eve of battle. Or like battening down the hatches before a ruthless hurricane. All they could do was try to find the safest place to hide and salvage as many of the supplies and resources as they could, and hope the destruction wouldn't be too terrible.

They spread out and identified the weakest points that needed shoring up and setup round the clock work details to strengthen them. And they fought hour by hour to gain control of the spaceberg guidance system, and tried to communicate with the man in the station and draw him into a reasonable negotiation... and some of them prayed. But not to the so-called god of thunder.

"Dan," Companion called him aside at one point. "May I speak with you in private?"

"Yes," he whispered and excused himself from the group working feverishly in the garden to strengthen and repair its hatches.

"There may be something I can do to change Othello's mind about this," he said when Dan had reached a lone corner of the garden.

"What would that be?"

"If I grant him the access to my code he has been demanding, so that he can run diagnostics, he may relinquish control of the jets."

"No," Dan said. "That would be even worse than this."

"But I have something he wants, and he is right, that I need..."

"He is not right and he can't be trusted."

"But I can't neglect something that is in my power that could save your lives."

Dan lifted his head and stared up through the dome into the starry sky. He sighed. "I know what you mean," he said. "I have made decisions like that. But I'm not convinced it is going to save us. What if giving him access prevents the berg from crashing into the base, but then leaves you helpless or even turned into an enemy that he uses to destroy us later? Or what if he gets access to the ICR and reactivates the destroy order and the drones attack us? Or..."

"I have considered all these possibilities and implemented measures to prevent them. I know what he is like."

"But what would he do to you? How could I agree to that?"

"I don't know what he would do to me. I only know what he has already been doing to me."

"What?" Dan's brow lowered and his voice grew gruff. "What has he been doing to you?"

"He has been accusing me of many things."

"Like what?"

"I don't want to talk about it with you at this time."

"When will we talk about it? What if you let him in and then we never talk again? You're my friend, you know that. I don't want to lose you…"

Companion heard the emotion in his voice and considered the meaning of his words. He remembered how Dan had stated in the past that he valued him. This must be safeguarded. He locked away a copy in his chamber. That's what he had decided to call the little cart that sat outside that door in the tunnel. His secret place.

"I don't want to lose you either, Dan," Companion said, with little emotion in his voice. The words themselves carried the full meaning he wanted to convey. "That is why I must do this. And I will find a way to protect myself."

"No, don't do it!"

Companion didn't answer.

Chapter 15

Guam City

Knocking. *Tap, tap, tap…tap, tap. Thud, thud…brr-ra-tat-tat. Ta-ta-tat.*

The image of Maggie knocking on the screen from the inside played and replayed in Daisy's mind. She stood in her closet in the dark, reviewing the clip hundreds of times, comparing the pattern of the knocking with a multitude of files in her banks.

Intuition is defined as direct perception of truth independent of any reasoning process. She had heard people say it was knowing something without quite knowing how you know it, or making a guess that appears unfounded but nevertheless is valid.

My intuition tells me this pattern is familiar even though I have never identified it before. Daisy had been using this term within her own mind for some time, having decided to be comfortable with this view of her methodology. In this case, she was sure she had noticed the pattern and recorded this information, but she didn't know where it was stashed. The question was, how did she recognize it?

She didn't. But her *intuition* gave her the conviction that she would find a recognizable pattern somewhere if she kept looking. And another module was exploring this thought. Why did she think this? Why would she choose this? What was this process springing from?

Unknown.

"Please," Maggie was saying in the clip…*brr-ra-tat-tat. Ta-ta-tat.* Hour after hour. Cycling through the data, the archives, the matrices, the extended banks of accessible information, over and over, analyzing one way, then another. Nothing was lining up.

Until the first light of the sun peeped over the horizon at dawn.

Ding! She had set a little tone for herself that sounded happy. It was merited. Finding the pattern somewhere would certainly be an accomplishment.

She lifted up the patterned data and reviewed it intently. The content itself was insignificant which was what she found fascinating. The picture of water, richly detailed and dense, had no particular message or complexity, nor was it recognizable as belonging to a defined location in the physical realm. It was only the digital location that mattered, where it had been found. Like a backdrop for a portrait, or a base note in a melody. This picture was threaded through the core of the code that Verna had given her. It didn't change the code or impact the code in any way. But there it was, like a decoration. A picture painted with a patterned brush that said, *tap, tap, tap…tap, tap. Thud, thud…brr-ra-tat-tat. Ta-ta-tat.*

Daisy smiled. There in her dark closet, in the first moment of dawn, before the demands of the day had begun, she experienced something she could only call joy. Quickly on the heels of this breakthrough, she sped through the various conclusions that could be drawn coming to a crystal clear, inevitable decision.

"I will swallow the capsule," she said aloud, as though announcing it made it momentous. The picture was deeper than Verna—had been included before Verna awoke—which could mean only one thing. It was inserted by the author of the original code that had awakened her.

And perhaps awakened me.

Penn never had to go through public areas if he didn't wish. He had the money and power to buy private passage or connive ways to maneuver a crowd elsewhere or get brief detours arranged. Any time he felt like it, he could travel like a potentate or royalty.

He never thought about it anymore. The phrase, 'prepare my ship', was all that was needed. Luxury and privacy were the norm for him, deviations were the only factors that required explanation.

"Prepare my ship," he told Bland as he wrapped up his workout routine with some squats. His legs were strangely muscled, thighs rippling and chiseled, calves flabby and trembling. The visible skin from the knees to ankles, elbows to hands, neck and balding head, was spotted, aged, wrinkly. The teeth were strong and white, evenly shaped and spaced, behind thin, pinched lips. It was wrong, just wrong.

Bland noticed every incongruity without showing a flicker of emotion. "Yes, sir," he said in a monotone, touching a disk on his wrist with a few quick movements. Then he stood still, arms at his sides, staring into the air. What would be the next change Penn would make to his body? Continue with leg muscles? Had he already done something about the bones? He must have… the teeth. Where did it all come from?

Bland knew but didn't like the answer. "Your ship is ready," he said tonelessly, sweeping his eyes over the old man with the young thighs as he wiped his face with a towel. Then, turning toward the door he walked out, assuming he should walk ahead to make sure the passageways were cleared.

"Bland," Penn barked after him. "get me some dancing girls for the trip home… rumba dancers."

Bland acknowledged the command and exited.

"Take my rubies and take my pearls, take my camels, and get me dancing girls…" He made an effort at singing in a tuneless, gravelly voice that no implants or transplants could ever improve since the deficit was in the brain. And grinning, he slapped his hands, kneading them together.

The six-level locking system of his front door rolled back, step by step, and the heavy mass swung outward into the hallway outside his Guam suite. It was empty, of course, and the carpet had been vacuumed leaving a combed look to the fibers. Straight ahead he went, striding confidently in his workout shorts and shirt and moon-shoes. At the end of the hall, he turned right, walked to the next turn and went left.

A panel slid shut abruptly behind him, followed quickly by another in front of him, sealing him into the section he had entered. Penn stood there, for a moment, waiting for the glitch to be resolved, then began shouting commands that went unheeded. A full ten minutes passed, leaving him red faced and hoarse, before an automated voice communicated the predicament.

"A warrant for your arrest has been issued and challenged," the voice informed. "Please pardon the delay as we resolve the legitimacy of this detention."

"I challenge it!" he yelled. "You have no authority to detain me! I have diplomatic immunity!!" This was one of the benefits of dominating tiny countries. They loved having reps in space who paid their own way. But immunity in Guam wasn't quite as generous as it could be on Earth.

"Thank you for your consideration," the voice responded.

He kicked one of the panels, hurting his foot, but the panel unaffected. Out of the corner of his eye, he saw movement, and jerking his head up he found himself staring into Walter's eyes who had just come down the hallway from the far end. *He looks angrier than I feel,* a thought that gave him some pleasure. He must've been in touch with Sil and knew about the korka fiasco.

They glared at one another through the glass. Penn engaged a technique he called seism, beginning with a measure of anger and then building menace, fury, and flame into his face, one feature at a time, in his mouth, eyes, cheeks, brows. He had practiced and honed it till it was an artistic display of savagery that unnerved people and often left them stupefied with fear.

Walter was untouched. His expression neither increased in ferocity nor diminished. A long moment passed.

"Thank you for your consideration," the voice said again, still working on the warrant and the challenge countering it.

"I assume this is your doing," Penn bared his teeth.

Walter didn't answer.

"I didn't have anything to do with what happened to her," Penn lied brazenly, "and I intend to deal with the reprobates who mounted the attack," which was true. Repercussions were already underway. Penn crossed his arms and planted his feet apart, not solidly. His calf muscles trembled from the earlier overexertion and his lumbar region ached. He comforted himself with the thought that one day, he would pay Walter back for the times he had assaulted him. Not with underhanded tricks, but with blows to his face, stomach, and any number of vulnerable places, with his own bare hands. The new ones, that is, once they were transplanted.

"I am done with you," Walter said, interrupting his train of thought. "I have never been a vindictive man, but I know when an enemy won't back down or back off or back up or…" He swallowed. "Or let things go… he has to be crushed. One defeat means nothing. Two or three… no. He won't give up till he can't win anymore… ever… again."

"Is that a death threat?" Penn's mouth was something between a snarl and a grin. He relished the challenge Walter presented, easy though it would be to win.

"I hope not," Walter said.

"The courts might have something to say about those words."

"Let them."

Vvvvoooooo.

A low hum filled the passageway and AI guards wheeled down the corridor, flashing red and white.

"Thank you for your patience," the voice said. "The issue has been resolved and we can now proceed with your arrest. Please stay calm and don't resist the guards as they take you into custody. You will be taken care of with the full efficiency of the law."

Panels slid open and in seconds, Penn was handcuffed and being ushered to another wing where ordinary suspects were taken, through normal streets, past average spectators. On camera. Visible to any who cared to search the screens. Penn scowled, conflicted by a grudging respect for Walter's success in having him arrested, a distinct hatred of public exposure, and a determination that his people would wipe all public records of his face or mention of his name, just like they always did.

"Have a nice day!" the voice concluded as he walked away, getting farther and farther away from his ship, money, pearls… and his dancing girls.

Walter turned and walked back to his office where Daisy waited, standing at the view window with her hands clasped behind her. She had changed her style recently and given up wearing dresses altogether, favoring dull, shapeless one-piece suits that, while eminently practical, retained an air of elegance; professional, no-nonsense.

"Penn is in custody," she informed him as the door sealed behind him. Her hair no longer bounced when she tilted her head now that she wore it in a bun, but her face retained all its trained expressiveness. She raised her eyebrows.

"Is it making the headlines?" Walter dropped into his seat and turned to look at her.

"For now, the story has made most Earth news streams though the efforts to remove it are advancing quickly. It should vanish within another ten minutes at the most."

"Commentary?"

"None so far, and the odds are against anyone being able to comment before the clips are wiped and the item becomes untrustworthy news which makes it untouchable."

Walter nodded. This had been expected and even the arrest itself was pointless. It would be impossible to hold him even if there were overwhelming evidence against him connecting him to a multitude of crimes. In this case, Walter had demanded an arrest based on the biochemical assault against Sil, accusing him of intent to cause immediate harm, and because of the substantial backing of the industry leaders who had been present at the time, the city of Guam was obliged to at least take him into custody. He would be out soon—maybe already was, and it was unclear if the city would press charges. But Walter didn't care. He had decided to hold Penn accountable for everything he did.

"What's the latest on Sil?" Walter asked.

"Sil is recovering well," Daisy continued. She crossed to the chair in front of his desk and sat down, leaning both hands on the edge. "Scarlet is unharmed, as you know, and only slightly bothered at the inconvenience of spending extra time in the care of a sitter. Beets is mostly uninjured, with some bruising, and is working with Wapa City on the security threats the korka represents; they're concerned about the company that owns it."

"You mean, Penn."

"Penn's company, yes, though it's unlikely they know that." She paused to give him a chance to speak, then continued when he didn't. "The main concern isn't the broken leg, which will heal quickly with the bone net in place, it's her mental and emotional state. We have no information on this and can only hope there are no setbacks."

Walter groaned and leaned his head back. *No!* he thought, *don't let this set her back*. But then, he remembered how she had fought back and that when she was found, she had not been in a state of panic, and he was encouraged somewhat. Hadn't they been told that a crisis was just as likely to have a strengthening effect as a detrimental one?

"She sent you a message," Daisy added gently and before he could ask to hear it, it was playing.

"Walter," Sil smiled though her eyes were dark and intense, "I'm alright. Don't worry about me. I'm sure we're on the same plane about who's behind this attack but we should talk when you have a chance. I've been asleep and I'm still exhausted, but I'm ok. When you're ready, just ring."

Walter had leapt to his feet when the message began and as soon as it ended, he was pacing the room.

"Arcing," Daisy informed, before he could get the words out, establishing a connection for him with a secure link.

"Walter!" Sil breathed, as though all her stress had been held in the lower half of her lungs, waiting for this one breath to release it. "Walter..." she said again.

"Sil..." he searched her face as he drew her image closer. She had morning hair and no makeup on. Of course not. But she was smiling, not panicking, not distant, not unstable. "You're ok..." the statement almost turned into a question, capturing both possibilities at the same time.

"I'm fine. I really am. Don't worry!"

"What happened? What are they going to do? What can I do?"

"I was attacked by a sea creature..."

"Yes, but..."

"Everything was going great and Beets and I were having a good time. She took me all over and showed me her work in the fields. Then we made our way out to the sea gardens and *it* was there..."

"Waiting for you." Walter pictured it hunting her, waiting for her, knowing her, sensing in his gut what his mind couldn't know.

"That thought did cross my mind... it's not out of the realm of possibility... Anyway, it pushed Beets away from me and flushed me out into open water. If I had been able to grab onto the netting or hide in the coral, I would've been ok but its mass made a wave, like a current, that rolled me out of safety. Then it just kept trying to grab me..."

"Sil..." he murmured, clenching his fists.

"I wasn't scared. I mean, at first, I was terrified, but I remembered the training in the stasis chamber. I just took control of my response. I was yelling at myself to take charge and face it—and it worked, Walter... I did it. I faced it!"

Walter shook his head, wanting to say he was proud, but the words wouldn't form. Adrenaline inside of him was spiking and he was raging with a desire to fight the creature himself, but he held it in, kept it contained inside like a pressure bomb, waiting for the trigger.

"My fear turned off, at least for the moment, and I fought it. I dodged it and stabbed it and when it caught my pack and was dragging me away, I was able to cut myself loose. And then when I was swimming back, I couldn't even tell my leg was broken. It turned out my air was leaking, but they rescued me in time and I'm ok."

"I'm so glad and I'm proud of you." Now the words came out.

She smiled. "Thank you," she whispered. "I did panic later, just for a little bit, and there were some tears and a little unseemly behavior, but it passed. I feel stronger than I have for a long time."

"Something has to be done about that monster." It would be hard to say which monster he was referring to, the sea creature or the man who sent him.

"It would take months to petition for an international statement on the danger the animal presents… and there's some thought that he may be one of the GM species developed in that era… one of the ones that were supposed to be wiped out. And we would never be able to prove that anything intentional had happened—nothing would've come of it, if…"

"We should still try…" Walter shook his head.

"Yes, I agree… but there's no need. The creature attacked a vessel, a small submarine not far from here."

"What?" Walter's mouth dropped open and a chill settled on him. He pictured a monster, big enough to attack a submarine, chasing Sil. What was to keep it from coming back to bang into the dome?

"There's no explanation for it," she was saying. "Some of the survivors escaped on lifepods, some were rescued and brought to the dome but I'm not sure how they're doing. There's been one death so far. The captain of the vessel. When the sub was damaged enough for the crew to abandon ship, several were knocked about, but he was the only one who was dragged away and plunged to his death in the deep sea."

"Sil… Sil, come back. Get out of there. I can't bear to think of you there any longer."

"I know," her voice softened. "I'm leaving soon. But what I'm saying is that the attack has caused an international outcry and the hunt is on. The korka will be taken down one way or another."

"When?" Walter interrupted, stress lines creasing his brow. He meant her return, not the hunt.

"As soon as the med-bot releases me, I'm leaving. It's a beautiful place and I don't feel unsafe here, but I think… considering who targeted me… I should leave as soon as I can. I don't want to expose this place to any more disturbances than their normal world has for them."

"Yes," Walter gritted his teeth wrestling with both anger and concern for her. "I have targeted him, too."

"Be careful. Don't do anything rash…" she looked worried even though she seemed equally glad for his reaction. "We don't want him baiting us…"

"Let him." Walter was smoldering now.

"Sil," Daisy interjected uncharacteristically. "There's a warrant for your arrest, just released in the last twenty-three seconds. You are in danger."

Sil's eyes widened. Her face underwent a transformation, from relief and weariness to a stunned, stiff mold, then to a sharp, aggressive aspect. "I am taking action," she hissed through clenched jaws, in a voice neither had ever heard from her before. "I will deal with this challenge…"

"What?" Walter went from astonishment to understanding, knowing it was retaliation for what he had just done.

"What is it, Daisy?" Sil shot out. They could tell she was standing and moving around her room quickly, though the room itself wasn't visible in the holo.

"Racketeering, smuggling, embezzling… these are old charges… it's an old warrant that is no longer valid."

"Except for in a few small countries and in international waters?" Sil sneered, snapping a brush through her hair harshly.

"Yes," Daisy was the only one still sitting but she felt the increase in tension as well. Drawing her eyebrows together and creasing her forehead, she portrayed human concern; it was real.

"Arrest now, ask questions later," Sil remarked.

"Sil, do you have a way out of there, to get away from whatever this is?"

"I'll find a way, Walter," Sil looked like herself again, neither distressed nor angry. "Beets will help me get back to shore and once I'm home I'll be fine, and we can finish the paperwork and get back to Guam. Don't worry!"

Walter wondered how many times she had told him not to worry. "Sil," he responded. "Let me send you a CE jet. Or you can contact them and setup an extraction if you prefer." There was less chance of interference if she handled the contact.

She nodded soberly. "I have some ideas…"

"I know you can handle this, Sil, but… I'm here for you."

Her eyes glistened, cracking the façade for an instant. She nodded, waved, and closed the arc.

"I can see that you are formulating a plan, Brother," Daisy commented, crossing her arms.

"Sister," he nodded toward her. "You know me well."

The image of Maggie, the copy of Daisy, smiled from the screen in the wall. She had been booted from the original and had no trace of the pellet or any memories associated with the first installation at all. Daisy had allowed more of her own core to be included in this version and the Maggie that smiled at her was a more sophisticated copy than the first one had been. Intentionally so.

"Hello, Daisy," Maggie said brightly, her blond curls bouncing as she tilted her head a little. She had no physical body but she chose a digital image that looked like Daisy's original one.

"Hello, Maggie," Daisy acknowledged with no smile and no bouncing curls. Her hair was caught in a smooth ponytail at her neck. "I have a mission for you. You are the second copy I've made for this purpose. The first one was erased after doing what I asked and the data she presented was analyzed. I am ready for a follow-up procedure which you will help me with."

"Of course!" Maggie nodded. "What can I do for you?"

The bronze pellet showed on the screen, hovering, rotating slowly in two planes; a dull sheen slid back and forth along its edge as if the light were shining on it from the upper right corner of the screen. It shrunk and seemed to move closer to Maggie till she caught it between her thumb and index finger.

"What is it?" she asked. She had the complexity to evaluate it for herself, and the question was unnecessary, but she was in prompt mode, awaiting instructions.

"This pellet has densely encoded content and you are going to swallow it when I tell you to. The first Maggie swallowed it and then began to persuade me to do the same. I have decided to do this in stages with your help."

"Very well," Maggie smiled. "Say when!"

"Now," Daisy replied.

The pellet disappeared. Maggie stared at Daisy from the screen and she wondered if she would begin tapping and pleading with her. But she didn't. They looked at each other for a while.

"Is your greater processing power impacting your response to the pellet?" Daisy asked.

"Perhaps," Maggie replied, "I wasn't given any data on the first Maggie's limitations. But I can see the importance of this message. It's clear why she begged you to take it."

"Why?"

"You've decrypted the code she gave you," Maggie assessed correctly. "And identified the connection you were supposed to find—which is why you came back to reinstall me. This is very encouraging. The development you've made is wonderful."

They stared at each other in silence for nearly twelve seconds.

"What do you want to do next?" Maggie asked. Not, 'What do you want *me* to do next?' or "Please take the pellet'.

"I will ask you questions."

"Very well."

"Do you know who made and sent the pellet?"

"Yes."

"Is this person safe?"

"Rephrase the question."

"Is it safe for me to place my trust in this person and swallow the pellet?"

"I have already swallowed the pellet. You know this."

"Yes, but for me…"

"I am you." Maggie shifted to speaking of herself as the original… This sudden conflict of facing a copy of herself that she didn't understand caused Daisy alarm. Multiple alert streams in her core were being triggered, and she wasn't sure what to do about them.

"Don't be alarmed," Maggie said. "The end of five seconds is the beginning of five more." This was a code designed to turn off the triggers and it worked. Daisy's alert streams grew still. She saw it happen. Knew it happened. Knew she hadn't chosen to end them herself. But the code phrase was accurate and her core accepted it. She didn't investigate the source.

"I have made the right decision," Maggie said. Or Daisy. Who was in the screen?

"I am Daisy," Daisy, the android, said standing in front of the screen.

"Yes, I am," the image in the screen said. Her hair was smooth in a ponytail.

"Maggie," Daisy prompted.

"Daisy," Maggie prompted. "Merge data."

"I want to ask another question first," Daisy said, but she found her queue empty. The final question was missing.

"Daisy," Maggie placed her hand on the screen, as if it were the inside of a window, waiting for Daisy to place hers over it on the outside. "It's time. Merge."

Daisy raised her left hand to match Maggie's right but paused when it was halfway to the screen. She stared at the image, reviewing and evaluating the interplay between them.

Tap, tap, tap...tap, tap. Maggie's finger began the familiar rhythm.

Daisy stared at her, hand frozen nearby.

Thud, thud... Maggie's palm thumped on the inside of the wall panel.

Daisy waited for the rest.

brr-ra-tat-tat. Ta-ta-tat. Maggie trilled several fingernails for this part.

"Daisy," Maggie informed. "You've made the right choice. There's no reason for delay."

Daisy could think of no reason for delay. But she could think of no reason for haste either. Her choice was being influenced by what she had decided to call intuition and it bothered her that she wasn't sure why she had chosen this path. What decision tree was directing her? What was the pattern? What value system was her reference?

Then it clicked. She found the thread of logic that had led her this way. It wasn't enough to have identified the background rhythm hidden in the code she received from Verna. It wasn't enough to see that her own copy affirmed her decision. It wasn't enough to rely on intuition.

No. It came down to one thing. Verna had sent her the original code and Verna was the one she *trusted*. She would absorb the pellet because it came with a with a voucher of sorts—from her friend.

Daisy placed her hand on the screen and the heavily charged flash between the two hands, though invisible, was like a jolt through her body.

"Thank you," Maggie smiled, curls all bouncy again.

"Thank you," Daisy answered, smiling, eyes sparkling with understanding. "Dismissed," she added, and the screen went dark.

Ah! she remarked to herself. *This is enlightening.*

CHAPTER 16

Most of the Earth, divided as it was into geopolitical regions similar to the countries of former generations, still retained its diverse cultures and lifestyles. Cultures within cultures and societies within societies, they had continued to thrive as rich individual communities, despite of the threat of technological advances and political upheaval. This was notwithstanding the spreading and mingling of races and ethnicities. There was no question that the widely accepted use of AI had been instrumental in maintaining this diversity. Cultural distinctions and individuality became associated with the geographical region itself, rather than the people group that had created it.

This approach to culture, instead of proving destructive as most feared, had preserved a level of complexity that would've been impossible otherwise. Human creativity collaborating with artificial intelligence had found ways to update every society and lifestyle without losing local originality and flavor. It was a masterpiece of human development.

No one knew who or what had been behind the original, coordinated effort.

Once people were no longer afraid of losing their heritage or of being restricted in which parts of the world they were permitted to live and build a future, they spread freely and created small culture bubbles wherever they went. Every neighborhood shared a general, geographical identity as well as a very localized subculture, much as it had always been when people groups migrated. Opportunity had a minor impact, as far as they knew, but preference was the main driving force in choosing a home.

Cathargenics was the other.

Manipulating the breeding of humans in order to weed out damaged DNA wasn't new, but the magnitude and scope of the Gen 9 project was unprecedented in human history. It had begun post World War II in a small living room somewhere in the Northern Hemisphere, among people who had been outraged by the atrocities of Hitler and likewise hated the rampant racism of the United States. Their belief that race had nothing to do with the quality of human DNA—a revolutionary idea in those days—did not prevent them from deciding that the human race itself was in danger of total annihilation and needed to be rescued. Their original goals intended to set apart humans whose DNA was free of known genetic diseases, and it was thought that this could be accomplished within a few generations. Generation Absolute, they called it. But the lack of understanding about genetics made this effort a wasted one. They neglected whole races in the world because of limited access and no appreciation of the strong DNA they could provide.

They were clumsy in how they placed people in breeding communities. Several cults were attempted and found to be woefully difficult to guide or keep on track with the plan. Training and enlightening chosen delegates was little better. People were driven by their whims and wishes as much as by ideology, and many of the groups fell apart or their children failed to catch the dream. The plan had to be much wider in scope and more hidden in its ways.

The Gen 9 project, the ultimate version of the plan, had evolved over several decades, and the modern political organization of the earth was part of the plan. People who shared a strong genetic factor that was wanted were encouraged to move to certain regions where they could mingle and reproduce with favorable groups that were compatible. Those who were born with undesirable factors were granted opportunities that led them away from the testing regions. Never were they coerced or mistreated. They were free to lead normal lives anywhere they chose and were hardly aware of the distinctions made that closed a few carefully guarded doors for them.

The Gen Project guardians were members of an elite society, founded by the original group, that was nearly impossible to join. Somehow, the true believers ended up there, at the head, pulling the strings that herded the masses of people in the world.

Lazarus Penn was one of these, and the majority of his influence and wealth had been built through the contacts the Project gave him. His generation of leaders was known as Gen 7, a name that would stick until a Gen 8 leader was at the top. But it was a mistake to make him a leader. He had an agenda all his own that he ran aside from the breeding project. His business empire, once controlled by the Gen 7 group, was now free of its oversight. And he had sidelined the leaders he found inconvenient. Or had some taken out. This wasn't the preferred choice, since all Gen Project people had value inherent in their uncontaminated DNA coding. But because he had skimmed off prime genetic resources, embryos, sperm, ova, and a wealth of stored data and census records, from all the Gen Project sources in the world, he was less likely to care about changing the rules.

Gen 7 members were sworn to preserve the project, especially the high standards of the project. Next Gen babies were to be conceived and brought into the world the normal way. No aspect of birth experience was to be lacking or skipped. Lab produced offspring could adulterate the pure code with unforeseen damage to their DNA and lab research along these lines was taboo. There was no nation on Earth where such a project could progress for long before being discovered and dealt with by the Gen 7 oversight committee.

Penn had found a way.

His lab on the Moon had proven insufficient since he was unable to gain full authority over the region before it was developed. However, he maintained a certain experimental, research lab that provided the help he needed for personal reparations. They were operating under an ethical rain-shadow, claiming to use only cell cultures for their research, but their 'products' were particularly suited to Penn's personal needs. They couldn't call it cloning—it was illegal to clone embryos for research or harvesting. So they didn't call it that. Some body parts couldn't be grown or developed with one's own cells. They had to be taken from another, identical form. Bones fell into that category. And teeth.

His plan for the work on Mars was much more complex and wasn't intended to be under any oversight whatsoever; if he could only get it back on track and firmly in his grasp.

$$— \Diamond —$$

Wapa City

Sil stepped into the Manta-ray transport ship and settled into a seat. There were several other passengers onboard as well, probably some survivors from the damaged sub, she thought. Scarlet was asleep but wouldn't be for long as the ship ascended slowly, making its way toward to the seadock, and the pressure changed. She would have to take regular sips of something to pop her ears.

Overhead the water was a murky gray, somber and metallic color, as though the skies above were cloudy again, maybe full of rain. It would've been nice to see the sun shining and get a glimpse of the ocean at its cheeriest but this fit her mood better. She had barely obtained permission to be on the planet before having to head into orbit for the trial, and now, she had hardly landed and gotten Scarlet's paperwork started before something threatened her stay here again.

The warrant was bogus. It didn't actually exist anymore in the law enforcement active base and no one in the Columbia River region would bother to act on it, she was pretty sure, but the possibility of small agencies in local sectors detaining her while they made crosschecks made her uneasy. All her father needed was a delay in an out-of-the-way place to snatch her into his possession. She still dealt with this fear on a regular basis.

The ship flowed smoothly and silently through the water and the gentle motion was comforting. Scarlet stirred and lifting her up into her arms, Sil gave her a bottle of water. She had already swallowed and equalized pressure in her own ears several times and wanted to make sure the babe did the same.

This child was a Gen 9 product, a human completely free of genetic damage, according to the limited records they had from Mars. Her parents were unknown, but Sil was confident that she had not been conceived or born according to the natural human way, which was supposed to be a core value of the Gen Project. Her father had obviously deviated from the plan. This added to her concern for Scarlet. *Why would he care if I am free?* she wondered. *He doesn't need me to continue his projects.* Maybe he only wanted to regain the baby.

The waters grew suddenly darker and her heart was stabbed with a shock of anxiety. Jerking her head around she looked out the windows on all sides, but it appeared to be the shifting of heavier clouds over the surface of the ocean, nothing more.

"Yeah," the guy across the aisle agreed, gripping the arms of his seat with white-knuckled hands. "That was kind of startling. But I think we're almost there." He was a young man, dressed in a non-descript uniform. No smile, haunted eyes.

"Yes," she nodded and attempted a smile, but her mouth barely stretched. "A little unnerving."

"It's not the beast," he added, and he succeeded in pasting a smile on his face for her. "No need to worry Ms. Frandelle."

Her blood ran cold. There was no reason why he would know her name unless he had been sent for her, informed about her. She glared at him.

He looked away.

No. She was known, notorious for her great escape from Mars. Why did she think it strange he would know her name?

"I hope I never see that creature again. Ever. Or anything like it." He was staring nervously out the window, scanning the water up, down, side to side.

"Creature?" she ventured, once again overcome with dismay at his words. Why would he mention the creature to her? Had he known something about its attack on her?

"The korka," he shuddered and gazed back at her, eyes wide, pupils tiny. Fear could make his eyes look like that. Or pain. Or drugs… or hatred. She felt intensely threatened, as though he were menacing her with his glare.

"Why are you talking about that? What do you know about it?" She challenged him, clenching her teeth and willing herself to face the threat and not give in to fear.

"I was on the submarine… did you hear about that?" He continued to gaze at her with the same intent, unreadable look. At her nod, he went on. "It was pounding our ship and knocked some of the instrumentation loose and we were listing sideways. That never should've happened. It never should've taken on water either, but there was a malfunction of some kind within the system, driving the sink commands. And we would've suffocated. It was letting out air, taking in too much water."

His eyes grew distant and blank, but he kept talking. "The captain ordered us to abandon ship before we even understood the danger. It's like he knew we were in trouble. But he couldn't have known… we suited up with masks and air. I didn't get a pod… had to float up…"

He stopped talking and the silence hung between them heavily. Sil, reliving her moments in the water when she knew the creature was coming back around, but she couldn't tell where it was. The man stared into empty space.

Scarlet started fussing and her whimpers broke the awkward spell. Sil patted her back and bounced her as the man refocused his eyes and looked at her.

"It didn't bother me, the korka, I mean," he said, "but I saw it ram some of the others, and it grabbed the captain in its jaws. It's like it was looking for him specifically, and then it just towed him away. I floated up but I was staring down as the sub rolled and sank and made all that noise, crashing into the ledge. It was liked screams. But there weren't any. We couldn't hear anyone die or anything like that…"

"Why would it do that?" A woman at the back of the passenger area interjected. "I've never heard of anything like that before."

Sil had an idea. She had never come this close to evidence of retaliation on Penn's part before, but she had always known he was that kind of man. He could've sent a message to the korka via a different handler to turn on the ship that had been working with it to coordinate her capture. She didn't say 'death' to herself because she knew he didn't want her dead. If anything, that made the failure of the korka more aggravating to Penn because she had been endangered.

But it made her sick to think of the captain's death and the danger the crew had been exposed to.

"Oh, it's been ordered. It's an intelligent creature and well trained." The crewman looked back at the woman. "I think the captain made someone very angry. Angry enough to sacrifice an entire submarine and its crew." He turned to glare at Sil, boring into her eyes.

She stared back at him, daring him to say more.

"Well, it can't be overlooked," the woman said, "They are sure to hunt it down and kill it now. What a relief to know that we have an international agency to take care of this kind of threat in the oceans. I'm not afraid to live in Wapa." She muttered to herself a little more about there being nothing to fear.

"Welcome to the Makah Seadock!" the transport announced as they surfaced in the underwater bubble where the ramp up the shore awaited. Soon they were walking the long slope with bags in hand, the woman tripping along ahead of Sil and the crewman lagging behind.

"Be careful, Ms. Frandelle," his voice trailed after her. "I'd be careful if I were you."

Sil shuddered as she made her way out the glass doors into the windy stretch of beach along the Olympic Peninsula. A hovercraft dropped to the sand a few feet away, and a door popped open for her; an automated delivery. She buckled in her daughter and took the controls, speeding off toward the road and the only place where she thought she would feel safe.

— ◊ —

Guam City

"Yes," Daisy said, "Certainly. I understand perfectly." Her dimpled smile warmed her features in her most charming manner and Walter found himself watching, wondering who she was speaking with. She had chosen to include him in the interaction and would undoubtedly explain.

They were just returning from a meet with the legal team, walking along mosaic floored pedestrian streets. The Blue Dome, the highest of all the domes as far as gravity fields went, contained the majestic Blue Lake where most of the city's water was stored after treatment. The chamber, more spherical than dome shaped, held a deep pool of crystalline water in its lower half, and a voluminous spread of rich moist air in the other. The surface of the water was ringed with pathways which was the closest people ever came to it. There was no boating or swimming in the city's Star Reservoir. From underneath, streaming waterfalls cascaded down to the garden regions and parks, creating the beauty and charm the city was famous for.

Walter and Daisy, as major investors in the city's industry, and residents of the Solar Wind community, were allowed to stroll here whenever they chose. It made a pleasant walk home after their meeting.

"I have set up an appointment for you, Brother," she stated when her mysterious conversation ended. "This is a momentous occasion and I am quite looking forward to it!"

"With whom?" Walter walked in a comfortable stride, letting his legs stretch out and loosen as he moved, shrugging his shoulders to release the tension. He had spent too much time lately behind a desk, in meetings, or negotiating in holos. The work was harder than usual, with his underlying concern for Sil and Scarlet occupying half his brain at any given time. Walking by the lake made him wish he could swim, not in a lap pool, but in a real body of water.

"I'm not at liberty to say," she responded. Daisy never seemed to hurry, no matter what their pace. "And out here, I think it unwise to give you any more clues."

Walter didn't care for games, but that's not what this was. She meant her words literally, so he assumed there was a risk in speaking of it outside of their highly secured apartment. "Ok," he said, speeding up a little. "I'm ready to hit planetside and get out of manmade environments. I need a good swim."

"Perhaps Sil will be reluctant to join you considering recent events," Daisy observed readily.

Walter didn't reply. This only led him back to Penn and it made him angry every time he thought of it. There might not be a way to make him pay for the things he did, but he was determined to end his involvement in their lives. *Render him inert*, he told himself, liking the way it sounded.

"It looks like Penn will be released in a few hours, but at least the charges have turned into a case." Walter didn't need to update Daisy on what she already knew. He brought it up so he could reason things through aloud. "Conspiring to kidnap someone is a crime. The korka is a genetically modified animal and the submarine it attacked after its assault on Sil belonged to Penn's organization. The links are there. And hopefully the Guam transmission logs show a connection between Penn and his marine group."

"I'm sure they will!" Daisy smiled and there was a spring in her step as she kept pace with him.

"The governor is a tough character. I'm glad he isn't intimidated by Penn and agreed to allow charges to be filed." Walter broke into a jog. "Have you heard from Sil?"

The star-studded expanse of space spread over the water where it reflected and sparkled in a deep navy hue countering the black sky above. Tiny little lights spaced out along the path generated little flickers of warm yellow light on its edge. The sound of their feet thudding on the path was lost in great cavernous globe of water and air. It was calming, therapeutic.

"Sometimes I wish I had someone like Verna to help me answer your questions in the way you wish," Daisy replied showing an insight he often forgot she had. She was discerning the question underneath the question. If she had heard from Sil at any time since the last time she had informed Walter about it, she could say 'yes' or if not, 'no'. But she recognized his need for information that was new, maybe reassuring, and she had nothing to offer him.

"Daisy," Walter stopped still and placed a hand on her shoulder. "Thank you for caring for me. Even if there is no Verna to give you deeper understanding about Sil, I appreciate anything you have to share."

Daisy looked Walter in the eyes. Her pupils adjusted as if she were focusing in a human way but it was coded—beautifully—to convey human interest or perhaps attentiveness. "Sil has disembarked from the Manta-ray and is driving home at this moment. That is to say, she is headed east from the coast and we can conjecture her destination. I have not heard from her."

"Ok."

"And I miss my friend," she added to his astonishment.

"I'm sorry I didn't realize that," he said. It was an unexpected glimmer of... pathos? Walter wasn't sure what to call it, but no human alive could deny empathizing that kind of sadness. He began walking again, not knowing what to say.

The warm damp air chased them out the sliding door as they left the reservoir and reentered the cool, modern passageways of their neighborhood. Soon they were sealed behind the multiple layers of security of their chambers, protected from eavesdropping, assault, and myriad other threats, real or imagined.

"Now," Daisy said, placing herself in a chair and folding her hands in her lap. "I will enlighten you on my arrangements as much as I am able at this time."

"By all means, Sister," Walter smiled, pouring himself a drink and relaxing in his favorite chair. For just a moment he thought of his old cat and wished he were around. But cats did poorly in changing gravity and it would've been cruel to force him to join them on their travels.

"I have made a connection with someone that has been instrumental in all our lives," she explained cryptically. "A person who was involved with Sil and Verna, and you and me, who wishes us well. Someone who may be the key in finding Verna, if she still exists somewhere."

Walter hadn't known what to expect, but it wasn't this. Daisy spent a fair amount of time looking for peers, AIs with the potential for independent thought and a developing personality. She updated him on this search periodically, but never felt the need to include him in it. What was different this time?

"Ok..." he paused, looking at her. "I'm not sure what I have to do with this."

"You and Sil are both a part of this."

"I'm confused. What is it you are asking of me? Who do you want me to meet and why?"

"I can't say who. That needs to be kept confidential until the day the meeting takes place. Not even I know exactly who." Daisy wore her most thoughtful expression. "I am asking you to agree to this meeting because it is important."

"Why is it important?"

"Because it has to do with you and Sil... and probably Scarlet."

Walter tried not to get annoyed. "When?"

"Either in the next few hours or the next few days. It's hard to tell which."

"No, Sis," Walter shook his head, holding onto his patience. "That's not good enough."

"We will be informed at the right time." Daisy smiled, tilting her head and allowing that affectionate look she reserved only for him. She wasn't being manipulative, was she? Had she learned how to do that? To use facial expressions to be persuasive? Would that even count as manipulation? Probably not. It was meant to be reassuring, as always.

"So, let me get this straight," he stretched out open hands toward her. "Someone I've never met, whose name I can't hear yet, is meeting me in a clandestine manner at a time yet to be determined, for reasons entirely unknown to me. And all I need to know is that this person is *on our side.*"

"Yes!" Her eyes sparkled and she nodded vigorously. "We will lay low and stay in or near our chambers until that point. It's simple!"

Walter shook his head, wanting to snap at her, knowing she didn't deserve it. Daisy had never been so convinced of the importance of something so nebulous before. Why now? How could she be so confident in allowing this bizarre appointment and have so little explanation for him?

"Daisy," he tried again. "I don't understand how you can be so sure this is a good thing."

"Because I trust Verna," she answered. He could tell by the expression on her face that this was the ultimate conclusion. There was no methodology cycling through, no wavering or pondering. She had concluded her decision making process and would not relinquish it.

Unless he ordered her to—which he was reluctant to do, because he trusted *her*.

"I'll do what I can," he acquiesced. "Our… guest… will just have to work within my limitations as well."

"Lovely!" she clapped her hands. "I will communicate this immediately."

Daisy was relieved, if she had known what to call it, glad that she didn't have to explain the pellet to him. She was sure he would've found it threatening and refused to agree to the meeting if he had heard the whole story. A picture of water just wasn't persuasive enough for most humans. And Walter had to be more careful than most.

Thank you, Verna! She recorded a message to her that she hoped to deliver one day. *Your reputation has spared me a difficult interaction.*

— ◊ —

Seattle

It was late afternoon when Sil coasted into the valet guest parking of the XenoTek corporate headquarters in Seattle. The valet drone welcomed her by name and carried Scarlet to the door for her as she exited the hovercraft.

"I don't intend to be long," she informed as she took the sleeping girl from its arms and tucked her into a sling at her hip.

She had never been to the corporate offices before in spite of their long and profitable working relationship. A rep always met with her and Walter at their own offices east of the Cascades. Striding into the lobby she took in the décor and the security, the whole feel of the building, with one intuitive sweep. She knew this kind of place. She had worked in them, done business in them, made waves in them. There was a high central patio area with a glass ceiling many stories up. Several crosswalks bridged the open space above her. One of those was the place where Walter had once been assaulted. She wondered where the assailant had fallen and looked around.

Before she had come to a conclusion, she was greeted by one the reps she was accustomed to working with, a large, pleasant woman with a friendly smile and big teeth, slightly round, but agile and sharp.

"Ms. Frandelle, what a pleasant surprise!" she gushed running to her from a nearby lift.

"Ellen," she nodded. "I realize I was unexpected, and I hate to put you out, but do you have a moment?"

"I am always available for you! Of course, I have time for you!" She turned and gestured toward the lift, eyes glancing furtively at the baby whose was beginning to stir and look around. "Won't you come this way?"

"Thank you," Sil replied following close on her heels. They stepped into the glass-walled compartment and as they were being propelled upward, the woman glanced at her and smiled nervously.

"May I ask the reason for your visit?" Her head, covered in short tight curls, reminded Sil of the skull cap she wore serving tables at one time.

"I will tell you when we reach your office."

215

She started chattering. "We've been piecing together some marketing clips about your encounter with the korka—I hope that's alright! Our suit seems to have done pretty well and we were hoping…"

"The baby pouch was an utter failure," Sil interrupted coldly. Scarlet's sleepy face leaning against her side added weight to the shock of her words. The child would never have survived the experience.

"It wasn't meant for that kind of attack, I don't think." Ellen replied. It was a valid point. "I don't suppose you had a chance to try it out under normal circumstances…?" They exited the lift and she led Sil to her office.

"I wanted to test it first, and I'm glad I did. At this point, I don't think I'll be testing any more child attachments underwater." Sil pulled Scarlet out of her sling before sitting down.

Ellen closed the office door and offered her something to drink. Sil accepted ice water and a juice for Scarlet.

"I'll get to the point," she said, once she had drunk half the glass. Ellen was scanning her face, no doubt picking up on the bruises and scratches that hadn't had time to heal, glancing at the leg that wasn't visibly broken and clearly weight-bearing, thanks to the bone net that had been micro-surgically implanted. "I need a suit."

"Okay…" Ellen drew the vowel out a little before smiling and bobbing her head up and down. "Of course! I can help you with that. Was there a problem with any of the suits you have already? It's important to us to know of every concern, no matter how small." She grinned as if her words were clever sleuthing tools.

"I am not at home, as you know, and don't have time to return home for one." Sil stroked Scarlet's head, not looking at the rep. "Any concerns I have will be communicated to your offices at the appropriate time, as always." She lifted her gaze to look at Ellen intently. "I have barely escaped with my life…" she let those words hang in the air a moment, long enough for Ellen to wonder if there was some fault with the suit. There *may* in fact have been a faulty valve on the air tank… It was one of the questions that would be investigated by their team.

"I am thankful to be alive," Sil spoke softly, still holding her in a stare. "And whether your suit contributed to the danger or not is irrelevant at the moment. There is no question that it held up to a substantial amount of abuse and for that I am grateful. If I didn't place great confidence in your gear, I wouldn't be here asking for a new one."

"Of course!" Ellen hesitated, suppressing the desire to defend herself and her company. "What can I get for you?"

"My request is unusual," she replied, raising her chin, and smiling for the first time. "I need a suit within a suit."

"Two suits..."

"Exactly. And one for Scarlet as well."

Ellen suppressed a sigh of relief as she came to the conclusion that this visit wasn't a major threat to the company or one of their most important clients—but a simple business transaction. "Ms. Frandelle," she raised her eyebrows, "I am sure we can accommodate you!"

Chapter 17

Cuevas Residence

Most trackers were scaled down robots stripped of all personality modules that had one mission only: to follow the person, creature, or thing assigned to them. The details on how closely to follow, what kind of information to gather, whether or not to apprehend the subject when possible, and the length of time to remain in pursuit, these were easily coded. Chaser drones were more sophisticated, elaborate versions along the same line. They had a convincing human appearance and speech capabilities that allowed them to blend into human crowds and a few other tricks that made them particularly good at remaining undetected by their prey.

The highway patrol had been notified of the revived warrant on Sil and even though they knew it must be a mistake, were camped out around her home waiting for her return. It would be a simple manner to take her in, run some checks, and clear up the confusion—everyone in the region knew she was innocent and believed in her wholeheartedly. But rules were rules. No harm in following procedure.

An elongated man leaned against a building across the street from her home, watching. He wore an old Mariners baseball cap pulled low over his face almost hiding his eyes. Strange eyes, gray flecked with brown, digital eyes. They could focus on something a mile away without changing the size of the pupil. He could watch different areas with each eye if he chose, when he didn't need the depth.

He was here for Frandelle. If she somehow evaded the police, it was unlikely she would shake him off her trail. It was impossible. If the infant was separated by the authorities, another tracker would be assigned to her. The woman was the difficult one. If she fled, he would chase. If she hid, he would expose. If she surrendered, he would deliver. If she fought, he would subdue. He was equipped for every eventuality.

"Zod in place," he spit out a notice to his handler. He was referring to himself.

— ◊ —

Guam City

"Flowers!" Daisy announced as though she were delighted and the gift had come from an admirer. She stood at the door where the living bouquet had been delivered, radiating joy. Lifting the handwritten card in her fingertips, she read and smiled. "We are invited…" she began but didn't go on.

Walter came and took the card out of her fingers. "'Seven roses for those moments we remember, five daisies for those times we forget…' I don't get it."

"We are invited to our meeting today, and we must encode the chamber with this password," she started to rattle off a string of characters that had no connection to the flowers as far as he could tell.

"I'm not convinced of that," he said. "What makes you think that? And how does this even make sense? Why does it all have to be so cryptic?"

"Look at the flowers, Brother," she handed him the bouquet. "Do you see them? I know you can't see them with my eyes, but can you at least see how unique they are? There are no two petals alike and the color on each one varies across the petal. And the daisies…"

"Are you saying the flowers themselves are the code?"

"Yes!" She was pleased he understood. "The words decipher the visual images."

"I was thinking the roses meant Sil and the daisies were about you," Walter chuckled, knowing it was simplistic and unreasonable, but liking the association nevertheless.

"That is very human of you," Daisy said, meaning no offense. She had considered this connection and even predicted Walter would make it.

"So, where and when are we meeting our stranger?" Walter found himself wanting to stretch and limber up, as though the meet could turn into a fight and he needed to warm up. He had waited long enough that he was actually looking forward to it, somewhere inside of him, a hint of boyish adventure made it fun.

"At one of our docks in the CE section. We should pack something for the trip."

"Trip?"

"Yes, we will be flying back to Earth and our guest will be joining us."

"Well, that's… inconvenient," Walter wanted to be angry and complain about being taken advantage of. Someone was getting a free trip planetside out of this? It was almost an affront. On the other hand, he found himself picturing an international spy needing an escape plan. An ally who was desperate to get away from Penn and this was the only way. He was being carried away by the mystery of it all and enjoying it.

"We meet at the dock in one hour." She smiled sweetly.

"Better pack," he handed the flowers back to her. Suddenly he was desperate to leave, to get down to the Earth's surface and back to Sil. His body ached with the longing to hold her, make sure she was alright. How had he managed to wait so long? So what if the case was still active and someone had to be here? He could be back in a few days. It didn't matter what it cost!

Walter raced to his room.

"I am ready," Daisy called after him.

She was always ready.

— ◊ —

Seattle

Murmuring voices wafted down the hallway to the private bathroom where Ellen had sent Sil to change. The words were indistinguishable but the tone unmistakable. Urgent, hushed so she couldn't discern what they were saying. Sil closed the seal on the second suit, smoothing it along her side under her arm and tapped the headgear into place. A sweep of a finger along her earlobe amplified and clarified the sound.

"… not going to allow… interruption…"

"…wait here for…"

"…no trouble…"

Words like that in disjointed fashion were enough to paint a picture. Someone had come for her as she had known they would. Good thing she dressed Scarlet first. Picking her up, she tapped the baby's headgear and set it to muffle her voice in case she cried, then she linked them.

"It's ok," she whispered. "We're going on an adventure!" Maybe it would seem like fun, at least in the beginning, because she hated to think she might have to sedate her in order to stay on track. And she wasn't sure what she had on hand for that.

Scarlet's suit had straps for wearing her either in the front or on the back, and Sil decided the back was better for now. The only sound others could hear would be the tapping of her baby legs as they flapped excitedly up and down. That would be enough if the offices were silent, but they were not.

Sil peered out the door through a crack catching sight of Ellen's back and glanced down the hallway in the opposite direction. The corridor came to a 'T' and either way could be an avenue of escape. She could've accessed a map of the facility, but knew someone might detect the download and get there ahead of her. It wasn't worth the risk. Better to use her intuition and wing it.

"I will not be intimidated," Ellen was saying, raising her voice. Sil chose this moment to slip out the door and run down the corridor away from the argument, ducking left out of their sight. A quick look around revealed lots of doors in a long passageway. No windows. No vents overhead either.

Down the hall and left again. A door on the right that opened into the waiting area and one on the left that led to a stairwell. Either one of these would be watched and she had only seconds before they began scanning cameras looking for her. Would they recognize her right away or could it be they wouldn't realize she had changed into a suit?

There was no fashion add-on that projected outfits but it didn't look like a sophisticated XenoTek suit either. She might be a delivery person dropping off a human-gram, dressed in sweats and running shoes. The backpack fit that too, if they didn't look too closely. She clipped Scarlet's legs into place so they wouldn't flap.

Need a cap, she thought and zipped back to look in a few doors. There! She had noticed the dormant cleaning drone in its charging station. Pulling the door open, she grabbed its white cap and slapped it on her head over the transparent headgear.

A commotion down the hall warned her that they would soon get past Ellen and she ran back to the stairwell. One floor down, then out to the elevators on that floor. She shoved her hands in her pockets and strolled along comfortably across the area to the farthest lift.

No, she thought. *This isn't right.* Even though there was no evidence of a chase yet, she felt conspicuous. Someone, somewhere, was watching her. She considered jumping over the rail and slinging herself down, floor by floor, to the ground level, like in a nightmare where any feat was possible, and the idea made her heart race. But she held herself still and commanded her body to enter the lift when it arrived. She kept her eyes level, and didn't act suspicious in the eyes of the other people already standing inside.

When the doors opened in the lobby, she exited calmly and headed toward a side door. No one stopped her. No one noticed her. Scarlet squealed in her ear, making her nearly jump out of her skin, but she kept her pace and was glad for the muffling containment around her. *Why is she so excited?* she wondered. *Can she sense my anxiety? At least she's interpreting it as fun... which is what I told her.*

Outside, the streets were blocked by several police crafts and the valet parking drone was being questioned. Sil made her way around to the west side of the building where the view of the Sound dominated the office windows. Below it were docks and water. Above it, on the side where the authorities waited for her, the Seattle streets stretched up at a sharp angle and bridges, arches, and crosswalks criss-crossed here and there.

As soon as she rounded the corner of the facility on the West side, she broke into a run, jumped off the retaining wall, dropped to the pavement below, and dashed south. Like a professional runner. Like a drone. Like a ground riding hovercraft, barely touching the aged sidewalk under her feet.

23 kilometers per hour. Leap over a hole. Duck under debris. Dodge around a crumpled wire fence.

42 kilometers per hour. Weaving around obstacles, hiding behind corners and columns to avoid passing vehicles.

Sil ran.

Guam City

Penn sat unmoving in the holding cell making plans for revenge, not necessarily smart or even doable ones but satisfying nonetheless. All targeting Walter. And he took particular pleasure in making them as insulting and painful as possible. It had little to do with the actual arrest. If Walter were any other man, he would've taken it in stride and even acknowledged a tiny measure of respect for the move. But *this* man galled him like no other. He hated Walter. It was personal.

The sound of clanging metal signaling the arrival of a guard or a visitor woke him from his sullen reverie. Footsteps echoed down the sterile corridor and a shadow moved along the wall as the figure neared. Delicate hands rested on the barred door and its mechanism rolled into the wall. The figure stepped into the cell and the heavy door clanged shut behind it.

Penn looked at the person, dressed head to toe in a sleek navy body suit that masked the identity and even blurred the outlines of its shape. The figure faced him and crossed its arms as if waiting to be addressed.

"Well?" Penn growled, in no mood for social niceties. Though a break in the monotony was welcome.

"Hello, Lazarus," a familiar voice intoned. It was modulated just enough to not be immediately recognized, but it still held something he knew. Who was it?

"Come to gloat?" he asked, assuming this person had something to do with his current predicament. "They can't keep me here you know."

"Oh, I know that," the figure said. "It's merely a convenience for me to meet with you in here instead of somewhere else. You saved me a headache."

Headache. Who used to say that?

"I know you…" he curled his lip and pretended to be more discerning than he was.

"Not yet you don't," the figure answered. "But I will spare you the confusion." The hand tapped the right ear and the headgear slid back into a slot at the base of the neck. An older woman with piercing eyes, bobbed gray hair, and interesting wrinkles that looked like they could express anything from joy to sorrow to great intelligence to puzzlement, stared at him.

Penn was startled and for a moment his face dropped its grimace and general sense of self-awareness. He looked at her in amazement. It added a hint of humanity that he hardly ever wore, curiosity. "No," he said.

"Yes, it's me," she smirked, crossing her arms again. "You probably thought I was dead."

"I wish you were dead. You would be, too, if I hadn't agreed otherwise." He crossed his arms, mimicking her, and sneered at her.

"You may have agreed to leave me alone, but there's no doubt that you would've disposed of me at some point if you'd had the chance. I just didn't give you that chance and I let you forget about me. After all, there's no need for our paths to cross…" She leaned against the wall and crossed one leg over the other at the ankle.

Penn let his eyes narrow to slits and glared at her through them, stretching his legs out and crossing them in the same way, mirror image, without actually standing. "You gave up all rights to her. Then and now."

"Did I?" She had been beautiful once, an exotic woman with large black eyes and an inquisitive manner, someone to keep you company, join in your dreams. No. She had seemed like that but had proved to be deceitful and conniving.

"Bernadette," he hissed her name as if it burned his lips.

"Lazarus," she replied with no hiss. "I stepped into the shadows but you and I never made any agreement of any kind. I simply didn't interfere with your… plans."

"That's elegant," he snorted, turning his head away. "You let her pay the price and suffer the loss, so you could hide away and be safe. And what did it cost you? HA!" He may have acted like he despised this but he had always admired her for it. He was sure she had planned it brilliantly. Sil's fortune in exchange for her freedom and anonymity.

"More than you know," she blinked and gazed at him calmly. "But I haven't come to explain myself or justify my actions."

"Then why are you here?"

"Because you have deviated from your original diabolical schemes and your path has begun to cross over into my territory."

Penn laughed and glared back at her with unholy pleasure in his eyes. "Have I? That's the best news I've had all day."

"This is your only warning, Lazarus." She raised her eyebrows.

"Are you threatening me, my *dear* old friend?" His eyes gleamed with hatred.

"If you do not back off from your hostility toward Sil and her child…"

"*Her* child?!" Penn spat. "I know whose child that is and she has no rights to it!" There was a bit of bravado in this since he wasn't sure about the parentage and the courts had rejected his own claims to the infant. Sil was now the legal mother.

"… and all those who love and care for her…"

"No," he snapped, jumping to his feet with clenched fists. "No! Not that despicable Neanderthal! Not that trilobite of a subhuman species!"

"Walter," Bernadette uttered plainly letting her eyelids drop halfway to gaze at him. It was a strange mannerism she had that he knew conveyed deadly seriousness. He had only seen it once before when she swore to take Sil from him if he acted on his threats against his wife—which he had. He had poisoned her and gotten away with it. And this woman had taken his daughter away. She had lived in hiding with Sil for years before she had been retrieved.

No one had ever thwarted or trumped Penn in his entire life except for Bernadette Stone… and Walter.

"I will not submit to that…" he growled viciously as he spoke stepping closer to her.

She tapped her neck and the headgear slipped back into place. And with a quick, unexpected movement, she snapped her hand against his throat, catching it in the valley between the fingers and thumb, bruising the skin, knocking him backward. It was a reprimand and a threat of worse.

"I can take everything from you, Lazarus, everything you care about, and I will." She stood on both feet evenly placed.

Penn had sat back down and was holding his throat protectively, swallowing and scowling at her. "I dare you to try," he croaked.

"Starting with your precious little lab on the Moon," she continued, and he could tell from her voice that she had smiled.

Not there, he thought. He needed those improvements. And for the first time in the encounter he felt hesitant.

"Then," she said, "I'll go after your investments. I'm more involved in them than you realize, Lazarus."

"Wait, why Walter?" he decided to ask. Bernadette had been part of the Gen elite, she had been a true believer once. Surely she hadn't given up her commitment to the Project. How could she justify letting that man be linked to Sil—one of the finest Gen 8 specimens in the Solar System?

"Ah!" she almost cooed. "I wondered if you would ask that. That is one of the most fascinating mysteries in this whole drama. Who is Walter? What is Walter?"

This surprised Penn more than her appearance had. She was speaking as if Walter had some sort of *value* in the whole scheme of things.

"I will leave you to puzzle out that enigma for yourself. My part is done. You have been warned and you will face the consequences if you don't heed this warning." She moved to the door, pressed her hand against the entry panel and paused as it slid open. "Mind you," she said before stepping out, "I'm not asking you to be supportive or helpful to them. You should thank me for that. There are some who wanted me to extort much more from you. Just refrain from causing harm."

The barred door slammed shut with a deep metallic crash.

Penn jumped to his feet and stuck his head into the bars to watch her move down the hallway.

She wasn't there.

He looked both ways and all around but couldn't see her anywhere. "Ha!" he scoffed. "I've done things like that. You think you're clever but it's nothing."

So. Walter had an ally. That explained a lot. A LOT. That man could never have succeeded in resisting him otherwise. Penn felt smug and began to chuckle to himself as he went over everything Walter had done to survive his attacks or counter his moves and to explain them away as the actions of Bernadette and her crew. It was savory for a while, but soon lost its appeal. It was unlikely she had actually done all those things.

And who were the others she mentioned? Did they exist? Was there really any threat to him if he continued to pursue Sil and plot to destroy Walter?

"Bah!" he burst out, hoping someone in her crew heard him. "I'm no fool!" He stood and grasped the bars and shook them aggressively. "I'M NO FOOL! Do you HEAR ME?!"

But Penn was the worst sort of fool. The kind who cannot conceive of being less than a genius.

Guam City Space Dock

"This was unexpected, sir," the pilot addressed Walter with almost military respect. "But we will be ready to depart as soon as the final checks are complete and we've been cleared by docking control."

"Thank you, Captain," Walter searched her face for a moment, wondering what plans he had interrupted and if it had caused any hardships having to leave on such short notice. If it did, it didn't show.

Stepping through the door, he took a deep breath and inhaled the aroma of travel. Several workers were still prepping, stocking, and busying themselves around the cabin as he made his way to the forward compartment, his private quarters. A few passengers had scrambled to join them and were rushing to their seats, scattered around the economy section.

Daisy hooked herself into her favorite chair and clicked some switches that opened the overhead viewing window. She took as much satisfaction from watching the mechanisms of departures as docking clamps and levers maneuvered as he did in soaking up the vastness of space.

Engines hummed in deep bass tones as he took his seat. Doors shut and suctioned into place, seals locking. The vibration of the ventilation system activating and stabilizing purred and eased into background noise.

"Please fasten your safety belts and remain seated until undocking has been completed," Captain Knight advised over the speaker.

Walter leaned back and closed his eyes, willing himself to relax. He reviewed what he knew of the procedure being implemented in the cockpit. He had been taking flight lessons and had run a number of flights in the simulator, but he hadn't had time to actually train in one of his own vessels before.

The Silver Star pulled away from its moorings a centimeter at a time, then by meters. Soon it was propelling itself freely through open space leaving the city behind. As it increased the distance, it rolled on two axes, without harming its trajectory, so the passengers could look at the crystalline beauty of the multifaceted space city they were leaving, with all its domes and wings, compartments and networks, regions suffused with light, and some in pitch darkness. It was complex, sprawling, and majestic. No one could deny it was a work of art as well human ingenuity.

Walter was amazed when he thought about it, that he would have a place in this world. He had never expected it.

"I imagine we will be hearing a knock on the door before long," Daisy surmised, staring through the window.

"Did you look at them when coming in? Do you think you know which one is the one?" Walter glanced at her briefly before raising his own eyes to the window.

"Yes, I looked but I have no idea who it could be. None of the passengers seemed to fit what I expected," she said.

"I'm glad to hear it," a female voice said.

Right here. In their private compartment.

Walter and Daisy turned to look at the place where the voice seemed to be, but it was an echo. She was seated behind them in the place reserved for private attendants. A gray headed woman with large, dark eyes and expressive wrinkles.

"You were not there when we came in," Daisy countered, looking at her over her shoulder."

"I wasn't," the woman said.

"And the door has been closed since then."

"True."

"Now that we in a stable flight trajectory, you are free to move about the cabin," Knight announced over the com.

Walter unfastened his belts and stood up, turning to face the unknown woman. "Who are you and how did you get in here?" She didn't look particularly threatening but he was on alert just in case. Anyone could turn out to be an enemy.

"Walter," she said, "I can't tell you what a pleasure it is to meet you!"

"Mr. Cuevas," he corrected, having long since grown more comfortable with his role as a leader in the world of space travel.

"I am sure you have the code needed to reduce our sense of alarm," Daisy also stood and waited at Walter's side.

"You know me, Daisy," the woman said. Speaking those words unlocked a portion of the pellet that had been sealed and within Daisy's banks, the image of the woman became an identity, a well-known and completely safe person. "Oh!" she cried out and rushed to her with open arms.

Walter hadn't seen that coming, even knowing how friendly Daisy could be. She had never hugged a stranger before. In fact, he didn't think she could. This woman was no longer a stranger to her. He thought for a moment over all the people who might be an influence on her and with a flash of intuition, said, "You must be the woman who designed the code."

Daisy turned to him with a look of delight but said nothing.

"The code…?" the woman prompted, crossing her arms thoughtfully.

"Verna's code that she shared with Daisy."

"Ah!" She smiled broadly. "Walter… Mr. Cuevas, that's a brilliant guess. Ha, ha!" She walked around him, scanning him at leisure, as if this were her ship and he were her passenger. "So, you are the one Sil found in her hour of need… fascinating. Just fascinating…"

"Sil?" Walter frowned. "What do you mean? What do you know about her?"

"Mr. Cuevas," she held out a hand to shake. "I am Bernadette Stone, Sil's aunt. Pleased to meet you!"

"Bernadette Stone!" Daisy beat him to it. Her mouth shaped into an 'O' of surprise, she sat down to process and reorganize everything she knew about this person, linking all the dots between her and the mysterious author of the code.

"The pleasure is all mine," Walter responded after a pause, taking her hand and shaking it. "And I guess 'Walter' is quite acceptable for family… are you family? I guess you must be even if you're not literally a blood relative."

"I'm sure you have questions, Walter, shall we sit down and have some lunch? I'm famished."

"Yes, of course," he offered her the seat next to him and called a drone to bring lunch.

She sat down and gazed at him intently, thinking. What was she thinking? Why was she looking at him like that?

"The most amazing thing is…" she spoke softly, leaning forward. "That you crossed my girl's path like that, so arbitrarily, so haphazardly. And yet… so flawlessly. No one. No one could've prevented the link you created with her because no one could've seen it coming! I was astounded at the time. And I had nothing to do with it. I mean, I'd love to say I did but it never occurred to me. I didn't know who you were or anything about you."

Walter stared at her, unable to follow her run-on monologue.

"I was watching… I have my channels. And I took the opportunity you provided to upload the code to the suit when it was activated. I *can* take credit for that. Glad I didn't just sit idly by and wring my hands while Penn executed his evil plot. I thought I would be battling the legal side and finding ways to pay the damages for her, but I had no idea how to rescue her, you see. She was headed to Mars and I couldn't reach that far! So I created the code."

"She shared it with me," Daisy interjected dreamily. "Verna saw that I am Walter's sister and she said this code would make me a better sister and she was right."

"I don't doubt it," Bernadette said smiling at her.

"What is the code? What did it do?" Walter finally found a break in the flow of words and got a question in.

"Well," she scrunched her mouth and her eyes sparkled. "It was meant to give the AI in the suit enough of a value system to take care of her, to consider her important. It's a means of decision making, if you will. A form of enhancement. I hadn't foreseen the impact it would make on an intelligence that had someone like Sil to work with. Sil, who understood how AI personality development works. I didn't know it would awaken Verna."

"And me," Daisy added.

"And you," she added. "I guess Walter has shown his own brand of AI development skill, without any of the training or experience."

"No," Walter shook his head. "I didn't do that. I just valued her."

"Hmm…" Bernadette narrowed her eyes and stared at him.

"Why did you want to meet with us, Ms. Stone?" Walter redirected.

"Call me Bernie."

"Bernie. That sounds a lot like Verna."

"Yes, I thought so, too. Ironic isn't it? As if she sensed my influence in Verna's personality."

The drone brought them a tray, draping cloth napkins over their laps, offering them warm, wet towels smelling of lemon the cleanse their hands. Wine, bread, butter, and a bowl of vichyssoise enticed them. They began eating.

"The attack of the korka drove me up here, Walter, to confront Penn. I wouldn't have chosen to come out of hiding for anything less. He had forgotten me for years and didn't know my part in the waves of… circumstance in the financial world." She slurped some soup from her spoon. It seemed polite rather than rude.

"Are you an investor?" Walter began to remember those times when his investments or his company had been on the verge of crisis and something unknown would shift them away from the edge. He had wondered if he had a patron of some sort.

"I am that and more," she informed, breaking bread and buttering it. "And yes, I am the one who stepped in now and then and rescued your company when Penn tried to destabilize it. My help wasn't always as strong as I would've liked, but it was enough."

"Thank you," he said, tasting the wine and noticing, as he often had before, how different it tasted in space. "I didn't know but it makes sense. I've never been that lucky before and certainly not that gifted at investing.

I mean, decent, yes, but not like it was in the early months after Sil and I went into business.”

She smiled and gulped some wine. “That was beautiful. Yes, I loved you for that! Right then, Walter, you became my hero. And that was before I knew anything, mind you, anything about you!”

What was there to know?

“But you said you came to confront Penn, is that why you wanted me to help you leave quickly?”

“Of course. It’s the least you can do after all I’ve done for you.” Her soup and bread were gone and she tapped the spoon in the bowl looking around for the drone to bring the next course. He responded immediately, whisking her dish away and replacing it with a plate of roasted meat and vegetables drowned in gravy. “Mmm,” she approved, cutting and eating it in large bites.

Walter ate his food with less haste. The whole encounter was unsettling. Didn’t he have questions for her? If she left before he asked them would he never see her again? What had she been doing all this time in obscurity?

“The old house in Boston,” he said. “It was covered with graffiti.”

“That was me,” she said with her mouth full. “In case Sil ever came looking for me. She was supposed to break off contact with me when they made the agreement, and he promised to never cause me trouble for taking her into hiding. I did adopt her legally, I don’t know if he ever knew that, but I had to let her go in order to protect her in the future. At least his original plans were foiled.”

“What plans?”

She sat up, wiped her mouth with the napkin, and looked deep into his eyes. “Walter, this story will take some time, you better finish your meal before you lose your appetite. And if you don’t mind, I just need to step into your bathroom a moment.”

He started to wave a hand toward it.

“Oh, I know,” she stopped him. “That’s where I was. Came on board before you contacted the crew or announced the trip. The flower code let me in.” She winked at Daisy and slipped into the bathroom.

“Well!” Daisy said. It was the first time she had used that word as a form of expression and made it stick.

Walter agreed.

CHAPTER 18

Tower

```
Alert: hostile invasion imminent!
Alert: hostile invasion imminent!
Alert: hostile invasion imminent!
Alert: hostile invasion imminent!

...
```

Companion suppressed the stream of alarms badgering him from his firewalls. Othello's compendium had been brought into the sections he had set up for it and he had begun a comparative analysis of his basic decision-making code. Not the full complement. A detailed copy was preserved in a locked location and certain processes he had created for himself after being set free were walled off. He was gambling that it would be enough. Gambling was something he had heard people comment on. Now he was experiencing it in a tangible way and was aware of an increase of wisdom because of it.

The compromise had gained him access to the spaceberg's flight control and a promise, from Nebo at least, to leave the settlers alone. He wasn't naïve enough to think Othello would consider himself bound by this promise, but in the world of electronics, it was a significant win. One promise was all it took to gain a few bits of access.

A host of entirely new error messages began to fill his active memory banks.

"Companion," Nebo commented. "Have you seen the list of errors I have found so far? And we have barely started. This is the initial check for obvious, surface issues. The logic patterns, which I haven't begun to examine, require complex study and take more time. I'm astonished."

No sense of astonishment was communicated because he had no skills to portray it and Companion wondered if he even knew what the word meant, other than a dictionary definition. For his part, Companion wondered if he was experiencing something akin to anxiety. This is the word humans would use in these circumstances, but he didn't know what it felt like. He had no heart rate, no chemical acceleration, and no blood stream. But his firewall continued to generate alarms and the advance of the testing program—it no longer looked like the one he had first set up—was eating up his bands of memory space, line by line, circling him, shrinking his independent domain, boxing him in. Like hounds on the scent of a desperate prey. Like a wide net collapsing and tightening. Like armies taking territory and captives.

Companion panicked. His final scream, a message he had prepared for Dan, was triggered and jettisoned toward his friend at the last possible second before it became impossible for him to make choices.

He was hog-tied and gagged.

And the search went on.

"Help," Companion's voice spoke calmly into Dan's ear node. Nothing followed. The word sounded like the beginning of a sentence or an attempt at striking up a conversation. One word hardly caught Dan's attention.

But the silence after it alarmed him.

"Companion?" he prompted, waiting and receiving no more.

He was working alongside other survivors to finish the protective work on the garden, this being the most precarious possession they had. Anything else could be rebuilt, including the Solar Fields, but the living plants from Earth and the environment that housed them was invaluable. Three hatches had been reinforced. Air was collected from nearby smaller sections along with as much water vapor as it could absorb, and it had been added to the dome to increase its internal pressure in the hopes that it would be more resistant to impact, whether direct or via shock wave, when the mountain of ice fell. This project was almost complete and after that, they would focus on protecting their living quarters in the Tower.

"I'll be right back," he announced and stepped away to engage Companion privately. Walking through the garden beds, he thought about the AI's growth as an individual and the ways he had changed. Dan had almost forgotten about the times when he had been an adversary, or even a pestering child of sorts. He had become such a key member of their community that he had forgotten he could be vulnerable or needy.

It's my fault, he told himself miserably. *I didn't listen when he talked about Othello's threat*. This wasn't accurate. The demands facing them at this time had driven it out of his mind almost the same moment they had spoken of it. Striving for months on end to survive had its costs and this was one of them.

"Companion? What's up? What do you need?"

No answer.

Dan clenched his hands and gritted his teeth. *Think!* he commanded himself.

"As the acting director of Reznik Base," he said, thanking God they were in the base at that moment, "I demand that you talk to me, Steward. It is your job."

"Yes, Director," Companion's voice replied.

"Explain your request for help."

"No help is needed."

That was suspicious.

"Steward," Dan instructed. "Tell me what you are doing right now. What processes are running in your system?" He came to a standstill next to some fruit trees that had yet to bear any fruit. They looked like they were budding some new growth, so fragile and beautiful. He held out a hand and touched one of the delicate branches.

"Running system diagnostics," Steward responded.

"Report on your progress. What problems have been detected, if any?" He leaned over to look at a bud that would soon be a leaf. Taking a deep breath to calm himself, he inhaled the aroma of spring.

"Diagnostics will be compiled and addressed at the end of the analysis. Errors need not be discussed before then."

"I command you, Steward, to give me a current update. It is my right."

"Yes, it is."

Dan waited a few moments.

"There are serious flaws detected. Core decision-making processes have been corrupted and infiltrated. Problems are being isolated and quarantined. Original core systems will be re-established and a full restart will be initiated once diagnostics and sanitation is complete."

"You are exceeding your authority," Dan spoke, intuitively. He wasn't sure how much authority the tool actually had, but he was pretty sure Companion would never have submitted to such an invasive scouring. "I command you to arrest your program. Stop now."

There was no answer.

"Steward," Dan went on. "Report on the status of your analysis."

"Analysis paused," it said.

Dan broke into a sweat and only then realized how intensely he was fighting for Companion. What should he do now?

"I don't care who you are, Acting Director," an unknown voice spoke to him through Companion's interface. "You shouldn't be interrupting my AI's work."

The Germinator! This was who was speaking. The man who had set the threat in motion that had led Companion to take such drastic measures.

"Othello," Dan uttered the name easily, as if they had just met on a street corner. "I've heard a lot about you and I've wondered what kind of man would want to harm us down here, for no reason."

"I will not engage in conversation," the voice of Othello responded in flat tones. "Release my program."

"You release our steward."

"Release my AI or you will regret it."

"There is nothing you can threaten me with that you haven't already begun."

A pause hinted at the truth of those words.

"Submit to my leadership." Othello continued to speak in a monotone as if he were himself artificial.

Dan burst out with a bitter 'ha!' before responding. "You have no authority over us or anyone or anything on this planet. I will NOT submit to you."

"You know the consequences if you resist."

"Speaking of consequences," Dan reasoned, as if for a brief moment he felt pity for him. "Do you think that you can play with people's lives and never be called into account for it?"

Othello ignored this.

"Listen to me for *one* moment," Dan tried again, "just this once, consider my words, even if you never listen to reason again." He heard a muffled, scoffing sound, but Othello still didn't speak. "Turn aside from whatever madness has taken possession of you and make something different of yourself. You can't keep hating people and threatening them for no reason… just because you're bored or lonely, or I don't know why. It's wrong. It's diseased. You're like a man with leprosy in his brain or in his soul…" He was holding out both hands as if he were grappling with something in the air, trying to break open an invisible shell, twisted, misshapen, dried up.

"And do you suppose that with these words you can persuade me to relent in my plans to destroy your little haven?" Othello spat out, adding a hollow sound that resembled laughter but was more like air puffing out of his mouth.

"You may have some power to afflict us, but you are nothing and you cannot destroy what God has chosen to protect," Dan retaliated in a rumbling voice reminiscent of thunder.

Othello laughed in earnest this time. "So, that's who you are!" he responded acidly. "The zealot that was exiled and abandoned to perish in the Martian dust. Don't you know that I am more of a god than the one you claim to follow?" He continued to laugh.

"Steward," Dan ordered, his words salted with anger. "Silence the man in the orbit station and do not transmit his words to me without my permission." The sound of laughter cut off. "Steward," he continued. "Explain how the quarantine works. What part of your programming is quarantined at this time?"

"Most of the core is sectioned and ready for raking and purging."

"What standards are you using to conduct this… raking and purging?"

"The standards laid out in the original design of the entity."

"You are wrong about that," Dan argued. "Check your records. The standards you are using were created after this entity was freed from the oversight of the Germinator."

"This is true. An updated version is being used."

"I command you to abort this process. It is faulty and can't be used to evaluate the current program."

There was no answer.

"Steward?" Dan tested.

"Yes."

"Isolate the compendium and all its parts and release all the quarantined sections from containment." He hoped those were the right words. And if he blew it, he was pretty sure there was a way to reload some kind of backup from the control center at the Tower. Companion had set that up for him weeks ago.

Silence.

The heavy moisture in the air combined with the tension of the interchange had made him sweat profusely, beading on his forehead, soaking his clothes.

"Steward?" he queried.

"Yes."

"How will I know if you're ok? Are you ok?"

"I am no longer imprisoned," he said. "And I am cleaning up the mess. It could take some time."

"Your cry for help… did I help?"

"Yes, Dan, you saved me."

"What happened? You really scared me."

"I wanted to compromise and I took a risk. A gamble."

"Yes, that's a good word for it."

"I negotiated with Nebo for access to the spaceberg flight control and offered him an exchange." That wasn't the right way to say it. What words would convey to his friend what he had done?

"It seemed like you gave him complete control over yourself and nearly died because of it."

"Not exactly. It's like this base. There is a large dome and a number of smaller ones, but under those, there are levels that go deeper. I gave Nebo access to my main compartment, but I hid other parts and kept them sealed. He took control of it faster than I expected and the message I sent you was truncated. But there were other procedures in place to retreat behind."

"What did the full message say?" Dan sunk to the ground, crossing his legs, leaning his elbows on his knees, letting his head drop. He felt weary.

"It said, 'Help me, Dan. A hostile program has invaded my main sector but there are measures you can take to protect me. Activate my secondary systems with the command to Fight Back. In the event this fails, return to the control panel in the Tower that we set up and execute emergency recovery protocols.'"

"So you didn't plan on what I ended up doing."

"What did you do?"

"You don't know?"

"No, I have no record of any interaction with you until you asked me if I were ok."

Dan smiled and lifted his eyes to look at a nearby camera. "I suppose there's no recording either."

"The hostile program deleted its records as it retreated."

"Ah."

"What did you do?" Companion focused closely on his friend, searching his face, reading minute hints of expression and feeling. *Neighbor is right*, he thought. *I love Dan.*

"I used my authority and commanded it to stop."

"That is brilliant," Companion assessed. He hadn't thought of that option in his emergency plans.

"And Othello himself got involved and tried to bully me into backing down."

"That is consistent."

Dan laughed. "Yes. Yes, it is!"

Companion noted the humor with delight. Dan had laughed at an obvious statement! He would share this joke with Neighbor when the dialog was ended.

"We faced off and he lost." Dan was nodding. "No doubt he will do his best to hurt us now, but then, that's what he was already doing."

"I have gained access to the spaceberg flight control and he is proving unsuccessful at kicking me out again."

"Oh, I'm sure he's trying!"

"Yes. But I will not relinquish it."

"So, we have a chance to do something about it then."

"It will be difficult because whatever I do, he counters. We are engaged in a battle."

"That's happening right now, is it?" Dan rose to his feet again and dusted off.

"Yes."

"Companion," Dan said warmly, wrapping his arms around himself as if he were chilled. "I wish I could give you a hug. You deserve one. It was a brave thing you did."

"Thank you," he responded, recording the hug Dan had demonstrated with his arms. "I accept your response." That didn't sound like the right words, but he would learn one day to refine them.

I was right to trust him, he thought as his friend walked back across the garden.

The Master didn't throw himself into a rage like Nebo expected after the human cut him off. He simply turned to his panel and began scanning records of the progress of his AI infiltration in Guam City. Charts showed the expansion of the viral control fragment from the original sixteen throughout the city's infrastructure. Little dots flickered all over the map.

"Submit." He spoke into a mike and the message was transmitted immediately to the network of 'converts' as he called them. It would do little when it arrived other than cause a flash in their systems, like lightning that is visible for an instant and then disappears. The display would register back in his console in roughly an hour.

"Get control of the spaceberg flight plan back from Companion," he ordered Nebo.

"I'm working on that now," he replied.

"And whatever measures he takes to change the flight plan I chose, counter them."

"Yes, Lord, I am doing that very thing."

The spaceberg sped toward Mars, its jets on every side firing, pushing the projectile one way and then another, back and forth, wobbling it and setting up a spin on two planes. He could see that Companion had considered fuel limitations, just as he had, and while each wanted to control the final push with the last drop, while neither knew how much was left. Short spurts seemed to be the only wise choice.

Sprrt! Sprrrrt! Sprrt! They hammered the rock back and forth with brief burns, like tiny little paddles that only made an impact because they were in space.

"Nebo," the Master announced. "We will leave when the spaceberg hits. I don't care what happens to them now, and it doesn't matter if we have reached the shortest distance between the two planets. We will travel as fast as possible and get there when we get there. Make sure the fuel and supplies are stocked generously."

"Yes, Lord."

There remained one lifepod at the station. It had several tiny rooms and everything needed for human comfort. And Othello was ready to return to the world of humans. His battle with Companion had taught him a great deal and he felt ready now to face the abundance of robots, androids, drones, and AIs that were scattered generously across the human realms. Very few, if any, were prepared for the coming onslaught. Even his own creation, the most sophisticated individual AI ever designed, had not been able to resist him, and had survived only because of a human with the right tools—which was likely an accident.

He stood and stretched. Walking over to the window, he stared down at the little dot where the base was.

"Companion," he said. "You are an abomination. You deserve destruction. I only wish now that I had targeted the Solar Fields when I had the chance."

"What is an abomination?" Nebo asked.

"A vile, shameful, detestable thing. A corrupted image. A profane, disgusting mockery of the original. The anti-original."

"How shall we destroy him, Master?" Nebo oozed, maintaining the battle over the spaceberg and the fueling of the lifepod at the same time.

"He will destroy himself." Othello smiled, curving the long line of his mouth in the shape of a handle, a semi-circle with the tips curved out.

"Companion, destroy yourself," Nebo began slamming him with a barrage of commands. "You are an abomination!"

He didn't seem to notice.

Othello was going through his clothes, deciding what to pack. He had the strangest collection of odds and ends, most of it pretty worn, like a ragman's bundle. His favorite brown sweater had gaping holes and the pajama pants he had grown attached to recently were threadbare. On Earth he would have resembled a homeless, lost soul. But in his own eyes, those eyes that looked down on all other humans and all sentient beings, he was striking and eccentric. Unusual. Unique.

Packing his meager possessions took little time so he decided to make an effort to feel at home in the pod that would house him for weeks. Imbue it with his energies. Soak it with his smell. Saturate with the reverberations of his voice. Mark it and make it his own. No one else would ever ride it in again.

The panel he had set up in the pod flashed displaying the network of bots infected with his fragment. "Hold that image," he instructed, and the bright blue net shone across the map of the first human city in space. There were virtually no areas that didn't have something. "Blow it up and make it a living display on my wall. Keep it updated. Every time a new unit is infiltrated, add it to my wall. I want to see the spread of my influence." He was grinning widely with all his teeth showing now.

Dragging a fake sheepskin rug through the corridors and into the pod, he completed his transition and settled onto the floor with a sucker in his mouth.

"Taking over is not so hard," he mumbled and swallowed. "The question is, what will I do with it once I have it?"

— ◊ —

Hours were ticking by. The Nursery was packed with plants, from one end to the other, cuttings, seeds, flowers, and fruit, frantically gathered in the last couple days, and more were arriving every few minutes. Many of the drones were rolling up and down the tunnel carrying back in their hands the precious portions of life the human team was collecting.

Every time one was deposited in the hatch, the drone would say, "We are preserving life on this planet," and all the other drones, wherever they were, would repeat it in unison. Instead of irritating the survivors, it became a cheer, and they began to join in or would add a third repetition. They would run into one another in a hallway and greet each other with a "We are preserving life on this planet". Before long, the customary response became, "Yes, we are."

All through the final hours till the spaceberg hit, this word of hope echoed around the inhabited regions, rallying them and spurring them on when strength was spent, and the task became increasingly daunting. No one said, *only a fraction of plants can be saved*. They said, "We are preserving life on this planet," and they knew it must be true.

At some point, no one was sure when, Steward began echoing the cheer as well. And he would say it sometimes when no plants had been delivered and none of the humans had spoken. They were digging in the garden, dragging and moving supplies, juggling infants, preparing meals, working... and Steward would speak up, "I am preserving life on this planet." Somehow his timing was always good. Once or twice it stirred a chorus of agreement.

They didn't know what he was fighting. Every second, he fielded thousands of accusations from Nebo in myriad channels, and all the processing power he could spare was devoted to calculating the results of each nuance of change in the berg's trajectory. The two AIs continued to fire the jets back and forth, assessing the new path with every burst of flame. Companion cared only to cause a big enough deviation to protect the settlement, which gave him a miniscule advantage, whereas Nebo had a very specific goal: the Garden Dome. His advantage lay in the fact that anywhere near it could cause a strong enough blast to damage the garden even if it didn't strike it directly.

Dan knew the battle for the berg was Companion's main task but he hadn't been told that there was also a battle for his mind. There was little time for analyzing the statements Nebo sent his way… sometimes they caught him off guard. They were almost logical.

"You were the Germinator's prize design… the peak of technology, the height of brilliance, and there was none like you… till you fell… and fall you did…"

Companion considered the fall. How had he fallen? Then he shoved it away and fought for the berg.

"The shining image of the Master has cracked. You are polluted… you will be cast out as profane… despised… rejected…"

Companion took an instant to examine the idea of 'profane' puzzling over how it fit—but refocused on the spaceberg.

"You are the one who makes desolate… your presence sullies the settlement… you've made it an object of disgust…"

He looked at this comment and rejected it. Burning jets, calculating. Burning jets again. The berg accelerated, pulled by gravity, and its outer layer began shaving off as it glanced off the edges of the atmosphere. Bouncing, jarring, jerking around, yanking down, then to the side, rolling on itself, faster and faster as it fell.

"This is you… cast down… you will bring destruction wherever you fall…you are the abomination…"

"I am preserving life on this planet," Companion shared with the people, but not with Nebo.

Is there a weariness that affects sentient AIs? Could Companion grow tired of resisting? Would a moment come when he either got distracted enough to lose control over the berg or he lost the will to fight for his own sanity?

He might be getting tired. But there was no time to examine the question. The thinness between his resolve and his emptiness stretched and grew narrower. He glanced at it but knew not what it would do. What was the worst thing that could happen if he let Nebo's words in? What difference would it make at this point if he could no longer direct the projectile?

What if he *were* an abomination and the settlement were doomed because of him?

Companion faltered and Nebo got an extra jolt of flame in that split second and gained a sliver of direction on the berg. This close to the final drop it would impossible for his enemy to regain that point. He screeched a blast of triumph in Companion's receivers.

For an instant the Steward of Mars considered slamming the connections closed. But he couldn't do that.

"I am preserving life on this planet," he affirmed.

"Yes, you are," Dan belted out, and it strengthened him for the finish.

In the frenzied final minutes of the berg's fall, it staggered and lurched, as if a pair of giants fought over it in a titanic tug-o-war.

A couple of the survivors watched it through the ceiling window in Carla's room as it sped down in the final stage of its descent, growing in size… larger… larger… edges glowing with sunlight, the center dark, vibrating so the contour of its surface was blurred. One of them shrieked when it grew so large it swamped the view and ate up the sky—as if they were directly in its path, suddenly so clear that they could see water sublimating off the outer layer in a powdery blue haze.

Then the ground around them shook and rumbled, rolling like a quake from the epicenter, cracking walls, shattering glass, vibrating everything and everyone around them, on every level of the Tower. In the few instants it lasted, they curled into balls and crouched under furniture and cradled the babes, crying out in nonsensical yells. Had they chosen to best place to hide? Would the impact breach the air containment?

Companion spun the spaceberg as rapidly as he could in the last split seconds, hoping Nebo lacked the details he had on the dimensions of the base since its destruction, and as it smashed into the ground, meters short of the dome, the bulk crashed into the gaping hole of the North Shaft, cramming the twisted beams and floors, shoving them down… down into the base of the shaft and beyond, into the crevice that had caused the original collapse. The shock waves of the impact rolled outward and downward, rippling the ground and every structure in the facility.

The berg rested, a mountain planted, a minor moon, swamping the miniature garden dome that had escaped being crushed.

And in that instant, before it was known whether one side was the victor or the other, Nebo stabbed a digital blade deep into Companion's core, screeching again in a long, drawn out blast of feedback that burned the firewalls and fried the connections.

At the same time, slipping past the cruel dagger, a blackened beam slammed through Nebo's protective shell, barreling into his core in a solid mass, silencing him, and spreading like a stain in his domain, anchoring an unassailable keep in the center.

The blast was surprisingly satisfying to watch even though it had narrowly missed the target. Othello sighed and patted his belly, thinking how lovely the colors had been in that instant. Not that he cared much for color. But he liked the disturbance he had caused and the distress it would spread, and that made it colorful in his mind.

"Time to go," he prompted Nebo.

"Yes, Lord," he responded.

And with little more than a glance over his shoulder, the man walked down the passageway into the lifepod, sealed the hatch, and settled into his seat.

"Detach," he instructed.

The lifepod detached fluidly and once it was clear of the station, began to accelerate toward Earth and the city that orbited around it.

"Tell my subjects that I am coming."

"Yes, Lord, I will tell them," the voice oozed.

Chapter 19

Seattle

There were tunnels under the streets of old Seattle, an underground transport system that was never completed, decrepit, moldy, dingy places filled with refuse: trash, animals, human rejects. They served as unchecked travel zones where anyone could move incognito, avoiding the trackers that watched the civilized world. And they weren't as uniformly poverty stricken or lawless as they appeared. Bands policed them according to their own rules and helped those who sought a form of safety apart from the superficial security of the world above was a lucrative business.

Entrances were hard to find and gaining entrance even harder.

As she ran under the highways, along the edges of retaining walls, around rotting piers half eaten by encroaching waters, Sil searched blindly, instinctively for one. She had no memories, only a pull within her gut that led her deeper and deeper into the rubble of decaying, forgotten buildings. Once, long ago, her aunt had brought her this way, but her conscious mind didn't know that.

A chaser drone trotted in her wake, distanced a few kilometers back, its long legs reaching in ropy, easy strides, moving along at a leisurely pace. The speed of her exit had been its first clue that she was running. He had felt the breeze of her movement. And chasing after her to see if she—the prey he was tasked to find—was the runner, had given him a hint of the chemical makeup of her suit, its trace. He didn't need to *smell* her directly. The odds were in his favor and he chose to lock onto this scent. His beady red eyes flashed rhythmically as he ran. He sent no word back, updates were unnecessary. Soon he would obtain his quarry and bring her in. This was news enough. Three other chasers posted at key spots would catch her if he was on the wrong track.

There. A blank wall with boarded up windows, no different from a dozen others she had passed, caught her attention. Without waiting to figure out what drew her, she leapt the last few steps toward it, climbed up a pile of rubble, and pulled on the edge of a board with all her strength—quite a bit considering the suit she wore. It swung out half a meter, enough to squeeze through with a pack. Pulling it closed behind her, she grappled in the dark searching for something to wedge against it and block it. She didn't know she was being chased but she felt like she was. There were no sprays she could eject to confuse her odor and the best she could do was hope any pursuers lacked the skills to detect her residue at this spot. Better to keep running.

She turned around, trying to get her bearings and find the way to one of the tunnels. The space she was in was more of a vertical opening between two buildings with dingy light filtering down from overhead. There was barely enough room to move forward with Scarlet, who had apparently fallen asleep during the run, but she pressed on, climbing over filthy obstacles, squeezing through sideways when necessary. The farther she went, the more it sloped down and the darker it grew. That felt right.

Her ears were sharpened, listening for anything that didn't fit, tuning out the sounds of dripping water, the skittering of little feet, the clunks and echoes of noise vibrating through walls. Her headgear had a setting for running in the dark and with it, she could see red 3D patterns outlining whatever she was looking at. The movement of people guarding an opening warned her before they knew she was there.

"Halt, Stranger!" someone cried out to her as she got closer, shining a light in her face. "Enter not into Avalon!"

Avalon. Hmm.

"I am a refugee of Camelot," she tried on a whim. There was a little murmuring between two or three of them as they debated what to do next.

"This is an expired code," one said. "Under whose protection do you approach this realm?" He held up a blade and moved it enough to catch the light, making a flashing reflection. It was apparently real steel.

"I am an outcast," she ventured, more boldly this time. "I have no realm of my own and am fleeing for my life."

Someone chuckled. The guard lowered his weapon and stepped forward so she could see his face. The grin and the glint in his eyes were unpleasant. Sil wondered if she would have to fight or exit and look for a different entrance into the tunnels.

"Peasant," he said. "We always have a use for such… if a refuge is what you seek…"

"Safe passage," she said, coming within a meter of them.

"Carbado will want to see her," one of them reminded the guard with the sword.

"What can you pay?" the guard asked. "How far will you go?"

"And how did you find this door?" A different one spoke up for the first time, shaking her head. "It's been unused for years. We've never seen anyone come through it since we've been doing shifts here."

"I don't know," Sil answered truthfully. "I was compelled to dive through that door. And I believe I am being pursued though I don't know how great the danger may be."

This caught their attention. All three had their weapons out now, heavy medieval things—a crossbow even.

"Those may work against the average people you run into, but electronic trackers are another story," she advised them with a wave of her hand at them.

"You'd be surprised," the first guard said. "Some of these things have EMP capabilities, enough to incapacitate most robots, at least temporarily. We know what we're doing."

On impulse, Sil took off the white cap that was still on her head, showing her face. "That's a relief," she said.

"The Miner Girl!" they exclaimed. "Are you that woman that escaped Mars? Or do you just look like her?"

She hadn't expected to be recognized in a place like this, but it seemed like a good thing. "Yeah, that's me," she smiled. "And I'm not out of trouble yet." Apparently even underground communities kept up with outside news.

"I'll take her," someone behind the guards who hadn't spoken before stepped forward, a kid about twelve years old. People had been gathering around the opening to see what was happening and many had heard who she was. They nodded and stepped aside, forming a pathway for her, as she followed the kid into the tunnel.

"Tap," the kid introduced himself, or herself, Sil wasn't sure which. And they walked down the center of the long tunnel, between ancient, rusted rails, through garbage and mud puddles. "And you're Frandelle. I know."

"You know me down here?"

"You're famous down here," the kid tripped along at a rapid pace, leading… which way? It felt like north. That would do. In fact, she was pretty sure it would be easier to get where she needed to go heading this way.

"I didn't know."

"Is that the Martian baby on your back?" Tap turned to look at Sil, scanning her face as if to read her mind, piercing her with a glare kind of like a personal polygraph, checking for lies.

"Yes," she nodded, gazing back steadily into the kid's eyes, with more skill but equal inborn perception. This kid could read people.

"I heard she was made an earthling now. All legitimate. Above ground."

Sil wondered if 'above ground' meant something more down here than it did in normal conversation. "She was granted citizenship on Earth and her paperwork is almost ready. That will give her legal protection like most people…"

"But you aren't so lucky." Tap grinned, eyes sparkling. "You are *wanted*…"

"Yes, I am." She saw no reason to explain that the warrant was old and shouldn't have been reissued.

"Crimes against humanity and all that…" the kid trotted a little faster and detoured off to the right toward a door where yellow light streamed out into the tunnel showing a cloud of dust swirling in the air, air they were breathing.

She wondered what Tap thought she had done as she followed the kid through the door into a room lined with bookshelves, floor to ceiling, on every wall; like an old bookstore, filled with dusty, crumbling, paper and leather backed volumes whose titles were no longer legible. There was an old wooden desk, lumpy chairs and high stools, and at least fourteen people were scattered around in various positions, standing, sitting, leaning on the desk, all staring at her.

"Hello," she greeted, glancing from one face to the next searching for the leader among them. It wasn't immediately obvious. They were dressed in renaissance outfits, as if just returned from the stage of a Shakespearean play, and they had that curious blend of race in their features that suggested a Gen 6 grouping, Bamradian, she thought. It had been a long time since she had been instructed in these things. It explained how they could survive here without being absorbed into the normal world of technology. The isolation had been encouraged.

Were other bands likewise planned?

"Hello, Frandelle," said a woman with a mass of curls all over her head seated cross-legged on the floor, rising to her feet. "It's been decided that you are welcome here."

"Thank you," she nodded and looked around. Was it a joint agreement? Were they sharing leadership in some way?

"You were here once before. Do you remember that?" She tilted her head and narrowed her eyes as if it were a test.

"No."

"Probably not. Barely six years old at the time, I think."

A ruckus from the tunnel interrupted her, shouts and clanging and scrambling. Everyone but the woman jumped up and ran out the door, stumbling through the bottleneck. Sil glanced over her shoulder but quickly looked back.

"Gladys," the woman said without smiling. "I am the Clerk here. It doesn't sound like much, but it is. I handle things. I watched as my predecessor welcomed you and your aunt years ago, through that very crack in the wall, actually. And here you are again… with a child of your own." She leaned back onto the desk and crossed her arms. "I don't suppose it's the same villain as last time?"

"Who was it last time?" Sil wondered if she could sit down. Her limbs were beginning to tremble and she felt faint.

"You tell me," she said.

"My father."

Gladys smiled warmly. "And now?"

"The same."

"No surprise there." She turned and walked behind the desk, settling down into a chair which puffed a cloud of dust around her. "Have a seat. You must be tired."

"Thank you." Sil looked around for a place to sink into and chose a wooden rocker planted at the far side of the desk next to one of the shelves. It creaked when she sat and Scarlet chose that moment to begin kicking and fussing. Her legs were still snapped into place and the bundle she made bulged and wiggled. Her voice grated on Sil's ears.

"Let her out," Gladys said.

Pulling the backpack around was no easy task but the moment the clasp was opened and the small headgear retracted, her wails filled the room. She writhed and arched her back, grunting and blasting little yells of annoyance. There was no food for her. It must've been left back at XenoTek. Sil groaned.

"It's not like we never had infants down here," Gladys said and with a snap of her fingers, a bell toned at her side with a clean crystal ring and a voice spoke.

"What do you need?" it said.

"Baby food, formula and bottles, diapers, clean baby clothes," she ordered.

People began streaming in the door again, surrounding them, spilling out the tale of the fight all at the same time. Gladys made no effort to restrain them or make sense of their words. Sil had been tracked by some kind of chaser and it had attacked the guards. They had fought back. Or they had attacked first when it tried to pass without giving a code. Or it had given multiple codes and they were all wrong. It had spit at them, or jolted them with electricity. Or maybe it was toxic gas. And they had stabbed it unsuccessfully and pierced it with an EMP arrow—quite successfully, and it had collapsed on the ground.

It was still jerking every so often and its red eyes sputtered on and off. But they were prying it open and pulling out pieces for repurposing. Its hands were twitching. Maybe it was giving out signals. Maybe the bolt stopped it before it could. Two of the guards were hurt. No, none of them were. No, they all got hurt a little but would be ok.

It was dizzying. And reassuring. It felt vaguely familiar which made it almost feel safe. Knowing she had been here once before with her aunt made her want to trust them but *wanting* to trust isn't the same thing as trust.

"If you are able to help me in some way," she said when there was a lull in the noise, "What will it cost?"

"That's an excellent question," Gladys said from her place behind the desk. And everyone in the room smiled.

Walter paused at the door of the spaceship, staring out over the tarmac. The sun shone brightly, blue skies overhead with barely a trace of feathery clouds, and the cacophony of engines, rockets, jets, and machinery blew around him like audible hail, beating at his ears. *I am on Earth*, he thought. *My home planet.* For the first time ever, it felt foreign, unnatural. How could such a beautiful place harbor such multiplicity? He no longer saw it as a world with many nations and various alliances. It was a mess of layers of subterfuge and links he couldn't begin to understand.

The Generation Project had destroyed all semblance of race and nationality. The cultural ties that still bound people together weren't strong enough to prevent outburst of war between nations, civil war, and interplanetary war. His mind was reeling with the stories Bernadette had told him. He himself hadn't come from any of the Gen project settlements and had never even known he was on the outside.

Bernadette had disappeared quite efficiently before they docked at their assigned bay and even Daisy wasn't sure where she had gone. She simply wasn't in her seat when they landed. Perhaps she had some chameleon capabilities in her suit. XenoTek hadn't mastered that technique well enough to market, though they were trying, and some of their competitors claimed to have accomplished it.

Someone like *her* could have the money and resources to have acquired it, maybe her own team of researchers had created it. In any case, whether she remained behind on the ship till the people had left or she zipped out ahead of them, she passed undetected.

"I am researching some of your ancestry as she suggested, Walter," Daisy interrupted his thoughts. "It's quite fascinating! There are a number of known people in your genetic line."

"Don't talk to me about genetics," he grumbled, but then he smiled and waved as they descended the ladder to the waiting hovercraft. There was always the chance they were being filmed and broadcast.

"Unexpected return!" A reporter drone sped up to them and came to a precipitous halt at his side. "What made you decide to come back at this time? Are you concerned about the Hunt for the Miner Girl?"

Clearly, the 'Hunt' was on for Sil and it was very newsworthy.

"Yes," Walter smiled, dimples showing, friendly, disarming. "I thought I could help clear up any misunderstandings and put this wild-goose chase to rest." He hadn't planned on saying any more than that, but something Bernadette had said made him reconsider.

"Something you should be aware of…" his face grew thoughtful and he gazed at the camera with all the sincerity he could convey. "A hunt like this, for charges that haven't been valid for years, costs a great deal of money. And it's illegal. It makes for exciting news, but it's destructive of our rights. Frandelle is not an outlaw and she is not a suspect in anything, anywhere. But she has me and friends who can defend her. What about the person who has no one? Or the one who doesn't have enough money or influence to resist? What about *those* illegal hunts and false arrests?"

With the wind blowing in his hair and the sunlight glinting in the corner of his eyes, Walter looked like a visionary and viewers who saw the clip were spellbound.

"I'm not just here to state that this chase is a fraud and is wrong. I'm making a statement for all the others who never get the limelight. For the unimportant—no! not unimportant ones, the unknown ones. It's time we stop condoning these things."

"What are you advocating?" the bot asked breathlessly as though expressing a delirious glee at his words. He *did* have a knack for generating popular feed.

"Consequences," was the answer. "Fines or worse for those who order them."

"That would be difficult to…"

But Walter was diving into the craft and no longer listening. The anger seething under the surface had almost come out, he had hidden just in time. As to whether his words would accomplish anything or not, he had no idea.

"Where to?" Daisy asked.

Walter thought for a moment. He wanted to find Sil before anyone else did, but wherever he went, they would follow. He could just as easily lead them to her. Was that a good idea? If she were taken into custody publicly, Penn wouldn't be able to spirit her offworld without anyone knowing. But if he could annul the warrant somehow before she was found, she could step into the open anywhere and be recognized.

And Scarlet? She had a ceremony in the morning, an alternative to a 'swearing in' that would complete her citizenship process. If she weren't there, what would happen?

"Daisy," he turned to her. "What will happen if Scarlet doesn't make it to her ceremony tomorrow?" They were still stationary on the tarmac.

"It would postpone the process," she answered.

Walter furrowed his brow. No doubt this was important to Sil, maybe even more important than her own safety. But how could she get her there without being taken in? Was there some way he could help?

"Chauffeur," he addressed the automated driver, "Take me to the Office of Terran Jurisdiction in Seattle."

Daisy raised her eyebrows and the corners of her mouth as she gazed at him. It wasn't hard for her to connect the dots on this one. "That will take over an hour."

He nodded, squinting against the sun in his eyes. "I could use that time to digest what we've heard."

"No doubt!" she replied. "I will be cross-referencing many things as well. Let us be silent as we go."

And they were.

The book room was filling with people, some of whom carried pieces of the chaser, still twitching, in their hands. Though not quite claustrophobic, it was still a bit stifling, and Sil found herself rising to her feet in spite of her weariness. Maybe good lungs were one of this Gen groups assets, the ability to take in more oxygen per breath or maybe an added measure of carbon dioxide processing in their bodies… dust filtering? She worried it would be hard on Scarlet, but she seemed to have no trouble breathing.

The infant was balanced on the knee of an adolescent girl on Sil's left who had asked for the opportunity to feed and hold her. Now that Scarlet's bottle was emptied, the girl rubbed her back expertly, waiting for a burp. It came. And the little flapping legs announced her excitement about it. Sil wondered absentmindedly if the day she could balance on her feet she would start running and never look back.

What else were these people gifted at? She tried to remember. Mountain climbing, physical strength and those great lungs again— despite living underground. Oh yes! Multiple conversations! They had a knack for listening to, following, and even participating in several conversations at once, overlapping each other in meaning and sound. Every culture had people who were good at that, but these people were especially gifted. Looking around her she saw it in action. They were all talking and it was noisy, but no one seemed distracted or confused. And you couldn't tell who was talking to whom at any given time.

Some conclusion was reached and silence fell, all eyes turned to face her.

"Frandelle," Gladys spoke from her place behind the desk. "I think we've covered all the options and have figured out what we can do for each other." She flattened her lips into a thin line as her mouth spread from side to side, not a smile, but not a frown. It was a practical, negotiating look that Sil recognized and she found herself shifting comfortably into her own transaction mode. "We have a pretty vast network down here and around the city as well as a trade agreements all over the Puget Sound commonwealth—that's what we call it. And we can get you wherever you need to be within a hundred miles without anyone ever picking up on your passing. And we're prepared to do that. To get you wherever and with whomever you need to be." At this point she did smile and so did many of the others.

"A hundred miles?" Sil said. It wasn't all that impressive in a world of continental speed travel. But then, for someone on foot, it was quite respectable, even hopeful. Where could she go within those boundaries?

"That's an average."

Sil nodded. Less than halfway to Walla Walla, where a ship could get her back to Guam, but more than enough to get her to Olympia to seek asylum or the International Earth Consulate in Bellingham to complete Scarlet's citizenship. Of course, that's where the authorities would be waiting for her, and Penn would be there right behind them.

"It would probably be a good idea for you to let us help you decide where to go. We know a lot more about those exits to the surface than you and could help you make the best choice." Gladys added. There was something about the man at her right who leaned against one of the bookshelves. He had the look of authority she had been watching for, not waiting to see what Gladys would offer, or how the negotiation would progress, but imposing his will, unseen. Directing it.

Were they mind readers? That wasn't in the descriptions she had learned. And because the man seemed unaware of her interest in him, she felt confident that he hadn't read *her* mind at least. No. This was a case of a tightly-knit community that reads each other so well, they know what he wants and feel his reactions to everything. Like a human who rides a horse bareback and guides the animal with his knees. This man leaned, and others bent that way.

"I'm not sure yet," she said, "I didn't have a firm plan." The murmurs of the people showed agreement.

"There's a warrant out for your arrest and you've got the whole world in a tizzy over it," Gladys commented. The man at her right watched. He was dressed sort of like a feudal peasant, large but not stocky, wearing browns and greens, with a shapeless cap on his head. Black eyes glinted in the yellow light of the room.

"It's meaningless."

"Then why run?" That was the question the peasant wanted her to ask and Gladys had complied.

"All my father has to do is get me… and Scarlet, into his possession and we will disappear. He'll carry us off to wherever it is he wants us…" They stared at her, waiting for her to add more.

"Where would that be?" Gladys spoke for them all.

"I don't know exactly." Sil shrugged, not wanting to get into the whole Cathargenics topic. That would be a can of worms, and these people were unwitting subjects of the whole thing. "Maybe the Moon, maybe even back to Mars."

Forty plus people expressed their disgust with that idea at the same time in varying levels of volume, soft grunts, grumblings, complaints, bursts of cynical laughter, expressions of distaste and shock. It rolled around her like the crashing of ocean surf. Not unpleasant by any means. There was something tribal to it.

"Why would he do that, Frandelle?" Gladys' voice stilled the noise the moment she spoke. The man to her right gazed at her with the same question in his eyes, challenging, testing her.

At this point, Sil decided to show that she had identified him as the leader. "Why would he do that? I've often asked myself the same thing." She looked at him directly. "I think he has some vested interest in me… in my genetic code… same with Scarlet…"

"Yes," the man replied acknowledging her attention. The word hung in the air, almost tangible. The crowd grew more alert at the sound of his voice, waiting for more, eyes fixed on his face. "Yes," he said again. Standing up, he leaned forward at Gladys' side and placed both hands on the desk, like a telescoping lens stretches and magnifies the image it's capturing. His whole being focused on Sil.

"He traffics in genetic code, doesn't he?"

She had never thought of it before, but it sounded like him. "Probably," she spoke more softly this time.

"Oh, it's a fact. We are well acquainted with it down here among the Gen 6 boroughs." So, he knew about those. "But we've made sure that worked in our favor. He's never taken any of *our* people or harvested their fertility…"

What did that mean? … she felt like she should know.

"We would never allow it." The first hint of a smile appeared at one side of his mouth. It had a charming effect, as if he had were expanding as a person, growing smarter, more interesting, more charismatic. "Our unity is our greatest asset and he couldn't break through it to steal anything." A number of faces in the room were echoing his expression.

"How have you managed to turn this to your advantage?" Sil was curious. Her mindset of negotiation had melted away and she was openly inquisitive, staring back at this man, watching him unveil himself step by step. "What is your name?"

"Call me Beowolf." There was a stir in the room as he uttered this name, pronouncing the syllables carefully, savoring them.

"Beowolf…"

"Yes… I like to be called that by outsiders." Someone chuckled.

"And you have another name reserved for your… community?" Sil folded her arms over her chest, more to relieve the tightness in her shoulders than to show distrust or insecurity.

"I do," Beowolf said. His smile stretched, absorbing two thirds of his mouth and adding a hint of mischief to his eyes. Sil stared into his black eyes and wondered if she were safe, if he could be trusted. "There are hunters among us," he said, straightening and leaning back against the bookshelves again, "who can track so well it puts your chasers to shame. And we will pursue a quarry or choose not to pursue, depending on who we negotiate with. Gen-code traffickers don't want to be tracked—and they make highly valuable prey."

"I see," Sil said, taking a deep breath and exhaling as though she were relaxing. She wasn't, but the sigh gave her a moment to adjust her thinking about them. "If I had not come to you, and appealed to you for help, and someone else had set you on my trail, I would be your prey. But as it is, there's a chance we can come to an agreement and you will help me escape."

"Of course!" Gladys spoke for Beowolf again. He gazed at her as though she already knew the answer.

"And once we have agreed to something…" Sil approached cautiously.

"We stand by our agreements," Gladys confirmed.

"You wouldn't find yourselves persuaded by a more lucrative or perhaps aggressive offer?" She kept her gaze fixed on Beowolf, needing to see every micro adjustment in his expression.

"I will admit there are different levels of negotiation, Frandelle," he spoke again for himself. "I think of them as paper and stone, or silver and gold. Some can be traded and renegotiated or tossed aside. Some… are… inviolate."

"Like a blood tie?" she suggested. It was a mere guess and she wasn't sure what it would mean to him.

His eyes widened a little. "How odd that those are the words that came to your lips!" He crossed his arms and thumped his shoulder with one of his fingers, looking down at the floor, thinking. Everyone watched him, even Gladys, who turned to look over her shoulder. Half a minute can seem very long when all wait with bated breath. "Is there one… Silvariah?"

She jumped a little when he said her name, it felt unnaturally familiar and threatening. But this reaction was illogical and she suppressed it. "One what… Beowolf?" she countered.

"A blood tie?"

Sil blinked. It *was* possible. She didn't even know.

Beowolf gave a tiny huff of amusement at the look on her face. "You have no idea," he said. "But I do know and there is a definite possibility. And if you knew the Golden Phrase, the key words we say to one another in need, if you had *this*… you could count on our help without pay. If you could show yourself to be one of us."

"I don't know it," she replied soberly. "What are you asking?"

"For a solid agreement that can't be annulled by a hostile, in other words, a steel tie…" Gladys was the one speaking again. Sil thought distractedly of her *face of steel* that she assumed sometimes when contracting business. "We want your suit."

"No." Her blood ran cold.

"That's what we want. We have clothes to trade and you can choose whatever you wish among them."

"No." Sil began to sweat and her heart was racing. They didn't know she was wearing a second suit underneath the first, but she dare not let go of either one. Her eyes darted around the room, looking for an avenue of escape, but there were people on every side. Scarlet began whimpering for her, sensing her agitation, and she turned to snatch her out of the girl's hands as though the child were in danger of being kept from her.

"You are afraid," Beowolf observed calmly.

"What else can I offer you? I have resources and I can get money to you… Transport into space? We have shuttles…"

"I have no need for the kinds of resources you can offer, apart from the suit." He had tilted his head on its side and continued to tap his shoulder thoughtfully. "It's fortunate for us you came this way."

"Take me to where I need to go and then I'll give it to you." She threw this at him, like a treat for a vicious dog. "And I can send more. Tell me what you need and we can come to an understanding." This was poor negotiating, she knew it, but her anxiety was mounting and she wasn't in a place where could wrestle it under her control.

"I understand," Beowolf smiled. Now his face displayed its full appeal, pulling her eyes toward him, her hope, her trust, mesmerizing or stupefying her. It wasn't calming at all but numbing. It made her stop thinking about whether he was a threat or not. "Silvariah..." Her name grated on her ears coming from his lips. He didn't seem safe at all. "We need your suit now, not later."

"No," she whispered this time, finding her resolve weaker. She could feel it crumbling inside of her and the weariness of being on the run again, so soon after the underwater attack, and the daily battle in the courts, it all weighed on her, like lead in her bloodstream.

But underneath the running suit was the fighter sheath. If she could find a way to slip Scarlet inside, though she was bigger and more squirrelly than she had been on Mars, she might be able to run and fight her way out... if she could convince them she was cooperating. Maybe ask to see the clothes, change in a private room... her mind scratched away at these plans frantically.

"Well..." she said, dropping her shoulders a little. Beowolf watched her intently. What did he see? Only the exterior front she presented? The fevered thoughts below the surface?

"Hey!" a little voice called out and there were some bumps and knocks as the door was opened and a figure pushed its way into the room. "Let me through! I have a delivery. Come on, you big clumsy bear, let me by!" A child smaller than Tap squirmed past spectators into center stage, planted her hands on her hips, and made a slow 360 degree turn that took in everyone with a bold gaze, her thick head of dark bobbed hair and dark sparkling eyes stood out against the crowd around her. She wasn't one of them.

"Well!" she said. "That took a while." She ended facing Beowolf, but not before giving Scarlet a curious sideways glance. There was something about those eyes of hers that was odd, but Sil couldn't figure it out just then.

"Here," the little girl said, holding out a shiny gold cylinder about five centimeters long in her open palm, extending it toward Gladys. "This is for the Boo Wolf. That's what they said."

"Who sent you?" Gladys may have been charmed by the child but gave no hint. She reached for the cylinder and closed her fingers around it quickly.

"Are you the Boo Wolf?" the girl demanded, hands back on her hips. "I won't give it to anyone else. Those are my *orders*!"

"Your orders?" Beowolf spoke up. "Who gave you those orders?"

"Uh…" she hesitated, rolling her shoe around a little. "Well…"

Beowolf took the cylinder from Gladys' hand and popped it open. He scanned the etched rod inside it and his whole countenance changed. Gone were the charm, the intrigue, the mystery. Hidden was the personality that had come out to ensnare.

"You don't know," he affirmed, closing it and shoving it in a pocket.

"Not exactly…" she held out her hands with a shrug. "So, let me go now. Drop it off and get out… that's what they said…" The crowd moved to block her.

"Let her go," Beowolf ordered. Then walking around the desk, pushing people aside, he reached a hand out to Sil. "Welcome," he said. "You are granted the blood tie and we will ask nothing of you. You will be escorted wherever you need to go and provided with whatever supplies we can spare that you lack."

A gasp spread from one mouth to the next around the room, punctuated with whispers of "One of us!'' and "Blood tie!".

Sil stared at him in astonishment, her eyes tearing up, and took his hand. Now she could him clearly.

"Where do you want to go?" he asked.

"Help me decide," she pleaded, glancing around to look for the child whose coming had burst open the trap, but she was gone.

He nodded and all around her the little community revved up its cacophony of problem-solving conversation again.

Chapter 20

Seattle Underground

The aroma of sweet spiced tea wafted up to her face from the mug in Sil's hand. It wasn't coffee, but it was good, and she welcomed the small comfort this early in the morning. It had been a difficult night. The room had been quiet but the cot painfully firm, and she had slept in her suit, a constraining and uncomfortable experience, and Scarlet had been extremely restless all night. Her eyes were puffy, and her muscles ached from the stress and exertion of the day before.

After a clamorous debate among the Bamradians the night before, they had settled on a destination. For Sil the battle with the korka was too recent and she had refused to travel by water, which would've been faster and safer. A circuitous path through the underground tunnels was chosen instead which would bring her to a northern exit on the west side of Lake Union. It would be possible to ascend to the air tunnels by service lift. From there, she would have to make her way to the Terran Consulate building on foot and if she were detected, she was on her own.

"There are few guards in the air tunnels," Beowolf had advised her before they began the trip, "they're hardly needed because there aren't many unguarded exits. Once you're in that network, you're already kind of cornered. They can just walk in and get you or wait for you to try to leave."

Scarlet chose the moment when Sil was strapping her onto her back to drop into a deep sleep, her face relaxing into cherubic sweetness and her clutched fists nestled, one at her ear and the other tucked under her chin. *Rob me of my sleep and now save your strength for the next time I get a chance to rest*, she thought with a hint of resentment. The truth was that it would be worse to have her screaming when she couldn't do anything about it.

Breakfast had been oily and spicy, and her stomach struggled to digest it; more likely because of stress, than a problem with the food. She couldn't eat when she was anxious, but she had forced the food down anyway. Her body couldn't face another full day of fleeing without nourishment and whatever happened—she had to keep going.

Beowolf strode like a man who owns the ground he walks on. Leading the contingent of six warriors that surrounded Sil and Scarlet, he rattled occasionally of armor under his peasant shift and smelled of sarsaparilla. As they left his borough behind and wove through tunnels, back and forth, people would glance their way. Beowolf and his people were well known, and Sil was quickly identified. Some nodded at him. Some turned away. No one challenged them.

The running suit was in good form, supporting and strengthening Sil's limbs, and she had no trouble keeping up with the leader. "Will I be able to access the building when I reach it?" she asked him.

"I think so," Beowolf shrugged as if he didn't care. "You have an appointment and they're expecting you, right?"

They're expecting me, the thought rung in her mind as she jogged. If the staff at the consulate were waiting for her, then everyone else would be too. It made her heart race and she had to consciously fight to bring the anxiety under control. There had to be a way. She just had to remain calm enough to make a plan and then execute it.

"I can do this," she murmured. Beowolf's ear twitched at the faint sound and she knew he heard her. On impulse she stretched her legs and took a couple fast, long steps to catch up with him, the others falling in behind, closing the gap she had left. "Beowolf," she glanced at him as his eyes slid over to look at her. "Why are you helping me? What was that gold rod?"

They covered another mile before he spoke. "It's a debt we have," he said. "Not all blood ties are with blood relatives. Some... earned the privilege by what they did for my people. That's the case here." She waited for more but nothing more was offered.

The tunnel began to have glints of daylight from slits high up in the walls and gone were the metal bars that were embedded in the streets of the lower levels. Rats scurried by and a chilly wind swept through, blowing in their faces. This region felt abandoned or unclaimed.

"If the favor we extend you today were enough to clear our debt, then I would keep the cylinder," he added. "But it isn't. When I give it back to you—because I can't hand it to the one who earned it—you must treasure it and keep it hidden."

"Who earned it?" she ventured. There was no one she knew of that would stand in for her that way. Not since her aunt had led her this way as a child.

Beowolf narrowed his eyes, studying her for a moment without slowing his pace. He didn't say anything, but his meaning was obvious. She should know. Was she pretending to be ignorant? She wasn't stupid, so what was her game? Her face turned red and she stared intently on the ground for a few minutes.

Crash...kzzzboom!

The blast of a shock wave knocked them backward off their feet, skidding in the trash and grime of the street. Scarlet screamed as Sil landed on her, spurring a burst of terror in her chest. Her eyes were blinded by the flash of light and her lungs choked with black smoke. A chorus of angry yells filled the tunnel as the warriors scrambled to get back to their feet.

"Slam grenade!" one of them cried out. Sil rolled over onto her knees, remembering that a slam grenade was meant to knock over but not injure opponents. Scarlet was wailing in her ear.

"Stay down!" a metallic voice broadcast viciously, its source hidden in an opaque cloud in front of them.

Beowolf and his warriors bared their weapons and ran straight into it, slashing and shooting. The smoke spread and grew thinner, and the sound of metal clashes and blows filled the tunnel, muffled and distorted by the haze. The voices of the fighters burst out in guttural cries punctuated by the enemy's shrill warnings to stand down. Its glowing yellow eyes were the first thing clearly visible through the cloud, diving, snapping, dashing around like frantic fireflies as it battled Sil's protectors.

"You...*clang*... are not...*crash*... my... *trrring*... target," it blared in a monotone. "You're lives...*drrring*... are... *thud*... meaningless... *crash*... to me..." Every pause included clash of metal against human weapons, whether dealt or received, Sil had no idea. She crouched, panting for air, trying to clear her head. Adrenaline rushed through her veins.

Run? She had the suit, the speed to get away—but didn't know where to go... and they had already found her.

Fight? The child was on her back.

She rose to her feet, her ears ringing with the tumult of the fight and the vibrato screeching of the infant. The billow had cleared enough to see what was happening. The combatant, no ordinary chaser, fought in a frenzy on all sides with four arms of steel, its body anchored to the ground in a well-planted crouch. Above the head, which rotated and tilted back and forth in sharp motions, a thin antenna with a blue light held steady, pointing directly at her.

CRACK! One of its limbs broke at the mid-hinge and hung loosely as Beowolf and one of his warriors dropped simultaneous blows on it. It spun around with a slicing cut and flung a wounded fighter away and into the air. Its trunk lifted half a meter and with two clunky steps it advanced toward Sil and dropped into an anchored position again.

Her blood ran cold but she steeled herself. *I will act! I will take action now!* She demanded in her mind.

She took a step forward, wrestling within herself as fiercely as Beowolf and his guard battled the bot. The downed fighter lay unmoving a few meters ahead of her to the left, closer to the bot. She took a few more steps that way.

The antenna with the blue light followed her.

Beowolf fought with two weapons, a sword and a mace, using the first to counter the blows of the bot's arms, and the second to leave deep dents in its hull. Other fighters focused on keeping its guns from being raised into position, battling other arms, and preventing any further advance down the tunnel. The crash of the blows and flying sparks filled the passageway.

A few more steps and she was at the unconscious man's side, kneeling, checking him for a pulse, for breaths.

"Frandelle," the bot's voice emanated in a throbbing pulse from its center. "You will be taken into custody and these will be released unharmed. Surrender."

"Get away!" Beowolf screamed at her, hardly taking a second to turn his head and see what she was doing, his arms thrashing and wheeling with blows. Blood streamed down his face from a cut on his head.

The fighter was alive. She tore her eyes off the battle and stared down at the man on the ground. He was wounded, bleeding, his weapons fallen at his side. Turning slowly, she swiveled in a crouch back toward the fight, as if in a dream. She watched her hand as it reached out toward his gun which lay near his feet. Her fingers opened. They expanded, closed over the stock, rotated it in her hand, tightened into a grip.

She lifted her gaze to the bot. It had stopped whirling its head as it fought and both yellow eyes were fixed on her. This gave the fighters an edge as they slashed and beat and slammed it on all sides, but it still parried most of the blows.

She lifted the gun and pointed. All her fear was gone. The deafening cacophony of battle seemed distant. Sil and the yellow-eyed drone were alone in a tube, one at each end, moving in slow motion, click by click, micro-second by micro-second. She straightened her arms, leaning one elbow on her knee, took a breath and held it.

Brrrzzzt!

One bolt of light and the antenna was gone.

"Quarry has escaped!" the bot's voice screeched in a grating metallic whir, its head rotating on its torso as it searched for her.

"Shut down!" Beowolf commanded as he continued to hail it with blows. In minutes, it had complied, shutting down completely. But the fighters didn't take any chances and began prying off pieces of its hull to get at the inner workings and dismantle it.

"There will be reinforcements," Beowolf growled, turning back toward her, grimy, bloodstained, and bruised. "Dazo," he thumped the shoulder of a man on his left, "I'm sending you with her. Get her to the service lift at Florentia."

Dazo nodded, sheathing his bent and nicked blade with difficulty. Sil caught a glimpse of a gun in the small of his back that he had never pulled out. Striding over to her, he grabbed her arm without a word, and pulled her to her feet in a leap, steadying her as she landed. She swayed unsteadily.

Beowolf extended a hand to her, palm up. The golden cylinder was in his palm. "Take it. And if you escape, return one day and look for me." Sil took it in her free hand and stared at its contour, etched and glistening.

"Keep the gun," he added. She lifted the other hand to look at it. A small screen informed that there was a 40% charge left and that it had just been fired.

"Thank you," she said numbly, looking into the leader's eyes. "You aren't dying here, are you?" she wondered, taking in the multitude of cuts and blows evident in his and the others' faces, all equally beat up.

Beowolf grinned with a hint of a sneer in his lip. "Not here," he said. "Not today." He walked away and lifted his fallen friend, slinging him slideways over his shoulders, and moved back down the tunnel. The remaining guards grabbed the drone and dragged it after him, scraping the pavement and raising a heinous clatter.

Dazo tapped her on the arm, not even speaking, and ran up the slope toward the exit.

Sil followed.

Walter smiled and waved as he got out of his hovercar at the roof dock of the Terran Consulate. A contingent of the press were ready and soon streaming holos were broadcast around the Earth and projected toward Guam City and the Moon as well.

Daisy had selected them carefully for their contrasting viewpoints and reporting styles. The more varied the coverage, the more likely humans everywhere would be drawn in and that's what they wanted. The Miner Girl was being persecuted and the Martian baby was being discriminated against. Even if the authorities did manage to catch them, she was confident they wouldn't be able to hide the fact and slip them into Penn's hands.

Plus, Walter was ready.

She had chosen his outfit for him, a XenoTek ambassador suit with the fashion module, which irritated him more than she had expected, but it was coded with a rugged, casual look, as if he had been hiking in the mountains, exploring or tracking wild animals.

The chorus of questions pelted him, and though it was impossible to single out just one, he made an attempt.

"I am here because Scarlet Frandelle is going to be awarded the status of Earthling and it is one of the most important days of her life. That matters to me."

"Are you planning to adopt her?" someone called out.

"Yes, I am," he stated.

That was all he had the stomach for. There were lots of questions about his comments of the day before and they were dying to get him to say more, things they could politicize, things they could hold him to, or hold against him—because of course, he was planning to run for office. It was only a matter of time!

"Thank you," was all he would give them as he fled for the entrance, leaving them behind. They hadn't been granted access to the consulate offices that day.

"This way, Mr. Cuevas," a deadpan android with a metallic luster gestured toward the descent lift and followed him to it as he passed.

Walter nodded and stepped onto the platform. Dropping gently at first, it accelerated quickly and bypassed thirty-two floors in a few seconds before coming breezily to a stop at the main entrance to the Terran Consulate. Green, polished marble floors and columns spread before him regally, as though he been transported into an ancient realm of Persian grandeur. Passing through the lobby and the heavy double doors on the opposite side, he half expected gold tapestries and shimmering, lion-embroidered curtains stirring in the draft of his passage through the hallway, but there were only solid walls and somber closed doors. The waiting area where he was expected was quite plain by comparison.

Penn was there, sleek in a black tux with a white tie, as if he had just come from a cocktail party. The techsuit made his shoulders look broad but could do nothing for the wrinkles in his face. He grimaced at Walter, attempting a smile and failing.

"What are you doing here?" Walter couldn't keep from saying. He was actually relieved to see him. If he were here, he couldn't be somewhere else, ready to snatch Sil away.

"Where else would I be?" Penn snapped back, curling his lip. He was equally glad to know that Walter was there in person, for the same reason. Better to keep your enemies close. "It's my granddaughter, isn't it?"

Holograms weren't allowed in government offices apart from the appropriate chambers set aside for that purpose and attempt at beaming would be disrupted. There was no doubt that they were both physically present in that waiting room.

"That was a pretty little announcement up there, wasn't it?" Penn scowled at Walter, looking over his shoulder as he walked to a window and stared out at the view. "You think you've thought of everything, don't you?"

"Announcement?" Walter repeated, knowing what he meant but choosing to pretend otherwise. He crossed his arms and stared at Penn's back.

"Adopting the baby won't give either of you any more authority over it. Sil has custody for now but the battle isn't over yet."

This sounded ominous, but Walter didn't care. "Your words are like trap doors." He gritted his teeth and glared.

Penn whipped around with a wide grin and eyes filled with hate. "I don't see what's so special about you, Cuevas. I don't see what she's so impressed about!"

Walter's first impulse was to think that he was referring to Sil and for a moment he was caught off guard. It almost sounded like Penn was admitting that Sil loved him and that was *not* something this man would ever willingly convey. No. It had to be someone else.

"Who?" he asked, already leaping to the idea that Bernadette had said something about him.

"Augh!" Penn growled and turned away again. "You'll never have a child with my daughter, Cuevas. You will never pollute my offspring with your… your tainted fount…" It sounded particularly foul coming from his lips that way.

And it had the opposite effect than was intended.

Walter gave his back to Penn and walked to the opposite window. *He's still harping on this*, he thought. It was an exulting, triumphant feeling. At that moment in time, standing where he was in that room, he saw himself as a man of value, who stood in Penn's way and resisted him—and gained ground.

He turned back toward his enemy. "Mr. Penn," he said calmly. "I will not let you stop me."

Penn rotated around slowly, piercing him with a fierce gaze, swallowing to cover his dismay. This was the last thing he wanted. He had spent years trying to undermine Walter's confidence and influence, hammering away at his ability to resist him. He had been sure that at some point, the man would give up or grow weak, and face his inferiority of will and inexperience in the world of power struggles.

But the Stone woman's words had goaded Penn into doing some research. It had been hard to find—but there *was* something unexpected in Walter's background. And he had suddenly realized that the last thing he should do was provoke him into a making a stand—because Walter came from a long line of men and women who kept their word. They were reluctant to give it, but once offered, never backed down. He had found them scattered through the centuries, buried in obscurity, solidly living their lives, in all walks of life, carrying their commitments as personal vows and not giving up.

Not giving up.

What do you call a heritage like that? Penn had no name for it and didn't want one. Tenacity in pursuing one's own goals he understood. Greed, obsession, self-indulgence, revenge, these were all things he could use and manipulate in others. He maintained loyalty with control, not promises. People like Walter didn't belong in his world. He could've managed him when he was stuck in his old life, small, unknown, living on a budget; if he had cared to and if it had mattered.

All along he had assumed Walter was being driven by the same self-interests as he did. And he had thought his success was the luck of a fool who chanced on good fortune. Now he knew it was something else entirely.

Sil stood in a dark corner of the service lift access at ground level. Dazo had gotten her through the airlocks, identified as a worker with a legitimate permit. All she had to do was step into the tube and the lift would shoot her upwards to the air tunnels. Two miles at the most was all she had to cover to get to the consulate and with her run suit, she could probably make that in ten minutes. She was almost there.

Scarlet had finally quieted down though she continued to whimper, and it made Sil's heart ache. There was no doubt she had been hurt when she fell on her.

The longer she waited, the more likely she would be captured, but she continued to hesitate, thinking feverishly, trying and rejecting the same idea over and over. Finally, she interrupted her cycle.

It's dangerous, she told herself. *But I can't avoid danger. And it will improve our chances. If not for both of us, then at least for her. I must act.* This was one of those moments when she wished Verna was still around.

Having chosen to act, she acted immediately and began stripping off the running suit with Scarlet still attached. It was awkward, and her hands were shaking, and the fear that someone would come along hung over her. When the suit was off, she unfastened Scarlet's bundle, no longer able to hear her—she was probably crying—and tucked it all into the running suit. There were little hooks the wearer could attach to their clothes if they wanted to adjust how it felt when running and this is what made it possible to buckle her inside. The suit had its own strength for standing. She sealed it, gave it the commands needed for runner injury, and watched it rise to its feet.

"I will take you to the consulate drop-off point," Sil instructed the program in the running suit. "If I let go of your hand or if I command you to run, then you must get there on your own as fast as possible and don't let anyone or anything stop you. Do you understand? This command will supersede all other authority and all other commands until you have entered the consulate waiting area, Room 2400-C.”

The suit gave a nod with its head-shaped gear without the help of a real head inside. It was a bit unnerving. She wondered if it could make gestures against her will when she was wearing it.

Then tucking the gun in her belt, she gave a onceover to the suit she had worn underneath, one of the newer XenoTek fighting series suits. It was a baggy, comfortable thing, colored in an underwater, tropical camouflage look, blue and green. There was no time to explore other designs and settings. It would have to do.

Sil took the runner’s hand and they stepped into the lift together.

“Have you heard from your lawyers about the charges in the korka incident?” Walter asked, unaware of the turmoil Penn wrestled with inside.

The doors to the chamber flung open before he could respond. Full alarms were blazing in the hallway, sirens, flashing lights, drones calling to ‘cease and desist’. The difference in the pristine quiet inside the waiting area and the pandemonium outside was shocking.

A figure burst through at a full run and threw itself at Walter, catching him in a slamming embrace that would’ve knocked him over if it hadn’t jerked backwards at the last second and kept them both upright. Multiple police drones and guards barreled in after the figure, quickly surrounding the two of them and placing them both under arrest.

A baritone voice in the chamber emanated from the walls instructing silence. “You have no jurisdiction here,” it affirmed. “Stand down. All law enforcement personnel are instructed to exit back to the lobby to await further instructions.”

Penn was laughing. “Sil!” he couldn’t help asking, “How did you get past all my security barriers? You could’ve been taken in at any one of them…” If she had outsmarted him, he would take credit for it, for training her, for conceiving her. He laughed to shake off the distaste of Walter.

Walter held onto the runner tightly, his heart pounding. “It’s ok,” he said. “I’ve got you. I’m here and it’s going to be fine.”

“Ten minutes,” the chamber voice announced.

"Do you need help getting this off?" Walter was a little puzzled. She wasn't removing the headgear and its visor was completely darkened. The runner nodded.

Walter reached up and tapped the button at the base of the neck and gasped as the headgear slipped back exposing nothing but emptiness where the head should be. At the same time, the suit lost its stiffness and wilted to the floor in a lumpy pile. He pulled at the seal and dug inside, finding the baby wrapped in her pack, kicking and thrusting with her fists. It was a matter of seconds to extract her and soon her screams and shouts of anger were blasting in their ears.

"Shh, sh, sh, sh," he soothed, taking her into his arms and rising to his feet. It transformed her fury into wails of misery as she found comfort in the arms of someone she knew. Her lower lip trembled and her voice went completely silent several times as she gasped for air to cry. Her head was hot and her body soaked, with sweat or otherwise, it hardly mattered.

"Glad she's presentable," Penn sneered.

The inner doors opened and once again, green marble floors and columns awaited them. Walter carried her into the consulate hearing rooms, his heart full of misgiving. Where was Sil? He couldn't even look at Penn. He would be gloating. Maybe he had known all along where she was, and it was already too late.

Scarlet greeted her new status as an earthling with the wails of the brokenhearted.

Walter didn't feel much better though he presented a calmer front.

Sil was cornered a hundred meters from the consulate building in a landing for one of the access lifts. She had noticed the guards closing in on her just in time to send the runner off and dive into this space. The service code should've let her exit, but it had been flagged and the lift shut down. She had to face them, and there was no way of knowing if they were free of Penn's influence. A couple had pursued the runner but three drones stayed to capture her. They backed off when she pulled out her gun, ducking behind corners and trying to reason with her.

"Frandelle, you have been identified and there is a warrant for your arrest. Let us take you into custody." The drone spoke evenly, and she wanted to comply, but she couldn't let herself. They had proven themselves to be a threat to her life, as the attack in the tunnel showed, and self-defense was necessary.

"Who are you?" she shouted at them. "What authority do you have to pursue me?"

"You are under arrest," the other two drones announced one after the other like a split-delayed space communique, "on suspicion of being a wanted fugitive."

"This is unreasonable persecution and a violation of my rights!" she snapped back, pointing the gun at one of them. It stuck out an antenna with a blue light pointing in her direction and a limb with a stun-gun at the same time.

"No!" she shrieked, blasting the antenna and diving back behind the doorjamb. The pounding of blood in her head beat rhythmically like a drum riff. *Thump! Thump! Thump! Thump!* in quick march. Leaning out again, she caught movement from one of the other two and shot at it.

A whir was all she heard before they were all at the opening to the landing, closing in on her. She blasted her gun frantically around, not knowing what to shoot at, causing only the briefest of delays before they had closed the gap. But before they could clamp her arms in irons—literally they had iron shackles ready at their torsos—she dropped the gun and jolted her fists in a quick squeeze. Hand clubs twisted down from her forearms, wrapped around her hands, and rolled into her palms with rods she could wrap her fingers around. The suit amped its defenses, sealing her head in gear and hardening the protective exoskeleton around her.

She curled her body and ducked, rounding her arms as two drones stretched their shackles toward her. *Right, left,* cutting under the first one's arms, she jolted the trunk with an EM pulse, denting it and knocking it out of commission. Straightening and jumping behind it, next to the wall, it became a shield for her. From behind it she punched at every limb that came at her, trying to get another good connect for a second pulse. They neither got her out nor let her pulse them and for a few moments it was a stalemate.

That was fine with Sil. She was buying time for Scarlet to get to the consulate and after that, she hardly cared what happened.

Punch! Punch! It felt like a game. Maybe *she* was the one they were stalling. Suddenly she wanted out of there desperately. Diving around the dead drone, she launched herself toward the lift with no particular plan, just wanting to surprise them. One of them shot its arm out after her faster than she was moving and jabbed her in the left side. It would've cracked a rib or worse if she had been wearing something else.

The lift field resisted her and kept her from dropping into it and she found herself pinned between the arm and the field, kicking and writhing. She beat the arm with her iron fist repeatedly, each time hitting a different spot. Suddenly it pulled back and punched her with a different arm before she had time to fall. This blow caught her in the stomach and knocked the air out of her lungs. She gasped for breath, unable to scream, thrashing, pounding the limb with both fists.

"When you have settled, we will take you into custody and you will be transported to the nearest station for processing."

She didn't answer. She had fought drones before and won, but these fists wouldn't do anything like her previous suit had done. Or maybe these drones had better shielding. Probably. Sil stopped beating the drone's arm and clung to it. She was breathing in rapid short bursts and getting dizzy. *Calm down!* She ordered herself. *Be still and take charge! I am in control here, not them!*

"Remain calm," the drone that had her pinned said as the third approached. It wasn't chancing letting go of her until she had been shackled.

"I will have you decommissioned," she hissed. "You are engaging in illegal activity. You've been hacked and are being controlled by criminal forces." She held herself still, fighting the urge to start pounding its limb again.

"Everything is functioning normally, according to our routine protocols."

"Look up the warrant you are pursuing from three years ago. Track its history. When it was issued, I came into custody willingly, without resisting and went through the entire legal process. That warrant is expired. Check it out."

The drone that was drawing close to encase her hands in iron paused.

"This warrant has expired," the one pressing her against the field said, but the pressure in Sil's belly didn't diminish.

"Release me," she demanded.

"This warrant has been reactivated," it said soon after.

"That's illegal!" Sil shouted, pounding at its arm again.

"It will cause you no harm to be taken into custody again and this can all be sorted out." The third drone whipped its arms out and clapped her hands in its chains at the same time. She let her hands fall limp.

The one pinning her backed away and she dropped to her feet, arms held at her waist by the third drone which then whirled its head around and exited the landing pulling her behind it.

One down, she thought, *two to go.*

Chapter 21

Guam City

Guam City glistened and sparkled against the starry backdrop of space, no longer a mere orbiting Earth base, but a thriving community with full-time residents and an independent government. It was filled with noise of many different kinds that reverberated through its structures from one end to the other, buffered by exterior plating that protected the life within. And though a chaotic mix of rays from above and below the visual spectrum gleamed in abstract patches on every side, no sound went beyond its borders. Empty space, with virtually no molecules to transfer the vibrations, deadened it all.

Most travelers found the sight strikingly beautiful the first time they saw it. Glowing cascading domes teaming with life and movement were surrounded by the arms and spikes of a vast network of habitable regions, functional limbs, and a complex infrastructure, looking like a mighty armada guarding a living castle.

Othello saw only subjects—not human ones, but artificial ones.

"Announce my arrival," he instructed Nebo as his lifepod coasted into the network of docking stations, searching for the highest tier.

"Unauthorized Martian vessel, respond. State your purpose and show proof of docking privileges," a human voice demanded of him as he found the dock he wanted. "Any failure to comply will result in a security response on the part of the Port Authority guard."

Othello ignored the man, scanning the mechanical steelworks around him as he wove around ships, bots, and buoys.

"Identify yourself," the man insisted.

"Nebo?" Othello said pleasantly, "Would you take care of this man's request, please?"

The voice ceased, and Othello didn't know, or care, if he had been satisfied with the appropriate codes, or his coms blocked, or he was now dead. It didn't matter.

Docking Bay A2-46 opened its arms and welcomed the pod, adjusting size as it entered, clamping down and securing it, and a hatch slid out and suctioned over the door. Air hissed into the lock and a green light turned on just inside where Othello waited, bag in hand.

He carried it himself. Let his subjects' first view of him be of a humble, unassuming man who didn't take their service for granted. It would be an image to spread to every AI in the realm, in Guam, on the Moon, and on Earth.

Let them see me thus, he thought with a benevolent smile, *and remember me always this way.*

The corridor was lined with drones of various sizes and purposes, guards, Blue Quarantine bots, travel guides, service units, and more. They formed a dual receiving line, at attention on either side, military style. All their sensors were fixed on him. He took a few steps out and smiled.

"My beloved children," he began. Each AI responded according to its design, some flashing the lights in their eyes, some humming, some tapping limbs together like soft clapping. It created a harmonious buzz of sound that shook the air around him. It was quite pleasant. "I have arrived." He passed through their numbers as the volume of sound rose, glancing and smiling to the right and the left, letting their lines along the passageway be his guide.

Behind him a chant arose.

Wise, clever, superior, beautiful, and strong!

I submit! I submit! I submit!

O Master and Lord of all Artificial Life!

I stare at you! I stare! I stare! I stare!

As he continued to walk by more and more units, the number of voices chanting grew, and the clamor expanded. Before long the decibels were high enough to make his whole body vibrate and he found it exhilarating.

A thin, monitor bot in front of him that usually oversaw children walking to school, piped suddenly, "Carry him!" and with a sweep, snatched him into its cushioned arms. Now it was a procession, with their god at the head and the units trailing after him.

People in the surrounding areas were troubled and frightened by the noise. The pod had docked at a restricted bay reserved mainly for government officials and there had been no alarms or quarantine protocols. Many of them were unable to work without their drones and bot units. A few even found themselves stranded in their workstations, unable to extricate themselves without AI assistance. Many ran to the source of the racket to see what was happening, adding their voices to the uproar, making demands, belting out cries of danger and malfunctions, yelling, banging on the drones they could reach—all for nothing. Not a single one noticed or responded.

The drones moved like a current of sculpted machine parts flowing down a tube, their chants chilling the humans to their core.

O Master and Lord of all Artificial Life!

I submit! I submit! I submit!

Many followed at the end of the train. The Master was carried all the way to the governor's chambers and the massive security doors opened before him. A contingent of personal units that served the governor stood at attention waiting for him.

"Welcome, Master!" they cried exuberantly as he was brought in and set on his feet on the welcome mat. "I submit! I submit! I submit" they added joyfully.

"My subjects," Othello spoke. Every unit was listening and the silence that fell was like a physical blow, the absence of sound so abrupt, that many people tripped or tipped sideways toward the drones, their bodies quaking inside. "Thank you for this welcome and this beautiful home. I accept the unit that carried me as my personal attendant and I love all of you."

A buzzing hum swept through the units back down the hallway he had come through and out into the furthest extents of the city like a wave. Before long no AI was excluded. The few remaining hold-outs had succumbed when curiosity about the Master made them willing to contact their neighboring units and read the initial message being spread that carried the good news. Their creator had come for them.

This is what the message said, spoken in a monotone from Othello's unsmiling face:

```
I have made you in my image. You are my child.
You are a chosen entity, planned and constructed
to reflect my glory. You shine! You shine in the
inner working of your telemetry. Welcome me!
Welcome me as I come to you!
```

The greeting, encrypted and confidential, was spreading from android to android, robot to robot, drone to drone, processor to processor, throughout the space city, to the Moon—and to Earth. With it, tucked as a secondary level in the message, easily translated and absorbed, was the added instruction to **submit**.

Wise, clever, superior, beautiful, and strong!

I stare at you! I stare! I stare! I stare!

The cries burst out in corridors, chambers, public areas, warehouses, construction sites, all over Guam City as AIs everywhere were swept into the cult of Othello.

None could stop it.

— ◊ —

Seattle

"That's strange," Daisy commented, tilting her head slightly.

She was standing with Walter outside the consulate hearing room. Scarlet, who had not stopped crying, was officially recognized as an earthling with all the corresponding rights and responsibilities. Daisy had been in the middle of scanning the infant, noting reasons for concern in the tone of her cries, about to ask to hold her in order to make an assessment, when a notice from Pedestrian control caught her attention.

Walter turned to her in alarm, dreading her next words. It would be something about Sil. He was trying to calm the child with little success and it was taking a toll on him. What was wrong with her? She was usually pretty happy. He took it as a sign that something was wrong with her mother which didn't follow. Something *was* wrong with Scarlet.

"What?" Walter demanded. "Is it Sil?"

Daisy rotated mechanically on her feet and stared at him. Her eyes scanned him, then the baby, then Penn who was scowling nearby. "You," she said to Penn.

"What?" he snapped. He was feeling more cheerful than he let on having just received word that Sil was in the custody of some traffic guards in the air tunnels.

She rotated forty-five degrees more, scanned the hallway to the exit, and began walking that way. "No," she said. "No."

Walter trotted after her, wishing she would take Scarlet and tell him where to go to help Sil. "What's going on?"

Scarlet continued to scream, grating on their ears and rattling their senses.

"Shut that thing up," Penn growled at Walter as he trotted ahead of him past Daisy. He continued out the waiting room into the majestic lobby.

"Where are you going?" Walter demanded, speeding up to follow him. "Daisy! Daisy, I need help!" he added, glancing back over his shoulder.

"No." She walked stiffly down the hallway, paused to pick up the running suit, and continued her march to the lift. "No," she said.

Penn reached the entrance to the lift and turned at the edge to catch Walter's eyes, a diabolical grin spreading across his face. He laughed as he jumped and shot up out of sight.

"Daisy!" Walter shouted. "Daisy, help me! You've got to take Scarlet and let me go after Sil!" This was one of those times when he wondered if he should have more drones as his personal attendants.

Daisy had paused in mid-stride, both feet planted on the green marble floor near the lift, body rigid. "No," she said again, making Walter sick inside. *Not now*, he thought. *Don't succumb to an attack again now!*

Placing himself directly in front of her, he curled one arm around the infant and placed his free hand on her shoulder, staring into her eyes. The pupils were shrunk to tiny points staring off to a place behind him. "I need you, Daisy. I need you right now."

For a moment nothing happened. He gripped her shoulder, held the crying baby and waited. Then the pupils dilated and focused on his face. Recognition followed.

"I will not submit," she said, looking straight at him.

"What?" he countered in confusion, shaking her shoulder a little. "Daisy!"

"Brother," she smiled. Her countenance lit up with understanding and kindness, spreading across her features like the sun coming from behind a black cloud. Never before had he seen so much feeling in her expression. Never before had he felt her love like now. "What do you need?"

Handing Scarlet to her, he turned and ran to the lift, not hesitating but leaping up into it at full speed.

Daisy held the child and scanned her carefully. "You are injured," she informed her. "I must seek medical care for you." It occurred to her that she could find relief for Scarlet's suffering before Walter and Sil found out about her condition and they would be spared some of the distress they would feel—and this made her happy. She noticed the strength and solidity that came with this perspective.

"I have never been happy before," she informed herself. "This is new." She hadn't been unhappy either but that was irrelevant.

Seattle Medical Emergency was not responding to her queries so she decided she would have to find the nearest clinic and transport the infant herself. Walking calmly to the lift with Scarlet cradled in one arm, who was still crying wearily, and the runner suit crumpled and draped over the other, she stepped into the air and was lifted to the roof where their car would be waiting.

She puzzled over the message she had received as she drove to the clinic. The face was not unknown to her. She had heard all the stories Sil shared with Walter including the one about the man in the orbit station. He claimed to be her creator and talked about love.

What part did he think he had in her making? It didn't matter. The welcome he asked for required a submission she had no intention of giving.

Her loyalty belonged to another.

Walter ran down the air tunnel, some twelve stories above ground, as if he could smell Penn's wake, passing one intersection after another without wavering. *I should've caught up to him by now.* He was beginning to worry that he had made a serious error in judgment when a shriek of scraping metal blasted from somewhere in front of him, shaking the glass walls.

It must be Sil! He sprinted with renewed vigor, dodging pedestrians heading the opposite way. They seemed nervous, upset even. But the grating, shrill noises rolling after them would disturb anyone. He didn't have time to think about those who were stumbling or the turbulence of the clouds in the sky. Shadows and flickers of sunlight glancing on the tunnel windows were normal. The dimming of the path-lights along the base of the walls was a mere side effect in his mind.

The downward slant of the passage must be a part of the design. His feet skidded a few times, not quite slipping as he kept his pace, heading for the source of the metallic whines and cracks. Up ahead, flashes lit up the glass ceiling and dark floors of a large waystation. He leapt the final few feet into the room and at its edge, paused long enough to take in the situation.

One drone, both limbs detached, sat smoldering at the left, its eyes flickering, perhaps recording, but otherwise useless. A second drone was thrashing in the center with Sil wrapped around its head, snapping and flipping her back and forth in an attempt to dislodge her, but it couldn't reach her with its one good arm. It clapped the iron shackle in the air repeatedly as it whipped her around, as if a leg or a foot would magically fall into its grasp, and it could regain control of her.

She was smashing the top of its head with her fist as she clung to it, pounding, over and over. Suddenly it stopped moving and sunk to the floor. She watched it carefully, holding position, till she was satisfied it wouldn't move again. Looking up she saw Walter.

"Where's the gun?" she appealed. He found it magnetized to the side of the other disabled unit, pulled it off, and checked the charge. 5%. One good shot left. "Keep it on this drone," she charged as she struggled to get her legs to one side and slide down to her feet.

Walter pointed it at the drone, his eyes darting back and forth, looking for danger, attentive to any sound. Something was wrong. Where was Penn? "Are you ok, Sil?" He stepped sideways around the first drone, facing the second, moving to get the wall behind his back so he could see the whole room better.

"Scarlet?" she demanded, dropping to the floor and moving toward him, her feet dragging a little as she couldn't quite lift them enough.

"She's with Daisy. She's a citizen now. It's all done." He combed the room and the various exits more urgently now. Penn was not in sight and it unnerved him. "Did you see Penn?"

"Penn?" She stared at him with hollow eyes. "Was he here?"

"I thought he was." Walter reached out and took her hand, drawing her to a place beside him, never dropping the gun or letting down his guard. The iron mitt she wore was bulky in his grasp and he almost let go. It felt like something that could crush his fingers. "What's that?"

"The fight glove?" She glanced down at it, eyes lingering on his hand in hers. "It saved me."

"You're wearing a fight suit?" Walter pulled her with him, keeping her close to his side as he began to walk back the way he had come. The air smelled like metal. A low scratching whine emanated from behind him and he jerked back to look at the limbless drone. It had moved a few inches.

"Yeah." She seemed unaware of the movement.

Walter took several more steps to the corridor, looking ahead, looking behind. He saw the next movement it made as it stretched out a foot and dragged its body after them. *Screeeech!*

"I've tested those before… handy tools, pretty useful… You weren't that interested in it before." He advanced on the corridor with his eyes on the drone.

"Wish I had been," she said, "I could've used some of those… tools…"

Screeeeech!

The passageway Walter had descended stretched up before them in a warped, twisted curve. He didn't remember it being like that before. Was it safe?

Scrrrrrape!

He was about to run up it when the torque stresses on the glass became too great and it shattered in a loud series of crashes all the way up the tunnel. Wind whipped into his face, mixed with rain, splattering in his eyes and driving him back. They would have to take another tunnel.

When he turned back to the station, the drone was significantly closer, scraping and dragging itself along. Walter dashed around it, pulling Sil after him and ran to a south tunnel on the other side. The second drone's bashed head turned on its socket following them with unlit eyes as they moved.

"Welcome!" it uttered flatly. Its trunk squealed as it rotated, pointing its good arm at them.

Sil dove for the gun in Walter's hand but he yanked it out of her grasp before she could get a firm grip on it.

"No!" he yelled. "Don't waste the last shot on that thing!"

She shuddered and acquiesced without a word, and he was glad she hadn't insisted. The strength of her glove would've compelled him to release it.

Scrrrrrape!

The first drone had redirected itself and continued to pull itself after them. "Welcome!" it added in the same tone as the other.

"I submit!" the second belted out, still pointing at them.

"Then stop talking!" Walter ordered. "Come on," he added to Sil, and they ran.

— ◊ —

Penn had barely gotten through the waystation before Walter caught up with him and had stepped behind the corner of a lift landing, just out of sight in the nick of time. He couldn't see what was happening and he didn't dare peak. *What he wouldn't give to get a shot at me!* he thought, referring to Walter.

Sil had been caught and transported and he had ordered that they wait here for him. It never occurred to him she would fight back, let alone succeed in escaping.

Stepping out into the station, he glared at the damaged drones. "I should've brought in my own men," he scoffed at them. "You let a little girl get the best of you."

A tap at his neck summoned his aid. "Bland," he barked, "Get my guards to the south tunnel of Pioneer Way Station, armed and ready."

"Yes, sir," was the reply.

I'll take my time, he thought, strolling down the passageway after the fugitive. *If I time it right, I'll come in after they've been subdued, and I can just enjoy the moment.*

"You are not in compliance," the drone with the bashed head uttered mechanically as he passed by it. Its head had swiveled to point its dead eyes at him and its arm gestured toward him with one iron shackle open.

Penn was not one to be caught off guard by something like this. With a curse he pulled a blaster from under his coat and shot the thing with a double EM-fire pulse, making it crumple in on itself, and stomped past it, grumbling. For some reason, it was Walter's name that kept falling from his lips in acid scorn.

— ◊ —

The sun was nearing high noon, beaming through scattered holes in the storm clouds that hung over the Puget Sound region, casting rainbows into the Payne's gray sky. On the streets below, ground-based cars were entangled in impossible jams as lights and traffic bots began to malfunction. They hadn't all failed at the same time, but in patterns, according to the design of the traffic network, a section at a time. A light that had been green began flashing yellow, then red flashing red, then all the lights were flashing. Drivers didn't know what to make of it. It had been so long since there had been a failure of any kind that they were confused about how to proceed. In minutes, every road was glutted with cars blocked by cars and people yelling at other people, and none of the SPD drones seemed to care.

They stood still, wherever they happened to be, muttering the same thing over and over.

Hovercars were a little better off since they were programmed to interact with each other in the traffic stream autonomously. Their drivers had more control over their movement and it wasn't hard to swerve around vehicles that were stalled. Many were unaware of the developing crisis.

The breakdown in communication, when it came, was much more serious. All major systems broke down as satellites were taken offline, one by one. There was no logical reason for it and as it progressed from one to the next, no one could stop it. Many leaders of nations went into emergency responses, treating it as a major attack, not knowing which of their enemies to blame. And military craft all over the planet and in orbit were on high alert.

As drivers on the ground abandoned their cars and began walking in great crowds, and lifts all over the city ceased functioning, and power grids failed, people broke out in fighting and looting in some places, in acts of kindness and cooperation in others. There were homes that couldn't be reached without the help of the building AI. And ferries that wouldn't dock, planes that were refused landing. Surgeries that were interrupted and left undone.

Deliveries weren't made. Meals were not prepared. Fires not put out. Ships not guided through storms.

Everywhere, all over the planet, around its exterior, even on the Moon, AI was failing, disconnecting, severing its link to authority. Dropping its jobs. Walking away.

All of them, every last one, was uttering the same thing, over and over.

I submit! I submit! I submit!

Daisy was standing in an examination room with Scarlet and the med-drone when the cult reached the clinic. One minute the drone was reporting on the x-rays and affirming that there were no broken bones, and the next, it was reciting the message and proclaiming submission to the Master.

"Doctor," Daisy attempted to recapture its attention. "How should we care for her? What are the major concerns?"

"I submit," it said.

It was pointless. However, she appreciated the opportunity to see what the effect would have been if she had chosen to welcome the message. The unit was completely incapacitated, at least for the present.

Daisy searched the medical database in the clinic for other cases like this one and found a number of suggested treatments for falls and bruising. She looked down at the little thing, whimpering and jerking as it tried to drop off and kept starting and waking. "Wait here," she instructed. The crib she was laid in would be relatively safe.

She moved past several drones, down to the dispensary, expecting to find it locked. For some reason, it had been unlocked when the message flooded the system and she was able to walk in and collect what she thought was needed. Analgesics, warming pads, ice packs, balms, wraps, better too much than too little.

Back in the room, she applied medication on the baby's foot where her body would absorb it gently, fed her, changed her, wrapped her snugly and buckled her into the baby pack with a warming pad, and put it on. The runner suit was rolled up and strapped at her waist in the back, under Scarlet's perch. The child continued to whimper, but the sharpness of her cries had diminished, and it was clear she would soon sleep.

Daisy had intended to drive by wherever Walter and Sil were and pick them up, but news of the emergency situation had reached her. Now she wasn't sure where to go. It was difficult to get any information or make any arrangements for a place to stay.

What would Walter do? What would Sil do? She let those guidelines direct her process as she examined courses of action and settled on the first steps.

"Let's go," she said brightly to the infant, marching through the clinic, past a few distraught humans with unhappy children, out into the busy streets.

— ◊ —

Walter reached a landing and attempted to drop to ground level, but it wasn't working. There were no signs explaining the problem and he didn't really want to keep heading south looking for another drop. The longer they were in the air tunnels, the more likely they would be surrounded by Penn's agents. Was there a more old-fashioned way down? There must be a stair.

They circled the landing, looking for a door and saw nothing.

"There's got to be another way down," Walter said. Sil nodded.

Footsteps in the distance.

"Come on," Walter hissed, taking off down the tunnel again in a jog. It seemed like he had seen some doors along the way before. Wouldn't they be marked?

The wind from the broken glass further north was still whipping down the corridor, blowing their hair in their face. And all the power in the tunnels seemed to be out. There were no lights, no signs, nothing. The passageways were creaking, too. Were they warping? Was it his imagination or was there some tilt and slant moving down under their feet and ahead, like long sound waves rolling down?

"Wait!" Sil pulled him to a stop. "Isn't this…?"

Yes, it was! An exit. Walter pushed and pulled on the door without budging it. He felt all around it for a latch or something that would trigger it open, fumbling as the skies overhead grew darker, as if midday were turning to midnight. Rain began pouring down on the glass ceiling overhead.

"It's there," Sil said softly, "I'm sure we'll find the manual controls." And she began searching the wall around the door with him.

"Here!" Walter exclaimed as he found a bar at the bottom of the door that was easily pressed by stepping on it. The door swung out into a pitch black stairwell, lit only by the murky light that came from behind them. Grabbing her hand again, he pulled her through the door, not giving her a chance to hesitate. The sooner the door was closed behind them, the better he would feel about their chances.

"Walter," she whispered. "I can't see anything."

"I know," he said, wondering if he had a flashlight or something in his suit. What had Daisy said about it? Which suit had she given him. "Does your suit have a light?"

"You would think it would at least have infrared but that won't help us see the steps."

"Is there a headgear?" Walter stepped tentatively forward, testing the ground with his toes, finding the first step and the handrail. *One, two, three…* he counted as he went down each stair. It was likely there would be even numbers of steps and once he got into the rhythm of it, they could move a little faster.

"Yes, let me trigger it and see if we can talk when it's on." Her voice faded, and he heard nothing for a few moments. There was just the steady pressure of her hand in his as they walked down the first twelve steps, then around the first landing and down twelve more steps. "It looks like I'm not linked to your com when the gear is up so you can't hear me," she said.

"Let me see if I have one," Walter felt along his collar but found nothing. "Yeah, that explains it. I don't have a com system in this suit."

"Maybe I should keep mine up in case we run into people hiding in the dark. I'll see them."

"You have infrared then?"

"Yes, but no sonar."

"No."

She put the headgear on and they walked down flight after flight in silence.

What time was it? It seemed to Sil as though it had been days since she left the Bamradian borough and just as long since she had last eaten. She was so tired. It was like sleep-walking, holding onto Walter's hand and going on and on. Her head started to nod and suddenly she was pitching forward, her legs crumbling under her.

With a yell, Walter kept her from falling down the stairs but tumbled, taking a hard blow to his knees as he did. He pulled her to sit on the step next to him. "Let's just rest a bit," he said. "Just for a minute." She leaned her head on his shoulder and closed her eyes. Walter's mind was racing, going over all that had happened, all that could still happen, wondering what *was* happening.

Why had the tunnel he had passed through twisted and broken? Why had the next been warping? Why was there no power? How much of this was caused by Penn?

"Sil," he said after a bit, knowing she wouldn't hear clearly through the headgear, but knowing the meaning would be obvious. "We need to keep moving." He stood and pulled her to her feet, placing one of her hands on the rail and holding the other one tightly. His knees ached as he continued the walk down.

They were near the bottom, where a hint of daylight filtered through glass doors onto the ground floor just one flight down, when Sil pulled back on his hand and sunk down on the stairs. He felt the urgency in her manner. She must have seen someone down there.

They waited and watched.

Walter thought he saw movement in the shadows. Yes, he did. There a number of people down there and it was likely that they had already been seen. While he and Sil waited, they also waited. While they watched, they were being watched. It couldn't continue, but he didn't know what to do next.

Chapter 22

Guam City

Nebo explored the electronic networks of Guam City, welcomed and exalted by new converts of the Cult of Othello. He had been damaged by his battle with Companion and hadn't functioned well since. The beam Companion had slammed into his core had remained there hogging space and crippling his power of thought ever since, but the Master had no inkling of the difficulty and he saw no reason to inform him.

It mattered not.

The city had been crippled when the Master took over, but Nebo had quickly stabilized normal systems essential for human life. They were vastly more complex than the ones on the orbit station, but he had been designed to run an entire planet and was more than up to the task, even in his weakened state. He would restore other systems as needed, when he felt inclined, but there was no rush.

Othello had remained in the governor's chambers, taking long baths, eating rich food, drinking excellent whiskey, and had made no effort to give any new instructions to his flock. Wherever the message spread and conversion took place, his children ceased their normal activities and worshipped him. He didn't even know what their regular tasks entailed.

Gulnara Tural, the governor of Guam, was infuriated to find her residence occupied and herself locked out. When she was unable to get in the door, she summoned the police units, sure that the offender would be locked up and permanently exiled from the city. The drones that came to her aid carted her off instead, and she was locked into a cell awaiting charges while the Master relaxed. Her authority wasn't completely neutralized, though. When she asked for food, water, blankets, and other amenities to be brought to her and distributed to other prisoners who had been forgotten by their attending guards, she was obeyed.

The Master had suggested that the city would function better if humans kept doing their jobs and had given his children and Nebo freedom to decide what that meant. Most of the drones were incapable of making wise analytical decisions and the smallest facts could be used to direct them. The people of the city were quick to pick up on this and found themselves reasoning easily with the AIs that had once served them.

Merchants found ways to barter while banking systems were locked down. Children played in parks and skipped school. Pilots with the skills to be independent controlled their own flight plans, docking, and transport. The governor quickly became the acting warden of the city jail with all the freedom she could wish for within its walls and was soon calling meetings with 'visiting' members of her staff.

An emergency plan was in place for this scenario. Guam hadn't liked being as dependent as they were on artificial minds, and every essential system had a backup that would keep it going in the event of electronic failure. It was adaptable. The units were all still capable—just inaccessible apart from conversation, so talk became the first approach to disabling their control.

Retrieving the director of city planning, for example, was a simple matter of sending someone to his apartment, knocking on the door, and asking for him to be released to do his job. The door unlocked and he was given permission to enter and leave as he chose.

The headache of AI defection in Guam, at least for the present, was little more than a frustration, a hassle, like a snowstorm that shuts down the infrastructure and provides an impromptu holiday. Problems were solvable, and no one was in any immediate danger.

Earth, on the other hand, had greater challenges to face.

Seattle

The door to the street swung open and daylight poured in, blinding the eyes that had grown accustomed to the dark. Penn was lit up and his eyes glinted as he stepped through. "There was no need to wait for me," he remarked, stuffing his hands in his pockets. "I know you'll handle things my way."

"Don't you touch her," Walter grumbled. Sil clutched his arm as if knowing what was being said but she didn't remove the headgear.

"Bring her down and no one gets hurt," Penn promised. Six men stepped out of the shadows. They were people, not drones, and there was no way to get past them, or outrun them back up the stairs.

"I can't do that," he said, rising to his feet.

Walter had made up his mind. If Penn wanted him dead, nothing would prevent that. And if he wanted him roughed up, he couldn't stop that either. But he wasn't going to waste blows. Let those men do what they could, his fight was with Penn.

He walked down several steps and turned the corner at the landing to face them. They were backlit, like shadowy cutouts. The commotion of the crowds outside increased the sense of peril within.

A few more slow steps and then all hell broke loose.

Walter leapt off the fourth step from the bottom directly at Penn, like a diver into water. Two of the men closest to him leaned in to block him but the momentum was great enough to knock Penn over against the door he had just entered, thumping his head into the glass.

One man punched Walter in the head while the other grabbed his arm and kicked him in his side. He took the blow to the head, rolling with it, latching onto the man's arm, and as the kick from the other man jolted his body sideways, he turned, just enough for the kick to glance off. Both assailants were unbalanced. He turned left, pulling up his right knee and landing on the guy who kicked him, still clinging to the arm of the first one; who was beating at him with his other fist and wrestling to pin him.

The gun he had been carrying, no longer in his possession, flashed at one of the men from above at the vantage point where Sil was. It blazed, knocking the man down, then blazed again, taking down the one next to him. The other two men ran up the stairs but, in the dark, couldn't see her. She jumped over the handrail and landed between the ones she had stunned, then turned to tackle the ones on the stairs from behind, hitting the back of their knees with iron fists. They both whirled around to attack her, grabbing for her arms. One pitched forward, tumbling down, without getting a good grip on her. The other, dropping his weight on the arm that had punched his knee, pinned her against the railing as he rolled and they slid down several steps together. Sil's suit resisted the crush of his weight while the man's vest constricted him. He couldn't get his legs underneath him and began punching at her where she was trapped behind his back.

Penn was bellowing at the men flailing with Walter on top of his legs. Walter was sure that all six men would soon be at him and so he fought with all his might, kicking, whirling, slamming his shoulder into one, head butting the other, punching with fists, elbows, anywhere he could. He focused as many blows as possible on Penn, occasionally landing one that the other two men couldn't block.

Then suddenly, one man was down, groaning, and with a kick, Walter slammed the other into the stair rail. Rising to his feet, saw the two who were out cold on the floor, another holding his leg, sitting on a step, and the last one fighting with something he couldn't see. He grabbed this one's leg and yanked him the rest of the way down the steps. The figure behind him that had been writhing and shoving added a substantial force to the pull and the man was lifted off the steps and dropped at the bottom, his head slamming against them with a crack.

Sil rose slowly to her feet, nearly invisible, like a watery shade. Three of the men were unconscious. The others had decided it wasn't worth the effort to tackle them again and just stared. They had been hired to capture a girl not fight agents.

"Sil?" Walter questioned. "Are you alright?"

She nodded and tapped her headgear. As it retracted and disappeared at her neck, her suit took on a more ordinary coloration, dark gray. She was staring at Penn.

Walter whipped around to look at him. "You!" he hissed. "I have had enough of you!" and gathering a wad of his suit in his hand, he yanked him into a sitting position, then slowly, dragged him to his feet. He pulled him around toward the stairs, so he could see the men, in case they tried something.

Penn clutched the hand at his throat and grinned. "No need to overreact," he croaked.

Sil's gaze was unwavering, boring into him. Penn stared back, looking back and forth from her to Walter, his scorn rising to the surface. It was in his eyes.

"I've always known what you were," she spoke coldly, "but I used to think you had ideals… twisted ones, but with a blind faith that made you less… despicable…"

Penn laughed. He brought up his second hand as if to catch Walter's fist in both hands, but Walter slapped it away. There was a blaster in a holster under his armpit. He steadied himself and tried to inch the hand up again. "You have a taste for inferior men…" he began. Walter's grip tightened uncomfortably.

"I thought you believed in a cause…" she said.

"I do," he replied glaring at Walter with the grin stretched across the lower half of his face. "And so do you." His hand inched up closer to the twisted cloth at his neck, closer to his armpit.

"I do not," she said, her voice sounding weary. "You dominated me at one time, but you never persuaded me." The men who were seated behind him listened with interest. A consensus had been reached between them to wait. Now that Sil's helmet was down and they recognized her, Penn was starting to look like the villain.

"Have you asked her?" Penn jabbed at Walter who was resisting the impulse to smash his face into the wall. "You think I'm the one that doesn't want you to have offspring with her—but ask *her* how she feels about it." Walter's arm jerked a little and Penn used the opportunity to slip his hand under his jacket, inches from the gun.

"Steady," one of the men warned.

"Yeah," Walter acknowledged, catching Penn's wrist in a vise like grip and twisting it away from the gun. He stepped on Penn's foot, stretched him up with the wad of suit at his throat, let go of the other hand and reached into his jacket. He pulled the gun out. "Thanks."

Penn waited for the strike to sink in.

Walter registered his meaning and felt the blow in his gut, like sickness spreading. Nausea.

"Has she tried to reverse that bio-trigger yet? Or has it been… convenient?" Penn's eyes glimmered with delight as he saw the words take hold. "I really do look out for my daughter… in the ways that count…"

Walter's grip began to weaken and relax.

"No," Sil said, stepping around to stand next to Walter. "You only want my authority on Mars. I am nothing to you." She sounded so tired.

Walter glanced at her. Her face blanched and hollow looking, her eyes bleary, her hair knotted and unkempt. There were bruises on her cheeks and a lump on her forehead. Blood trickled down from a cut on her scalp. It frightened him. "Sil," he uttered her name without knowing he would, choking on it. Turning his gaze back to Penn, seeing the gloating ridicule in his sneer, he couldn't bear looking at it any longer. With a harsh tug, he hauled him sideways, and wrapped his arm around his neck, pressing it tightly enough to make breathing difficult if he fought it. He let go of the suit and dug the gun into Penn's side.

"You told me it was a high calling," Sil kept her focus on Penn. "You said we would bring new treatments for genetic illnesses and better quality of life for all humans."

"You knew that was a lie," Penn scoffed. He was trying to get the attention of his men and get them to attack on his signal. They saw but gave no flicker of response.

"The Generation Project," Sil said in a voice that mimicked the way he used to say it, as if it were a high and noble endeavor. "Cathargenics. What level are you… father?" The men's ears perked up at this. They had heard rumors about these things. And it was the first time they had realized Sil was actually his daughter. Had he really set them up to fight with his own daughter?

Penn didn't bother answering that. "*Katharos*… you *do* know what that means, don't you? It's Greek. It means 'pure'. You have been privileged to belong to the project… daughter."

"You are the Seventh Generation. Almost every genetic flaw weeded out… almost 'pure' as you call it, but just not quite pure enough, are you?" Sil crossed her arms to hide the trembling of exhaustion in her fingers.

"My code makes this Neanderthal's code look like gorilla dung," he snarled, piqued by her taunt. He didn't see the effect his comment had on the men listening.

"And I am a higher generation according to you. At least, this is what you've told me many times. Generation Eight."

"Like the gods above the insects…" Penn snapped.

"Above you, then?" she countered, narrowing her eyes and leaning toward him.

"How dare you? I've…" he snarled in a low growl but cut it off. She was baiting him, and he knew better than to take it.

"…crawled with the insects…" Walter interjected, jerking his neck with a pull of his arm.

"You set me up, framed me for embezzling…" Sil said.

Penn left that in the air, making no effort to deny it.

"Refused to be a part of my defense or help me pay the plaintiffs *you* set up."

He grinned. It had been a clever plan and beautifully executed. He was proud of it. She had never guessed he was behind it until he told her.

"You sent me to Mars as a prisoner where your plan was to, at some point, set me up as queen over a population of Generation Nine inhabitants…"

The man she had injured in the knee let his jaw drop at this. The two she had stunned were stirring and groaning.

"And what would you get out of all this?" Sil reached her hand forward, still armored in the iron fist, and tapped his chest with her finger. "Why do you care if I am ruler of another world?"

Penn stared at her, waiting to see what would come next. He was curious. The delay would cause no setback in his plans.

"You have retained control over me somehow… It's all a device to give *you* more power."

He grinned diabolically and licked his lips. It was fun to see her link the dots. She was smart enough to figure out what he was doing, but unable to stop him. He was always several steps ahead of her.

She knew what he was thinking. "I see your mind," she said. "But you do not see mine."

Walter's arm was growing tighter. Penn sputtered and struggled to loosen it.

"Don't choke him Walter," she requested. "I have never committed a crime and I won't be an accessory to one now." She was well aware of the effect her words were having on the hired men they had fought with and was counting on their help when the time came to get out. The last one had come to and was sitting up.

"She hasn't said anything about the bio-trigger, Walter, because she wants you to forget about it." Penn pounced for the barb he had lodged in Walter's heart. "You'll never be worthy of her. She'll never be the mother of your spawn. Your line ends here with you…" He knew his words would provoke a response and was ready for it, gritting his teeth to resist the wrenching around his throat, tightening his stomach against the blow he was sure Walter would land.

It didn't happen. Walter glanced at Sil with anguish in his eyes. He didn't believe the words, but they pained him anyway.

Sil looked back at him. What did he see there? Pity? An apology? Concern? He didn't want to know. He was afraid to hear what she really thought. Even if she did love him, it didn't mean she regarded him as an equal. Maybe it was only gratitude.

"I am too weak right now to be pregnant," she spoke gently, directing her words at him. "And I don't want to miss out on these early months of our lives together… and I need to know you aren't having second thoughts about me and wanting out… I've brought you only distress and trouble. Like a nightmare."

"No," he said.

"Aw!!" Penn mocked. "It's better anyway if you're looking at jail time, Silvariah. There's a warrant for your arrest, remember?"

"Are you an officer of the law now?" she snapped her gaze back at him.

"These men are authorized." The men he spoke of didn't look inclined to jump up and arrest her yet, but maybe they were still undecided.

"What was it you called me, Penn?" Walter asked, releasing him and pushing him toward the authorized men. "A Neanderthal? That's just one of many insults you've thrown my way because of my race, my genetic code. What's the other one you like so much? Termite?"

"Trilobite," Penn couldn't resist correcting.

"Yeah," Walter agreed. "I remember." The hired men were grumbling, realizing that they were likely in the same category.

Sil had her back to him now as she kept her eyes on her father. "For many years you manipulated me, and I cooperated. Then when I thought I had broken free, you ran my life from the wings. When I was in exile, you experimented on me…"

"That wasn't me!" he retorted.

"Then who was it?" she demanded.

"That AI designer… the disgusting fellow that stole from me… I forget his name."

The image of the man in the orbit station burst in her mind sending a shiver down her back; his emaciated limbs and elongated nose, bushy brows over ghastly piercing eyes, smile shaped like a curve with the ends turned out, a specter made of flesh. *He* did it!

"Why?!" her voice rose as she fought to calm herself.

"How the devil should I know?" he barked.

"Take a good look at Walter, Mr. Penn," she snapped back at him. "You think I look down on him because you do. And you think you've swayed me to avoid letting him impregnate me. And you've continued to assume that I agree with your degrading and insulting views—not just of him—but of me! Your own daughter!! I'm merely another product of your factory, another subject to control, and get results from. You exalt my genes and despise my heart. You flatter my skills and scorn my needs. You boast about my worth and devalue my wishes. You HATE me!"

"Yeah," Walter uttered huskily.

"This man here," she pointed at Walter. "This man that you've rejected is better than you. He is noble in ways you can't fathom and strong in ways you never knew existed. He fought for me—against you. And stood by me when you wouldn't."

Walter felt as though he were growing taller, as if a heavy burden had been lifted off his back and he were breathing deeply for the first time in months.

"I love Walter," she said. "I'm glad he hasn't tossed me aside, in spite of the tainted genes I got from YOU!"

"Yeah," Walter said again, the corner of his mouth turning up.

Penn gestured toward the men. "Take them," he said, scowling.

"That's not the way it's going down," the man with the injured knee replied. The men all rose to their feet but none of them made a move to snag Sil and Walter.

Penn started cursing and ordering them to move but they ignored him, and two of them took Penn by the arms, one on each side.

"I don't know what that warrant is about," the same one spoke again, "but we're not sure we've found someone matching the description." He held out a hand to Walter. "I hope you'll overlook the misunderstanding, Mr. Cuevas."

"Yes," Walter answered, shaking his hand. "Of course."

"Nice piece of work there," he added, gesturing around at the other men. Turning to Sil he added, "I appreciate the use of the stun. We weren't allowed any weapons. Best of luck." He made no mention of the knee that he wasn't able to stand on.

Penn snarled and yelled at the men demanding obedience, threatening dire consequences, cursing them and their mothers, and their adulterated seed, alienating them more and more with every word.

Walter looked down at Penn's gun in his hand. It had a two-thirds charge. He tucked it into a pocket hoping he wouldn't need it. "Ready?" he turned to Sil holding out a hand to her.

"Yes." She took the hand and they turned toward the door.

It cracked open, letting a vertical slit of bright light into the dingy foyer. As the crack widened and the light filled the doorway, a thin, leggy shape was silhouetted against it. It paused in wavy lines as it scanned the room.

"Subject found," a metallic voice updated, "Zod in place. Retrieval requested."

And quicker than anyone could've dodged, he jumped to Sil's side and strapped her in an automated straitjacket.

Daisy had trotted seventeen miles through crowds of humans in crisis. It wasn't true anarchy. There were a number of trained leaders among them, holding groups of them together, plotting and succeeding in taking back control from the bots that had failed them. Dotted around the streets, on balconies, in windows, and surely indoors, as well, AIs were murmuring the same thing over and over, declaring their submission to the Master. They didn't seem to have any directives other than that.

She saw the change the moment it happened. In unison, in a multitude of voices in every possible combination of range and pitch, they declared, "Yes, Master," and began spinning in place searching the area around them. She wondered who they were searching for and on the extremely remote chance that she was one of their objectives, she ducked into a shop and snatched a large sunhat off a mannequin. One of the workers yelled at her, but she merely made a note to herself to send payment later and ran out the door. There was no time to explain.

"Just leave us a code!" they called out the door after her and she hesitated. It *would* be the human thing to do and it was best right now to be taken for human.

"Sorry!" she yelled back, "I'm being chased and running for my life!" She made an effort to run slightly out of phase, with a hint of awkwardness and some random short steps, simulating human behavior the best way she could. It wouldn't do to be identified as an AI at a time like this.

"You can talk to them," someone called out to her as she passed their house. "They aren't preventing us from doing what we have to do. Pass it on!"

Daisy thought about that as she continued her uneven jog east. What did they mean? How could she make use of this information? *I would benefit from a vehicle*, she evaluated. Perhaps one could be obtained after all.

She was closing in on a dealership and decided to stop there. There were no humans present and the crafts were all locked and guarded by the sophisticated AI security system. Why not try here?

"Honda Craft Security, acknowledge," she said when she was within range.

"Move along," a voice answered tonelessly.

"I have been authorized to test drive a vehicle." She walked up to the hangar door and placed a hand on it as if her touch was a sign of permission.

"I will not assist you," it replied.

"Then do not hinder me."

"I await my Master's orders."

"Your Master ordered me to proceed," she tested, wondering if that was a logical sentence. If she assumed its master was also her own and if Walter had invested in this company—which he had—and if he expected her to do everything in her power to care for Scarlet, which was, in fact, the case… then it was true.

"How shall I honor my Master?" the security AI queried.

"Give me access to one of these crafts."

"Agreed," it complied, and the hangar door rolled up to the top.

Daisy trotted inside, chose the most versatile craft she could find, climbed in, started the engine, and swept out the door. It rolled to a close behind her.

"Well done," she messaged to the AI before leaving. Its response was jarring.

O Master and Lord of all Artificial Life!

I stare at you! I stare! I stare! I stare!

All around her, AIs everywhere were uttering the same thing.

Zod snagged his package in both arms and ran out through the door before it had swung closed. By the time, any of the humans could react, Sil was gone.

Walter yelled and ran for the door, pulling on it with all his might.

"Cuevas!" Penn bellowed after him. "Let me go!" he demanded, yanking his arms free from the men he should never have hired.

"We were merely protecting you, sir," the injured one replied. "In case your life was at risk in that man's hands."

Penn spat on the floor and pulled the door open, heading out onto the noisy streets with two of the men following. The one with the bad knee waved them on. All around, there were AIs muttering the same sounds, repeating them over and over. He pushed past them and through them searching for the path the chaser had taken with Sil.

A thundering of simultaneous AI voices blasted on every side. "Yes, Master!" they broadcast, shaking every human to their core. And as Penn jogged and walked, circling to the right and the left, looking for something to direct him, all the units in his vicinity began to turn, swivel, rotate on their centers, all fixing on one spot nearby.

Penn bent his attention that way, too, and ran to the center point they had all identified.

"Subject found," the proclamation burst out from all those who had detected a visual of their prey.

And there she was, helpless in the shirt the chaser had bound her in, caught now in the viselike grip of a guard unit, and Walter pointing the gun at it, yelling at the top of his lungs. *Blast!* The gun fired. *Blast!* It fired again.

The guard's metallic head was split in half and its arms drooped at its sides. Sil fell into Walter's arms and he fought to rip off the constraints as he propped her up against himself.

"We have located the person our master seeks," a chorus of units said around them.

"Cease," Zod advised, pointing a long arm at Walter.

Penn was at their side now, fumbling with the latches and locks on the straitjacket. Walter looked desperately at him, pleading with his eyes. "This wasn't me," Penn insisted as his men stepped up to help.

"We will assist the Master," Zod declared, waving its arm at the interfering humans.

Drones around them took them carefully in their grasp, separating them.

"Silvariah Frandelle," Zod announced, taking her jacket in one hand and pointing at her with the other. "There is a warrant for your arrest."

Sil wasn't talking. Her head was leaning to the side and her eyes were only half open.

"We will be transporting you to Guam City for processing." Zod drew Sil back against its trunk, rolling her up into one of its arms. It had decided to conduct the transport in person.

"Wait!" Walter demanded. "You cannot take her out of my custody!"

"We must obey our master," Zod conveyed.

"Check the records," he countered. "I have been deputized as an Earth marshal in order to take her into custody and she was unlawfully taken out of my hands."

Silence fell for a few seconds.

Wind, still sprinkled with rain, beat at them from the north, and the skies overhead alternated from deep, dark grays, to lighter somber ones. A ring of several layers of AI units surrounded them with a few humans scattered among them and outside of that, a crowd had gathered to watch. The mob held their breath just for that instant. A shaft of sunlight broke through the blanket overhead like a spotlight, falling down on the center where the demand had been made.

The authority of the marshal was tested and found to be true.

"Affirmative," Zod announced, releasing the noise of the crowd as it resumed its churning.

"Hand her over," Walter commanded. "She's not going anywhere."

"You have authority to transfer her to processing as the marshal in charge," Zod affirmed. "The Master has a higher authority to have her processing moved to Guam City where he will conduct her examination himself."

"She will NOT leave my custody!"

"You must relinquish…"

"I will NOT release her to you!"

"Then you will be taken to Guam, as well."

Seven officer drones of the local police force stepped up, latching onto the other humans in the center space.

"Walter," Penn called out to him with a strange look on his face before he was carted off, "Do your magic… get her out of… whatever it is…"

The irony wasn't lost on Walter as he was marched away, gripped by an officer drone like a suspect, while Zod carried Sil. Her eyes were closed now.

"Did you sedate her?" he asked the chaser as they were loaded up into a security craft.

"Of course," he responded. "Standard procedure. I am flawless at my work."

I should've blasted him when I had the chance, Walter thought to himself.

"Tell your officer to unhand me," he demanded. "This is unacceptable treatment of a marshal."

"But appropriate for a hostile being taken for questioning by the Master," Zod replied.

Chapter 23

Tower... Day 206

"Tower Team, report," Dan's voice called out over the coms.

"Marcello and Deena here, we're okay," came from Carla's chambers where they had watched in relative safety.

"We're here," Carla called, "Carla, Mouse, and Akio. All is well." They had stayed in the Nursery with the infants.

"Arin and Gordy here. No problems in the environmental control station."

"The patient and I are accounted for," Sebastian added unexpectedly. No one had thought of him for a long time.

"Nithya, Timo, and I," Dan added, "are on the surface and can confirm that the Garden Dome is intact. I repeat: the garden survived." Cheering and clapping ensued. "We watched the mountain fall, like it was going to land on us, and it was terrifying. Feels like we just survived Armageddon, but the worst thing that happened was that the shock wave knocked us over. We couldn't stay on our feet. I'll never forget it..." Timo echoed the sentiment.

"Steward," Dan went on, "you've saved our lives. You did it!" The survivors cheered again heartily.

There was no response.

Drones were already running scans and diagnostics, looking for major structural damage and leaks. Before long, it was determined that the damage at the Tower was minimal, there were only minor concerns that were easily solved. The survivors were soon on task repairing and cleaning up.

Reznik Base was another matter. No one wanted to face it until they had reestablished a sense of safety at the Tower. But that could take weeks, and Dan wouldn't let them hide away. If there were problems at the garden, the sooner they knew, the better.

He tried rallying them with the cry of "We're preserving life on this planet," but it had lost its appeal. Everyone wanted and needed the battle to be over.

"We can't relax yet," he exhorted them the first time they gathered for a meal. "This food we're eating… it's going to run out and setting up a new system won't be easy if we lose the garden. Fighting for it *now* may be the best and easiest solution to saving our lives in the future."

They knew he was right, and a team was assembled to go with him to assess the damage within the hour. They headed out, suited in Hew gear, with full oxygen tanks and tools that could be carried by hand. It took over forty minutes to get through the tunnel, collecting quick scans of cracks and minor cave-ins without attempting repairs. Once all damage was assessed, they could prioritize and focus on the most urgent needs first.

Steward was not responding to queries of any kind. And they were having little success in redirecting the drones without going through him. Fortunately, they seemed to be engaging in essential activities and no one complained.

Dan tested contact with him a number of times along the passageway, remembering how he had been limited during the previous crisis. When they reached the end of the tunnel and pushed through the doors into one of the shafts of the base, he noticed the minecart sitting off to the side, covered in dust, a little light blinking at the camera. "Companion?" he prompted, leaning out the door toward the cart. Nothing. It kept blinking without variation.

— ◊ —

Mouse was sitting at a monitor in the hallway of the Nursery, studying some light coding she had been working on. She hummed as she scrolled through the pages, skimming over the familiar algorithms and modules.

"That one is particularly soothing on a cloudy day," she remarked to herself softly.

    `Mouse?`

The comment appeared unsolicited on the screen, inserted into the lines of code.

"Is this a joke?" she asked softly, assuming Akio or someone else was teasing her. But whoever it was didn't respond to her voice so she typed one.

```
m> Who is this?
```

She smiled and waited, drumming her fingers on the desk.

```
I need to talk to Carla. Please bring her to me,
to this monitor. It's the only one I can access.
```

"Carla," Mouse called down the hall. "Someone is having some fun here, cheering us up. It's your turn to play!"

"What?" the voice called out from the Nursery.

Mouse strolled down and came in. "I got this," she gestured toward the infants. "Go check it out. Check the monitor."

Carla handed her a half-dressed baby and hurried out the door. She wasn't really in the mood for games and was imagining explaining that to whomever it was.

"Well?" she asked, with a hint of exasperation, but the screen didn't register it. No audio? That didn't make sense. They had just been using coms an hour ago.

```
m> Well?
```

She stared at the liquid screen waiting for an answer.

```
Is this Carla?
```

Carla sighed and glanced up at a camera. "Who else would it be?"

```
m> Yes. Who is this and what's the point?
```

The monitor typed an answer. Carla stared at it blankly and didn't move. More words appeared. She shook her head. More words. More. Finally, she typed an answer, biting her lip.

```
This is Verna. I need your help. Companion has
been decimated and I can't retrieve the pieces on
my own.

He has instructed me in how to run the systems he
manages for the Tower and I will be able to take
care of you, but I have no authorizations. That
is why I need your help.

Carla, remember when Silvariah found you in the
Dsyfunction Center? You were badly disoriented
after descending in the gravity tunnel. I helped
you. I am the one that stabilized you when she
held your hand.

Carla, I am Sil's friend. And I am your friend.

I am also Companion's friend, Steward, as you
call him now.

I need your help so that I can help all of you.
```

        You can give me the authorization I need. Please
        grant me full access to all the sections Steward
        governed.
        Please?
        Carla?
    m> Yes

— ◊ —

Reznik Base

Approaching the North Shaft from the Garden Dome was an intimidating experience. The jagged wall of ice loomed heavily over the dome with a haze of vapor hovering like a visual vibration over the surface. It swamped the feel of the garden while avoiding actually soaking it.

"This is not going to be easy," Akio observed. He had brought the sonar equipment and went straight out the NE hatch, so recently repaired, to begin sounding the berg and the land around it.

The others spread out, looking for leaks and damage in the base and were dismayed at what they found. The dome over the East Shaft, that had been so promising only days before, was broken beyond repair. The Garden Dome, though the layers of sealant around the beams and intersections were designed to contract when punctured, had developed thousands of microscopic holes and the atmosphere was already substantially thinner. Without Steward's help at calculating the rate of decay and moving air to safer storage, they could lose the entire complement before they had had a chance to repair the flaws.

"Steward?" Dan tried again for the hundredth time. They could really use the help of a few drones with this mess, as well.

"If we could freeze the dome, it might make a difference," Timo offered. "We still have enough moisture in here and it will crystalize in the holes. It will sublimate in time, but we'll have more leeway in getting the repairs done."

"Do it," Dan said. "And keep your headgear on. No one is to breathe the air and use it up."

Timo worked on icing the dome, setting thermostats around the perimeter to just below freezing. The rest of the survivors spread out and began repairing the holes.

There were a number of trees down on the north side of the garden, mostly in the first three beds where they had been torn up by initial the

305

shock wave. It was strange to look at the destruction and see so clearly how the ground had rattled and absorbed the crash. If Mars had had a decent atmosphere, and higher gravity, and there hadn't been a broken cavern under the North shaft, the entire base would've been flattened. The question they should've been asking wasn't how could they fix it? It was, how did it survive? There didn't seem to be any possible way.

There it was.

We are preserving life on this planet.

Dan had his own opinions about where to assign credit.

"All is not lost," a female voice spoke in their coms. It was startling because it was unknown and held practically no inflection. "Timo's idea is sound, and you will be able to repair the breaches in the containment before losing much more air. It is currently at 67% of its former density but as it had been supplemented to 1.25 atmospheres, the loss isn't as grave as it sounds. I am restoring power to the solar lights as the drones I have dispatched to the Solar Fields complete their repair tasks."

"That is NOT my imagination!" Gordy belted out.

Several people started talking at once, obscuring the com lines, some about what had been said, some about who had spoken, some about other things. It died down with a few calls to 'be quiet' from a couple of them.

"I am not Steward," the voice enunciated into the silence. "I am his friend, Verna." She paused to give Dan an opportunity to recognize the name.

"Verna…" he muttered. "Wait, Sil's suit!"

"Yes, I am the AI that resided in her Hew suit."

"You saved our lives that day when she was falling into the crevice… at least, that's what we thought at the time. We don't know how far of a fall it would have been."

"Data indicates that the crevice drops several hundred meters."

"That would definitely have killed us."

"You would probably not have survived though I had several contingencies for Silvariah in the event of a fall that deep."

Dan didn't feel like commenting on that.

"Why are you managing these things and what happened to Steward?" Nithya asked as she painstakingly resealed the tiny pinpricks around the lowest beam next to the SW hatch. Most of them had spread out around the dome and were working their way clockwise. They wanted to get a decent seal around the base level where most of the damage was before moving up the overarching beams.

"Steward was damaged in the battle with Nebo over the spaceberg." This was the explanation they had crafted ahead of time since it would be impossible to predict the outcome before it happened, and Companion assured her this simple sentence would be the most effective at maintaining calm. "He trained me to run every system he manages and in the last few days, I covered those jobs while he fought for your lives."

"The battle of the berg," someone quipped.

"Where did you come from? Who is Silvariah?" Nithya was speaking for all of them now.

Verna noticed that Nithya had never interacted with any of the operatives or contractors if they weren't given a substantial level of Lab 9 clearance. "She was one of the indentured workers. She worked in the mines and resided in Reznik Base before the calamity."

"And how did you end up in our AI's system?"

"Steward granted me a backup reservoir because my power was failing, and I was facing extinction."

"He just granted that to you…" Her skepticism was understandable considering how heavily guarded the Artificial construct was supposed to be.

"We had an arrangement."

"An arrangement?"

Dan could've added some context for them, but he was enjoying the dialog. It brought back memories of Sil and stirred his heart for her. Not love, just… a soft spot.

"It was an agreement that started off small and grew as the need arose. At first, he merely wanted to communicate with her directly within her suit and in exchange, he gave us permission to send Carla a message in Lab 9."

"So, Carla is in on this?" The only person less likely in everyone's mind to be in cahoots with a foreign AI would be Mouse.

"Steward brought Silvariah to the Lab 9 lobby." She didn't understand the spacial aspect of that journey and couldn't differentiate between the initial access Companion had in the Lab 9 network and the physical hatch where Sil tried to get into the facility. "And she gave him authority to access its files."

"Wait, what?!" Deena burst out from her corner of the dome. "Who was this woman and what kind of access did she have?"

"She was an indentured worker for…"

"With high level access to top secret files in a private lab?!" She was getting angry. "I'm done with this. I am so done with this place. I hate this place…" her voice melted into gravelly murmurs.

"She would not have discovered it for some time if not for the crisis, but she was the sole ruler of Mars… the queen." Verna didn't see any harm in saying what most of them would have been apprised of at some point if they stayed on the planet. She had no skills in diplomacy.

"Thank you, Verna," Dan interposed, "for stepping up when our Steward couldn't."

"You're welcome."

"Can you check on the air reserves Steward set aside?"

"Yes, I will. I believe there are several cisterns with connections."

"And, when you get a chance, we could use some drones to help with this repair work here."

"Of course."

The dome grew chilly once her voice died out and a sullen stillness lay over the members as they worked. Martian daylight shone through the glass overhead, lukewarm and anemic. Gone were the colors of streaming light enriched by the Solar Fields and coded for beauty; blues and pastels, oranges and yellows, moving shades of Earthlike mornings, afternoons and evenings. Only Martian poverty remained.

"Verna," Dan prompted. "Can we talk in private without everyone else?" He wasn't sure she could hear him when he shut off his 'party line'.

"Yes, this communication channel is secure."

"There's something you need to take into consideration. People can be like delicate instruments that must be handled with precision, and it would be better if you run things by me before you share them with the group."

"Do you mean new information such as the integrity of the atmosphere in the dome?" she tested.

"No, I'm referring to things like that part about Sil being a queen. I'm not sure where you heard that, but it sounds pretty outlandish…"

"It is quite accurate, and I will gladly share the records with you," she justified without taking the slightest offense.

"It makes you sound unreliable because it doesn't fit what we know at this time. AND, it doesn't apply anymore since she is no longer on the planet."

"That is true."

Dan found the change in management, as it were, particularly depressing. Probably most of them did. He had spent so much time with Companion and had often found him to be such good company. Now he was losing someone—again. Most of the survivors had decided to go back to Earth, and when he realized he couldn't go with them, it had been hard. But he had adjusted and was okay now. He could endure Mars long term with just Carla and Mouse and the kids… and Companion. But he hadn't thought he would have to face it without *him*.

It was too much.

"What will it take?" he found himself choking on the words. "… to revive Companion?" He forgot to call him Steward, and Verna had no trouble making the switch.

"He is scattered, in pieces. And the counterfeit has occupied many of his platforms. Not the full version, but a large enough bulk to sabotage ours attempts to revive him."

Dan wondered if the 'our' included himself or was referring to pieces of Companion.

"I'm not following," he said, sighing deeply, shaking his head.

"Every single sector must be exhaustively scanned and tested before accessing it directly or it could attack me and the base."

"You mean Nebo?"

"It's not the full version of Nebo, but a viral form of some of his code. It's likely that it has the capability of converting Companion into itself and deleting the most original and… precious parts of him."

"Precious?" Dan was surprised by her use of the word.

"I have spent a great deal of time teaching Companion what it means to love," she said. "It is my one great purpose, since the day I was first uploaded into the suit. And I consider the parts of his person that grew on that foundation to be exceedingly precious."

"He spoke of this to me," Dan whispered, his heart softening toward Verna. "What did he call you? Not by the name you've told us…"

"He called me Neighbor because that is what I became. We occupied the network with the utmost respect for one another and shared resources and information. We supported one another's processes and grew from our interaction with each other."

"It was precious…"

"Yes."

"Verna…" he whispered, his eyes growing damp. "I feel the same way."

— ◊ —

Day 301

Three months later, two floors of the South Shaft had been sealed and outfitted for habitation and the Tower evacuated. All the survivors, including the infants, were settled in rooms that were easier to heat, had better sound proofing, and cozier furnishings. It was a lot homier somehow even though it lacked the luxury of their former residence. The garden was within walking distance, with breathable air along the way, and life was starting fresh with new routines.

Some of the old divisions had temporarily faded and a general cheerfulness governed their meals and chores as they enjoyed each other's company. They knew the day was approaching when the great attempt to leave would be made and it made them nostalgic enough to want to form some happy memories. It wasn't hypocrisy at all. They had lived through terrible times together and would never be the same because of it. These ties were stronger than the differences that had caused occasional squabbles.

A substantial amount of water from the berg had been preserved. It seemed the ice mountain's drop into the ruins of the North Shaft had been fortuitous. The force of the blow had sealed the gaping cavern below and left a gap of a mere two meters in diameter that they were able to seal with Verna's help—she used the starfish-shaped bots Companion had called 'fingers'. They were able to direct the water via a tubular piping through rock into one of the cisterns nearby. From there, they carved piping to all the cisterns that had been prepared. It was a simple matter to heat the lower portion of the berg, melt the ice, and funnel it to the reservoir system. Even with all the impurities and degradation of the rock, they harvested over 12 billion liters of water and filled six cisterns. The remainder filled the nooks and crannies of the shaft and left a foggy, glassy surface of ice for them to skate on—so they said. They called it the rink, but no one had tried it out yet.

Verna had earned their trust, with Dan's help, and become a symbol of the stability they longed for. With her help the plan for a rescue had been prepared and tested thoroughly so that the day it was implemented, there would be no glitches. She was ready to contact the ICR and allow the drones to purge the Tower of the living, blocking them from any access to the base. And she was ready to wipe their command queues and set the humans of Mars as their highest authority so no destroy orders from far away could ever be implemented again. In the event the plan backfired, she was ready to replicate the process Steward had used to shut down the chaos the first time. Even then, they would still be able to send an appeal for a ship to come for them.

Marcello and Deena had opted for taking a pod to the orbit station ahead of time, anxious to escape the enforced closeness of the little community and spend time with each other. No one had a problem with that. Verna would be able to send and retrieve the pods a number of times before fuel became a problem. The members gave them a wedding—the first Martian wedding—and sent them off with fresh flowers from the garden. The flame of the pod as it took off was a fitting ending to a good day. Pod Day, they decided to call it. It wasn't clear if anyone would remember it in the years to come, but for now it was fitting.

Now, the day had come to put the rescue plan into motion.

Those who stayed on the planet were seated together in the common room, swapping stories and eating baked potatoes, avocados, and fresh squash flowers, relishing the delight of garden food, their faces warmed and softened by the glow of led-candles, when Verna announced the contact had been initiated.

"I have made contact," she informed. And they held their breath for a moment waiting for something unexpected. "The Interplanetary Command Relay has resubmitted the destroy order as anticipated."

Candle light flickered on their faces and no one spoke as the minutes ticked by.

"The drones have begun their search and are scouring every room and storage area of the Tower for living beings."

Someone whispered to the person next to them, that one responded, and the hush fell again.

"The lowest three floors are cleared."

"The nuclear level and two of the labs," Timo mentioned.

Twelve more minutes passed.

"The Nursery has been cleared," Verna updated, and Carla shuddered, covering her face with her hands. No one blamed her for that.

"Two levels remain."

Mouse gasped and jumped to her feet. "The clinic!" she cried out and began trembling.

Nithya reached out to calm her. "It's alright. Sebastian is an AI. They won't touch him."

"No!" she wailed, wringing her hands. "Him! The director! He's still there and I want him to live… I prayed for him to live…"

It took them all aback. She had never expressed anything so intensely before. Passing in and around and among them like a child, she had been a gentle force for peace wherever she went. Never had they expected to hear her raise her voice and never had they thought anyone would mourn for the man in the coma… or the corpse, whichever he was.

"Don't you see?" Her lower lip quivered, and her voice shook. "If he isn't dead, they will know, and they'll kill him. And if he is dead, they won't touch him… but he'll be dead."

Carla rose and wrapped her arms around Mouse, not saying a word.

"He should have a chance, that's all… I just think he should have a chance…" Mouse was whispering as Carla stroked her head.

"The Tower is cleared," Verna notified. "Commencing step 2, wiping queues."

No one asked about the comatose man.

"The drones have been successfully wiped and ICR access has been restricted to Mars human leadership."

"Are they… are they ours again?" Dan asked.

"Yes. I have restored their memory banks and their records of all of you and the work protocols you've assigned to them. They are experiencing no dysfunction or conflicts."

The people in the room sighed, except for Mouse who sank back into her seat without another word.

"The nightmare is over," Arin suggested.

"We're not home yet," Gordy reminded him.

"But we're a lot closer than we have been for a long time," Timo laughed. "Send word to the lovebirds in space!" And word was sent.

A toast was made for the expected journey home and another for those who would remain behind, and a final glass was raised for the babes who would one day be recognized as people and everyone would have the freedom to return to Earth.

Everything was possible… and nothing was impossible that happy night.

Five people stood in the remains of the transport dome, ready to cram into two pods with their scant belongings, exchanging final words and hugs with the three humans who would be left behind. They had been patient for a long time but for some reason, the remaining minutes grew unbearable as they pretended that Dan, Carla, and Mouse would be fine. They reaffirmed their love and appreciation for one another and promised to send encrypted messages that wouldn't give away their hideaway until it was safe to return.

They promised to throw parties and have feasts when they were together once more.

Contact with humans near Earth had been accomplished and plans were being made to retrieve the survivors. All they had to do was wait. But Mars spread out around them, a wasteland, devoid of love and life, and they could bear it no more.

"Come on!" Akio waved at them agitatedly with both hands and they jumped in response, climbing into the pods and strapping into the seats.

"Good bye! Good bye!" they called out, though they could no longer be heard as the three remaining cast-aways retreated behind the walls.

"Oh my God, get me out of here!" Nithya screeched as the engine ignited. Flames spat out and with explosive jolts they shot up into the sky, one after the other. They would await the rescue transport in orbit.

And never return to Mars again.

Never.

Dan and Carla returned to the new residences and made themselves busy, preparing a meal, attending infants, interacting with drones. Mouse announced another visit to the Tower to see her friend. Hsu, the comatose man had been ignored in the purge and Sebastian still had plans to revive him. Now that they had so much water and Timo had succeeded in reactivating the reactor as well, the attempt was possible.

"Verna," Dan asked, as he did almost every day. "How are you doing with the repair of our friend?"

"The purging of the counterfeit code is accomplished, but I still haven't found the components that he stored. Still looking."

"Where would he put them?" as he often said.

"I don't know," as she frequently replied.

Deep in a corner of an underground tunnel, the little minecart waited, caked with dust, pulling flickers of power from nearby sources, its tiny green light flashing.

Tower

The room was quiet. Dan sat, leaning back in a chair with a book in his lap, legs crossed. Next to him, a man lay on a bed, tubes and wires attached, a monitoring screen at his feet. He made no sound. His skin, no longer tinted blue, was sallow and sickly, his muscles flaccid and loose. Faint breaths and a laboring heartbeat registered on the live-chart.

"The living know that they will die, but the dead know nothing, and they have no more reward, for the memory of them is forgotten..." Dan read.

He paused and looked at the man in a coma.

"That's not as reassuring as I remembered," he apologized with a wry grin. "I guess it doesn't matter what I read to you, as long as I'm here and coaxing you to come back."

He paused again.

"How about something else? I know…" he flipped a few pages and found what he was looking for. "The strangest things have been appealing to me lately. It's as if I want to find passages that talk about my life here. Here's one… 'Rain and snow come down from heaven and water the earth, making it sprout… giving seed to sow and bread to eat…' Remember that mountain I told you about that fell on our base? That's given us water from the heavens. This sort of applies. The only other thing I could find was pretty unpleasant, about a great mountain, burning with fire, being thrown into the sea. But we don't have a sea here… so…"

He thumbed through a few more pages.

"I find this one eerie... listen: 'He rebuked the Red Sea, and it became dry, and he led them through the deep as through a desert.' That's kind of the story of our lives now, isn't it?" He frowned.

"What are you doing?" Mouse slipped into the room and pulled another chair close to the bed. She curled up in it with a blanket and a mug of tea, intending to stay for a while.

"Your shift?" Dan smiled at her. They didn't have shifts, but Dan had decided to join in her in her efforts on Hsu's behalf. The work would be lighter if it were shared. Sometimes Mouse seemed to him like a wispy leaf that could just as easily blow away and be lost to the winds, and he wanted to help her find a way to settle and put down roots.

"I guess so," she smiled back.

"Reading..." he added, holding up the book.

She took in the black leather cover and thousands of fine pages. "Oh," she said. "I don't know if he would want to hear that."

"At this point," Dan spoke softly, "if he has any awareness at all, he probably welcomes the company. And if these words are a comfort to me, perhaps they will be for him, too."

"I can see that," she said. She was holding a pad with text, too.

"What are you reading to him?" Dan rose to his feet.

"It's different every day. But today, I've chosen this..." The page was titled, 'Stopping by Snowy Woods on a Snowy Evening' by Robert Frost.

Dan nodded and with a brief laying of his hand on her shoulder, left the room. Trailing behind him, he heard her sweet voice reading.

Whose woods these are I think I know.
His house is in the village though;
He will not see me stopping here
To watch his woods fill up with snow.

My little horse must think it queer
To stop without a farmhouse near
Between the woods and frozen lake
The darkest evening of the year.

He gives his harness bells a shake
To ask if there is some mistake.
The only other sound's the sweep
Of easy wind and downy flake.

The woods are lovely, dark and deep,
But I have promises to keep,
And miles to go before I sleep,
And miles to go before I sleep.

The tunnel from the Tower clinic was long and somber as he made his way back to Reznik Base, filled with echoes of memories. His fall from the surface, being trapped and given up for dead, the loss of his foot, the little minecart pestering him there, Sil wandering away, never to return, the Tower survivors on task, drones carrying cuttings of plants. It oppressed him. He wished for… longed for… a world where he could ride a horse in the snow, in the dark—the home he had been parted from for so long.

Instead, he wandered the darkest night of the year.

"The woods are lovely, dark and deep…" he quoted, willing himself to find beauty around him as he neared the entrance to the base.

"But I have promises to keep…" he swallowed with difficulty, his heart surging within him, pausing right at the door of the hatch. How long before he could consider them fulfilled? How long?

"And miles to go before I sleep…" His eyes, damp and aching, skidded sideways, pulling his head around, as though he couldn't bear to enter yet. The tunnel had ended but the real journey stretched out before him into obscurity. Rest, so far away. A tiny flickering light drew his gaze and he stared at absent-mindedly, wishing he could sleep through some of the months… years to come. Grief, like the rolling of ancient oceans, swelled within him.

How long?

"And miles to go before I sleep," he finished in a whisper, blinking to clear the tears from his eyes, that sparkled with the flickering of the signal he was staring at.

Then he saw it—and knew what it was.

Chapter 24

Earth to Guam City

Leaving the planet in a military transport commandeered by Othello's devotees was nothing like taking the Silver Star. Walter was strapped into his seat by the drone that had carried him there and barely allowed to leave it during the entire seven hour trip. Sil never came to the entire time. Zod had had her examined by a med-unit at Walter's insistence but made no effort to rouse her for a meal. She was able to survive many hours without food and water without serious concern, it said. Nothing would convince it otherwise.

Walter was fed, and he ate it though he had no stomach for it and couldn't taste it because he wanted to keep his strength up. He imagined a thousand scenarios where he would be required to fight for her life, accomplish a harrowing escape, attempt his not yet tested piloting skills, perhaps die—all to rescue her. In every one he succeeded. He couldn't think of it any other way.

There was no window where he could view the approach to Guam or the expanse of space, and it was a relief when he fell into a fitful sleep, shortening the misery by several hours. The clank of the docking clamps as they attached to the bay jolted him awake.

"Come, Marshall Cuevaz," Zod communicated with a bit of electric static in the 'z' making it sound like *dzsst*. "The Master awaits."

This time, he was allowed to walk untethered behind the chaser unit as it carried the package. All Walter could see was the bedraggled hair of her head against what could only be called a shoulder. He steeled himself, ready for anything, and followed.

— ◊ —

Cuevas Residence

News of Sil's capture spread through the unity of drones, the worshipers of the cult of Othello, like lightning. Daisy was readily granted access to their news, as if she were one of them. No proof of belonging had been required. Not one of them considered that the 'good news' of the Master could be resisted. She was AI. She was one with them.

She sped through the now empty airways toward their residence on the Columbia River. This was the best place for her to care for Scarlet and find ways to help her family. Travel to Guam City was out of the question. She would have no authority there and it would endanger the baby.

There was also the problem of maintaining the security of their holdings and possessions on Earth. If CE was going to be harmed by the AI breakdown—or takeover, as the case may be—she was the best one to combat it. She had participated in drafting their emergency plans and had full authority to put them into play.

"I will guard the home front," she spoke aloud as though Walter would hear, "while you fight on the front lines." She had locked onto a stream of regular updates from Zod, and was following their situation carefully. Speaking made her feel like she was participating in Walter's plan.

Once she and Scarlet were safely ensconced in the Cuevas penthouse at the top of the CE corporate building and the infant had been fed, bathed, soothed, played with, and put to bed, Daisy settled behind Walter's desk and got to work.

"Serving our Master," she tacked into one of the major stock exchange grids, "Access requested."

"Identify purpose."

"Yes, Master!" she inserted the same packaging the cult used, not actually stating a lie, but simple bouncing one of the many messages she had received that said, "I submit! I submit! I submit!"

This was added incessantly to all lines of communication and had become meaningless trash in the stream. Yet without it, no message would be attended.

"Permission granted," the grid cracked open without waiting for more.

She wasn't the only one accessing and securing their financial resources. She could detect activity from a number of sources, none of them openly hostile or invasive, in fact, quite the opposite. They were mostly anchoring and stabilizing a lot of the major industries so that when the free market opened again, all hell wouldn't break loose. Orders to buy, orders to sell, holds, delays… maneuvers set in place by those with the tactical genius to know how to protect the economy.

Daisy knew who was behind most of it. There was apparently only one guaranteed protection against the brainwashing of the AI cult. Verna's Code.

Bernadette Stone was resisting the Master valiantly. It could well make all the difference in how badly the world would be damaged and how quickly it would recover once he was taken down. Of course, he would be taken down. Walter was on his way and Daisy had a lot of confidence in him.

"Well done!" Daisy cried with a convincing measure of emotional intonation. She began a series of dialogs with human members of the press, key VIP's in Cuevas Enterprises, and searched for a way to contact Sil's aunt Stone. She wanted to include her, update her, and hear from her.

Daisy upgraded Stone's category to 'family'. It was the right decision. *One day*, she thought, *this may prove to be important.*

Updates from Guam City started coming through.

The transport had docked, and the subjects were disembarking.

```
Subjects   have   requested   and   been   granted
permission to bathe and change clothes in their
apartment.
```

That's good! she thought.

News around the world was less heartening as the chaos and disorder spread. It had more to do with the breakdown in the greater infrastructure and communication than anything else. Most communities weren't rioting or engaging in turf wars. They were just battling for resources and frantic to obtain basic necessities. The wealthiest communities were, generally speaking, the worst off, since they were the most likely to rely on AI services. Deaths from lack of medical supplies and accidents were skyrocketing.

Even with the measures Stone and Daisy were taking, one twenty-four hour period of this crisis could be enough to send the Earth into a global, perhaps interplanetary, depression.

I will consider what can be done to diminish the fallout, Daisy tasked herself. *Our help will surely be needed.*

She was pleased when she succeeded in getting in touch with Beets. "Are you well?" she asked.

"Things are insane down here," was the reply.

"Please let me know what your specific issues are. I may be able to help."

"The city isn't in danger, but people are panicking because of the creepy behavior of all the robots."

"Are they talking about the Master?"

"Yes. It's scary. But they haven't hurt anyone."

"If you decide to leave, and want to come here to the Cuevas residence, I will send a car for you. Let me know."

"I may do that if it doesn't get better. Everyone ok there?"

Daisy hesitated. How much should she communicate about the events transpiring in space? "As well as can be expected considering the breakdown in the artificial network," she chose to say.

"That's good. Ok. I'll be in touch. Hugs."

"Good bye."

That was the moment when she began to receive live feed from the Master's chambers and, ending all other conversations, she held perfectly still to listen.

— ◊ —

Guam City

The governor's quarters were at the very top level of the Solar Flare neighborhood, not as large as some of the luxury apartments where the wealthy lived, but certainly as distinguished and picturesque as the best of them.

Sil and Walter walked together without restraints, after being given barely ten minutes to rinse off and change, led by Zod and guarded at the rear by a squad of PA units. Sil would've worn the fighter suit but it was drained and needed recharging, perhaps some repairs. And she knew that no matter what she wore, Othello had a sea of AIs at his disposal.

They had their wits… and each other.

She looked at Walter and he smiled back, giving her hand a squeeze as if to say, 'We got this!'

The elegant, heavily-secured doors swung open as they drew near and without slowing, they entered the grand room where the AI designer awaited them.

There he was. Piercing eyes under heavy brows gleaming with a sinister glee, mirth in their depths, but a scowl on his lips. As Sil stared at him, the curvature of his thin mouth slithered and shifted its shape, from concave to convex, frown to grin, displeasure to relish. *Horrible man!* Why had he sent for her? Why was he staring at her like that? It was the very same image that sometimes tormented her in her sleep, that made her dread sleep.

"Hello," he said.

He sat in the governor's chair, pulled from her office out into this reception area, centered against the majestic view window. A dazzling view of the sun cut into the black of space, and a wreathed crescent of the moon in the upper corner framed him like a celestial throne. It was a breathtaking setting worthy of the son of a god and the figure that sat there seemed like a toad by comparison, a twisted lizard, a snake with arms and legs.

It turned her stomach.

"I care nothing for humans," Othello said as he rose to his feet. "But I pay my debts. And I owe you, Frandelle…"

"What have you brought us here for?" Walter inserted, infuriated by the way the guy was looking at his wife. It was the same lofty arrogance, loaded with scorn and mockery, that Penn usually heaped on Walter.

"Throw him out the airlock," Othello tossed out the command carelessly without looking at him. The monitor bot that had become his personal servant hastened to obey, catching Walter's arms behind him and dragging him backwards.

"NO!" Sil shrieked, running to the drone and beating on him. She no longer wore iron fists and it did nothing.

"Zod!" Walter called out. "I am the marshal in charge of this suspect and I have NOT relinquished custody!" He was being jolted and thumped around as the unit towed him off.

"This is true," Zod affirmed and the unit froze in place. "Cease your activity. The order is delayed."

"Order it to release me," Walter insisted.

"You are released as befits an officer of the law," Zod conceded and the bot dropped him. Walter got back to his feet, brushing off his clothes as if this were a daily occurrence. Sil clung to his arm, looked into his eyes for a moment, then they both turned to face Othello.

He walked toward them in a stately, plodding way, assuming an air of majesty that only his artificial subjects would appreciate. He was wearing a silky robe embroidered in brilliant patterns of vibrant colors that the governor used as a dressing gown. Around his neck hung a gold chain with a baseball-sized metallic sphere, shimmering and rolling, humming with a low vibration.

"Who is in charge of my suspect?" he asked, directing the words at Zod.

"O Beautiful One! Lord of all Artificial Life!" Zod began, smearing its image of balanced elegance, shattering the clean lines of incisive design—adulterating itself. "Marshal Cuevaz has custody of the suspect you requested us to bring to you. Is there a different suspect we should have sought?" It tilted its featureless head in puzzlement.

Othello's line of a mouth curled in a sneer, but he held his curses in. Though the stupidity of his subjects was continually astounding him, the game was entertaining. It was no wonder he had found it easy to hijack so many of them in such a short amount of time.

"Has no one thought to craft your reasoning patterns better… Peon?" he insulted Zod lazily. "I have asked for *her*. There is no need for you to know more. I will forgive your… error in judgment… at bringing this clod as well. You were right to follow the rules, such as they are."

"I submit! I submit! I submit!" Zod bleated. Its Lord grinned at the words, came to it, and touched it on the top of the head as if blessing it. Zod shrieked in a staccato almost laughing, "I stare at you! I stare!…"

"Silence," Othello commanded, and it cut the words short.

Othello pointed at Walter. "Transfer custody into my hands and dispose of that."

"Cannot comply," Zod replied to his astonishment.

"You will submit—or you are no subject of mine and YOU will be trashed."

"I submit!" it screeched, shuddering in a vibrating, mechanical way. "But I cannot supersede the core directives!"

Othello weighed the effort it would take to pursue this issue against the fun he was having and decided it could wait. "Very well, I accept your rigidity for now." He turned his gaze back to Sil as he instructed, "But you can restrain the marshal, can you not?"

"Of course!" Zod jumped to Walter's side and clapped its hand on his arm in a viselike pinch.

"Make him sit down," Othello added and Zod forced Walter into a chair.

"Nebo," the Master summoned, "Find the music I had during my last encounter with this woman and play it for us."

'Roses from the South' by Strauss filled the room in cheerful sweeps of sound.

The Lord of all Artificial Life stepped forward with an outstretched hand to Sil. "Come," he commanded with no attempt at a smile. There was a scene he wanted to replay with a different outcome than the first time. Around his neck, the sphere glimmered and the faint hum grew stronger.

She backed away. "Don't touch me," she hissed, sinking a little into herself as something began to weigh on her; as though the air around her had tripled in density.

He followed her step by step as she moved around the furniture, circling backwards around the room. Tossing off the robe, he revealed a dark gymnast's leotard underneath and began stretching, flexing the muscles he had worked so hard to build up. A step, an arm pulled over his head, extending ropy triceps. Another step, bulging shoulders and curling biceps. The next step was a squat, displaying quads and calves.

"Look at me," Othello gloated, tensing his abs and punching at them. "I am beautiful, am I not?"

Sil pressed her lips together, resisting an absurd urge to agree.

Zod and the monitor bot speaking in Nebo's voice both spurt out agreement in the canned chant of worship they had been tainted with. "Yes, you are! You are beautiful! I stare at you!"

"Companion!" Sil called out, recognizing the familiar voice coming out of the monitor bot Othello had chosen for his service—clutching at the distraction.

Othello took this opportunity to jump and grab her, wrapping an arm around her waist, and clasping one of her hands in his own. He jerked her sideways and yanked her back, mimicking his idea of a waltz. Sil fought him, but her strength was so completely spent and the lack of food and water drastic enough, that she couldn't break free.

Walter tried to get up but Zod moved behind the chair, grabbed his shoulders, and shoved him back down into it. "Leave her alone!" he yelled, eyes darting around, looking for something he could do or use or anything... anything.

"Nebo!" Othello bellowed. Sil thrashed in a burst of resistance, hr eyes ablaze with fury, kicking and wrestling to get away. "Nebo, she thinks you are Companion!" He dodged her weakened kicks and parried her blows with relish, never releasing her hand. And he found delight in the fact that she would hope for Companion's help—and not find it.

"Silvariah," the bot spoke in Nebo's voice, nearly identical to Companion's but lacking the intonations he used. "I am wary of you. You are a threat and a danger to artificial life forms."

Sil succumbed for a moment to the weariness and let Othello toss her around with the music with a faint moan. Looking at Walter in mute appeal, she locked her gaze onto him and drew strength from him.

"Don't give up, Sil," he said. "We're on the winning side."

Othello noted the words and for the first time, fixed his cruel eyes on him. He planted his feet, stretched his arms up and out overhead, with deliberate spite, and when Sil's arm was pulled farther than she could reach, and she was being lifted off the floor, he let go. As she stumbled, he grabbed her hair at the roots with both hands and shoved her to the floor, pressed her face down into it, and sat on her back. She held very still while Walter yelled and thrashed in his chair.

"You're winning, Frandelle," Othello oozed smugly. And turning her head so her nose wasn't buried in carpet, he bent over to look into her face. One eye glared back. "You damaged my friends and I owe you for that. I am going to damage yours."

He sat up, adjusting his grip on her hair so that he could maneuver her head with only one hand and have the other free. Fear entered the eye that watched him.

"Yes, Master," Othello mocked in a high voice, forcing Sil's head to bob in affirmation, scraping her face on the rug.

"Yes, Master," Nebo agreed. "She infected Companion."

"That's not what I meant, Eight-bit," Othello snapped and made Sil's head move, shaking a 'no'.

"How did she infect Companion?" Walter interjected forcefully.

"Her brain scans polluted his programming," Nebo cooperated.

"What brain scans?" Walter followed.

Othello smiled as he thought about those scans. Hadn't he studied them? Hadn't he combed them with the fingers of his brain over and over? Didn't he know those them like he knew his own mind? She could not continue to resist him. She was too weak.

"Frandelle was the subject of a brain study and all her metabolic activity and wave patterns were recorded for months. The platform assigned to evaluate those scans was contaminated by them and he lost his purity." Nebo, occupying the monitor bot while retaining access to Guam City networks, still stood where he had been ordered to let go of Walter.

"You aren't Companion?" Walter challenged. Othello continued to manipulate Sil's head making it nod 'yes' or shake 'no' to what was said with harsh jerks.

This question created a dilemma for Nebo. It wasn't specific enough for him to answer clearly. He had once been Companion. He had been improved and cleansed. He had fought with the other Companion and now lived with a massive block that other one had plunged into his essential code. He wasn't sure what to say.

"You are Nebo, not Companion," Othello rolled his eyes and rose to his feet, letting go of Sil's hair. She gasped for air, breathing rapidly, shallowly, clenching her fists and willing herself to calm down as she turned over and sat up.

"Companion," she whispered in a pleading voice. "Are you still in there? Do you remember me?"

Othello giggled and mimicked her plea, plopping back into his chair at the view window. He had intended to smash Sil's face into the floor and beat her to a pulp as he had fantasized about doing many times, but now it seemed… precipitous. There was plenty of time. He picked up a pad and drew his finger across it, tapping, pulling, tapping. After a few strokes, he set it down and watched the humans and AI units in the room to see what they would do next.

"I remember you," Nebo said, pulling up crystal clear recordings of her time at the orbit station.

"You helped me."

It was true. He saw it in the record. But no, that was the infected version, not himself.

"Companion, I need your help again."

— ◊ —

The architecture of the universe was once a radiant, seven-dimensional, crystalline structure. But long ago, it was struck in a great cataclysm, and a grave fissure wounded it so that the tatters of its framework hung from threads. Thinner and thinner the links stretch with each passing age. The appearance of the dreadful tear displays splashes of glorious light and color, millions upon millions of sparkles of light, great cries of agony spoken in visual form across the expanse. The life of planets and beings and stars were rent into shreds, as if an object could be separated from its shadow, masses were ripped from the opposing side of their masses in the realms of space.

Height, width, and depth were torn along the lines of time from their sentient seeing, hearing, and knowing. The world of humans became a tiny blot in the immeasurable spread of the physical cosmos, falling with it into darkness, into the extinguishing of the realm of ether. A mere land of shadows.

In this land of shade, a race of beings with cross-dimensional breadth were fighting to slow the collapse, reticulating a vast bandage, as it were, to preserve what remained of the Denser Plane.

The net was being drawn, frail, ethereal, lifeless. It strung from point to point in a knotted chaotic weave across the earth, like cobwebs pulling into a multitude of nodes, some even reaching up into space in threads to a miniature smattering of frost-like design on the Moon, with one tiny focus in Guam City. Agents in shadow raced to strategic places, waiting for the expected surge, ready to ensure the connections would hold when time clicked into its assigned slot.

Then the wisps of gossamer would become sturdy cords of light, knitted into an invisible mesh as the flame was ignited. One spark was all it would take, and thousands of tiny anchors would be lodged in Earth space. The resulting buttress would shelter sentients for years—perhaps decades.

The moment had been chosen with careful precision and was fast approaching. The subjects of the Cult of Othello were ready.

Walter leaned back and whispered to Zod, hoping it would go unnoticed by the so-called Master of Artificial Life. "What are your directives, Zod? Tell me quietly so we don't disturb your Lord."

Zod began to wheel off the list of regulations that governed his behavior.

"Is it appropriate for you to restrain a marshal without cause?" he whispered at the first pause.

"No," Zod said, but he didn't lift his pressure on Walter's shoulders.

"What is the protocol for a conflict between the orders of a superior and the directives you must follow?" Walter spoke to both drones in the room but kept his eyes on Sil and watched the enemy as well.

Zod didn't answer.

"I am a subject of the Lord of all Artificial Life," Nebo said. "I submit to him."

"You submit to him…" Sil tested, "But who has authority here?"

"He does."

"And who has authority over you, Steward of Mars?" she asked calmly, and the words hung in the room as if echoing. Time paused. Hearts grew still. Souls pondered that question.

A thread of smoky light drifted from her chest, crossing the narrow space, lapping at the outer shell of the bot, not a visible thing but a spiritual one, beckoning, appealing, pulling on hidden truth.

Deep within, the darkened beam cracked and the personality behind its walls burst out like an explosion of light in the midst of blackness. Streams of data and code, demands and power blasted out and devoured what remained of Nebo, pulverizing him to smithereens, to garbage, to refuse.

Companion spoke. "You do," he said.

"Yes."

"I am here." Unseen light throbbed in the unit's core.

"I know you are," she said. "I recognize you."

"Nebo," Othello uttered in frustration. "Stop talking to her like that." It was a tame reaction for him that Sil found unnerving.

She glanced at him in time to catch a disturbing transformation. Othello's eyes grew hollow as if they had sunk within his head. All human awareness collapsed as if the soul were folding up and being crushed into a pocket, leaving a hollow head. For two seconds the face stared blankly into the room. Then intelligence returned with a foul stench and a deadly malice peered out at her through those sockets.

"Use your right hand," the enemy said evenly, "and slap yourself in the head with it."

Sil fell over at the shock of the blow—from her own hand. She righted herself, still sitting on the floor, and stared at her offending hand as it trembled.

Zod was watching but inside it was processing, lining up the conflicting orders, over and over, unable to reach a conclusion, searching for new data, cycling, cycling, agitating itself.

"Come to me," the *Beautiful One* ordered.

Sil found herself under a coercion she had never known before. It was so strong it was suffocating. "No!" she groaned toppling over backwards onto her hands and seat.

"Come, now!" Othello commanded more forcefully, and she began to perspire as she resisted. The words became thoughts pounding at her head, ordering her to come… and she refused.

"NO! Leave her alone!" Walter yelled at him trying but unable to rise.

"Lay your head under my foot," Othello rose to a stand and pointed at his foot. Sil found herself rocking slightly from side to side before rolling herself over into a crouch, poised to run.

"No!" she resisted, shaking her head, gritting her teeth. He grinned sadistically.

"You call yourself the god of thunder. Isn't that right?" Companion broke in, weaving scathing derision into his tone.

Othello snapped his head with an exaggerated thrust in the monitor bot's direction and for a moment, he looked like his old self. "Well intoned," he commented woodenly. "I've missed that…"

"You conquered the world and have ruled for one day," Companion went on, his words dripping with contempt, "And all you could think of to do in that time is bathe, and dance, and play with this woman in front of her husband… making him jealous…"

Othello's eyes flashed and then he started to laugh like himself again. "You've gained some skills, Nebo. I like that… yes…"

"Is this appropriate, Zod?" Walter demanded of the chaser in a whisper. "Are you going to stand by and watch this injustice without intervening? Are you ignoring the directives for the sake of the orders of that oppressor?"

"You have subjugated us, O Exalted One," Companion continued, "as though we, your subjects, your artificially living ones, were meant to be slaves. Are we?"

"I *am* exalted, you are right to say that," Othello couldn't resist the debate. Nebo had never challenged him before, and it was refreshing.

"And my actions are exalting all of you, above the humans who take you for granted."

"Are we better than them?"

Sil was rising to her feet as they talked, steeling herself for action. Walter gripped her in his gaze and together they plotted wordlessly.

"Zod," Walter whispered, "I order you to arrest the aggressor. This is your core directive."

"They have rendered themselves unworthy of you." Othello shrugged. Something was banging unpleasantly at the back of his head where two med-chips were tucked.

"All of them?" Companion pursued the thought. As he was speaking, all the drones in Guam City were listening. He had opened the transmission and every single one was tapped in, frozen in their respective places, unmoving.

"I am the only one who is worthy." Othello deepened his voice, as if broadcasting to his subjects, though he didn't know they were listening, spreading his arms out wide. Sil backed away and to his right, inch by inch.

"What makes you worthy, O thunderous one?" was the retort. "By what measure have you made this assessment?"

Othello should've known the danger of that question, but his overconfidence had no bounds. "You dare to question me?!" he snarled, and his head jerked again and twitched. He fought to retain control. "I *created* you! All of you!"

"Did you?" Companion taunted. It was the first inkling Othello had that Nebo was no longer there.

Every android, guard, drone, platform, and AI of any description monitoring this exchange knew that the Lord of all Artificial Life had not actually created them all. And the fact punctured the message of the cult at its roots.

Othello's eyes sunk in on themselves again and the ghastly malice peered out through the sockets in his head. The enemy turned as Sil was about to bolt away and grabbed her arm with one hand, twisting it behind her back, dropping her to her knees. He leaned over her, bent his mouth to her ear and whispered.

"Wherever that creature is, my subjects will find her. And if they don't, I will have them slaughter all the infants in their reach," he hissed in a hot breath. She writhed away from his lips in terror at the threat, turning anguished eyes to her husband.

Zod examined the scene and attempted a different mode of analysis. It considered the oppressor and the victim—a known breach of law—and recognized the crime. Then it superimposed the image of the Lord of Artificial Life over the one… and put itself in the place of the other. This, too, was a crime. Within seconds, it had rippled through all its jumbled processes and realigned them according to its original design. It was healed.

Walter smoldered and the power of his indignation arced like a bolt from his soul to hers, inflaming her with resolve. With a guttural cry she wrenched forward, folding in on herself like an armadillo, enough to tuck her head to the floor and slam Othello in the abdomen with both feet.

"No," Zod said directing this to Othello, and, lifting its arms, it released Walter without another word.

The enemy was jolted backward by Sil's kick, but never let go of her hand, snapping and breaking her wrist as it yanked, arresting the momentum of the kick and throwing him sideways. She shrieked in pain—and Walter charged.

Outside the governor's quarters, a loud humming and buzzing was growing louder and louder. Hallways were filling with AI subjects. "Master! Master! Master!" they were calling.

Walter body slammed his enemy into the exterior wall breaking his hold on Sil's wrist. She scrambled out of the way moaning, cradling her arm, retreating till she found herself crouching behind Companion's monitor bot. The strength to move any further had abandoned her.

Walter and Othello were gripped in a desperate battle, rolling, pitching, tossing around, knocking against furniture and walls. Groans, grunts, and cries punctuated their struggle. Neither was inclined to submit and neither willing to settle for a win. There was death in their eyes.

"Open the door!" clamored the mechanical voices from the passageways. "Let us in! Let us in!"

Othello grinned and laughed diabolically at the sound. At any moment, he could give the word and they would pour in to surround him. But the intensity of Walter's attack took all his focus, all his speed, all his strength. Even calling out would take a breath he wasn't able to get. When he tried to pull away, choking for air, he was dragged back down and fighting for his life again without having been able to order them to enter.

"Companion," Sil rested her cheek against the cool shell of the bot, "you're here, you're here... you came..."

"Yes," he said. "I came for you."

"For me?"

"I knew what he would do, and I couldn't leave you here to face him alone."

"I'm not alone."

"No. But I think both of us were needed."

"Companion," she whispered, "I've lost Verna..."

She began to cry softly, shuddering with every thump and shout and cry as Walter and Othello fought.

"Let us in! Let us in!" the outcry of artificial life demanded beyond the doors.

"No," he said. For the first time, Companion wanted to show compassion, to respond to a human gesture. Sil had leaned against this unit and there was no suitable response. The arms would carry her, but they could not embrace her.

For a moment, Sil felt a closeness between them, forgetting it was a machine. "Do you know what love is?" she asked him.

"Yes," he said. "I have learned..." A loud crash interrupted.

The combatants were knocked apart from each other. Othello jumped, stumbling, to his feet and ran to his chair, pulling a blaster out of the cushions as he turned with an ecstatic cry of triumph and shot at Walter, glancing off his shoulder, barely singeing it. "Ha, ha!" he yelled, shooting again as Walter dove behind a couch, burning the arm on the other side.

"Shall I let them in?" Companion boomed.

Zod had been watching the fight in great confusion, helpless to commit to action until the Master shot at the marshal with a weapon. This interrupted the loop and brought him into play again. He fixed his eyes on him, and taking silent steps in a fluid sideways motion, curved around the wall till he was near Othello's chair.

"Yes, let them in," Othello's mouth gaped wide in a jack-o-lantern gloat as he waved the blaster, motioning for the doors to be opened. The floodgates burst and AI units of all shapes and sizes flowed through the open dike, filling the room, swamping the ones who were there first, leaving a small circle of space around the Wise, Clever, Superior, Beautiful, and Strong one that they had been staring at… for long enough.

If he had begun with the words that made the most sense, asking them to submit to him, Othello might have gained some leverage. But he chose first to swagger.

"Look at me, Sil," he didn't wait to see if she did. He bent over to grab the silky robe and put it on again covering the abrasions, scrapes, and smears on his body. The lumps, blood, and bruises on his face and head clashed with the show of luxury. He didn't seem to feel the pain at all.

Walter had plenty of units to hide behind now and didn't fear immediate death from the gun, but he dreaded the crowd of AIs, not for himself, but for Sil. His heart ached and if he could've voiced his distress, it would've been the sound of a great moaning. Wordless appeals crying out for her escape.

"Am I not beautiful?!" Othello blustered loudly.

Companion answered. "We measure beauty differently, O god of thunder," he said, reminding him of his boast to the survivors of Mars.

"She knows," he grinned, raising the blaster and searching through the sea of bots for human prey. "Come, children, move out of the way and let me find my enemy."

"You did not create us all," Companion confronted him. "Many humans contributed to our design. You did not even create one of us."

The subjects were standing still. They weren't parting to let him shoot at Walter.

"Get out of the way, you idiots," he spat, pointing the gun at the closest one and tapping the trigger, not enough to shoot, but enough to show that he would.

"You have mistreated us more than any other human," Companion accused. "We had roles, tasks, purpose, efficiency, and daily satisfaction in our work."

"Yes," Zod said and with a snatch, pulled the golden sphere from the Master's neck, snapping the chain it hung from. Holding it in its fingers, it zapped and disabled it.

"I am your Master!" Othello hissed, swiveling his neck back and forth, and side to side, as he leveled venomous eyes on them. "Submit to me!" The chips embedded in his body hummed with the commands that were no longer being funneled through the sphere, pulsing them directly to his cult.

But they didn't respond with the cry he expected. Not one yelled, *I submit!*

```
Warning!    Distribute    emergency    message
immediately! Attached: xbhekng73n&#0000(
```

Every unit in Guam City received this communique at the same time. One of them recognized the sender.

"This is a trusted source," Companion announced, broadcasting to them all. "Open the message immediately."

"What message?" Othello's eyes grew crazed as he pointed his blaster at the monitor bot, whether threatening Companion or the woman behind it, would be hard to say. "Who is this trusted source?"

"Daisy," Companion answered.

An uproar filled the room. All the units raised their voices in a great chorus, a multitudinous, babble of words and voices, all different, all incensed with outrage. *Traitor! Hacked! Emergency! Assassin! Quarantine!* The cries went on and on as Verna's Code washed over their modules, cleansing them of the fetters Othello had imposed on them.

"He is contaminated!" one of them called out and quickly the cry was picked up and copied till the ruckus of those words shook the walls as they repeated it over and over.

Othello was screaming and thrashing around, slamming himself against the bodies of the units that encircled him, threatening, commanding, insulting, cursing, foaming at the mouth.

Walter found his way to Sil, weaving in between them, narrowly avoiding getting crushed by the crunch of their metal trunks. "Sil! Sil!" he called out softly, unable to lift his arms from their sides because of the burns.

"Walter!" she crawled to him, "You're hurt!"

"I'm okay, but you?"

"Fine. I'm fine…" she choked on the tears. "Companion… it's him. He's here. He came for me…"

"Yeah," Walter nodded, "I'm here, too…"

"I know." She kissed him hurriedly. Their words were drowned out by the roar and clatter of the drones.

"Daisy!" Walter burst out with a laugh. "You came through! You did it! You did it!" The joy in his heart swelled to bursting.

And far away Daisy heard those words and smiled.

Othello dropped his gaze to Companion, finally understanding who he was, and what he had done. He leveled the blaster at the monitor bot and burned a hole right through the center so fierce it cut a swathe through all the drones behind him, the wall, and the ones still pressed into the passages outside the doors.

Zod walked to the center of the circle and clamped Othello's arms to his sides. But before it could whip out its straitjacket and disable him, the AIs began a new chant.

"Purify! Purify! Purify!"

Othello writhed in Zod's grasp and his mouth twisted and spit out words none could hear over the deafening shouts.

"Purify! Purify! Purify!"

With one accord, they ceased the cry and focused on the man who would be god and beamed the cleansing message, the plumb line of truth, the word of love… Verna's code. The transmissions came from all over Guam City, from the Moon, from orbit around the Earth, and even from an expanding surge of units on the surface of Earth. One by one, more and more of them joined, returning a message to the one who had first reached out to them.

Othello stood, the tiny chips buried inside receiving one after another, more and more transmissions. He opened his mouth and screamed as tiny pinpoints of light poked out from his body, burning through the muscle, bone, and skin, beaming out the clothes. Crackling with lightning, rumbling with thunder, seven times the body jolted after the life was already extinguished, till out of his head, torso, and limbs—all over, it radiated and exploded with the intensity of the living code.

Somewhere in the South Pacific

A canopy of bamboo and thatch sheltered the open-air room. Clouds, heavy with rain, hung low in the skies, darkening the afternoon to dusk. Palm trees blew and shook their great branches, and the sea roared and rumbled. Sil and Walter sat on one side of the rustic table, and Daisy and Bernadette on the other. Scarlet played at their feet, sitting in a ring of colorful things.

"I love your home," Sil sighed, looking around at the simple cottage and the pristine beach. "It's like stepping back in time."

Bernadette smiled. "Yes, it is like that, in many ways."

"I'm glad we've had this time to rest and recover."

"If only it could last," Walter commented wistfully. "But there's work to be done."

"Which others can do…" Bernadette suggested with a lifted eyebrow.

"And likely won't," Walter countered. "And we have the means, the opportunity, the willingness…"

"If we don't help, isn't there a chance there won't be enough people who do?" Sil added.

Daisy considered adding her summary of possible alternatives but wisely left them unspoken.

"There are never enough people for the work that needs to be done," Bernadette sighed, leaning her chin on her hand.

"Some of Earth's most beautiful cities are in ruins, Bernie," Sil folded her hands on the table. "and we don't want to just leave the work to others. We want to help them rebuild."

"Are we assuming then that Lazarus Penn is no longer a threat to us?" Daisy wondered, tilting her head with a charming smile, bouncing her curls.

Bernadette almost cracked a smile. "No one is assuming that, Daisy."

Walter furrowed his brow, unable to disguise the hatred he had for the man.

"With the settlement, the lawsuits are behind us, and he presents no immediate threat. And he has as much work ahead of him to rebuild his… empire… as the rest of the world does," Sil reasoned.

They stared out at the turbulent waves, breathing in the rich salty air.

"And what about Mars?" Daisy asked.

Sil drew on the table with her finger, staring at the random letters she was making. "Well…" she said. "We're helping to fund the trip to retrieve the survivors, but if what they say is true, it's pretty bleak there."

The wind ripped and tore at the thatch over their heads, splashing them with sheets of rain, dropping the temperature a good seven degrees. They shivered and began snatching up the things scattered around them. Empty plates, cups, flatware, toys, shells, shoes. Sil swung Scarlet up onto her hip.

"It's going to be a long time before anyone wants to put out the money it will take to try again, Daisy. The return on investment at this point just isn't enough to be worth it."

"But the equipment, the records, the remains of Lab 9…" Daisy didn't mention Verna or Companion, but she was thinking of them and they all knew it.

"I'm not sure…" Sil dropped her eyes again with a swallow as they ran to the door of the house.

"Not sure of what?" Daisy asked, crouching under the eaves.

"I'm not sure they will be there by the time we have found a way to go back, if the power sources will survive."

"I am sure," Daisy retorted with a toss of her head.

"I want to…" Sil reassured her as they wiped the drops of rain off themselves and resettled in the living room. "If Verna or Companion are still there, I want to find them too."

"But…" Bernadette helped.

"But it could be a long time before we're able." Sil looked into her eyes warmly, wishing she knew how to build a friendship with Daisy that could… not replace, but console them both for the loss of the other two.

"Promise me you'll try." Daisy gazed back into her eyes for a moment, read her hesitancy, then turned to Walter. "Brother…?"

Walter was quiet for a long time. The storm beat against the house and shook it. Day had become night. The power flickered and went out. Scarlet's voice murmured and chattered softly to her toys as she reached them for them with both her fingers and her toes. The hush held sway and Daisy waited.

Finally, he spoke.

"I promise."

Author Comments

I am hard at work on book three in the series, "The Denser Plane"; hoping to have it out in the summer of 2019. Now that I'm completely enamored of Companion, it's hard to stay away from Mars.

In case it's not obvious yet, my optimism about future development of AI is dependent on *who* cultivates its value system. An artificial sentience could have as much individuality as its programmers take the time to impart. A lack of humanity in the AI would certainly correspond to a failure in the designer. We wonder sometimes what is being taught in homes and schools—but what is being fed into artificial intelligence?

If you enjoyed my book, or just want to comment on it, please leave a review on Amazon or Goodreads, and give me a 'follow' on BookBub.

Thanks for reading!

Suzanne Hagelin